"Full of marvelous yarns, colorful customs, genuine humor and pathos. . . . You are going to love *Cold Sassy Tree*. . . . Exuberant, funny, touching, and so full of the sheer joy of living that the amiable exercise of turning the pages will make you feel ten years younger!"
—*The Plain Dealer* (Cleveland)

"A hilarious and passionate book. One of the best portraits of small-town Southern life ever written."
—Pat Conroy,
author of *The Lords of Discipline*

"Lovely. . . . Burns charms the dickens out of the place."
—*People*

"Will Tweedy is brother to such literary immortals as Huck Finn and Holden Caulfield. *Cold Sassy Tree* will be read and reread and laughed and cried over for many years to come."
—Anne Edwards, author of *Road to Tara*

"A toothsome book, with passages that will make you pucker with pleasure."

—*Newsday*

"It's a winner, it rings with authority, it moves fast, and its use of language is as surefooted and convincing as any in *The Color Purple*."

—*San Jose Mercury News*

Cold Sassy Tree

Olive Ann Burns

Delacorte Press

LARGE PRINT EDITION

Published by
Delacorte Press
Bantam Doubleday Dell Publishing Group, Inc.
666 Fifth Avenue
New York, New York 10103

The trademark Delacorte Press® is registered in the
U.S. Patent and Trademark Office.
ISBN: 0-385-30842-6
Reprinted by arrangement with Ticknor & Fields
Manufactured in the United States of America
Published simultaneously in Canada
October 1992
10 9 8 7 6 5 4 3 2 1
BVG

**This Large Print Book carries the
Seal of Approval of N.A.V.H.**

To Andy
My beloved

To Becky and John
Our grown children

And to my father
Who was fourteen in 1906

ACKNOWLEDGMENTS

Cold Sassy is a lot like Commerce, Georgia, at the turn of the century. I couldn't have understood small-town life in that era without the oft-told tales of my late father, William Arnold Burns. He grew up in Commerce, was fourteen in 1906, and, like Will Tweedy, could always make a good story better in the telling. Another rich source of information was the delightful *History of Harmony Grove–Commerce, Jackson County, Georgia, 1810–1949*, by Thomas Colquitt Hardman. I am indebted to the Atlanta Historical Society for access to old Atlanta newspapers, and to C. Vann Woodward's *Tom Watson: Agrarian Rebel* (The Macmillan Company, New York, 1938) for filling the gaps in my knowledge of conditions in Georgia at the time of this book.

I have many reasons to thank my husband, Andrew Sparks; also the children's book author Wylly Folk St. John, who for years urged me to try a novel; Norma Duncan, my neighbor, who saw what was right and wrong with the early manuscript; Eleanor Torrey West at

Ossabaw Island, Mary Nikas at the Hambidge Center, and Dr. and Mrs. T. E. Reeve, who provided places where occasionally I could get away from home to write; Menakhem Perry, literary critic and University of Tel Aviv professor, who read the first four hundred pages and helped me believe it was good; Anne Edwards, author of *Road to Tara,* who recommended it to her publisher, Ticknor & Fields; Chester Kerr, former president of Ticknor & Fields, and his wife, Joan, without whose encouragement I would still be finishing the manuscript; Katrina Kenison, my editor at Ticknor & Fields, and Frances Apt, manuscript editor, both of whom helped make *Cold Sassy Tree* what it is today.

1

Three weeks after Granny Blakeslee died, Grandpa came to our house for his early morning snort of whiskey, as usual, and said to me, "Will Tweedy? Go find yore mama, then run up to yore Aunt Loma's and tell her I said git on down here. I got something to say. And I ain't a-go'n say it but once't."

"Yessir."

"Make haste, son. I got to git on to the store."

Mama made me wait till she pinned the black mourning band for Granny on my shirt sleeve. Then I was off. Any time Grandpa had something to say, it was something you couldn't wait to hear.

That was eight years ago on a Thursday morning, when Grandpa Blakeslee was fifty-nine and I was fourteen. The date was July 5, 1906. I know because Grandpa put it down in the family Bible, and also Toddy Hughes wrote up for the Atlanta paper what happened to me on the train trestle that day and I still have the clipping. Besides that, I remember it was right after our July the Fourth celebration—the first one held in Cold Sassy, Georgia, since the War Between the States.

July 5, 1906, was three months after the big earthquake in San Francisco and about two months after a stranger drove through Cold Sassy in a Pope-Waverley electric automobile that got stalled trying to cross the railroad tracks. I pushed it up the incline and the man let me ride as far as the Athens highway.

July 5, 1906, was a year after my great-grandmother on the Tweedy side died for the second and last time out in Banks County. It was six months after my best friend, Bluford Jackson, got firecrackers for Christmas and burned his hand on one and died of lockjaw ten days later. And like I said, it was only three weeks after Granny Blakeslee went to the grave.

During those three weeks, Grandpa Blakeslee had sort of drawn back inside his own skin. Acted like I didn't mean any more to him than a stick of stovewood. On the morning of July 5th, he stalked through the house and into our company room without even speaking to me.

Granny never would let him keep his corn whiskey at home. He kept it in the company room at our house, which was between the depot and downtown, and came by for a snort every morning on his way to work. I and my little redheaded sister, Mary Toy, always followed him down the hall, and he usually gave us each a stick of penny candy before shutting the company room door in our faces. While our spit swam over hoarhound or peppermint, we'd hear the floorboards creak in the closet, then a silence, then a big "H-rumph!" and a big satisfied "Ah-h-h-h!" He would come out smiling, ready for the day, and pat Mary Toy's head as he went past her.

But this particular morning was different. For one thing, Mary Toy had gone home with Cudn Temp the day before. And Grandpa, instead of coming out feeling good, looked like somebody itching for a fight. That's when he said, "Will Tweedy?" (He always called me both names except when he called me son.) Said, "Will Tweedy? Go find yore mama, then run up to yore Aunt Loma's and tell her I said git on down here."

Lots of people in Cold Sassy had a telephone, including us. Grandpa didn't. He had one at the store so he could phone orders to the wholesale house in Athens, but he was too stingy to pay for one at home. Aunt Loma didn't have a phone, either. She and Uncle Camp were too poor. That's why I had to go tell her.

I ran all the way, my brown and white bird dog, T.R., bounding ahead. As usual when we got to Aunt Loma's, the dog plopped down on the dirt sidewalk in front of her house to wait. He couldn't go up in the dern yard because of the dern cats, of which there were eighteen or twenty at least. They would scratch his eyes out if he went any closer.

I found Aunt Loma sitting at the kitchen table, her long curly red hair still loose and tousled, the dirty breakfast dishes pushed back to clear a space. With one cat in her lap and another licking an oatmeal bowl on the table, she sat drinking coffee and reading a book of theater plays.

Mama never knew how often Aunt Loma put pleasure before duty like that. Mama liked to stay in front of her work. But then Loma was young—just twenty—and sloven.

When I told her what Grandpa said, she slammed her book down so hard, the cat leaped off the table. "Why don't you just tell him I'm busy." But even as she spoke she stood up, gulped some coffee, set down the cup still half full, and rushed upstairs to change into a black dress on account of her mother having just died and all. When she came down, carrying fat, sleepy Campbell Junior, her mass of red hair was combed, pinned up, and draped with what she called "my genteel black veil."

Campbell Junior pulled at the veil all the way to our house, and Aunt Loma fussed all the way. When we got there, she handed the baby over to our cook, Queenie, and hurried in where Grandpa was pacing the front hall, his high-top black shoes squeaking as he walked.

I couldn't help noticing how in only three weeks as a widower he already looked like one. His dark bushy hair and long gray beard were tangled. The heavy, droopy mustache had some dried food stuck on it. His black hat, pants, and vest were dusty and the home-made white shirt rusty with tobacco juice. Granny always prided herself on keeping his wild hair and beard trimmed, his shirts clean, his pants brushed and "nice." Now that she was gone, he couldn't do for himself very well, having only the one hand, but he wouldn't let Mama or Aunt Loma do for him.

"Mornin', Pa," Aunt Loma grumped.

"Is that y'all, Will?" Mama called from the

dining room, where she was closing windows and pulling down shades to keep out the morning sun. We waited in the front hall till she hurried in, her hair still in a thick plait down one side of her neck. I always thought she looked pretty with it like that—almost like a young girl. Mama was a plain person, like Granny, and didn't dress fancy the way Aunt Loma did every time she stuck her nose out of the house. Even at home Aunt Loma was fancy. She wouldn't of been caught dead in an apron made out of a flour sack, whereas Mama had on one that still read *Try Skylark Self-Rising Flour* right across the chest. The words hadn't washed out yet, which I was sure Aunt Loma noticed as she said crossly, "Mornin', Sister."

Taking off the apron as if we had real company, Mama said to me, "Son, you go gather the eggs, hear? With Mary Toy gone, you got to gather the eggs."

"Yes'm." My feet dragged me toward the back hall.

"Let them aiggs wait, Mary Willis," Grandpa ordered. "I want Will Tweedy to hear what I come to say. He'll know soon enough anyways." Then he stomped toward the open front door and put his hand on the knob as if all he planned to say was good-bye —or maybe more like he was fixing to put a match to a string of firecrackers and then run before they went off.

My mother asked, nervous-like, "You want us to all go sit in the parlor, sir?"

He shook his head. "Naw, Mary Willis, it won't take long enough to set down for." He took off his black hat and laid it on the table, pulled at his mustache, scratched through the white streak in his beard, and turned those deep blue eyes on Mama and Aunt Loma, his grown children, standing together puzzled and uneasy. When he began his announcement, you could tell he had practiced it. "Now, daughters, you know I was true to yore mother. Miss Mattie Lou was a fine wife. A good cook. A real good woman. Beloved by all in this here town, and by me, as y'all know."

Hearing Grandpa go on about Granny made my throat ache. Mama and Aunt Loma went to sobbing out loud, their arms around each other.

"Now quit yore blubberin', Mary Willis. Hesh up, Loma. I ain't finished." Then his voice softened. "Since yore ma's passin' I been a-studyin' on our life together. Thirty-six year we had, and they was good years. I want y'all to know I ain't never go'n forget her."

"Course you w-won't, Pa," said my mother, sobbing.

"But she's gone, just like this here hand a-mine." He held up his left arm, the shirt sleeve knotted as usual just below the elbow. Grandpa's blue eyes were suddenly glassy with unspilled tears. He struggled to get aholt of himself, then went on. "Like I said, she's gone now. So I been studyin' on what to do. How to make out. Well, I done decided, and when I say what I come to say I want y'all to know they ain't no disrespect to her intended." Grandpa opened the door wider. He was about to light his firecrackers.

"Now what I come to say," he blurted out, "is I'm aimin' to marry Miss Love Simpson."

Mama's and Aunt Loma's mouths dropped open and their faces went white. They both cried out, "Pa, you cain't!"

"I done ast her and she's done said yes. And Loma, they ain't a bloomin' thang you can do bout it."

Aunt Loma's face got as red as if she'd been on the river all day, but it was Mama who finally spoke. In a timid voice she said,

"Sir, Love Simpson's young enough to be your daughter! She's not more'n thirty-three or -four years old!"

"Thet ain't got a thang to do with it."

Mama put both hands up to her mouth. With a sort of whimper, she said, "Pa, don't you care what folks are go'n say?"

"I care bout you carin' what they'll say, Mary Willis. But I care a heap more bout not bein' no burden on y'all. So hesh up."

Aunt Loma was bout to burst. "Think, Pa!" she ordered, tears streaming down her face. "Just think. Ma hasn't been d-dead but three w-w-weeks!"

"Well, good gosh a'mighty!" he thundered. "She's dead as she'll ever be, ain't she? Well, ain't she?"

2

I thought Mama was going to faint. She stumbled toward her daddy, arms outstretched, but Grandpa glared at her and she stepped back.

"I'm lonesome." He said it kind of quiet. Then he hugged each weeping daughter and walked out the door, hitching up his trousers with the stub of his left arm.

On the veranda, Grandpa turned back and spoke his defense. "I ain't go'n be no burden on y'all. Not ever. Which means I got to hire me a colored woman or git married, one, and tell you the truth, hit's jest cheaper to have a wife. So I'm a-go'n marry Miss Love. And I ain't got but one more thang to say. All y'all be nice to her. You hear?" He said *all y'all,* but it was Aunt Loma he glared at when he said it.

With that, my grandfather stalked tall down the steps. We watched as he strode past Mama's pots of pink begonias and Papa's life-size iron stag and walked through the iron gate. Banging it shut, he passed the tall pink crepe myrtles that lined the dirt sidewalk in front of our house, crossed the dirt street called South Main, went over the railroad tracks onto North Main, and headed for the store.

Soon as Grandpa got out of sight it was as if somebody had wound Mama and Aunt Loma up and let go the spring. Mama wailed that she could never show her face in Cold Sassy again, she was so embarrassed. Aunt Loma was just plain mad. "Remember Ma's funeral headline, Sister?" She spat out the words.

Mama nodded into her handkerchief. "Y-yes, of course I do. It said, 'Grieving Husband Left to Walk Through Life Alone.' "

"I can just see the engagement notice: 'Grieving Widower Finds Woman to Walk With.' "

"You know Bubba wouldn't do that!" Mama cried. Bubba Reynolds was editor of the *Cold Sassy Weekly*.

"He will if he thinks of it," said Loma. "Sister, that woman ought to be ashamed. And I'm go'n go tell her so."

Mama was alarmed. "Now, Loma, once you get started, you don't know when to hush." Then she added, "But it might do some good to tell her how stingy Pa is, and how hard he is to cook for. That might make her think twice."

There was a silence, except for Aunt Loma pounding her right fist into her left hand, bam, bam, bam, glaring at me as she did it. Finally she said my daddy might could talk Grandpa out of it.

Mama didn't think so. "Hoyt don't even dare ast Pa to raise his pay. Get your Camp onto him." She was being sarcastic. I'd heard her say that Grandpa thought Uncle Camp was still in knee britches. Aunt Loma didn't answer. She knew—they both knew—that nobody could stand up to their daddy.

Then Loma shook both fists in the direction of the store. "Dog bite your hide, Love Simpson!" she screamed. "And dog bite yours, Pa!"

"Loma, hush. The neighbors will—"

"How could he do it, and her a Yankee!"

Mama was always fair, even when flustrated to distraction. "Now, Loma, everybody calls Miss Love a Yankee and she does kind of talk like one. But Maryland is not a Northern state." Then, as another thought struck her, Mama collapsed onto the leather davenport there in the front hall. "Loma," she wailed, "Pa didn't have on his black armband!"

"Well, should he, Sister? When he's engaged?" Aunt Loma like to choked on the word *engaged*.

"But they cain't marry for a year or more. I don't see why Pa couldn't wear an armband for Ma."

"While Love Simpson wears an engagement ring for Pa?"

"Surely he won't give her a ring! He just

said he wanted us to know, not the whole world!" Mama jumped up and stuck her nose right in her young sister's face. "Now you listen to me." Loma backed off a little. "I want you to keep your mouth shut. It may all blow over, and nobody'll ever know. Maybe— maybe Pa just thought she said yes."

"Grandpa ain't hard of hearin'," said I, but they didn't seem to notice.

I was amazed at Mama. She was usually just the mildest sort of person. Ordinarily if anybody was saying hush up around here, it was Aunt Loma, despite she was fourteen years younger than my mother. No doubt Aunt Loma marveled, too, because she didn't say anything sassy back. Just jerked off her genteel black veil and threw it hard as she could toward the front door.

"Sister, I was fixin' to ast Pa for Ma's piano," she burst out. Tears of flustration wet her red face. "And I want the mirror that Cudn Pearl painted Saint Cecilia on. Just think, while I was waitin' a decent time to ast for a piano and a mirror, come to find out he was astin' for a wife!" Screaming the words out, she stomped her foot.

I knew Mama wanted the piano so Mary Toy could take music lessons. Mama always liked the Saint Cecilia mirror, too. Everybody in Cold Sassy except us had Saint Cecilia painted on something. And though Mama wasn't the kind to ask for things, I'd heard her tell Queenie she was go'n see if her Pa would let her swap our mismatched parlor furniture for Granny's nice parlor suit. She knew he wouldn't care one way or the other.

"I just cain't understand it," Mama fumed, getting up to pace the hall just the way Grandpa had. "I thought Love Simpson would marry Son Black. I know his mother don't approve, but he's not gettin' any younger, and they been courtin' a year or more."

"And Love deserves him," said Aunt Loma. She used to be sweet on Son Black herself, so I reckon she knew what she was talking about when she added, "Son's right nice-lookin' and smart, but his mouth sure isn't any prayer book. And he's meaner'n a snake."

"Yeah," I chimed in. "I heard he had him a pet snake one time that bit him and the next day the snake died."

They ignored that. Mama said, "Love is too used to town life and dressin' fashionable. Maybe she don't care to stay out there on the farm with Son's mama and raise chi'ren. Maybe she thinks she's too good to marry a farmer."

"Shoot," retorted Aunt Loma, "what about that rancher out in Texas she was engaged to before she came here? A rancher has lots of land and money but he's a farmer just the same. Lord, I wish to heaven she'd married him. If only he hadn'—"

"Sh-h!" Mama nodded toward me.

I knew Loma was fixing to say "If only he hadn't got Miss Love's best friend in trouble and had to marry her." Everybody in town knew that story. I don't know why Mama thought I didn't.

Nobody asked my opinion, but I had always admired Miss Love, with all that wavy brown hair piled atop her head, and that smiley, freckledy face and those friendly gray-blue eyes. She was a merry person, like Grandpa. Always wore big flowered hats and bright-colored dresses, never "quiet" clothes like nice ladies were supposed to wear on the street. I could see how Miss Love could cheer up a man whose wife was short of breath for four years, dying for ten days, and dead for three weeks.

Aunt Loma's face suddenly went redder

than ever. Clearly she'd had a new thought. "Sister, with Love bein' Pa's milliner, and them seein' each other down at the store every day, people are go'n say—"

"Will, I thought I told you to go get the eggs," Mama interrupted with a mad sound in her voice. "Now go on, right now. Mind me."

I minded her. But she needn't think I didn't know what Aunt Loma was driving at. Well, there couldn't have been any carrying-on down at the store or we'd have heard about it long time ago. Anyhow, Miss Love wasn't that kind and neither was my grandfather. And heck, he loved Granny. Even now I couldn't hardly imagine him kissing another lady, or slapping her playful on the backside like he used to do Granny when he was in a teasing mood. I guess what I really couldn't imagine was Miss Love kissing him, much less marrying him. It was easy to see he needed looking after, but what did she need that an old man could give when she already had a beau her own age who was anxious to marry her?

3

I sat down on the back steps to think. I didn't see why Mama and Aunt Loma weren't glad Grandpa Blakeslee had found him a lady to marry. The sooner the better, if you asked me. The wedding couldn't be for a year or more, of course, but after that he wouldn't have to keep coming to our house for dinner or to Aunt Loma's every night for supper, which he'd been doing ever since Granny passed away. And Miss Love wouldn't have to bring a quart Mason jar full of hot coffee down to the store for him every morning like she'd been doing.

Papa kept trying to get Grandpa to eat breakfast with us, being as he came by home anyhow for his snort. It wouldn't of been much trouble for Mama; all Grandpa ever wanted in the morning was four cups of coffee and some yeast bread, toasted hard and dipped in boiling water and then buttered. But when Papa said, "Sit down and have a bite with us, Mr. Blakeslee," Grandpa would say he just et. I reckon he thought if he took dinner and breakfast both at our house, it wouldn't be any time before Papa would be after him to move in with us.

Well, this time next year Grandpa would be married, and if he didn't like what was put before him it would be Miss Love's little red wagon, not Mama's or Aunt Loma's. Also, they wouldn't have to see after him if he got sick. He was hard to take care of when he was ailing. Liked to groan and carry on. He'd lie down before supper on the daybed, moaning, "Oh, me, me. . . . Oh, me, me," and Granny just about went crazy listening to it, knowing that next morning he'd go on to the store anyway. The last year or two, no matter how bad he felt you couldn't make him stay home. He could have a cold so bad it sounded like pneumonia rattling around in there but he wouldn't stay home.

That really used to worry my grandmother. She'd beg him not to go to work. "Mr. Blakeslee, I nurse everybody in town but my own husband. Please stay in bed t'morrer. Hear?"

But he'd say, "I ain't thet big of a fool, Miss Mattie Lou. Ain't you ever noticed? Folks die in bed."

Anyhow, now there wouldn't be any more worrying about Grandpa living by himself.

Aunt Loma had already declared he couldn't live with her. Said she didn't have room. I don't know how she could say such as that when her daddy had given her husband a job and provided them a house to live in. Mama couldn't have said it—even if he didn't own our house, too, and even if Papa didn't work for him. Papa had been keeping the store ledgers since he was sixteen.

Grandpa wouldn't of lived with Aunt Loma, of course, on account of her cats. The first time he went there for supper after Granny was buried, the next morning he started fussing about her cats the minute he got to our house for his snort. "I swanny to God, I seen one a-them cats jump up on Loma's kitchen stove last night! Tiptoed across thet red-hot stove on his dang claws and et right out of the pot!"

I had been hoping Grandpa would come live with us. But even though she never said so, I knew Mama dreaded that possibility. Tell the truth, she was scared of her daddy, as if she wasn't sure he'd got over her not being a boy and her marrying a Presbyterian— though the way I heard it from Cudn Temp, Grandpa was all for her marrying my daddy,

and had a fit when the Baptist deacons tried
her for heresy.

Heresy was his word for their word for her
marrying a Presbyterian.

According to Temp, the deacons voted to
put it in the church records that "Mary Willis
Blakeslee has swapped her religious birth-
right for a mess of matrimonial pottage." It
made Grandpa mad as holy heck. "Anybody
calls Hoyt Tweedy a mess of matrimonial pottage," he roared, "thet man is a-go'n answer
to me." The deacons struck the pottage part
from the record. But they turned Mama out
of the Baptist communion just the same, and
her only seventeen.

That was one reason I didn't like the way
Mama was carrying on so about Grandpa getting engaged. He had stuck up for her when
she wanted to marry Papa. Why wouldn't she
stick up for him now?

I wasn't surprised at Aunt Loma, of course.
She was the only child of Granny and
Grandpa's to live more than a few years, besides my mother, and she'd been spoiled all
her life. I reckon they thought they had to
keep rewarding her for not dying. Anyhow,
Loma never could think about much else for
thinking about how to get her own way. De-

spite she was married now, and a mother, she hadn't grown up any that I could see. If it didn't suit her for her daddy to marry again, why, he just wasn't going to.

Miss Love having worked for Grandpa at his store for two years or more, she must already know he was stingy and set in his ways. She also knew that, because of his having just the one hand, he needed special looking after. He bit off his fingernails, so keeping them short was no problem. But tough meat had to be cut up for him, and he needed help with his high-top shoes. Timmy Hopkins had been coming by to tie Grandpa's shoelaces ever since Granny took sick.

But though Miss Love might not be a good cook after boarding so long, and probably couldn't of outworked Granny in a vegetable garden or rose garden or sickroom, most anybody could outdo Granny with a broom and a feather duster. She used to say, "A house will keep, whether you weed it or not, but that-air yard will git away from you in the bat of a eye." The only thing she liked to do indoors was cook and tend the sick. I remember one time she pulled off her apron after two days and nights nursing a neighbor lady and said, "They ain't no feelin' in the world like takin' on somebody wilted and near bout gone, and you do what you can, and then all a-sudden the pore thang starts to put out new growth and git well."

I hadn't ever heard of Miss Love nursing the sick. But that wasn't any reason for Grandpa not to marry her. I just couldn't see why Mama and Aunt Loma were having a fit about it. The fact that I liked Miss Love didn't mean I hadn't loved Granny, and I figured it was the same with him.

I was just fixing to get up off the back steps and go gather the eggs when Campbell Junior started squalling in the kitchen. I heard Aunt Loma go in there. "I got to get on home," she told our cook.

"Yas'm," said Queenie. "B'ess his li'l heart, he be's hongry."

"And I be's full as a Jersey cow," said Aunt Loma, mocking her. "Seems like all I do is nurse this bloomin' baby."

"Shame on you, Miss Loma, talkin' lak dat. Some peoples cain' nuss dey baby, and some ain' got nary baby to nuss. You be's lucky."

"Humph," said Loma, and left.

Before I had a chance to move, Mama came out and lit into me for sitting there doing nothing. Said I was no-count and shiftless and why hadn't I gathered the eggs and I was supposed to have weeded the lower garden two days ago and to go do that "but first you gather the eggs like you been told to. You go'n let the rats get'm. Or that no-count egg-sucker dog of yours."

I resented that. T.R. didn't suck eggs. But I said yes'm.

Mama went inside, and I was hardly down the three back steps before she stuck her head out of her bedroom window upstairs and hollered to me to watch for Papa and my grandpa when it was time for them to come to dinner.

"Yes'm."

"I got a sick headache," she said, like it was my fault, and put her hand up to her forehead as she faded back into the room. The window slammed shut and the shade came down to keep it cool in there.

In a kind of furious daze, forgetting the eggs, I got a big old gray peach basket off the porch and dragged it down the path. The garden was to the left of the barn and the pasture, hidden from the house by the smokehouse and a pecan grove and a row of little peach trees that because of the drought had dropped hard knotty fruit not even fit to make spiced pickle with.

Gourd leaves that yesterday drooped down like a hundred little half-closed umbrellas were now freshened with dew. But it was already hot, great goodness, and the dirt was powder-dry. I hadn't weeded since the last rain. I started pulling up the grass and weeds as if they were Miss Love Simpson—like I thought getting rid of them would get rid of her and bring Granny Blakeslee back from the grave and let us be a normal family again.

Nothing had been normal since Granny died. Mama was grieving herself to death, Papa was sterner than ever, Aunt Loma was meaner, the laughter had gone out of Grandpa, and if he was about to sell the store, it wouldn't of upset everybody any more than him aiming to marry his milliner.

Worst of all, for me, was being in mourning.

I just didn't think I could stand any more mourning. For three whole weeks of summer vacation they hadn't let me play baseball or go fishing or anything. I couldn't mention the camping trip I'd been planning all spring with Pink Predmore and Lee Roy Sleep and Smiley Snodgrass, and I had missed a chance to ride in a Buick automobile all the way to Atlanta. Pink's uncle over in Athens invited him and me to go so we could fix his flat tires and push the car up hills—and out of ditches if it rained and the roads got slick. Pink went, but Mama wouldn't let me go. Also, I didn't get to go downtown for the Fourth of July parade, and they hadn't let me read the funny paper since the day Granny passed on.

Papa never had let us read the funny paper on Sunday. That was a sin. We had to save it till Monday. But now we were having to save the funnies indefinitely, and sometimes the newspaper got taken to start a fire with before I could tear out the page. The Katzenjammer Kids had dropped clean out of my life. Seems like I missed them about as much as I missed Granny. Maybe more. They were up there on the shelf in Mama's chifforobe with things happening to them, whereas Granny wasn't anywhere.

I wished she could come back for just a minute. I'd ask her wouldn't she hate my giving up the funnies and the automobile trip when there wasn't a thing I could do for her anymore. Despite she had wanted a nice funeral, I knew she wouldn't expect a boy to walk around with a long face the rest of his life.

I was just fixing to quit weeding and rest a spell under the big hickernut tree when I noticed my shadow was underfoot, nearly straight down. It must be right at dinner time. Gosh, Mama had told me to watch out for Papa and Grandpa. Dashing past the barn, the smokehouse, and Mama's flower pit, I ran through the house and got to the front door just as Papa hurried up the walk. He was by himself.

"Where's Grandpa at?" I asked.

"Where's Mama at?" he asked. He was sweaty and red-faced from rushing home and he looked upset.

"She's gone to bed, sir. I think she's sick."

Even now, eight years later, I remember how my papa looked that day—like a thundercloud, but also like a pitiful, lightning-struck tree. Taking the stairs two at a time, he didn't even notice me following behind.

As he burst into the darkened second-floor bedroom, he said, "Mary Willis, guess what! Your daddy just left in his buggy with Miss Love Simpson! Said they were off to Jefferson to get married!"

Mama bolted up. "You mean already?" she screeched. "Today?"

"You knew it?" roared Papa. "Why didn't you tell me?"

"I didn't dream he meant today!" Then she blurted out what all Grandpa had said that morning. "Hoyt, he said it didn't matter, said Ma havin' just passed away didn't matter! He said . . . he said Ma was d-dead as she—" she started crying. "Dead as—oh, Hoyt, I c-cain't bear to repeat his w-words! He said . . . Ma was dead as she'd ever b-be!"

Peeping in the doorway, I saw my mother was laying across the bed, on her side, pressing a handkerchief to her mouth. Papa had sat down by her and was patting her shoulder. He kissed her forehead. "There, there, Mary Willis hon. Don't carry on so. I admit it, I was surprised myself. But Lord knows, Mr. Blakeslee needs somebody to see after him. Hon, I'm sure Miss Love will be good to him. She'll—"

"She'll get the store, that's what she'll do!" cried Mama. "And this house! Maybe everything he owns! What if she has a baby, Hoyt? Did you think about that? And what if she marries again after Pa dies? Oh, Hoyt . . ."

I knew my mother thought the marriage

was a scandal, but this was the first I guessed that she saw Miss Love as a scoundrel, a villain, out to steal hers and Aunt Loma's inheritance.

Slowly it dawned on me that if Grandpa Blakeslee died and left Miss Love the store, she really could marry again and let her new husband run it. And if he was somebody like Son Black, he might just push my daddy and Uncle Camp clean out. The threat was sobering even to me.

But somehow the picture didn't fit. Maybe Grandpa didn't care what folks said or thought about him, but he cared a lot about Mama and Papa and Aunt Loma. I mean, he didn't *like* Aunt Loma a lot, but he loved her. Also, he set great store on a man doing right by his family.

Peeping in again, I saw Papa had his arms around Mama. She was crying. "When a woman m-marries a man old enough to be her f-father," she said, "you can b-b-bet your . . . bottom dollar it's for . . . w-what she can g-g-get out of him. . . . Pa's a fool, Hoyt! And I just don't see h-how we can start all over when he d-dies. Oh, Hoyt . . . !"

She kept wailing and Papa kept patting her. I didn't know what to think about all that, but

I knew I didn't want them to catch me out there listening. Tiptoeing around to the other side of a golden oak bureau that was in the hall near their bedroom door, I squatted down.

"I'm sick over the whole thing," Mama muttered. "Just sick! No tellin' what kind of fam'ly she comes from. There's a milliner in Athens who trained with Love in Baltimore and she says Love's daddy fought on the Union side in the War. That by itself should of made Pa think twice, feelin' like he does about Yankees. Hoyt, we don't even know what her father does, for heaven's sake, or whether the fam'ly has any education or background, or any standin' at all in their community." Mama was a great one for not marrying beneath yourself.

Papa argued that the family surely must be educated, judging by the way Miss Love talked so proper. "She seems like somebody with background."

"Well, one thing I know, Miz Predmore says the only letters Love Simpson gets from Baltimore are from the millinery company that trained her. The postmaster told her. We figure she must be ashamed of her folks. If she don't write them and don't hear from them and don't ever say pea-turkey about them to anybody, something's wrong."

"Please, hon, don't let yourself get all wrought up."

"Her fam'ly could be common as Camp's folks, for all we know. Ignorant. No-count. Even low-down. I still don't see how Loma could of married into that sharecropper white trash. With all her education and advantages, she's got a daddy-in-law who cain't read or write and a mother-in-law who dips snuff. And Camp's sisters work in the fields just like colored girls. Thank the Lord they didn't come to the weddin'."

Papa couldn't stand it when Mama got to low-rating Uncle Camp's people. "Now, hon, that don't have anything to do with your pa."

"It does, too. Even if Love's folks ain't ignorant, they could be dead-beats. Jesus said take up your cross and follow Me, but He didn't ast us to go out and nail ourselves to a board. Some fine day, mark my words, Love's fam'ly will get off the train from Baltimore to come live off of Pa. Just like Camp's folks are go'n be livin' off of he and Loma before it's over. Or maybe livin' with them. Only reason Loma married Camp, she was mad cause Pa wouldn't let her go off with those actors.

That's just exactly why. She was bound and determined to get her way about something —just to spite Pa."

It was true. A touring Shakespeare company had let Loma try out after their performance in Cold Sassy's brush arbor and then asked her to join the troupe. Everybody in town said Lord help Loma if she ends up an actress. Even if she got rich and famous and did command performances for Edward VII, like she said she would, she couldn't ever live down the taint.

But Grandpa said, "Loma, I ain't a-go'n let you do it. Ain't no tellin' what kind of a life you'd live with them kind a-folks."

She stomped and cried and carried on something awful. "I wish I was a boy so I could go off on my own!"

"I wish you was a boy, too, but you ain't," Grandpa retorted, "and you ain't go'n be no actress, neither. So hesh up." Loma went to her room and threw things, but Grandpa didn't hear it. He had gone on back to the store.

I myself used to wonder why Loma didn't find some more actors to run off with—a thing she wanted to do—instead of marrying Campbell Williams just to spite her daddy.

Well, and now her daddy had married Miss Love—maybe partly to spite Cold Sassy.

"Loma and Pa, they're just alike." Mama was fuming. "They don't ever consider anybody else. Neither one of them. When I think of the nice widders Pa's age who'd be happy to marry him, I don't see why he had to pick an old maid from Up North who's had to work for a livin'."

In Cold Sassy, ladies who work for pay are looked down on—except schoolteachers or widder women with no close kinfolks to turn to. Milliners are considered in a class with store clerks and telephone hello-girls.

"Why wouldn't Pa let me look after him?" Mama went on. "We could of moved up to his house."

"And go back to usin' lamps and privies?" asked Papa irritably. "And give up Queenie?" Grandpa didn't have electricity or running water and didn't believe in hiring colored help.

That silenced my mother, but only for a minute. In a new burst of tears, she said, "Hoyt, Pa has disgraced the whole f-f-fam'ly. The whole t-town!"

Most likely Papa was patting her shoulder again. "It's go'n turn out all right, hon. Just don't forget I work for him, and Camp works for him. Y'all have got to be nice to Miss Love. Now, hon, I need to get back to the store. Please, let's go eat."

"You and Will eat." Mama's muffled voice came out of her pillow. "I'm not hungry. The nerve, that woman thinkin' she can take Ma's place! And everybody's go'n say—you mark my words—they go'n say Pa must have been sweet on her from the day he laid eyes on her. It's like he just couldn't hardly wait for Ma to p-p-pass!"

I guess my mother didn't notice that Papa had left the room. I waited till he got downstairs before I crept down myself. I couldn't stand hearing her keep on talking against Grandpa.

4

I used to try to undress Grandpa Blakeslee's face in my mind and think how he'd look clean-shaved. I never could picture him like that, but I liked looking at him the way he was—his eyes merry, his upper lip hidden under the droopy mustache, his bushy gray

beard usually stained here and there with tobacco juice.

Most people thought I was his spittin' im-
age. Granny used to say I walked like
Grandpa, twitched my shoulders like him—
"cain't neither one a-y'all set still"—and
looked like him "cept for yore eyes bein'
brown and his'n so blue, and the fact yore
nose ain't humped." Grandpa's nose had got
broke three times, and it showed. First time,
he was trying to fly: "I was maybe twelve year
old. Jumped out'n a hayloft holdin' a dang
umbrella and it turned inside out." The other
two times, his nose got busted in fistfights.

At fifty-nine, Grandpa still had all his
teeth, which should be a comfort to Miss
Love. He only wore glasses to read. He was
lean, strong, straight, and taller than most
men—the way I was taller than most fourteen-year-old boys. My grandmother was
small. She could stand under his arm if he
stuck it straight out, and never could keep up
with him when they walked together. His long
legs swung in giant strides; she trotted at his
heels like a good little dog.

Grandpa was a buster all right.

He was a Democrat, a Baptist, and a de-
vout Confederate veteran. The words *Abra-*

ham Lincoln couldn't be spoke in his presence. His only hand was soft and smooth, not like the rough, red, calloused hands of farmers. In a fight he used the elbow of his left arm as a deflector and his "fightin' right" to punch with.

The fights were embarrassing to the family but real entertaining to the Baptists, for he would stand up at the next Wednesday night prayer meeting, in the testimonial and confessing part, and tell the Lord all about it. One Wednesday night he ended a long prayer with "Lord, forgive me for fittin' thet man yesterd'y—though Thou knowest if I had it to do over agin I'd hit him harder."

Grandpa was a good shot with a pistol. He never went hunting, but he could prop a Winchester rifle on a fence and shoot into the mouth of a Coca-Cola bottle fifty feet away and not even chip the glass, except for the hole at the bottom where the bullet came out.

I never could figure why Papa and Mama let him keep his quart jars of moonshine in the closet in our company room. At the time, Papa made and drank locust beer, and Mama made scuppernong and blackberry wines for church communion. After the Georgia legis-

lature declared a prohibition against alco-
holic beverages in 1907, Papa quit making or
drinking beer—he believed in being law-abid-
ing—and the churches started using fruit nec-
tars instead of wine. But even before Prohibition, neither Papa nor Mama could stand
whiskey-drinking.

Yet there stood those jars of corn whiskey
on our closet shelf.

Why couldn't my daddy ask him to keep
them down at the store? Or after Granny
died and wasn't there anymore to disallow it,
why didn't he take the stuff to his own house?

My parents never once spoke of his drinking in front of me or Mary Toy. Acted like he
just went in the company room to hitch up his
suspenders or something. But I doubt they
could of said anything even if he hadn't been
Mama's papa and Papa's employer. Grandpa
had the manner of a king or duke: when he
said do or don't do something, you said yessir
before you thought. And if he said he meant
to do something—like keep his corn whiskey
in your closet or marry Miss Love Simpson—
if you couldn't say yessir, you sure-dog didn't
say no sir. Not out loud.

What I admired most was his flair for practical jokes. That was a way of life you could learn early, as I discovered when I was little bitty and Cudn Doodle told me to lick a frozen wagon wheel and my tongue stuck to the ice. Playing jokes didn't have to stop because you got grown. Grandpa must of been twenty-five at least when he turned over the privy at the depot with a Yankee railroad bigwig in it.

I didn't want to be like my grandfather in all ways. I thought I wanted to be like Papa, at least sometime in the distant future. But right now Grandpa was more fun than Papa and didn't worry near as much, if at all, about sin. And he was real proud of me. I was the son he never had.

While I was still in dresses he put me to sorting nails at the store and getting out rotten apples and potatoes. By time I was seven, he let me make deliveries for him in my goat cart. It was his notion that when I got grown, he would give me an interest in the store and take me into partnership.

It was my notion to be a farmer. Papa wanted to buy the old home place out in Banks County from his daddy and let me run it. But at the time Grandpa Blakeslee married Miss Love, I still hadn't got up the nerve to tell him my plans.

Most folks thought, as Miss Effie Belle Tate put it, that Grandpa was "both rich and well-to-do." For sure he was one of Cold Sassy's leading merchants. Had him a big brick store with mahogany counters, beveled glass mirrors, and big colored signs for Coca-Cola, Mother's Friend (*Take to Make Child-birth Easier*), Fletcher's Castoria, Old Dutch Cleanser, McKesson and Robbins liniment, and all like that.

I liked to look at the advertisements in the mail-order catalogues he kept by the cash register. *Manhood Restored* was my favorite:

Nerve Seeds guaranteed to cure all nervous diseases such as Weak Memory, Loss of Brain Power, Headaches, Wakefulness, Lost Manhood, Nightly Emissions, nervousness, all drain and loss of power in generative organs of either sex caused by over-exertion, youthful errors, excessive use of tobacco, opium or stimulants which lead to infirmity, consumption or Insanity. Can be carried in vest pocket. $1 per box address Nerve Seed Co., Masonic Temple, Chicago, Ill.

Grandpa had him a big sign out front over the entrance to the store. In fancy red letters outlined in gold it said:

GENERAL MERCHANDISE
Mr. E. Rucker Blakeslee, Proprietor

Besides keeping the store's ledgers, my daddy took a lot of the buying trips to Atlanta and Baltimore and New York City. I went to New York with him one time when I was little bitty. I'd heard about damnyankees all my life and there I was in a city just full of them. It scared me to death.

Granny's Uncle Lige Toy, who used to have a restaurant business feeding county prisoners, was in charge of Grandpa's cotton warehouse, one of the biggest in north Georgia, and also the store's cotton seed business. Uncle Lige was the one to talk to if you wanted to put your bales in storage till you could get a better price.

A third cousin of Papa's, Hopewell Stump, from out in Banks County, clerked and took care of the chickens that folks brought to trade out for nails, flour, sugar, coal oil, coffee, and chewing tobacco. There used to be smelly chicken coops out on the board sidewalk in front of every store in town, but after Cold Sassy was incorporated in 1887, the Baptist missionary society ladies petitioned the town council to get rid of them. So when Grandpa built his brick store in 1892 he put a great big chickenhouse in back, and every Friday Cudn Hope shipped hens, roosters, and frying-size pullets to Athens or Atlanta on the train.

Uncle Camp mostly swept the floor and put out stock, and in the wintertime broke up wooden shipping crates to burn in the stove. Grandpa called him "born tired and raised lazy." Said getting him to finish something was like pushing mud. "Money don't jump out at you, boy," he'd say. "You got to work for it."

Campbell Williams was Uncle Camp's whole name. He was a pale thin fellow with pale thin yellow hair and a pale thin personality. He was always checking the time so he could show off his gold pocket watch.

He wasn't but nineteen when he came to Cold Sassy from over near Maysville, Georgia. The day Camp walked into the store and asked for a job, Grandpa took one look and said he didn't need no hep right now. Camp got him a job at the tannery, working for

Wildcat Lindsey, but soon lost it, and then worked a while at the gin. Grandpa didn't bring him into the store till after he married Aunt Loma, and never did have any respect for him.

Love Simpson was the first woman Grandpa ever hired. She grew up in Baltimore and had never married but didn't look or act like any other old maid in town. She was tall, plump, and big-bosomed, stood very straight, moved lively, and wore flouncy, fashionable clothes. Miss Love had a sparkly way of talking and she laughed a lot.

I remember the first time I saw her. I had been standing in front of the store watching a flock of turkeys trot through town. If a turkey strayed, a man would snap a long whip around its neck and pull it back in line.

When I went inside, there was the new milliner, seated at a table littered with feathers, bird wings, satin bows, stiff tape, bolts of velvet, linen, silk, and so on, and several life-size dummy heads. She had one of the heads in her lap, wrapping folds of pink velour around it and sticking pins here and there to hold the cloth in place. Looking up, she saw me, smiled and said, "What's all the commotion outside, honey?" She had two pins in the corner of her mouth and had to speak around them.

"A turkey drive, ma'am. The men are rushin' to get'm through town before first dark, cause when it's time to roost, they go'n fly to the nearest tree and they ain't go'n budge till daybreak."

I was only twelve then. It was before I got long-legged, so with her sitting down and me standing, my head was just about level with hers. I forgot all about the turkeys, I was so busy smelling her perfume and looking at her freckles. They were like brown pepper. She had gray-blue eyes, long black lashes, a tilted-up nose, a big smiley mouth, and thick wavy brown hair piled high and perky on her head.

Miss Love took the pins out of her mouth. "I guess you live here in Cold Sassy," she said, smiling extra friendly.

"Yes'm. I'm Will Tweedy, ma'am. You must be the new milliner."

"And you must be Mr. Hoyt's boy." She nodded in the direction of Papa, who was over by the cash register.

"Yes'm."

"He is a very nice man, and good-looking, too." That pleased me. Papa was stocky, not tall, but he was neat about his clothes, had a

handsome face, and shaved every morning.
Most men in Cold Sassy had a beard or just
shaved on Saturday night to get ready for
Sunday.

Miss Love held up the dummy head with
the pink velour wrapping, turning it this way
and that to get the effect. "You like this hat,
Will Tweedy?"

I didn't have much opinion about hats, or
much interest either. "Well'm," I mumbled,
"I cain't hardly tell what it's go'n look like
yet."

Miss Love laughed. A hearty laugh. Her
lips were so red they looked painted almost.
"You're a good diplomat, Will Tweedy."

One thing I noticed that day was how
proper Miss Love spoke. Till then, I never
met anybody who could talk as proper as
Aunt Carrie. Aunt Carrie was taught to speak
cultured at a private school in Athens run by
a French woman, Madame Joubert.

I found out later that Miss Love learned to
talk right from a rich educated lady in Phila-
delphia that she used to go stay with every
spring and fall, making hats for her and her
daughters.

"Mrs. Hanover was always correcting my
grammar and pronunciation," Miss Love told

me. "If I mumbled or made the least little mistake, I had to say it over and over till I got it right. I guess Mrs. Hanover liked me. She said that with my flair for fashion, her friends couldn't tell me from one of them till I opened my mouth. 'Cultivate good speech, Miss Simpson,' she'd say, 'and you can marry above yourself.' She gave me her finishing school grammar book. I still have it. I felt certain if I memorized that book I could marry the Prince of Wales—or at least a railroad president."

Grandpa was real proud of the store having a milliner trained at the Armstrong and Cater Company in Baltimore. In 1901, the company had sent Miss Love and her best friend out to a big store in Texas. When she wanted to leave Texas, Armstrong and Cater sent her, sight unseen, to Grandpa. He had written asking for a milliner and Miss Love was available, so that's all there was to it. But for weeks after she came to town, men would poke Grandpa in the ribs, nod toward the milliner's table, and say, "You shore know how to pick'm, Mr. Blakeslee," or, "You got you a real looker, ain't you?" Grandpa would grin and say you dang right.

At first Miss Love stayed at Granny and Grandpa's house, in their company room. Later she boarded with Mr. and Mrs. Eli P. Crabtree, whose son Arthur was bad to drink and took an overdose of laudanum in the cemetery one cold night. They found him dead the next morning, huddled up against his sweetheart's tombstone, and now Miss Love was renting Arthur's old room. The Crabtrees thought she was real nice, but she didn't tell her business to them or anybody, and didn't have close friends. The only thing Cold Sassy knew about her was what that milliner in Athens told Aunt Loma.

Besides about her daddy being in the Union Army, the woman told it as gospel that after Miss Love got engaged to a rich Texas rancher and went home to Maryland to make her trousseau clothes, her best friend got you-know-what by her fee-ance, and they eloped. Aunt Loma said if her fee-ance and her best friend were that kind of trash, "it don't speak so well for Love Simpson."

You have to take into account that Aunt Loma was just eighteen when Miss Love hit town, and the jealous type. Aunt Loma was blue-eyed and had the thickest long curly red hair you ever saw, with little tendrils around

her face that made her look sweet and inno-
cent. Till Miss Love came, she was considered just the prettiest thing in Cold Sassy,
and also the most fashionable. While visiting
one time in Atlanta, Loma went to M. Rich
& Bros. and bought herself some handmade
French drawers with lace-edged ruffles, and
also what she called "a blue poky-dot foulard
dress with an overskirt of Georgette crepe."
Grandpa like to had a fit about her spending
the money, but after she cried, he let her
alone about it. The only thing not fashionable
about Aunt Loma was her bosom.

She was so flat you didn't have to be big to
be bigger, and Miss Love Simpson was definitely bigger. At some point Miss Love made
the mistake of remarking that Loma had just
the perfect figure for the stylish new shirt-
waists with lots of tucks and ruffles in front.
That was because of Loma's flat busts, so
though it was meant as a compliment, she
was insulted. She hadn't had much to do with
Miss Love since, especially not after one Saturday when she wanted to buy a little blue
hat with white bird wings on it that Miss Love
was wearing and didn't want to sell. I heard
what was said because I was down at the store
washing fly spots off the show window.

"You've sold hats off your head before," Aunt Loma argued, pushing out her bottom lip.

"I know," Miss Love answered sweetly. "But I made this hat special to go with this dress. Let me fix up something else for you."

Aunt Loma's face flushed red as her hair, she was so mad, and she flounced off acting like a store-owner's daughter to a hired hand. "I must say, Love Simpson," she hissed, "you'd do well to quit thinking you're good as your betters!"

As they say in Cold Sassy, Aunt Loma was behind the door when they passed out the tact. And her temper was such that if King Edward VII or the Lord God Almighty Himself had been around when she got mad, she wouldn't of talked any less awful. In fact, she'd of been glad of the extra audience.

I just couldn't stand Aunt Loma. As long as I could remember, she'd bossed me like I was her slave. She was only six years older than me, for gosh sake, which to my mind didn't give her any right to lord it over me like she was a hundred. God help Miss Love Simpson if she really had gone off and married Grandpa against her will—against Aunt Loma's will, I mean. I hoped Miss Love understood what she was up against. I could of told her, because I had been up against Aunt Loma all my life.

There were some people in Cold Sassy who called Miss Love "that Yankee woman" or made fun of her for being a suffragette. Not a man in town thought it mattered a hoot about women voting, and only two ladies went to the first women's suffrage meeting Miss Love set up. Either nobody else was interested or their husbands wouldn't let them come, one. After that meeting, most folks felt a little uneasy about Miss Love. Still and all, just about everybody liked her.

The men liked her because she was pretty and friendly and, as Mr. Cratic Flournoy put it, full of ginger and pepper.

The ladies liked her because she made hats that could of come straight out of New York City. Also, she had a pattern book of the newest styles and would order patterns for anybody who wanted her to, and she showed the ladies how to fix their hair fashionable.

The congregation at the Methodist Episcopal Church, South, liked her because her piano-playing was loud and lively. Ever since Miss Love started playing for preachin', folks had sung out good, patting their feet and generally getting in shape to shout and amen during the sermon.

Just the same, Cold Sassy thought it was one thing to like Miss Love and another thing entirely to marry her. Especially if your wife died just three weeks ago.

5

As Mama expected, there wasn't anybody in Cold Sassy who didn't wonder if Grandpa hadn't been sweet on the milliner a long time, and maybe was relieved to get shet of Miss Mattie Lou so he could marry Miss Love.

For sure Miss Love wasn't a bit like Granny, except they were both feisty. Granny always wore her skimpy gray hair pulled straight back behind her ears and fastened in a ball. I never saw a frill or ribbon on her and I figured she had never been pretty. She told me that when she and her cousin were young, they walked by the harness shop one day and chanced to hear an old man say what nice girls they were. Another man said, "Yeah, but one of'm shore is strange around the eyes."

"We never knowed which'n he meant," Granny said, laughing.

I knew which'n. It was Granny. Her eyes were the farthest apart I ever saw. She had big ears, too, and the last few months a peculiar knot came on one side of her throat. It wasn't a goiter. Doc Slaughter said blamed if he knew what it was. Grandpa teased her about it. "You look like you done swallered a goose aigg, Miss Mattie Lou, and it got stuck in yore goozle."

She just laughed. She was kind of worried about the knot, but really didn't care how it looked, and Grandpa didn't either.

Her not having a boy baby was the only thing Grandpa ever threw up to her. Once I saw tears come in her eyes when he mentioned it.

Granny used to say she never did see why Mr. Blakeslee married her. "When he come back to Cold Sassy after the War, he was the handsomest man you ever seen and I was a old maid. Twenty-one year old and never had a beau in my life. I was fixin' to go in to church one Sunday mornin' when this good-lookin' feller, he tapped me on the shoulder and said, 'Ain't you Miss Mattie Lou Toy? You don't need no sermon today. Stay out

here and le's talk.' I ain't seen him since the
fourth grade but I knowed it was Rucker
Blakeslee. So we stayed in the churchyard,
like a reg'lar courtin' couple, and talked one
another's ears off. Afterwards it was dinner
on the grounds, and we talked some more.
Fore that day was over Mr. Blakeslee said he
was a-go'n marry me, soon as he come back
from peddlin' in the mountains." I remember
she laughed about how quick Grandpa could
make up his mind. "Maybe he thought I was
rich," she added, laughing again.

There were those in Cold Sassy who had
the same idea. They said the land Mattie
Lou's daddy owned was why Ruck Blakeslee
was so taken with her. She knew they said
that, but it never worried her.

She always called him Mr. Blakeslee, and I
never heard him call her anything but Miss
Mattie Lou. Once when I was little bitty and
Papa and Mama went to Atlanta on the train
to buy for the store, I stayed at Grandpa's
house and slept on the daybed in the back
hall. About daybreak I heard him stand up to
use the pot. The bed creaked as he flopped
back down, and I heard him say, "Turn over,
Miss Mattie Lou, so I can put my feet up to
yore stomach. They's cold."

At the time, I wondered how Grandpa could get his feet up that high, tall as he was and short as she was. Only when I was older did I think how funny for a man to call his wife Miss Mattie Lou when it was just the two of them in bed. Papa called my mother Miz Tweedy in front of Queenie or neighbors, and Mama in front of me and Mary Toy, but I knew she was "hon" or Mary Willis when they were by themselves.

Everybody in Cold Sassy admired my grandmother. At her funeral, I heard somebody say, "Miss Mattie Lou just reeked of re-fine-ment, didn't she?" and I knew what was meant.

Her refinement wasn't like Aunt Carrie's. Granny didn't sit on the porch reading Greek and Latin and Shakespeare, or get up lectures for children, or recite poetry. She didn't think she always knew best, the way Aunt Carrie did, and didn't throw off on people who said "I seen" or "I taken," like Aunt Loma, and didn't make children practice manners, like Mama. But Granny was a fine lady anyway, never mind her grammar or her country ways and never mind how plain she was.

To my thinking, it was refined that she

didn't fuss at Grandpa about not having the house wired for electricity. When Mr. Sheffield, the mill-owner, bought a Delco generator for the mill and contracted with the town to install twenty street lights and run wires to all the houses and stores on both sides of the railroad tracks, practically everybody got electricity except Grandpa and the mill workers and the colored folks in Pigfoot Bottoms. But you didn't hear Granny complain about having to trim wicks, clean smoked-up lamp chimneys, and fool with kerosene when other ladies could just pull a ceiling cord to get light.

Grandpa wouldn't pay to hook into the new water main and sewer system, either. Said he didn't mind going to Egypt, which was what everybody in town called privies. He never seemed to notice that Granny was still drawing well water and emptying slop jars after other women were turning faucets and pulling tank chains.

Still and all, Grandpa loved Granny. Nobody would doubt it if they'd been down there with him and her like I was after she had her stroke.

She got took one night early in June. I remember I was at a magic show in the brush arbor and they called me out.

The family sat around Granny's bed till nearly daybreak. She moaned a lot and hiccupped, but never spoke a word. Not even to Grandpa. We went home for breakfast, and I remember how Papa kept patting Mama's hand. "Please, God, don't take her," she prayed between bites.

We could hear Queenie moaning in the kitchen as she fried salt mackerel, her tears splattering in the hot grease. Then she went to singing a Nigerian grief song learned from her daddy, who was lured onto an illegal slave ship in 1848, when he was only twelve. The slavers brought him to an island off the Georgia coast and hid him there till he got bought for Mr. Bubba Tate; that's how he ended up in Cold Sassy. Queenie always sang her daddy's African words, but you knew by the wailing and moaning that they meant death.

"Don't you dare sing that!" Mama yelled from the breakfast room.

Soon as we could, Papa and I hurried to the store. We knew Grandpa wouldn't get down there that day.

We were so busy we none of us went home to dinner, not even Miss Love, who put aside her hats to help wait on customers. All we had was crackers out of the barrel and rat cheese off the wheel. Dr. Slaughter came by the store from the sickbed about one o'clock. He told me Granny was "tol'able." But when he went over to the cash register where Papa was, he said, "Hoyt, she's dyin'. And she cain't stop hiccuppin'. Hit's wearin' her out."

You have to understand that Dr. Slaughter was a fine physician. He had not only read medicine for six months under a doctor over in Athens, he'd gone two whole years to medical school up North. So if he thought Granny was dying, I never doubted it was going to happen. "God's mercy is our only hope," he said as he went out.

I went back to the storeroom and knelt down on a sack of cowfeed and prayed harder than I ever had before in my life. "Oh, Lord Jesus Christ, have mercy on Granny Blakeslee," I begged. "Please, God, spare her. If Thou wilt just let her live, I promise I'll be a better boy. Please, God. Please. . . ."

6

It was all over town about Granny's stroke. Several ladies who went down to the house came by the store later and told us how she was, but at three o'clock we still hadn't had any direct word from Grandpa or Mama or Aunt Loma. Papa said he sure did wish Mr. Blakeslee had a telephone at home. Finally Miss Love said, "Mr. Hoyt, why don't you send Will up there?"

So Papa said, "Will, run and see how your granny is and how Mama's holding up. And ask Mr. Blakeslee if that case of Castoria ever came in from Athens. Chap Cheney's wife needs some for the baby."

Aunt Loma was at the door to greet people. When she saw it was only me, she turned away without speaking. Her eyes were swollen and she held a handkerchief to her mouth. As I went in, Mrs. Means came out with her baby, who had not only spit up but had soiled his diaper, I could tell. The front hall and parlor were full of neighbor ladies, but instead of it being a gaggle of sound like at church meetings, the talk was all whispered. My mother hurried toward me. I was fixing to ask her about Granny, but her face told me.

"Pa won't let anybody in the sickroom," she whispered. "Not even me and Loma." Tears welled up in her eyes. "But he'll want to see you, Will."

"Is she still hiccuppin'?" I whispered back.

"No, it fine'ly stopped, thank the Lord."

Granny was propped up on pillows in the big high-back walnut bed. Her eyes were closed. Her face looked gray. I thought she was dead, but when I stared hard at her chest, I saw a faint rise and fall. Not knowing what to say or do, I tiptoed in and just stood at the foot of the bed, one bare foot on top of the other, and looked at her and Grandpa.

He hadn't seen me come in. Sitting in a cane-back rocker pulled up by the bed, he was resting his left elbow near Granny's head. The empty knotted sleeve lay crumpled against her gray hair, and he held her small right hand in his big bony one. He was staring at Granny like she could hold on to life if only he didn't blink. But all of a sudden Grandpa's chest started jerking in the strangest way, and his eyes squeezed shut. Between the heavy mustache and the bushy, white-streaked beard, his mouth stretched across his teeth in a fierce smile. Then his lips squeezed shut. Though he made no sound, his chest kept jerking. I didn't know what to think. It scared me.

But then he gasped, and tears ran down his cheeks as he buried his face in his hand.

I had never in my life seen a grown man cry that way. Preachers and sinners cried at revivals, and old Chickenfoot Creesie, a colored man, would cry when he came to our back door begging vittles for his children on a cold winter day. But not silent like this.

Grandpa would of hated being seen. I sneaked out of the room, went out on the back porch, and stood watching Granny's White Leghorn rooster chase the dominecker hens and the Rhode Island Reds. Then I went in the kitchen, where several ladies were talking. The table was just full of good things folks had brought in, and I ate some fried chicken and a piece of lemon meringue pie.

When I peeped into the sickroom again, Grandpa was bent forward in the rocker, his arms and head resting on the bed by Granny's side. Her eyes were still closed, but her right hand brushed across his mane of dark hair.

"You need . . . y' hair . . . cut . . . Mr.

Bla'slee." Her words came weak and slurred. The left side of her mouth drooped like a rosebud gone too long without water. "Soon's I git . . . better . . . I'm go'n . . . cut it . . . trim y' beard."

At which Grandpa got up quickly and stood a spell before the window, getting aholt of himself. After he sat back down in the rocker, he gently pushed the hair off Granny's damp forehead, then blew his nose loudly—like a foghorn, tell the truth—and said, "I seem to of caught a li'l cold, Miss Mattie Lou."

That's when he saw me standing in the doorway.

"Grandpa," I said, "why don't you go get you some lemon meringue pie? I'll sit with Granny."

He started to argue, but Granny smiled a tiny one-sided smile and said, "Let Willy . . . I ain't hardly . . . seen . . . m' Willy. . . ."

Soon as he tiptoed out, she closed her eyes. I think she slept. In a few minutes Grandpa was back with a dark red rose in his hand, biting off the thorns and spitting them out as he walked toward the bed. When Granny roused a little he held the rose close to her face. His hand was trembling. He said gruffly, "Here."

She tried to take the blossom but it fell to the sheet. Picking it up, he sat staring at it, then spoke real low to her. "I remember you had a red rose like this'n in yore hair the day I decided to marry you. Recollect thet Sunday, Miss Mattie Lou?"

She kind of nodded and just barely smiled, her mouth listing to the left.

"I hadn't laid eyes on you since you was a li'l girl, till thet day. You was sech a sweet thang," he said softly, his face close to hers, his hand caressing her cheek. "Yore eyes was all feisty and yore feet patted out the organ music whilst we talked. Was thet really the first time you ever set outside with the young folks, Miss Mattie Lou?" There was a twinkle in his eyes, a slight teasing in his voice, almost like he'd forgot how sick she was. "Gosh a'mighty, girl, thet rafter-rattlin' preacher give us plenty time to git acquainted thet day, didn't he? And I was after you like a charged-up bull. You recollect thet day, Miss Mattie Lou?"

She struggled to speak, her voice a whisper. "'Member . . . the brush arbor . . . Mr. Bla'slee?"

As Grandpa held her hand tight and tears rolled down his cheeks, I thought how Granny used to tell me about them camping out under a thick brush arbor their whole first married summer while Grandpa and Uncle Ephraim Toy built her a two-room house out of poplar logs so big it took just five to make a wall.

I had figured out long time ago that my mother must have been conceived under the brush arbor—and I blushed to think about that now. Whether such memories were stirring in Grandpa, who can know. What he said next was "Miss Mattie Lou, try real hard and git well. You hear? Please git well. I don't want to live 'thout you."

But Granny was asleep again, and soon was breathing so loud and deep it was like—I don't know what it was like. I'd never heard anybody breathe that way.

He looked over at me. "Will Tweedy, git on yore knees, son. Hit's time to pray."

I knelt down on one side of the bed and Grandpa on the other. Holding Granny's right hand, he rested his bowed head wearily against the edge of the feather mattress. Then for all the world like we were at testimonial time at the Baptist church with forty-

five people listening besides God, he commenced to pray.

The way Grandpa prayed wasn't like other
people prayed. You'd of thought God was an
old crony of his instead of somebody who
could strike you down dead if He had a mind
to. "Lord?" he began, then stopped to honk
his nose into a handkerchief. "Lord, I'm
tempted to ast You to make Miss Mattie Lou
well, like You was one a-them Atlanta doctors, or maybe Santy Claus and her a Christmas present You could give me if'n You jest
would. I know Thou don't mind me hopin'
she'll git well, Lord, or wishin', but hep me
not to beg You to spare her. . . . Oh God,
You know my sin!" he cried suddenly. His
voice had an awful sound, like he was about
to break half in two.

What could be his sin?

Granny's harsh breathing and the hushed
voices in the parlor filled the silence. Finally
he went on. "If'n she lives, Lord, I'll be thet
thankful. If'n she don't pull th'ew, I ain't go'n
say it was Thy will. You wouldn't kill her,
Lord, to punish me. . . . Hep me remember
my faith that Yore arrange-ment for livin' and
dyin' is good. Hit ain't fair or equal, Lord, but
it keeps thangs movin' on. Hep me not forgit

my faith thet whatever happens, it's all right.
. . . Hep Will Tweedy here see thet we got to
accept dyin' in exchange for livin' and
workin', and havin' folks like Miss Mattie
Lou to love. And be loved by."

My grandfather's voice was stronger and
calmer now. "Lord," he added, like it was a
postscript on a letter, "please forgive the
ways I ain't done right by Miss Mattie Lou.
Please, forgive me. She don't know, and ain't
nobody else knows, but I know and You
know, Lord, what I'm a-talkin' bout. And
please hep her stand the sufferin'. Hep her
not be skeered. And wilt Thou please comfort them grievin' daughters in the parlor,
Lord, and Will Tweedy here, and li'l Mary
Toy. Give them heart's ease. And me, too,
Lord. A-men."

Granny didn't die that day. Next morning she
was better. She could talk clearer and she
took some chicken broth and sassafras tea
when Mama brought it in to her.

Everybody except Grandpa said it was
God's will. Some said He spared Miss Mattie
Lou because so many folks were praying for
her. The Presbyterians said her getting well
was preordained. Brother Belie Jones, the

Baptist preacher, said God just wasn't ready to take her Home, praise Jesus, or else He had something more for her to do here before she passed into the Great Beyond.

Grandpa didn't say anything at all. But there wouldn't of been more joy on his face if he'd just won a fist fight or made a hundred dollars on a land deal. If Cold Sassy folks would bother to remember that day and how happy he looked, they'd know Miss Love was nothing more to him at the time than a way to make a profit on ladies' hats.

7

Mrs. Avery down the street kept saying, "Now don't y'all git your hopes up too much. I seen it many a time—a sick person gits better just fore they go'n die."

We didn't pay her any attention. Granny really was better, no doubt about it. In the days that followed she slept a lot, but not with that awful unnatural deep breathing, and she could talk plainer and move her left hand, and the left side of her face wasn't dead-looking.

The first sign that Mrs. Avery might be right, or at least that there was a change, started one evening about a week later. It was about five o'clock. I was the one sitting by the sickbed. Granny had been dozing when all of a sudden she roused up and grabbed my arm. "Willy, look-a-there at them two coats fightin' in the corner! That littlest coat don't have a gnat's chance!"

Before I could answer, she whispered, "They's a old woman in Mr. Blakeslee's cheer. Go away, woman! She's hid-jus, Willy —face all puckered like them doll heads made out'n dried apples. Go on, git!"

"Ain't nobody in the chair, Granny."

"Ain't now. I got rid of the old booger." She sounded proud of herself. Then in a panic she whispered, "Willy, she didn't leave! She's up on the wall!"

I was scared. I didn't know what to do. Mama had gone down to our house to change clothes. Grandpa, wore out, was sound asleep on the narrow daybed in the back hall. I was just fixing to call him when Granny smiled and said, "Old booger's gone, thank the good Lord!" Then she drifted off into a perspiry sleep.

Trying to cool her off some, I picked up the

cardboard fan that said BIRDSONG'S FUNERAL
PARLOR in big letters and under it *Rest in the
Lord.* The fan seemed like an omen. A chill
goose-bumped my arms. I fanned fast so as
not to read the words, but they had already
brought to mind Great-Granmaw Tweedy,
how at her first funeral she sat up in her coffin at the graveyard and screamed. They were
fixing to close the lid on her and nail it down,
and she wasn't dead.

I shuddered, and just then Granny Blakeslee's eyes opened wide in a horror of her
own.

"Willy?" she whispered. "What's them two
men doin' over yonder? See? Look on the far
side a-the cemetery." She pointed. "They got
shovels. They comin' over here! They go'n
steal me!" Grabbing my arm, she pulled me
down on the bed—pulled so strong that if
she'd really been pulling me into her grave, I
wouldn't of been scareder.

"Grandpa!" I yelled. But then she loos-
ened her hold and looked up past me, as if
seeing a wonderment. "Y'all come for me?"
she called out, real friendly.

Granny listened, like to somebody talking
. . . looked disappointed . . . then smiled
politely and said, "Well, when y'all ready for

me, just holler." Then in a strong, trembling voice she said, "Ain't they a sight, Willy!"

"Ma'am, I don't see nothin'."

Granny kept nodding and smiling, like greeting folks at church, and reached up like to touch somebody.

"What you see?" I asked eagerly.

"Angels! Son, this here room's just full a-angels!" Her voice sent another thrill up my spine. "They got lacy wings, and they's all dressed up in quilted robes. . . . The softest, prettiest colors, Will! Lordy, they keep a-comin'. They's flyin' out'n the quilt chest! You cain't see'm? They come out, and then they float up and on off—clear th'ew the ceilin'! They's just beautiful, son! Bye-bye now," she called. She kept looking this way and that, smiling and waving. "Y'all come see me agin, hear." Every time one batch of angels left, another batch came out of the chest.

"Go git your grandpa," Granny ordered. "I bet he can see'm. They's just ever-where. . . ."

When Grandpa stumbled in, rubbing his eyes, she said to him, "Lookit the quilted angels, Mr. Blakeslee! . . . Aw, shoot, they done gone." Granny sagged down weak against the pillows, exhausted, her fingers plucking the sheet.

Mrs. Avery always said you know death's on the way when a sick person goes to picking at the covers.

"Mr. Blakeslee, I seen the most beautiful bein's. . . ." As Grandpa plopped down in the rocker, she went to telling him about it and got all excited again. "I wouldn't take a pretty for them angels!" She said it over and over. "I just wish you—"

"Forgit all thet, Miss Mattie Lou," Grandpa said finally. He spoke soft to her, like you would to a child. "Hit were jest a dream. You all tangled up in yore mind. Go to sleep now." He slid his left elbow under her neck, circling his other arm around her, and pulled her close to him, rocked her against him.

"Mr. Bla'slee," she mumbled, "if you'd a-come . . . a mite sooner . . . you'd a-seen'm. . . . I seen a . . ."

"Sh-h-h. Go to sleep now, Miss Mattie Lou," he whispered, his strong arms holding her, gently rocking, slow and gently rocking. "You all tuckered out. Sleep now. Go to sleep."

She drifted quickly into a deep snoring stu-

por. By next day you could hardly wake her—
and if you did, a minute later she'd go right
back into that loud, awful breathing. The last
time Grandpa got her roused up, she looked
scared and said, "Sump'm terrible . . .
Sump'm awful's a-matter . . . w' me. . . ."

Grandpa smoothed the damp hair from
her forehead, spoke soft. "Tell you the truth,
you been pretty sick, Miss Mattie Lou. But
you gittin' better now. You jest real tired and
need to rest. So go on back to sleep, hear. I'll
set right here by you. I ain't go'n go leave
you, Miss Mattie Lou." He choked up. "I
ain't ever go'n leave you. . . ."

But she left him. That night the angels
came back for her, like she'd asked them to.

And nobody who saw the heartbreak on
Grandpa's face when Granny breathed her
last would have thought for one minute that
he was glad to get shet of her so he could
marry Love Simpson.

8

After Grandpa and Miss Love eloped, a lot of people felt sure he had never so much as looked at the milliner till after Granny died and he needed a housekeeper.

But those same folks were sure as certain that Miss Love had had designs on him ever since Miss Mattie Lou took sick, and was after him from the minute he became a widower.

"I was onto Love Simpson from the beginnin'," skinny old Miss Effie Belle Tate told Mama after the elopement. "Nobody else suspicioned what was goin' on, but I did." Because of living next door to Grandpa, Miss Effie Belle acted like God had sent her a special delivery letter explaining all the goings-on. "Miss Mattie Lou's body wasn't hardly gone to the funeral parlor before that woman was down to your pa's house, washin' and moppin' and dustin' and sweepin'." The pink wart quivered on her thin upper lip. "I knew the minute Miss Love got out a broom that she was after the nearest of kin. Why else would a white woman go over to your daddy's house to get it cleaned up for the funeral?"

she asked Mama. "Hit wasn't like he didn't have you and Loma to do for him."

But at the time of Granny's funeral, Miss Effie Belle had sung a different tune entirely. I remember how she talked across the coffin to Mama. "Ain't Love Simpson sweet to pitch in like this? After workin' for your pa two years, I reckon she knows how economical he is. He ain't go'n hire nobody to hep, and Lord knows, you and little Loma got your hands full. Not to mention your hearts bein' full to overflowin' with grief."

All Miss Effie Belle did for Grandpa that day was bring over a chocolate cake and a caramel cake. Being eighty-nine years old, she'd had plenty of practice and was by far the cake champion of Cold Sassy. Still and all, two cakes weren't anything like equal to the trouble Miss Love went to on the day before the funeral. Besides all the cleaning, she had washed and dried dishes for hours in Granny's hot kitchen. The house was full of sad people, come to cry and eat and drink tea, and Granny didn't have enough dishes without somebody being in the kitchen to wash each plate and glass as soon as it got set down.

If Miss Love had notions about Grandpa

that day—the way Miss Effie Belle claimed later—having to use a privy and draw well water and go to the back porch to throw out the dirty dishwater would have been enough to make her think twice.

That night after supper, Aunt Loma, Uncle Camp, us Tweedys, and Grandpa sat in the parlor with the remains and the visitors. But Miss Love was still working in the kitchen— by lamplight, I might add. I remember Grandpa went back there two or three times to tell her to quit. She said she wasn't tired a bit, but she must of been about to break half in two.

Mama and them had expected we would all sit up with Granny that night. But at ten o'clock, when Miss Love finally got through and came in the parlor and asked if there was anything else she could do, Grandpa not only told her to go on home, he told all of us to. "Ain't nobody go'n set up with Miss Mattie Lou but me."

"Pa, we don't mind a bit," my mother said. "We want to. You need us."

"I don't need nobody but yore ma."

While we were saying good night, I saw Miss Love put her hand on Grandpa's arm.

"You done too much," he told her gruffly.

"Not at all," she said. "Sir, the first winter I was here, when I had the flu, Miss Mattie Lou came and bathed me every morning—like she was my own mother. I won't ever forget that. I want to do anything I can to help you now." She said it so sweet, with tears in her eyes.

Grandpa blew his nose loud. "Uh, well, good night, Miss Love. I'm much obliged."

When I was halfway down the front steps, he called me. "Will Tweedy? Git up here fore sunup, boy. I want you to hep me."

Anybody who had been with us next morning wouldn't ever wonder how Grandpa had felt about Granny—before she died or after.

I got there at daybreak. The parlor door was shut where Granny was, and I could see the flickering glow of lamplight under the door as I walked down the cool dark hall. I wanted to go look at her, but I was scared to, by myself. I hurried to the back porch.

In the half-light I could see Grandpa out in Granny's rose garden. He was cutting rosebuds, which for him wasn't easy with just the one hand, and dropping each one into a big zinc tub. Without even a howdy or good morning as I walked toward him, he called, "Git out yore pocketknife, Will Tweedy."

"What you want me to do, sir?"

"Hep cut them roses."

When it came to feeling close to Granny, being in the garden was a sight better than sitting by her coffin. Out there amidst all the growing things, it seemed like maybe she'd just gone to the shed room to get a hoe instead of being off in Heaven.

I stood and looked for a long time. Over yonder were what she called her "word plants"—the wild flowers she planted because they had names she liked. Creepin' Charlie, Lizzie run by the fence, love's a-bustin', fetch me some ivy cause Baby's got the croup. . . . In the next bed were medicinal herbs she used in potions for sick folks: squaw weed, hepatica, goldenseal, ginseng for the brain, jewelweed for poison ivy rash, wolf milk for warts, and fleabane and pale bergamot, which Granny would rub on her face and arms to keep off mosquitoes and gnats.

But on that early June morning, the heavy scent of roses was what made my heart ache. It was hard to believe the roses could be so alive and her so dead.

"Make haste, son. Come hep me." Grandpa was impatient.

"How many we go'n pick?" I asked, coming up where he was.

"All of'm," he said, waving his arm stub over the big garden. It had been a late spring and there were still masses of roses. Red, white, light pink, dusky pink, yellow. All colors, all kinds. The garden had a border of climbing Seven Sisters on the west side, a hedge of red roses on the side next to Miss Effie Belle's house, white roses against the henhouse, and yellow tree roses at the far end. "Just git the buds," ordered Grandpa. "The wide-open ones won't last out the funeral."

Grandpa had him an idea.

I toted tubs full of roses to the back porch. Drew buckets and buckets of well water to pour over them. And about time the first rays of sunlight hit the back steps, I sat down out there with my grandfather.

First he took a square of Brown Mule out of his pocket, bit off a plug, and settled it in his left cheek. Then he leaned his chair back against the porch wall and got to work. While I trimmed off the lower leaves and thorns, Grandpa took a big split-open croker sack

and poked each rose stem into the loose bur-
lap, weaving it in and out, then in again, like
a pin being stuck into cloth. In no time at all
he had him a solid blanket of roses. It was
beautiful.

I noticed for the first time the pile of big
croker sacks by his chair.

He spat tobacco juice in an arc that just
missed a Rhode Island Red pecking dirt in
the swept yard. The hen shrieked, flapped her
wings, and ran off. Handing me what he had
done, Grandpa said, "Now, son, git this here
thang down under some water. Yore granny
always soaks roses under water fore she
puts'm in a pitcher." He didn't notice he was
talking as if Granny was in her kitchen, fixing
to cook us some grits, instead of laid out in a
coffin in the parlor.

It will help to show what Granny meant to
Grandpa if I point out that it wasn't a cheap
homemade coffin she was in. It was a fine
readymade one he'd ordered years ago when
rich Mr. Sheffield was thought to be dying
and didn't. It had been upstairs at the store
ever since, alongside the stock of corn plant-
ers, fertilizer spreaders, mule collars, iron
washpots, hat trees, and extra brass racks for
readymade dresses. When I was little bitty, I

used to close my eyes whenever I had to walk by that coffin.

There were some who said later that Grandpa, stingy as he was, wouldn't have used that expensive coffin for Miss Mattie Lou if he wasn't trying to make it up to her for something he'd done wrong—such as lusting in his heart after Miss Love or being too stingy to give Granny electricity and a bathroom.

If he wasn't ashamed about the lights and plumbing, maybe he should of been. But personally I didn't think guilt had anything to do with the nice coffin. I thought he used it because he loved her. Despite all I found out later, I still think so.

Grandpa told Granny one time that dead folks ought to be put right in the ground as the Lord intended. I was there and heard it. "And I want me a party when I die, not a funeral. Remember thet."

She didn't act shocked like Mama would of. As a matter of fact, she laughed. "Don't go talkin' bout dyin', Mr. Blakeslee. I druther live in the past than dwell on that part of the future. Still, since you brung it up, I'll say this: my feeling bout buryin' ain't the same as your'n. You remember that." She said the dead body was sacred, it having been a house for the mind and soul, and as such it deserved proper respect. "A nice funeral is a sort of thank-you," she added. "A person's body oughtn't to be treated like no old dead dog."

What she said didn't change Grandpa's thinking about buryings in general, but that being the way she felt, then he was going to see to it she got her thank-you. For Grandpa, that was a sign of love, because usually he did what he wanted to and never noticed that Granny might welcome a little consideration.

By the time he finished covering another sack with roses, he was as excited as a little boy digging worms to go fishing.

They were really something, those rose blankets. It seemed a shame to plan on covering up a fine coffin with them, but they were sure pretty.

I stood up to stretch and scratch. I was hungry. After milking that morning, I had poured me a big glass of sweetmilk, warm right out of the cow, but that wasn't enough to call breakfast. I slumped down in a chair, tilting it against the side of the porch. "We picked way too many roses," I said, yawning.

"No, we ain't. Now make haste, son. I don't want no kinfolks or neighbor ladies

seein' what we done and buttin' in with sug-
gestions. Fore you know it, half a-Cold
Sassy'll be down here a-cryin' and carryin' on,
tryin' to see how I and yore ma and Loma is
a-takin' it. I cain't stand thet. So we got to git
th'ew."

I figured the real reason he didn't want
anybody to see the rose blankets, it would
spoil his surprise for the funeral. But of
course he couldn't admit that.

Before long we heard somebody at the
front of the house. Probably Mama, but I
knew he was scared it was Aunt Loma. He
made me drag the zinc tubs full of watered-
down rose blankets into the shed room by the
back porch. Then, with me on one side of the
tub and him on the other, we toted the rest of
the roses to the barn and finished out there.

When he thought we had enough, he told
me to cut a sack half in two for him. Leaving
an oval space the shape of a head on a pillow,
he put the last rosebuds around the oval. I
guessed what he aimed to do with it.

First I had to go ask Mama to clear folks
out of the parlor where Granny was. Then me
and Grandpa went in there from the dining
room. I couldn't believe how many big vases
and baskets of yard flowers had been brought

in and set on tables and on the floor around the coffin.

It gave me the creeps, helping Grandpa slip his pillow sham of roses under Granny's head. But touching her didn't seem to bother him. He patted her face and smoothed her hair, and even pried up her stiff hands and moved them a little. Then all of a sudden his face scrooched up, and in a choky voice he ordered me to leave and tell Mama not to let nobody come in on him.

It was ten o'clock, and like I say, I was hungry. Folks had already brought over more cakes and pies, and platters of fried chicken and ham, and their good china bowls full of string beans, butterbeans, okra, and tomatoes. Enough to feed a ox, really. So I ate. I was in the kitchen finishing a piece of Miss Effie Belle's caramel cake when Grandpa found me again.

My mother stuck a glass of buttermilk in his hand and he drank it, but I'm not sure he even noticed. He was all business. "Will Tweedy?"

"Sir?"

"Go hitch up Big Jack."

"Yessir."

He walked with me to the back porch. As

soon as we were out of earshot of the others he said, "When you git Jack hitched, lay them rose thangs in the buggy and bring it on up here."

"Yessir."

When I got back with the buggy, Grandpa was out on the porch picking long nails from a dusty glass jar on the long-legged, blue-painted old slab table. A hammer handle stuck out of his pants pocket. "Load up, son."

"Yessir."

The mourners were all up front with the corpse—admiring the roses that framed her head, I expect. So not a soul except Mama saw me bring the zinc tubs out of the shed room. She marveled, I could tell, but said nothing as I dragged each one to the edge of the porch, tilted it to drain the water out, then loaded "them rose thangs" on the back of the buggy. I didn't know how many blankets we had, but I was sure it was too many.

Grandpa said, "Naw, son, it's jest enough."

Enough for what? He didn't say, I didn't ask, and neither did Mama, who watched as we drove off.

He let me keep the reins. Said we were bound for the cemetery—"but first, son, we'll go by yore house." I didn't have to wait till the whiskey was on his breath to guess why.

The grave was already dug, of course, close behind all his and Granny's children that hadn't lived to grow up, and just a little ways from the Toy plot, where Granny's daddy was buried between her mama and his second wife. He had a granite tombstone. His wives had slabs of brown marble off of washstands.

I always thought a single marker joining the graves of a man and wife looked like the head of a double bed. In the moldy old Crane plot was a wide granite headstone that joined three graves—like a triple bed, you might say. This is what it said:

Here Lies Luzon Theophilus Crane
A Good Man

Eugenia Lamson Crane	*And Lucy Wylie Who*
His Wife	*Should Have Been His Wife*

"Did the Wylies put that up, Mama?" I asked her one day. "I know it wasn't the Cranes did it."

"Aw, shah!" she snapped, jabbing a cone-shaped tin cemetery urn into the ground for the jonquils we brought. "Quit readin' that trash and bring me that quart jar of water for the urn."

Not far from Mr. and Mrs. Crane and Miss Wylie was a little bitty headstone that said *"In Memory of Tweety, Jan. 4, 1894."* I used to think that was a baby cousin of mine with the Tweedy name spelled wrong, but Mama said it was somebody's pet canary. "The Tweedys are always buried at Hebron," she reminded me. "I mean the older generations. This family"—she solemnly indicated the grave of my baby brother—"has started bein' buried here."

Always before, the graveyard had seemed real interesting and peaceful. Just a quiet and reverent place. But in mid-June, 1906, the deep yawning hole that would swallow up Granny looked horrible, like it could suck me down.

"What we go'n do, Will Tweedy, we go'n line yore grandma's grave with these here roses."

It took two of the blankets to cover the floor of the pit. The others he nailed into the grave's damp red-clay walls while both of us lay on the grass, me holding a croker sack blanket and a long nail, him propped on his left elbow, hammering. It was only as the last nail went in that Grandpa sagged. As if he was too tired to get up, he lay there looking down, and so did I. It wasn't awful anymore. The heavy smell of roses drifted up, and I thought I'd never seen anything as beautiful.

A tear dropped off Grandpa's nose and watered a red rose. Seeing that, I choked up. I ached for Grandpa, grieving. And for Granny. I knew she wouldn't want to be dead. And then I thought about my friend Bluford Jackson, the one who got lockjaw after firecrackers burned his hand last Christmas. He had died soon after New Year's Day and now nearly six months later I was just finally seeing that Blu was gone for good.

"Why'd Blu Jackson have to go and die, Grandpa?" I hit my fist on the grass. "Why'd God take him like that? He hadn't lived yet. He wasn't old like Granny. He had so many things to do. . . . He was scared of dyin'. . . . I bet Granny was scared of dyin', too."

Grandpa put his arm stub around me, and we lay there, staring down into the grave. "Like they say, the old must die and the young may die," he muttered softly. "Hit's what you git for livin'. But thet don't seem so

awful as you grow older, son. You'll see." He
gave a deep sigh.

"How you go'n stand it, Grandpa? I mean
goin' home every night and she ain't there."

"Thet's what I don't know, son. Thet's
what I don't know. Yore granny was—" He
choked up again. When he could go on, he
stretched both arms down into the grave,
dropped them, helpless-like, and said, "But
do I got a choice, Will Tweedy? I got to stand
it, ain't I? Livin' is like pourin' water out of a
tumbler into a dang Coca-Cola bottle. If'n
you skeered you cain't do it, you cain't. If'n
you say to yoreself, 'By dang, I can do it!'
then, by dang, you won't slosh a drop."

We lay there a while longer. Finally
Grandpa sighed again and said, "I wouldn't
ast the Lord to steady my hand for a thang
like pourin' water into a Coca-Cola bottle.
But I'll be astin' Him for hep on this." He
indicated the grave. After a moment he said,
"Miss Mattie Lou shore was a fool about
roses." Silence again. "Two or more year ago
she was out workin' in her rose garden one
mornin'—did you know, boy, she's got over
sixty different kinds out there?—and she said
to me, said, 'Mr. Blakeslee, I wouldn't even
mind dyin' if'n I could be buried in a bed of

roses.' Thet's jest the way she put it. I laughed and said it would be her luck to die in the dead of winter. . . . Well, son, we better go git cleaned up for the funeral. Wisht it was over with. I'm plumb wore out." We both got up. "If'n I had my way, wouldn't be no sech a thang as funerals. They's jest a long hot time full a-hypocrites and kinfolks— grievin' some maybe, but mostly bein' glad to be alive theirselves and tryin' to pretend they ain't havin' a good time seein' one another."

"It wasn't like that at Blu's funeral."

"No, course not. They ain't no hypocrites at a youngun's funeral."

When I brought up the buggy, Grandpa stood by old Jack, absently stroking the huge gray forehead, and looked back at the grave site. Then he spat a wonderful stream of tobacco juice and climbed in beside me. "She was a plumb fool bout roses," he said softly.

Later, remembering that morning, I had no question in my mind: Grandpa's eloping wasn't a matter of him not loving Granny or not respecting the dead. He just needed a cheap cook.

9

To me, all that went on during Granny's sickness and dying and getting buried was more like a dream than real, till we got back from the cemetery and I watched Grandpa stop at the little pine desk in the front hall and write down her end in the Toy family Bible.

Miss Love Simpson was standing nearby, come to think of it, as Grandpa put on his glasses and opened the Bible to the page where his and Granny's life together was written down in different handwritings and different shades of faded ink. Miss Love and I watched as he read it, muttering out loud to himself:

"Matilda Louise Toy, born April 10, 1850, in Cold Sassy Community, Jackson County, Georgia.
Married Enoch Rucker Blakeslee May 27, 1871.
Children:
—Mary Willis, born March 5, 1872.
—Trix Esperance, born Jan. 19, 1873. Kicked by a mule and died July 1, 1880.

*—Rachel Aleez, born Nov. 25, 1875.
Died April 5, 1877, of the smallpox.
—Emma Frances was born Dec. 29,
1876. Died April 30, 1877. Pneumonia.
—Missouri Mathis, born Wednesday Spt.
2, 1878. Died Spt. 5, 1878, of water on
the brain.
—Loma Louise was born Dec. 6, 1886.
—Fannie Marie was born January 28,
1888, died a little Lamb of God the
same day."*

Then Grandpa wrote in fresh, black, final-
looking ink beside Granny's name: *Died June
14, 1906.*

The *Cold Sassy Weekly* said it was "one of the
saddest deaths that has ever grieved the people of Jackson County, because Mrs. Blakeslee was so beloved by so many."
I saved the write-up. It had a black border
and was long and fancy, beginning,

*Asleep in Jesus, blessed sleep From which
none ever wake to weep. . . .* Mrs. Mattie
Lou Blakeslee, a sacred mother of Israel,
has gone to receive the crown of righteous-

ness which God has promised to all those who love His appearing. Born Matilda Louise Toy, great-granddaughter of Capt. Josiah Toy who pioneered the settlement of Cold Sassy in 1804, she embraced the religion of our Blessed Master when young. Since that time her life and character has been that of a pure Christian ministering to the comfort of all, especially her beloved husband and consort, E. Rucker Blakeslee of this city, who now must walk alone. She gave up this life *"As one who wraps the draperies of his couch about him and lies down to pleasant dreams."* We must believe that the gates of Heaven were thrown open to receive her ransomed spirit, and that a crown resplendent with glory was placed upon her peaceful brow whilst the plaudit *"Well done, thou good and faithful servant"* echoed and re-echoed through the mansions of bliss. . . .

There was a lot more. Grandpa read it all, but instead of tearing it out to put in the Bible, he just dropped the newspaper on the floor, the way he always did when he was through with it, put his glasses in his pocket, and got up to go feed his mule.

He went back to work the day after the funeral, which most folks thought not fitting. But as I said before, he wasn't the same. No laughter in him. No jokes or funning. No neighborly talk, and wouldn't talk about Granny, either. If a customer started saying her condolences, Grandpa would nod and cut her off with "You be needin' anythang else, ma'am?"

He treated Uncle Camp awful during that time. One morning Grandpa pointed to a keg of nails and said, hateful, "Camp, see thet keg? I want you to roll it from one end of the store to the other till I say stop." He made Uncle Camp roll the keg all day long. When Papa asked what it was all about, Grandpa said, "I'm jest sick a-watchin' thet boy do nothin'."

I didn't like my grandfather much that day. But I didn't like Uncle Camp, either. If he'd been a real man, he would of refused, and then either walked out or set to work like his job depended on it.

We soon found out that Grandpa didn't go home at night when he left Aunt Loma's after supper. He went to the cemetery.

"Yore pa walks by here and we're settin' on the veranda but he don't speak or so much as nod in our direction," Miss Alice Ann Boozer told Mama. "He don't even see us. Just turns at them iron gates and disappears like a ghost. We always stay out there till the night air cools off, you know, and many a night he still ain't come back by time we go to bed. It ain't good for Mr. Blakeslee to be by hisself at the cemetery in the pitch-black dark—or in a full moon, either, for that matter."

I've mentioned Miss Effie Belle Tate, who lived next door to Grandpa. She told Mama that sometimes Grandpa's lamp was still on in his bedroom at two and three in the morning. "And lots a-times he goes out there to Miss Mattie Lou's rose garden in the middle of the night to pace them paths. If it's a moon I can see him just a-walkin'. Up and down, down and up. Pore man, he's a-grievin' hisself to death. One night I come close to takin' some sweetmilk and cookies out there to him, but I didn't know what to say. He's shut us all out. I keep out'n his way."

Miss Effie Belle wasn't the only one who didn't know how to take Grandpa.

Folks felt a lot more easy with Mama and Aunt Loma, who would sit and cry with them and carry on about God's will and how He surely had a purpose in letting their ma die or else needed her in Heaven, one. They'd talk on and on about the final illness, the dying, the funeral, and especially about the grave being lined with roses. "Such a sweet thing," folks would say. "Such a sweet thing Mr. Blakeslee done."

Nobody seemed to of been told that I helped.

Then somebody would bring up about Granny's ancestors leading a wagon train from North Carolina, how they camped here on the ridge under some big sassafras trees while they were building their houses. If somebody didn't know how come the settlement was named Cold Sassy, it would be explained that mountain wagoners on the way to market used to call the place "thet cold sassyfras grove" or "them cold sassy trees."

As often as not, before the conversation got back to Granny, somebody would say, "I think we done outgrowed the name Cold Sassy. Hit's old-fashion and tacky. We ought to do like Harmony Grove and git us a name like Commerce."

Then they'd talk a while about how hard Miss Mattie Lou worked all her life, hinting but not exactly saying out loud that she had worked herself into an early grave—which was the same as saying Grandpa could and should of hired her a cook and a colored boy to work her garden.

Nobody mentioned that all my life I had been her colored boy. Knowing Grandpa wouldn't hire anybody, Papa had expected me to put in a piece of every day down there. And I didn't mind. What I did mind, now that she was dead, was being in mourning.

Because of her hair, my sister didn't feel like I did. She was glad to hide at home. What happened, while Granny was on her deathbed, Mama got up a black outfit for Mary Toy to wear to the funeral—black taffeta dress, black stockings, black slippers, and a little black bonnet. "It'll give her something to wear on trips later," said Mama. "If everything is black already, the train sut won't show."

Unfortunately, Aunt Carrie decided early the morning of the funeral that Mary Toy's fiery red hair looked "inappropriate" for such a sad occasion. Her solution was to dye it black. "Just for today, sugarfoot," she said when my sister had a conniption fit. "We'll rinse it out tomorrow." By time Mama heard about it, it was too late to argue. And anyhow, who could argue with Aunt Carrie?

She wasn't really kin to us. She had latched on to Granny's mother long time ago. Granny inherited her, and now she was ours—for Christmas and Thanksgiving and all the Sundays between. She used to be rich, but wasn't anymore, having lost everything during the War, including her husband. But she still acted rich and, like Grandpa, had the manner of one who expects to be obeyed. She lived in an old three-story, rundown plantation house with morning rooms and sun rooms, and porches wrapped around every floor. Aunt Carrie looked rundown herself, in her frayed sweaters and canvas and rubber Keds shoes. She wore her thin hair in a knot, and except in winter always had a flower stuck behind each ear.

One summer she held weekly "cultural gatherings" for children. You had to recite a poem to get in. She gave us lectures on women's suffrage, Shakespeare, Beethoven, English history, and horticulture, and always had two freezers of homemade ice cream, which was why we all went. Her last lecture was on what she called "human excrement." Taking a rose out of her hair, she said it wouldn't be nearly so lovely if it weren't for human excrement, and told us children to go home and get our folks to empty our slop jars into our manure piles. Nobody let their children go to Aunt Carrie's gatherings after that, but she kept letting everybody know what happened to the excrement at her house. Aunt Carrie was stubborn.

Which is why nobody thought to argue with her when she decided to dye Mary Toy's hair black for Granny's funeral.

Halfway through the service Mary Toy got to sweating. Trickles of black liquid started running down her face. Seeing it, the preacher could hardly keep his mind on how good Granny had been or how it was God's will and all. Mama kept glancing at Mary Toy and finally dabbed at her face with a lace handkerchief.

About then, Mary Toy noticed the black that was smearing off her hair onto her sweaty arms. Thinking it was black blood, she went to wailing. People in the pew behind the family said later they thought she was just missing her granny, pore child.

Soon as we got to Grandpa's from the cemetery, Mama took Mary Toy's taffeta dress off and stuck her head in the wash basin on the back porch. The black leached right out, just like Aunt Carrie said it would. Only thing, her hair wasn't red anymore. It was purple. Soon as she looked in the mirror, Mary Toy went into mourning for her hair. She cried for hours and then days. It was a relief to everybody when, after our Glorious Fourth celebration, Cudn Temp said to her, "Sugarfoot, come on home with me and stay till the color grows out." Cudn Temp lived out on a farm in Banks County.

Like Mary Toy, my mother was partly in mourning for herself. Because of Granny's dying, she couldn't go to New York City with Papa on the buying trip they'd been planning ever since February, when a wholesale house in New York offered the store two free tickets on the boat from Savannah and Grandpa said for Mama to go. The morning after the funeral, she insisted she wouldn't even want to go now. But tears were brimming in her eyes and all of a sudden she left the room and ran upstairs, I guess to cry. I felt sorry for her, and I knew she couldn't help feeling sorry for herself. Mama had never been anywhere much except to Atlanta, once to Raleigh, and once to Social Circle, Georgia, for a two-week visit the summer before she married.

At first I didn't mind being in mourning. I didn't want to do anything anyhow but think about Granny. It was like I was trying to memorize her.

One thing I already missed was pork. Granny had been providing me with ham and sausage ever since Papa decided if the Lord thought hog meat was bad for the Jews, then we weren't going to eat it, either. "Southern Presbyterians are as much God's Chosen People as Jews are," he said.

Grandpa had laughed about that. Said he heard Presbyterians were God's Frozen People, haw. He and I thought that was funny, but Papa didn't. Anyhow, we gave up pork and got sanctified. I reckon us and Mr. Izzie, Cold Sassy's only Jew, were the only folks in town who never ate a piece of fried ham for breakfast. Well, and my friend Pink Predmore's mother. Pork gave her the trots. Mrs. Predmore was the last of seventeen children and always said the family gave out of strong stomachs before it got to her.

Well, Granny saw to it that Mary Toy and I had our share of hog meat. After Papa's big decision, she kept leftover sausage or ham or fried streak-a-lean in her warming oven in case we came by after school. Pork didn't matter all that much to me, but the fact Granny saved me some mattered a lot. It was like getting hugged, or knowing that at the Friday speakings she would be out there in the schoolyard with Mama, sitting on a saw-mill puncheon and perking up when it was Mary Toy's turn to quote from "Lord Ullin's Daughter" or my turn to give an oration from Demosthenes. No matter how bad we recited, Granny always clapped loud.

I went up to her house about a week after her passing. I guess I hoped she would seem less dead there.

Everything was a mess. Grandpa's bed looked like he got caught in the cover when he flopped out that morning. The top sheet trailed onto the floor. His bureau drawers were all open, and the clothes jumbled. His spit cup on the night stand was full of stale tobacco juice and smelled awful. A pile of *Atlanta Constitution Tri-Weekly*s littered the floor by the cane-back rocker.

In the kitchen I found coffee grounds spilled all over the table and burned toast in a pan on the cold stove.

Like I said, it had never been a spic-and-span house. Granny wasn't much for cleaning up. But though her windows didn't shine and her curtains drooped with dust and nobody could of eaten off her floors, she kept the bed made, the dishes washed, and things in place. She always said if a house looked neat, folks didn't notice cobwebs in the corners or dust on the mantelpiece.

Well, it was a sight now. I guess Grandpa had been looked after for so long, he didn't know how to do for himself. Mama had tried to help him. A week after the funeral she went up there and cleaned, but next morning when Grandpa came by for his snort, he told her she had her own place to see after "and anyways, I ain't a-go'n let you work like a colored woman at my house. Hit was yore ma's duty. Hit ain't yore'n." The place looked so lonesome without Granny that I couldn't stand it. My feeling was that if I called out, she would answer from the next room. But my knowledge was that I could go from room to room all day long and never catch up with her.

Despite I used to scour the porch for Granny and row her garden and all, I'd never done woman's work there or anywhere. But I did it that day. I wiped the kitchen table, rinsed out the spit cup, put clean sheets on Grandpa's bed, picked up clothes and newspapers. After which I just had to get out.

In the backyard, the hens clucked and murmured as they scratched for bugs or pecked at the last dirty crumbs of wet cornmeal that Grandpa had put out for them. The chickens didn't seem to miss Granny. The garden and the flower beds did. It being June, nothing looked tired of growing yet, but it all looked neglected.

I should of gone to weeding. Instead, I got Granny's gallberry brush-broom off the back porch and swept the dirt clean around the steps. Then I sat down on the bottom step, put my face in my hands, and commenced to mourn.

To mourn is not the same as *to be in mourning,* which means wearing a black armband and sitting in the parlor, talking to people who call on the bereaved. At first you feel important. The armband makes you special, like having on a badge. But after a day or two it stops meaning anything.

But *to* mourn, that's different. *To* mourn is to be eaten alive with homesickness for the person. That day, I mourned mostly for Granny, who had lost more than any of us, but also for Grandpa, for Mama, and for myself. I didn't want to visit Granny at the cemetery like Grandpa was doing. That was just her empty shell over there, whereas here I could touch things she had touched, look out on the flowering plants she had looked at, and walk through her house. Of course, it never dawned on me then that another woman was about to come in and take over.

This had been the Toy home place ever since it was built in 1837. Granny lived here till she got married. It was still a farmhouse in 1890, when her daddy died and her step-mother went to live with a grown son, Mr. French Gordy. Granny moved back there with Grandpa and Loma, who was four years old at the time. Mama had already married, so she never lived in this house.

A long time later, when I was telling Miss Love about the home place, she asked me what happened to all the Toy farmland.

"Grandpa chopped it to pieces," I said. "He'd always made his livin' and sellin', so when all that land was left on his hands, why, the only thing he knew to do with it was sell it." The railroad was finished in 1877 or around then, I explained, and with new businesses starting and folks wanting house lots close to town, the Toy farm that used to yield cotton was soon sprouting homes, outhouses, gardens, stables, and small pastures.

Granny never questioned Grandpa's selling her land or using the money to build the brick store. But as she once admitted to me, "I looked at him kinda hard one day and said, 'Cain't we use part a-that money to make the house modrun?'" She had been cooking in the dining room fireplace—that was easier than going outdoors to the old kitchen—and she wanted to join the old kitchen to the house. So it was placed on logs and rolled close to the dining room, and what they called a "butler's pantry" was built between. While he was at it, Grandpa also bought her a new walnut bedroom suit and a big iron coal-burning stove. He put in a nice new privy, and had a new well dug right by the back porch so you didn't have to go in the yard to draw water.

But that was the last time he ever put a dime into improvements.

Now that Granny was dead, you'd think he'd ask the Lord to forgive him for not letting her have plumbing, electricity, and a telephone. But I doubted he could repent of that. He had skimped so long to get ahead, he didn't even notice how stingy he was—something like the way my daddy had gotten everything wholesale through the store for so long

that he didn't notice how much he spent anymore; just noticed how much he saved over
retail. When Grandpa wouldn't even put in
one bathroom, my daddy had put in two—
one on the porch upstairs and another on the
porch near the kitchen. The same year, Papa
replaced our old-fashioned white picket fence
with a fancy iron one and set up the iron stag
between the pittosporum bush and the
elaeagnus.

Well, so Granny had died without ever getting much she wanted. But she had sixty vari-
eties of roses, and most everybody in Cold
Sassy was beholden to her for nursing a relative back to health or laying out the body for
burial.

If she'd been a man, Granny Blakeslee
would of made a dandy doctor or undertaker,
either one.

One thing I got onto that morning, with the
house full of Granny and empty of her at the
same time, was the notion that she'd of hated
dying so plain.

Like doctors and undertakers, she really
told good dying stories. There wasn't a grown
person in Cold Sassy who couldn't pass away
the time after Sunday dinner by recollecting

who'd died of what when, but Granny was the only one I ever heard be interesting about it.

Just for instance, her aunt Beppy—the one they say had the power of levitation—died with typhoid fever. That by itself wasn't enough to mention. Lots of folks died of the typhoid. But Beppy died at seventeen, on her wedding day. "They give her Bible to Mr. Billy," Granny would say.

She used to tell about a Confederate soldier from Cold Sassy who got sent to Andersonville to guard Yankee prisoners and passed away in the smallpox epidemic there. He was buried at Andersonville. His family never forgave the Confederacy for not marking his grave. "In that cemetery," said Granny, "you couldn't tell Abner from a dead Yankee."

If Aunt Carrie wasn't there, Granny would tell how Carrie's husband, Mr. Horace, went to the War right after they married and never was heard from again. "Everybody figgered he died on some Yankee battlefield, but you cain't be sure for certain," said Granny. She never liked Mr. Horace.

Granny's cousin Selah Toy had been a boatman on the Savannah River and named his daughter Vanna, after the river. Not long after he got the top of his head shot off in the Battle of Chickamauga, Cudn Vanna married an Englishman, a blockade-runner for the Confederates. When the Yankees caught him, they stood him up on a barrelhead and, without a trial or anything, shot him. After the War, Cudn Vanna married three more husbands and lived to bury them all, even the one that was forty years younger than she was.

Uncle Buson was the one I liked to speculate on. He didn't die. He just disappeared.

"We never knowed what happened to him," Granny would say cheerfully, "but he was dead to the fam'ly from the day they read Grandfather's will. Hit said, 'My son Buson has not acted in a becoming manner so I leave him nothing.' That night, Uncle Buson he took off on my granddaddy's best horse and ain't nobody in Cold Sassy ever heard pea-turkey from him since. Somebody said he went out West and married one a-them Mexican women, but we never knowed if it was so or not." Once I asked Granny what Uncle Buson did that was so bad, but she wouldn't tell me. Said I was too young to hear such. It must of really been worth hearing about if it was too awful to mention.

Granny's favorite was the Stokeses. "They was mighty wrought up about the South losin' the War," she would begin. "When the carpetbaggers commenced takin' over, them Stokeses built a rock wall around the fam'ly graveyard and took off for Brazil, lock, stock, and barrel. The whole lot of'm went, and never wrote one word back to Cold Sassy. Hit was like ever last one had passed away."

When Granny passed away herself, I thought how dying was a lot like what happened when the Stokeses went to Brazil or when Uncle Buson rode off into the night. Whether you were up meeting God, down in Brazil hating Yankees, or out West somewhere loving a Mexican woman, to those left behind, you had just plain disappeared.

The morning I was mourning up at Granny's house, I thought how disappointed she would be to of died so ordinary. She wouldn't call heart trouble, a stroke, kidney failure, and malignant spring fever worth mentioning alongside having two funerals, like my great-grandmother Arminda Tweedy, or being buried alongside Yankees at Andersonville, or dying on your wedding day.

But after Grandpa went off to Jefferson in the buggy with Miss Love, it dawned on me

that now Granny's passing wasn't so plain after all. Like everybody else in Cold Sassy, she
would call it worth mentioning that her husband got married just three weeks after she
went to her grave.

10

Purely on account of being in mourning, my
family missed most of the July the Fourth
parade.

Grandpa had thought up Southern Independence Day way back in February as a
practical joke on the United States of America. Like everybody else in Cold Sassy, he still
carried a grudge against the Union, and I
reckon he had a right to. Grandpa was just
fourteen when he joined the Army of the
South with his daddy. They served all through
the War in the same outfit: Echols Battery of
Georgia Light Artillery, Company K, 6th
Georgia Regiment.

Grandpa went in as a drummer boy, but
one morning when the 6th Georgia was in
retreat, he put his drum in a supply wagon

and took up a gun, and that was the last he saw of the drum.

His lieutenant told them one time not to get captured. Said the Yankees would hang you by your heels and split you down the middle like a dang pig. Grandpa claimed he never believed that. But he believed starving. They got so hungry, one night his daddy roasted a rat and parched some acorns, "and we was glad to git it. But right then I made up my mind, if'n I got home alive, I never was go'n eat nothin' I didn't like agin. And I ain't."

One time when my mother complained about him being so hard to please about food, Papa said, "Hon, what if you'd had to eat a rat?"

Besides losing his appetite and his drum, Grandpa always said the War cost him half his left arm. He claimed a damnyankee shot it off. Granny told me it happened in a sawmill accident after the War. "But they ain't a bit of use mentionin' that in front of your granddaddy," she said. "For one thang, it don't matter. For another, you know how he is. He tells a thang a few times, he believes it hisself. For another, when that-air arm goes to hurtin' on a cold winter night, it's a comfort to him to cuss the Yankees. A man cain't hardly cuss no sawmill."

Be that as it may, 1906 was the first and only year we've ever celebrated the Glorious Fourth. Usually nobody even mentions it.

Cold Sassy is the kind of town where schoolteachers spend two months every fall drilling on Greek and Roman gods, the kings and queens of England, the Crusades, the Spanish Inquisition, Marco Polo, Magellan, Columbus, the first Thanksgiving, Oglethorpe settling Georgia, and how happy the slaves were before the War. A good teacher could cover the history of the whole world in two months and spend the rest of the school year on the War of the Sixties and how the Union ground its heel in our faces after it knocked us down. Seems like we never got much past the invasion of Yankee carpetbaggers before school let out for the summer.

The Declaration of Independence and the Revolution were mentioned at school, of course, but just barely. In Cold Sassy, nobody under forty had ever made or waved an American Flag. Even today, in 1914, there's not but one United States flag in the whole town. The post office being in one corner of the drug store, Dr. Clark is required to fly a

U.S. flag. On July 4, 1906, he put it down to half-mast.

Just the way Grandpa planned it, all the stores closed that day, and folks white and colored lined North Main and South Main, waving their Confederate flags. The parade was led by the town band and the Negro band, which rode in a mule-drawn wagon. Both bands were playing "Dixie," but not in the same style.

Our cook's husband, a giant, tar-black Negro named Loomis Toy, blew the alto horn in the Negro band. His trick was to sit with the horn in his lap for the first half of a piece, then start at the beginning and, tooting double time, hit the last note right with the others.

Behind the bands came a big cotton wagon draped with Confederate bunting and pulled by a double team of mules. It carried Cold Sassy's disabled veterans and the moldy old ones. Most were in uniform, sitting up there stiff and proud in rows of chairs. As the wagon rolled slowly along, grown men and women watched silent, with tears in their eyes.

Next came old Ab Pulliam in his goat cart, the pants of his gray uniform folded under his thigh stubs. He had a double sign hung across the goat's back that said, WE LOST THE WAR BUT WE AINT ON OUR LAST LEGS!

Behind him walked Miss Love Simpson and Aunt Carrie, Cold Sassy's only suffragettes. The banner stretched between them read, "Ladies, How Long Must We Wait for Liberty? Demand the Right to Vote!"

Grandpa Blakeslee was supposed to be next, leading the column of younger, gun-toting veterans who were to charge up North Main Street, playing like this was the Battle of Gettysburg. He had planned on riding a bicycle, just to be funny, and even went so far as to order one from Sears, Roebuck and Co. But him never having ridden anything smaller than a horse, buggy, or train, the bicycle scared him to death. After one try, he fell off and wouldn't get back on. Said he would lead the charge bareback on old Jack, his mouse-colored horse-mule.

In the planning stage, Grandpa said I could be the drummer boy and march right behind him. As it was, because of our being in mourning for Granny, Mama wouldn't let me so much as follow the army downtown, much less beat the drum. I just watched what I could from our front veranda.

Grandpa wasn't in the parade, either. When Granny took sick, he said he didn't have any heart for the battle and wouldn't be in it. Mr. Toot Withers took his place, riding a high-stepping white stallion, and waving a sword in one hand and a big Confederate flag in the other. Mr. Toot being drunk, as usual, nobody knew how he stayed on a horse that didn't like rebel yells, drumbeats, rifle fire, or firecrackers, all of which erupted when he shouted "Charge!" and the marching soldiers went into action—dashing, tottering, or limping back and forth across the railroad tracks, firing their guns toward the sky and poking bayonets at imaginary damnyankees.

It was a grand sight!

At that point I do believe Grandpa would have left our porch swing and joined in if he could of found his uniform right quick. But only Granny knew where she had packed it away, and Granny was dead.

The very next day, Grandpa got married.

11

Mama didn't come down to dinner at all after Papa told her Grandpa and Miss Love had run off to Jefferson together.

I wasn't hungry, and Papa's appetite was down, too, judging by the way he picked at his food and picked at making conversation.

He had a habit at meals of telling things he'd heard at the store or read in the paper. But whereas I thought the big news today was Grandpa's eloping, the first thing Papa said was something about the average life span in America being forty-seven years.

Thinking any minute he would tell me what was really on his mind, I just said, "I declare." But what little he talked, it was about other things. Like for instance Papa said old man Plunket told him the train hit a mule and a cow at the same time yesterday just outside of Cold Sassy. "Killed'm both," Papa said, and reached for the pully-bone, my favorite piece of fried chicken except for the head. "And might-near wrecked the train."

By then I was just barely listening, because it had dawned on me that our time of mourning must be about over. If Grandpa could go get married, maybe I could go fishing.

Well, I'd just go. Today. I'd go to Cussin' Creek. Leave just soon as Papa went back to the store.

I never did like to fish by myself. So after whistling my dog out of the garden, where he was digging a hole to lay in and get cool, I went by the Predmore house to find Pink.

"He ain't to home," his little brother Harkness told me. "Him and Daddy rode the train down to Athens this mornin'."

Pink's mother was in the yard, hanging out clothes. "I was hopin' Pink could go fishin' with me," I told her.

"Well, he's gone to Athens."

"That's what Harkness said."

Mrs. Predmore didn't even mention Grandpa and Miss Love, so likely Mama was all wrong about folks being scandalized.

But when I got to Smiley Snodgrass's house I found out Mama was likely right. "What's this I heerd 'bout yore granddaddy, Will?" asked Mrs. Snodgrass, wiping her hands on her long white apron as she came to the door.

I couldn't tell how much she knew, so I just said, "I don't know'm."

"When they gittin' hitched? Not any time soon, I reckon."

"I don't know'm." They were already hitched, more than likely.

"I hear tell Loma's bad-mouthin' thet Simpson woman all over town. You cain't blame her." She waited for me to say something. When I didn't, she said, "Pore Loma. Pore Mary Willis. What a cross to bear, and Miss Mattie Lou not hardly cold in the grave. How's yore ma a-takin' it, Will?"

I couldn't make out whether Mrs. Snodgrass was embarrassed for pore Loma and pore Mary Willis or if she was thinking Mama and Aunt Loma would be pore in the future if Miss Love got aholt of their inheritance. One thing I did know, my mother sure would be upset when she found out Aunt Loma was talking outside the family—especially now that there wasn't any chance of changing Grandpa's mind. Mama thought private family matters ought to be just that. Private.

"Mama's takin' it all right, I s'pose," I said, as if widowers getting hitched right after the funeral was an everyday thing.

"I betcher Son Black's madder'n a wet hen, losin' Miss Love to a old man."

"I don't know'm. . . . Miz Snodgrass, where's Smiley at?"

"Down to the barn, cleanin' out the stalls. Bein' punished for back talk, so don't you go git him to slip off. You hear?"

"Oh, no, ma'am." I backed off the porch. Knowing that Mrs. Snodgrass would likely watch to make sure I left, I struck off down the street, pitching sticks for T.R. to go fetch. But after passing by the French Gordy house next door, I ducked around back to the Gordy stable and went through it to the pasture.

Mr. French had three cows. One of them, a tan Jersey named Blind Tillie, was Cold Sassy's champion milk producer. Born with milk-glass eyes, she was named for Blind Tillie Creek, where I sometimes fished. She always walked with her chin resting on the rump of another cow. That day, Tillie and the other two cows and I were all headed for a big oak tree near the barb wire fence, on the other side of which the Snodgrass's mule-headed Jersey cow had already laid down to chew her cud in the shade.

I crawled under the barb wire, stepped

around a wet cow splat, and headed for the Snodgrass barn. There was old Smiley, leaning against a fence beside a big pile of manure, staring at the sky with his mouth open and his hands resting on the pitchfork handle—dreaming about girls, most likely. Seeing a pile of dried horse biscuits, I got me one and threw it just as Smiley's mouth stretched in a wide yawn. It went in nice and neat, like a baseball into a glove.

Boy, was he mad. He and I had us a great manure war then, throwing dried cow cushions and sheep pills and horse biscuits at each other and dying laughing. Just as I was fixing to talk about fishing, Mrs. Snodgrass yelled from over near the smokehouse for Smiley to come catch her a chicken. So that was the end of that.

Lee Roy Sleep was still out of town. He and his folks were up in the mountains at Tallulah Falls, visiting his grandmother. I thought about Dunson McCall, but remembered Dunse was picking peaches for Mr. Angus Tuttle, the depot man, who had an orchard out on the edge of town.

Mr. Tuttle hadn't offered me a picking job since that time us boys pulled up an acre of his onion crop to dam the stream between his pasture and ours. We were making a swimming hole. Our daddies paid for the onions and we all worked out the money, but Mr. Tuttle never forgave us.

Well, so I didn't have a soul to go fishing with but T.R.

T.R.'s real name was Theodore Roosevelt. He was just a puppy when Papa took me to Atlanta to hear the president speak; I named him Theodore Roosevelt when I got home that day—then shortened it to T.R. so folks wouldn't think my dog was a Republican.

Naturally I didn't carry a fishing pole. No use looking disrespectful of the dead. In one pocket of my overalls I had me a line, and my sinkers and my hooks stuck in a cork. Stuffed in another pocket were some biscuits, to wad up into dough balls to bait the hooks with, and five pieces of Queenie's fried chicken in case I got hungry. I would cut a pole at the creek.

Cussin' Creek was where us boys usually fished when an hour or two was all we had between chores. It wasn't far. Just a piece down the railroad tracks near Mr. Son Black's farm. Our train was a branch line of the Southern Railroad, which ran north from Athens through Cold Sassy, Commerce, and

Maysville, connecting at Lula Junction with the Airline Railroad, which went on to Atlanta and Charlotte. I would get on the tracks at the depot just past the Cold Sassy tree.

That tree was close to a hundred feet tall and the only sassafras still left of the big grove our town was named for. On a bright fall day when the sun lit up its scarlet leaves, you never saw anything to equal it. People would ride the train to Cold Sassy just to look. Usually they'd read the plaque that was nailed to its trunk: "Sassafras: family *Lauraceae,* genus *Sassafras,* species *S. albidum.* Note how the leaves vary in shape on the same twig, some having no lobes, some two or three." Considering the number of train travelers we had, I thought the plaque ought to tell how unusual tall the tree was and something about how Cold Sassy got its name.

We used to have another big sassafras tree, which stood next to this one and had a knothole where bluebirds nested. Us boys used to rob the nest of its bluish-white eggs and blow out the insides. The railroad had taken that sassafras down some years earlier to make room for a bigger depot platform.

I saw Mr. Angus Tuttle out there on the

platform now, but he didn't see me. He was too busy arguing with a fat old farmer in overalls. Like all depot agents, Mr. Tuttle was cow coroner for the railroad, so I guessed right off that this was the farmer whose cow and mule got killed yesterday. Death by train isn't unusual out in the country. Farmers don't keep their livestock tied or pastured up like we do in town. I gathered from the argument, which was getting pretty loud, that the farmer was mad about the amount Mr. Tuttle had offered to settle the claim against the railroad. I could still hear those two fussing after I passed the foundry, but then everything got drowned out as the 1:10 from Athens approached.

Stepping off the tracks to let it pass, I watched as the engine screeched and ground to a halt at the depot, belching smoke and steam. Back on the tracks and heading toward open country, I had a thought. "T.R., hot day like this, ain't no fish go'n bite at Cussin' Creek." I remembered then that Queenie's husband, big Loomis, said they were biting real good now under the trestle at Blind Tillie Creek.

There were hazards. The shortest way to get there was to follow the tracks in the opposite direction, which would not only take me back past the depot but also past our house and Grandpa's store, where I might be seen. Also, I'd have to go through Mill Town.

I had walked through Mill Town plenty of times, but never by myself.

I was about to call it a dern fool idea when it came to mind I might see Lightfoot Mc-Lendon. I hadn't laid eyes on her since school let out for the summer. Whistling to T.R., I turned and headed back—past the foundry, past Grandpa's house, past the Cold Sassy tree and the depot, past our house, which I detoured around, and on toward the hotel and the block of stores.

Walking along, I wondered about Grandpa and Miss Love. When would they get back? Would she come in and work on her hats, or would Grandpa drop her off at his house so she could sweep up some and cook his supper? Or since he was used to eating supper at Aunt Loma's, would they both go over there tonight?

I wondered if an old man who just buried his wife would take his bride on a wedding trip. I decided he wouldn't. Not just because of being stingy but also because, at fifty-nine, Grandpa had his mind on the store and not on what Queenie called "de sweet'nin' on de gingercake."

Well, right now my problem was not Grandpa and Miss Love but how I would get past the batch of stores without Papa and them seeing me, or old Crazy Tatum, who always sat in a rocking chair by the door to keep people out of his store. He put the chair just inside if it was cold, and out on the sidewalk if it was summer. If it looked like you might try to come in, he'd flap his arms like a bird and leap around, hollering and whooping. I knew if he went to whooping at me, Papa might chance to look out the store window and wonder why I wasn't weeding the garden like he said to.

I had figured on going behind the brick stores till I was clear of them, but when I saw the 1:10 leave the depot, headed toward us on its way to Lula, I whistled to T.R. and got off the tracks on the South Main side. Seeing me, the engineer put an arm big as a leg of mutton out the window and waved.

Since the store was across the tracks on North Main, we were hidden behind the moving boxcars, and I decided to keep on walking. The train was so long that before all of it passed us we were beyond the stores, the

Confederate monument, the livery stable, the tanyard, the cotton gin, and Sleep's Ice and Coal, and nearly to Mill Town.

The factory soon came in view and, just beyond it, the river that powered the machines. On a railroad siding off the main tracks, men in linty overalls were loading big pasteboard boxes full of cotton thread onto a freight car. At a huge square opening in the factory wall, other men were taking bales of cotton off of a wagon. I recognized old Charlie Rowley up there on the driver's bench of the wagon. Old Charlie and his mule were both string-halted, each having a tight ligament in the leg that made him limp. But that didn't keep them from hauling for Grandpa's big warehouse—delivering to the mill or depot when farmers who stored their cotton with us finally sold it.

Charlie saw me and waved, and I waved back. Too late, I realized if he saw Papa later he might chance to mention seeing me on the train tracks going through Mill Town.

Hurrying by the factory, I came to where the mill hands lived in close-together little shotgun houses—three rooms in a row, like long boxes, with public wells and privies that served two or three houses each.

Cold Sassy was proud of its cotton mill, just as it was proud of the trains coming through. "Get you a railroad" and "Get you a cotton mill" was what big businessmen in Atlanta advised any town that wanted to grow. Having both, we were bound to grow, but Grandpa said he didn't see how the population could change any. "Ever time a baby's born, some boy joins the Navy." Still, Cold Sassy was considered up-and-coming. And like I said, already folks were talking about changing its name to something less countrified, the way Jugtown had been renamed Winder, and Garden Valley was now Pendergrass, and just four years ago Harmony Grove became Commerce—all of which, to my mind and Grandpa's, were awful improvements.

Our mill houses were a long sight better than in lots of places, but they looked more like repeating blobs of white than homes. There weren't any trees. No shrubbery. Families sat crowded on the hot little porches, cotton lint from twelve hours in the mill still clinging to their hair and overalls and dresses. I guessed they were night workers who hadn't gone to bed yet. Who could go to bed in those little houses on a hot day in July?

I kept glancing at the blank, stony, pinched faces of the men and women staring at me from steps and doorways, and at the children, all white-headed just like you see them in the Appalachians. They stared at me with sullen, mean eyes, like I was a strange animal. But whenever I looked right at them, their gaze dropped to the ground.

Mill Town was watching the Town Boy pass.

Nervous, I hurried my steps on the cross-ties. And T.R., who'd been running ahead like a brown and white flash, now walked stiff-legged close beside me, growling at any bony mangy dog that slunk too near. I went from hoping I'd see Lightfoot to hoping I wouldn't. It was one thing to like her at school and nobody know it. Here in Mill Town on my crosstie stage, folks would suspicion her if they saw me acting friendly. Also, I knew I'd be embarrassed if she was sweaty and lintheaded from the factory or if, Lord forbid, I saw her coming out of a privy.

I decided it was a lot harder to walk through Mill Town than to have our school cluttered up with snot-nosed children who had cooties and the itch, and who at dinner-time stayed at school to eat biscuits and syrup, making us town children feel guilty for going home to a big hot dinner. The mill boys were always picking fights with town boys—tripping us up or calling us names. Of course we did our share of tripping and worse. But it was our dern school, for gosh sake.

Before Lightfoot, I had a healthy disrespect for all mill children. Since Lightfoot, just being around them was like getting fussed at for wearing shoes in winter and having a cow and a family cook.

Lightfoot wasn't like the other mill children. Wasn't like any girl I ever knew, for that matter. Wasn't silly, wasn't always twiddling her plaits, didn't tattle or gossip, didn't hit boys over the head with books or scrape the back of your neck with a sweetgum burr when you weren't looking. She was quiet and sweet and smart. Ragged, of course, but real clean, and thin without having the bony-faced, sunk-eyed look of mill children who've been hungry all their lives. Lightfoot had what I thought of as the fresh free look of the hills on her.

The way I got to really know her, I had to stay after school one day for flipping spitballs, and she was staying late so Miss Neppie could help her catch up. This was back in January, soon after she came to Cold Sassy from the foothills of the Blue Ridge. At some point, when Miss Neppie went to Mr. McCall's office, I asked Lightfoot how come she left the mountains. "My mama always wanted us to move to Cold Sassy," she said. "My mama she had the TB, you know. Last summer, jest fore she passed, she wrote her brother in Mill Town and he said we was more'n welcome to stay with them. Mama kept sayin' Pa would have steady work in the mill and I could git me a good education and amount to something."

The girl didn't seem to have heard yet that nobody in Mill Town ever amounted to anything.

"So after the fall crop come in, my daddy he sold his plowin' steer and his piece a-land, and we caught the train to Cold Sassy."

"You got any brothers and sisters in the mountains?" I asked.

"Yeah, lots of'm. But they all married or dead, one."

As T.R. and I walked the railroad tracks past the sweaty, dirty, hostile faces of Mill Town, I couldn't help wondering if a summer of slaving at the spindles would take away Lightfoot's hopes—and my notion that she walked in a cloud of fresh mountain air. Fixing my eyes on the repeating crossties, I walked fast. And even faster as it dawned on me just how much I didn't want to see Lightfoot McLendon with lint in her hair.

I also didn't want to see Hosie Roach, a snot-nosed twenty-one-year-old mill boy in my class who stunk like a polecat and had tow-colored hair so thick and tangled it looked like a cootie stable. Hosie wasn't big as me, but whenever we had a fight—about once a week—he usually won. Gosh, what if he and a bunch of other mill boys ganged up on me.

Getting beat to a pulp might have been better than what happened later at the trestle. But of course I didn't know it at the time, so it was a grand relief when my dog and I got past all chance of seeing Hosie or Lightfoot, either one.

Once we were out in the country, we had a high old time. The dog romped through the daisies and weeds and tall grasses growing along the tracks. He scared up rabbits, barked at terrapins, caught gnats and flies in his mouth, and every few minutes looked back to be sure I was still coming along behind. Two bobwhites scooted across the tracks right in front of us, heads up and backs straight as tin soldiers', but they flushed before T.R. could point.

That dog must of wet every black-eyed Susan and every head of white Queen Anne's lace we passed. I never saw such a dog for doing Number One. Grandpa called it the sweet-pee trick. I know that's how dogs stake out territory and also how they find their way home, but looks like T.R. would know by now that all we had to do to go home was turn around and follow the train tracks.

Two or three times he stopped and stared back like he thought somebody was coming behind us. But then he would lower his head for a new scent and run ahead.

We saw a few mill people near the tracks, picking blackberries into lard buckets, and a whole family of colored people. The Negroes smiled and waved and held up their buckets for me to see. The mill people didn't.

It was hot, good gosh. My straw hat shaded my eyes, but that was all in the world good it did. "I guess I got about two hours," I muttered out loud. I knew the southbound train would cross the trestle over Blind Tillie

Creek about when I ought to head home to milk.

You couldn't exactly tell time by that train, but it would be close enough. It always came back through Cold Sassy with a load of lumber from the sawmill at Lula, bound for the lumberyard in Athens, and usually there were some passenger cars carrying folks who'd been to Atlanta. In the fall there were always cotton buyers, and usually four or five drummers who would set up their merchandise in a hotel room, stay a few days, then move on to another little town. Grandpa called them "Knights of the Grip." When Mama and Aunt Loma were young, he never let them hang around the depot. Drummers liked to flirt, were fresh-shaved, and wore suits, patent leather shoes, and big smiles. Girls always liked them.

Less than a mile past Mill Town, I rounded a bend and saw the train trestle up ahead, marching through the air high above the wooded gorge where Blind Tillie Creek ran. Just before we got to the trestle I whistled for my dog and went slipping and sliding down a red-dirt path, past dusty briar bushes that reached out to scratch me as I ate my fill of blackberries.

It was a sight cooler by the creek than up there on the tracks. I cut me a pole and was soon perched on a stump, fishing and eating fried chicken. Later I cut a blackgum twig to chew on and settled myself comfortable on the ground with the stump for a back rest.

It was nice and peaceful there. Watching the shallow water splash and churn over rocks, I almost forgot how mad I was at Mama for making me stay in mourning, how mad I was at her and Aunt Loma for fussing about Grandpa marrying when he clearly needed a housekeeper, and how mad I was at him and Miss Love for not caring how the family felt. But then I got mad at Papa. Here I was at last—fishing—and I couldn't enjoy it for feeling guilty.

I had sense enough to know my daddy really needed me to be home working the garden. But I wished he knew what it felt like to have fun. All Papa had ever done was work. Before he was knee-high to a gnat, his own daddy had him picking bugs off of cotton plants, and he was hoeing as soon as he knew the difference between a weed and a cotton stalk, and milking soon as his hands were big enough to squeeze a cow's tit. I bet he never in his life had sat in the shade of a train tres-

tle holding a fishing pole and watching drag-
onflies walk on water.

Grandpa Blakeslee bragged a lot about my
daddy being such a dandy worker. I was
proud he wasn't lazy like his own daddy, who
spent the summer days on his porch swatting
flies and even had him a pet hen to peck up
the dead ones. Grandpa Tweedy always
claimed he couldn't work. "My veins is too
small," he'd say. "My blood jest cain't git
th'ew fast enough to let me do much." Naturally he had a beard. He was too lazy to
shave. He was even too lazy and self-satisfied
to go anywhere, except to preaching over at
Hebron or to Cold Sassy to sell his cotton.
Wasn't ever on a train but once, when he
went to Dr. Mozely's funeral in Athens. All of
us went, but first Grandpa Tweedy and my
daddy had to decide if it was all right to ride
that train. Being Sunday, it might be a sin.

Like Grandpa Tweedy, Papa worried all the
time about sin on Sunday. He never let us
read anything but the Bible and the *Christian
Observer* on the Sabbath, and once talked Mr.
Tuttle into locking up everybody's Sunday Atlanta papers at the depot till Monday morning. The fact that Cold Sassy put up with that
for a month or more shows how much they

respected my father. I respected him, too, as I said before. But I wished he knew what it felt like to need to go fishing.

My bait was gone again. I wasn't going to catch anything here. It was too hot and the creek too low. Might as well go home and get to work. But glancing around, I saw a mess of logs and brush on the other side and remembered the deep hole there. If any fish were in Blind Tillie Creek, that's where I'd catch them. I was just fixing to get up and wade across when I chanced to look up at the train trestle.

I had walked trestles plenty of times. I used to play on one out in Banks County with Cudn Doodle and them. But I'd never been on Blind Tillie Trestle. From where I sat, leaning against my tree stump and looking up, it seemed higher than a Ferris wheel. Higher even than the new Century Building in Atlanta, and it spanned a wide, deep gorge.

Miss Bertha at school had told us about the si-renes—the mermaids who used to sing to Greek sailors and they'd go off course to follow. Looking at that trestle, I felt like I was being sung to. Or maybe it was more like when the fire bells clang on Cold Sassy's horse-drawn fire engine and you just got to go chasing after it to where the smoke is billowing up.

That's how Blind Tillie Trestle called to me that day.

The longer I stared up at it and the blue sky and fleecy clouds beyond, the more it seemed like a bridge across the world. I wanted to see how things looked from up there. I don't even remember winding the fishing line around my pole, but all of a sudden I was clambering up the bank. Old T.R. raced me to the top and then barked at me till I got up there.

At the edge of the trestle, a brisk breeze had whipped up, and the tracks seemed to soar across the sky.

It never once occurred to me to be scared. But it occurred to the dog.

12

Following behind me, T.R. crouched low and took a few careful steps onto the trestle. Then, whining, he turned and crawled back to solid ground, tail between his legs, and commenced begging me to come back, too.

When the dog saw I was laughing at him, he wet on the rail, scratched with his back paws in the dirt, and dashed off, trying to get me to play chase. After that didn't work, he bounded down the brambly path to the creek below, where we had just come from, and splashed over to the other side, trying to show me a better way to get there. Standing in the shallow water, T.R. barked and bragged his white-tipped tail like he'd done something to get praised for.

"Old yeller belly!" I called down to him, laughing. My voice echoed spooky between trestle and water and gorge. I sure wished Pink Predmore and them were up here with me.

I put one bare foot on the rail. It was hot but not enough to burn, so I walked on it a piece, arms spread-eagle, balancing with my fishing pole like a tightrope-walker at the circus. I remember wondering if any birds ever walked through the sky up there instead of flying over the gorge. I soon passed the sand barrel that was bolted onto the trestle beside the tracks. People have been known to jump into a trestle barrel if a train comes at the wrong time and they get trapped.

Two thirds of the way across, I stepped off

the rail onto a crosstie and sat down, elbows
on knees, to look around. I thought about
putting a penny on the tracks for the train to
flatten, then decided not to. The penny would
fall in the creek. So I just sat there, looking
way off, and tried to think who lived in that
little white farmhouse with green shutters
down in the valley. From up here the house
looked like a fresh-painted toy. I wondered
why nobody ever painted their houses out in
Banks County, where Grandpa Tweedy lived.
He didn't know what a can of paint looked
like.

Enjoying the breeze, I stretched out, face
down, to look through the crossties at the water below. Leaves floated on the creek like
tiny boats. And here came a long stick, a
wake trailing behind it. When the stick
turned against the current to swim toward the
bank, I saw it was a water moccasin and threw
a cinder at it. I missed the snake, but my next
cinder hit the white spot on old T.R.'s rump.
He barked at me till he got distracted by a big
terrapin crawling on the creek bank.

It sure beat being in mourning.

All of a sudden I saw T.R. raise his head to
listen. Then he dashed up the path on the far
side of the creek, barking all the way, and

went to jumping around at the edge of the trestle. He like to had a fit for me to come on. Shoot, you'd think he heard the train or something. Wasn't near time for the train. I didn't hear anything myself except that dern dog barking.

But just to make sure, I moved my head over to the rail and put an ear against it, lazy-like, and—I could hear the clickety-clack! The train was coming! Well, I could make it easy. But as I scrambled to my feet, the fishing pole got wedged somehow between the rail and crosstie. Couldn't leave it that way. Might derail the train. By the time I got it loose, the clickety-clacks were plain as day and getting louder, *louder,* LOUDER!

I stumbled and fell. Jerking myself up, I saw I couldn't possibly get off the trestle before the train moved onto it. Like a fox who runs into a hound, I turned and sprinted the other way. From somewhere, as in a dream, I heard a scream and looked back just as the big smoking engine roared around a bend.

I knew the engineer saw me. His whistle was going *whoo-whoo-whoo* in quick fast blasts. The trestle shook like a leaf as the train hit it.

I thought to aim for the sand barrel.

God A'mighty help me, I wasn't go'n make it! *Jump!* No, too far, creek too low. . . . Whistle screeching in my ears. . . . Train heat almost at my heels. . . . *Whoo-whoo-whoo!*

At that moment I thought FALL!

Like a doll pushed from behind, I fell face down between the rails and lay flat and thin as I could, head low between crossties, arms stretched overhead. As I was swallowed up in fire and thunder, I hugged my arms tight against my ears.

The engine's roar pierced my eardrums anyway, making awful pain. I was so scared I could hardly breathe, and there was a strong smell of heated creosote. Hot cinders spit on me from the firebox. Yet even as the boxcars clacked, knocked, strained, ground, and groaned overhead, it came to me that I wasn't dead. If there wasn't a dragging brake beam to rip me down the back, I was go'n make it!

Boy howdy, I did some fancy praying. All it amounted to was "God save me! Please God save me!" And then it was "Thank you, Lord, thank you, God, thank you, sir. . . ." I guess what made it seem fancy was the strange peaceful feeling I got, as if the Lord had said, "Well done, thou good and faithful servant," or something like that. I wasn't dead! Boy howdy, boy howdy, boy howdy! I was buried alive in noise, and the heat and cinders stung my neck and legs and the bottoms of my feet. Still and all, that was what kept reminding me I wasn't dead.

I found myself counting boxcars, by the sound of them, which was a long sight different in this position, with my eyes shut tight against the dust and cinders, from being in Cold Sassy waiting for the train to get by so I could cross from South Main to North Main. The train had to end. Trains always do. It seemed like this one never would, but brakes were screeching and the clickety-clacks on the rails were slowing, so I knew the engineer was trying to stop.

I felt blistered from the heat. My straw hat was gone. My arms were so tight against my head that my ears felt numb, yet it wouldn't have hurt more if knives were being jabbed into my eardrums.

But boy howdy, I was alive! Thank you, Jesus.

All of a sudden I felt sunshine overhead. Opening my eyes and raising my head, I saw the red caboose getting smaller and smaller as it neared the end of the trestle. The shaking of the trestle stopped. All sounds were muted, as if I had a wad of thick cotton in both ears or was shut up in a padded closet. I felt limp and dizzy. And as knowledge of what could of happened hit me, I started shaking and crying.

I heard T.R. barking from what seemed like far off, but all of a sudden his tongue was on my face! By gosh, he had run out over the trestle he was so scared of! I grabbed and hugged him, crying, "Good ole dog, good ole T.R.!"

When the train finally stopped, its caboose was maybe a hundred feet beyond the trestle. Just then, despite being deafened, I heard a girl's voice scream out, "Will! Will Tweedy! You awright, Will?"

And then she was on the trestle running toward me, her arms outstretched. "I'm a-comin', Will!" she called. "I'm go'n holp you!"

13

The girl running toward me was Lightfoot McLendon, which didn't surprise me at all. If you've been run over by a train and you're alive to know it, what can surprise you after that?

She ran over the crossties barefooted, sure-footed, lightfooted like her name. I wanted to quit crying and shivering, but what did it matter, anyhow? I was alive!

I no longer felt so boy-howdy about it, though. I was numb, I was half-deaf, I was sick, shaking, stinging, and smudged with dirt and oil. I fixed my eyes on Lightfoot as if she was one of Granny's angels come to fetch me, and put my arms tight around T.R. He crowded me—licking, wagging, whimpering. When Lightfoot reached us, I grabbed her, too, and the dog licked both faces. Hers and mine, hers, mine, hers, mine. She was crying, too.

She said something that must of been "Lemme holp you up, Will," and tried to pull me to my feet. WHOOP! Both of us nearly toppled off into the creek below. I tried not to look down.

"I don't . . . I cain't . . . I don't know if I can stand up," I mumbled. My voice came out of a well inside my head. She said something I couldn't understand.

Lightfoot bent so close that her long flaxen hair brushed against my face. It was tied with a string instead of plaited and I can still remember how sparkly white it looked in the sun. She yelled into my ear, "Kin you crawl, Will? If you cain't, them men comin' out'n the train can holp you."

I looked up to see men, women, and children rushing toward the trestle, and others swinging themselves out of passenger cars. Reminded me of bugs pouring out of a rotted cantaloupe if you kick it on the ground. The sight was enough to get me moving. Nobody was go'n tote me off that trestle.

"You go on first, Lightfoot!" I yelled. I reckon I was thinking if I couldn't hear her very good, she couldn't hear me, either. "I'll come behind you!" Grabbing a rail, I pulled myself up to a squat—but didn't have the nerve to turn loose and stand up. I was still shaky. The girl stood up, but swayed and then dropped down to her hands and feet, like me, and we moved on all fours, holding to crossties. Later somebody said we looked like spiders coming off that trestle.

As we neared the end of it, there were shouts and whistles and cheers from the folks crowded there, and finally a burst of clapping. The last few steps of the way, hands reached out to pull us to our feet. Then I was caught up in the arms of a huge man wearing overalls and a train cap—the engineer who'd waved at me in Cold Sassy. Giving me a bear hug, he shouted, "God a'mighty, boy! God a'mighty!" It was like I was his own son. He'd never even seen me before that day, I don't think, but it was like I was his own son.

In bed that night, going over and over what all happened, it dawned on me that by saving myself, I had saved the train engineer from running down a life, never mind it wouldn't of been his fault. That's why he was so glad to see me.

He was still holding me tight when I looked back and saw that T.R. was right out there where we'd left him on the trestle. Yelping and whining, he crouched forlorn between the rails, yearning toward us but not moving.

"T.R.!" I yelled, pointing at him, and the crowd took it up.

"Come 'ere, boy!" a man called, giving a loud piercing whistle.

"Here, boy! Here, boy!" from someone else.

"Come on, pup, you kin make it!"

More whistles. Arms outstretched toward him. And me shaking worse than ever, too weak to yell again. The dog wouldn't budge. Howling, barking, whimpering, he finally tried to crawl, but quit when one hind leg slipped through the crossties. He just let it hang there. He was frozen.

"Won't somebody g-go get him?" I was weeping now. "That's my dog!"

But the engineer, one bulging arm still around my shoulders, suddenly yanked me toward the train. "We gotta git outer here, boy! Come on, folks, git back on the train!" he hollered. "They's another'n comin'!" Then, handing me over to the conductor, he and the fireman sprinted toward the engineer, way up the tracks.

The conductor, a tiny man in a beaver hat and Prince Albert coat, was jumping up and down like a tin clown. "Make haste, folks!" he yelled, waving his hat and pushing me toward the caboose. "We had to put on two trains! Other'n will be along any minute! Got to clear the tracks!"

"I ain't go'n leave my dog!" I said, turning back.

Lightfoot sprang forward. "I'll go git him, Will!"

The conductor grabbed her. "We ain't got time! I ain't go'n let you be on that-air trestle for the next train to hit. Besides, you cain't tote that big dog, honey. You too little bitty."

A new voice swept by like a wind, deep and booming. "I's gwine git him, Mr. Will!" It was big black Loomis, Queenie's husband, six feet six and three hundred pounds, hat on and coattails flapping. Racing by me, without even slowing down he hit the trestle like it was no different from the tracks in Cold Sassy. T.R. recognized Loomis right off and started crawling in, belly scraping the cross-ties.

Some of the passengers rushing to get back on the train stopped to watch as Loomis loped over the trestle. It was like they were hypnotized. But the conductor and the regular train travelers sure weren't hypnotized. They kept yelling for us to come on.

As the crowd pulled and pushed me toward the cars, my head corkscrewed back just in time to see the black man swing T.R. up and drape him around his neck, like in the Bible picture of the lost lamb and the shepherd. Then I got handed up to the conductor, who stood on the steps of the caboose—Lightfoot right behind me. The conductor was screaming for folks to run on up to the other passenger cars. "Ain't room for nobody else on this here caboose!"

But they let big Loomis on. He handed up the dog. Then, ducking, he swung himself through the door just as the train lurched forward. T.R. licked my face, wagging his tail into a blur, while I and the others cheered the black giant.

Some of the passengers didn't make it back onto the train. We saw men, and women, and children pull back into the bushes and brambles as the train got rolling. They looked anxious but most smiled and waved. Those of us who were by a window waved back.

Big Loomis had moved onto the little platform at the back. I figured he didn't feel right, being in the same car with white folks, though Lord knows nobody cared right then. All of a sudden Loomis yelled, "Jesus save us, dare's dat dar udder train! He ne'ly at de trestle!"

Fear spread over faces. A lady screamed. I felt like screaming. Clapped a hand over my mouth so I couldn't. Lightfoot caught my other hand and held it tight, her eyes wide, her face gone white. Somebody yelled, "Conductor, cain't you run faster?"

The oncoming engine hit the trestle, whistle screaming WHOO-WHOO-WHOO. The question was could it be braked fast enough and could we speed up fast enough. . . . The chasing engine got bigger and bigger as the gap between us closed, then shrunk as our engineer picked up speed. The last I saw before we rounded a bend, the other train had stopped and was picking up everybody we'd left beside the tracks.

Lightfoot sat by me on the short run to Cold Sassy. T.R. lay across my feet. Loomis had come back in, and he stood with one hand on my shoulder, his black face shining with pride and sweat. Hot as he was from running, he kept on the long black jim-swing coat till he saw me shivering, and then he put it around me. Queenie had sewed that coat. Weren't any white men in town big enough to where Loomis could wear their old clothes, so she had to make nearly everything he had. The cloth smelled sweaty, but I didn't care. I didn't know there was lubricating oil on my overalls and in my hair, where it had dropped off the engine parts, and I'm afraid it got on the coat that Loomis was so proud of. Shouting above the train noise, I told him much obliged for saving T.R.

"You be's welcome, Mr. Will. You know dat."

I loved Loomis. His whole name was Annie Mae Hubert Knockabout Loomis Toy. After his mama had ten boys, she said the nex' baby gwine be name Annie Mae no matter whut. She always called him Annie Mae, but nobody else did. His daddy was owned by the Toys is how he got his last name. Loomis worked for us off and on all my life—milking till I got big enough, plowing the garden till I got big enough, fixing fences and chopping wood till I got big enough. He beamed down at me now, showing his two gold front teeth, and rolled his eyes toward Heaven. "You sho got you a frien' Up Yonder, Mr. Will. Sho nuff! I speck it cause yo daddy and mama be sech good peoples. Lawdy, Lawdy, it gwine be a happy time at yo house t'night!"

I hadn't thought that far. Good gosh, Papa would be mad as heck about my sneaking off!

The train rocked on toward Papa.

Lightfoot was scrooched up in the corner of the bench, swaying with the motion of the train. I looked over at her, red-faced from the heat and sweaty and dirty as me. Her long whitey hair hung in damp strands and there were briar scratches on her hands. Tears brimming in her blue eyes suddenly spilled over. I figured she was picturing me flattened like a penny on the trestle rails. But what she said, in a wail hard to understand over the train racket and me still part deaf, was "I left my bucket in the blackberry bushes, Will! Hit were might near full!"

I couldn't think what to say. If she hadn't rushed to help me, she wouldn't of lost the bucket, and I knew those blackberries weren't picked to make a pie with or to put up as jam or jelly or wine. They were for supper. Like as not, all else her folks would have was fried fatback, cream gravy, and corn pone.

The girl blushed, like it just dawned on her that she had let out how poor and hungry she was, and turned her face away from me.

Trying to sound like I thought berry-picking was just something she did for fun, I said, "Why'n't we go pick some more early in the mornin'? Mama's been astin' me every day when am I go'n get her some blackberries."

As a matter of fact, Mama never asked me to pick anything anymore, except in our garden. Between her and Papa and Grandpa I was too busy with home chores and store work to go hunting wild fruit. Mama bought our blackberries and yellow plums and muscadines from little colored boys who came by, or from doddery old colored men, or from fat black women with shy stair-step children, each toting two lard buckets full.

"If we go back to Blind Tillie Trestle we can find your bucket," I said. "How bout tomorrow?"

Soon as that was out of my mouth I didn't know why I said it. For one thing, I didn't particularly want to walk through Mill Town again. For another, I felt sick. Sick at my stomach. For another, I'd never hear the last of it if Pink and them somehow found out a girl was waiting for me under Blind Tillie Trestle. Guffaw and haw!

And if Mama and them found out it was a mill girl, I'd be hard put to explain it. No town boy or girl from a nice home would be caught dead with a linthead.

I was about to make up some excuse when I felt the clickety-clacks slow down and saw Cold Sassy going by the train windows. Remembering Papa, I forgot all about Light-foot's blackberry bucket. Him laying on the strap wouldn't be the half of it. He'd keep me in the store, garden, and stable the rest of the summer.

Sick at heart, I knew I didn't even want to meet Lightfoot tomorrow.

I tried to think up some excuse, but no matter what I said, it was such in Cold Sassy that she would read *mill girl/town boy* written all over me and she'd hate me the rest of her life, despite she had helped me up from under the wheels of death, so to speak.

Passing the Cold Sassy tree, I felt a new wave of nausea. Amidst the jolts and grinds and the whoosh of steam as the engineer braked into the depot, big Loomis pulled me to my feet and said again, "Lawdy, Mr. Will, yo ma and pa dey gwine be sho nuff proud dis eeb'nin'."

I never found out why Mr. Tuttle was way back there at the caboose when the train pulled in. I just knew that when I looked out the window I found myself staring right into his hard little eyes.

Loomis half pushed, half carried me to the door. I was shaking like the palsy and scared to death I'd puke or start crying. If the earth had opened up and dropped me clear to China, that would have been just dandy with me.

14

When I try to put together the rest of July 5, 1906, it seems hazy. And not just because eight years have gone by now. It was hazy at the time.

I remember worrying after I got to bed that night about not telling Lightfoot good-bye or thanking her. I guess she followed me and Loomis and the dog off the train, but I never saw her after I got surrounded by the other passengers. They were touching me, patting my arm, congratulating me. A tall old man with bulging eyes and a big goiter on his neck pressed a five-dollar gold piece in my hand and got back on the train without saying a word. One little boy begged for a piece of my shirt. I felt foolish, but I pulled off a loose button and gave it to him.

Loomis pushed me through the crowd, bowing and scraping to the white folks, but pushing all the same. "Pleas'sir, let dis here boy pass. . . . Please'm, we's gotta git dis here boy home."

There were Cold Sassy folks at the depot and of course they were puzzled why I was such a hero. I saw Shoeshine Peavy, a young colored boy. He was staring at me, and so was the dwarf, little old Thurman Osgood, who always watched the trains come in. Mr. Beach drove up in his buggy, bringing his wife and little girls to catch the train to Athens. They and others pressed around me, asking questions. "What happened, Will?" "You git hurt?" "Somebody tell us what happened!"

"Please, white folks, let dis boy pass. He don't feel lak talkin'. . . ."

Then the big engineer ran up. "Lookit this 'ere boy!" he shouted, like he was a barker at the county fair and me the prize pig. Waving in my direction, he boomed out his news: "This 'ere boy just now got run over by this 'ere train! Look at him good, folks! Ran over by a train on the trestle and livin' to tell it! Not a hair on his head hurt, folks, not one Goddamn hair, praise be the good Lord!"

Normally I didn't mind being on stage. But what with shaking and shivering and about to cry and vomit and all, I just wanted to get home. It was awful, everybody crowding around like I was a side show, asking how'd it happen and what was I doin' on the trestle anyhow, and what you mean, ran over?

"Mr. Will he ain't feelin' too good," Loomis kept insisting. "He need to git on home." He was still talking polite, but not smiling.

About then Mr. Tuttle got to me. "Engineer said you was on Blind Tillie Trestle. You know you shouldn' a-been up there, boy!"

I didn't answer. I figured Mr. Tuttle was picturing me cut to pieces and himself down at my house trying to settle, cheap, my folks' claim against the railroad. Gosh, would I be worth any more than a dead cow and mule? Or would Mr. Tuttle have sat in our parlor and argued about it.

When Mr. Beach offered to carry me home in his buggy, I said, "Thank you, sir, I'd sure be much obliged." We just live across the street and two houses down from the depot, but I wasn't certain I could walk it, and I sure as heck didn't want Loomis totin' me like a sick calf.

You can imagine how it was when we got to my house and Mr. Beach told Mama what happened. Trying not to cry, she led me in and made me lay down on the black leather davenport in the front hall. I was shivering like a wet dog; she put a heavy quilt over me. She was wiping the dirt and grime from my face with a wet washrag when Papa tore through the front door.

"Loomis said—" he began, then must have been too mad to say any more, because he just stood over me. Fastening my eyes on his knees, I saw they were shaking. I waited for him to take off his belt. When he didn't, I got the nerve to look up at him.

Tears were streaming down Papa's cheeks. He had his straw hat across his chest like folks do when a Confederate veteran's funeral procession passes on its way to the graveyard. I stared up at him, tears wetting my own cheeks. Suddenly he knelt down beside Mama, put his hat on the floor, grabbed my right hand in both of his, and held on like he'd never let go. I couldn't help it; I sat up and threw my arms around my daddy's neck. He held me tight for a long time, till I quit shaking. He didn't say a word.

Papa hadn't hugged me I don't reckon since the day I was twelve years old.

Well, then he put his arms around Mama. "Oh, Hoyt," she whispered. "The little grave we've got in the cemetery . . . I don't think I could stand it if—oh, Hoyt, our boy is alive!" Then she grabbed aholt of me and cried like I was dead.

At some point my daddy walked toward the back hall and was gone a while. When he came back in he said, "You don't have to worry about the milkin', son. I did it."

It's not to my credit that I had forgot all about the cow. Well, I reckon he needed to go get aholt of himself.

I didn't want any supper, and they didn't, either. Mama just brought some buttermilk and cold corn lightbread and they sat there by me in the hall to eat it.

About first dark, Cold Sassy arrived.

Good ole Loomis, he must of galloped all over town telling about my escape on the train trestle, because everybody seemed to know all about it. Just the same, they kept asking questions that I didn't feel like answering.

Lots of ladies brought cake or pie—like if somebody had died.

I wanted to see Grandpa Blakeslee. I almost asked if him and Miss Love were back yet from getting married, but there wasn't any use giving Mama another headache.

I remember Aunt Loma and Uncle Camp coming in. The baby, fat and sweaty and dumb-looking, was fast asleep on her shoulder. I don't know if I mentioned it before, but Campbell Junior was the fattest baby ever seen in Cold Sassy. Aunt Loma looked furious. She didn't so much as ask how I was feeling. Why would my getting run over make her so mad? Maybe she was mad because I'd lived to tell it.

But for once it wasn't me she was mad at. "How could Pa have run off with That Woman!" she whispered to Mama.

"Hush, Loma," said Mama, placing her hand on my arm. "That's not important right now. Not compared to Will."

I felt like the Prodigal Son. When my mother headed for the dining room, her eyes shining with joy, I knew she was fixing to get out her gold and white china dessert plates.

Pink and Smiley and Dunse McCall came in, tiptoeing over to me like I was a haint or a corpse, or like they planned to yessir and nosir me from now on. Finally Pink mumbled, "You didn't have to go do a fool thing like that, Will." He was proud of me and jealous both, I could tell.

"Aw, go get you a piece of pie," said I. Propped on my elbow, holding up my head with my hand, I grinned at the three of them.

They grinned back, and Smiley kind of joshed my shoulder as they moved toward the dining room, where Aunt Carrie and Miss Sarah, French Gordy's wife, were slicing cakes and pies. I could hear the dessert plates rattling as Mama took them out of the china cabinet.

I could also hear several ladies talking low over near the front door. I knew by the crackledy voice that Miss Alice Ann Boozer was one of them. She said somebody seen Rucker Blakeslee and the Simpson woman havin' supper at the ho-tel. "A weddin' supper, I s'pose you'd call it. Rucker didn't never spend one dime takin' Mattie Lou to no ho-tel. Bet you she haints them two t'night."

"Well, I heard little Loma threw a pure fit down at the store today," said somebody else. "You want my opinion, Rucker's been hopin' to git shet a-Mattie Lou ever since he laid eyes on the milliner. But be ye not dis-encouraged. The Lord says vengeance is His'n."

Miss Sarah heard this last as she came through the hall with the big plate of sliced cake. Going over to the talking ladies, she whispered, "I saw her and Rucker right after they come in from Jefferson. He called me over to say they'd just got married. 'She wants a weddin' pitcher,' he said, and they went in Mr. Hale's photo shop. I couldn't believe the nerve."

"I heard Mr. Hale refused to take the pitcher," said Miss Alice Ann.

"Well, good for him," said somebody. "Imagine, a weddin' pitcher this soon after Mr. Hale took a funeral pitcher of Mattie Lou laid out in her coffin and all them baskets of flowers around her."

I knew Mr. French would be upset about the wedding. His mother having married Granny's daddy, they grew up together like brother and sister. The day Granny died, Mr. French said to Mama, "Mr. Blakeslee is a good decent man. But Mattie Lou done all the givin'."

The talkers moved on then, because a covey of Presbyterian ladies were coming in. I shut my eyes like sleeping as they marched over to stare at the corpse.

"Dear boy, hit just wadn' his time to die," Miss Looly said softly.

"S'pose it wadn' his time to die but it was that trestle's time to fall?" her sister breathed, touching my cheek. "Or what if it was that train engineer's time to die? What would of happened to Will?"

"Shet up, Cretia," whispered Miss Looly. "Hit ain't for us to ast sech questions. Hit were the Lord's will for the boy to live. All we got to do is be thankful."

For a moment I swelled with importance, getting talked about like that. Then for no good reason I saw myself as Raw Head and Bloody Bones, spinning into nothing under giant wheels and thunder. I felt sick again, and scared. I didn't want to be a nothing.

I wished Grandpa would come, but I knew he wouldn't. Not on his wedding night.

15

Who came instead of Grandpa was the Methodist preacher. Standing over me, he said, "Son, John Wesley got saved from a fire as a boy and he started the Methodist church. Now you been spared, Will. Miraculously spared. Maybe the Lord's got special plans for you, too—like preachin' the gospel."

Miss Lizzie Mae Tuttle came in the door as he said that. She hooted. "God sure better get to work if He's got in mind to make a preacher out of Will Tweedy." Everybody laughed, including me. "Mr. Tuttle's go'n be on over terreckly," she added, like she thought I'd asked for him personal.

Cudn Hopewell Stump spoke up from the parlor. "God spared Li'l Beulah Samples in that cyclone back in 'eighty-four. Y'all recollect them Sampleses? Used to live over on the Athens road."

Raising my head, I saw Cudn Hope lean forward in his chair, taking aim at the brass spittoon on the hearth. But him being known as a poor shot with tobacco juice, I reckon Mama cringed, because he said, "Jest a minute, folks," and went outside to spit over the banisters.

When he got back, his wife, Cudn Agnes, had taken over the story, telling how Big Beulah sent Little Beulah over to take Miss Winnie Blalock a basket of sweet potatoes. Miss Winnie lived in a sharecropper house on the Stedman farm. "Jest fore Li'l Beulah got thar, a storm come up and hailstones big as this commenced a-fallin'." She made a circle with her plump thumb and forefinger.

"Lord, some them hailstones was big as teacups and weighed a pound," Cudn Hope said, sitting down again. "I seen'm. If one had a-fell on Beulah's head, she'd a-been with Jesus 'thout ever knowin' what hit her."

"Pore thang had jest jumped under a bridge to git shelter from the hail," said Cudn Agnes, "when here come a great big ole dark funnel-shape cloud, full a-planks and trees and dust. Hit was a-roarin' like a freight train!"

Cudn Hope grabbed the story back. "First it sucked up the Stedman house, like 'tweren't no more'n a leaf, and—"

"And after that house went whirly off into the sky, dipped down agin and tuck Miss Winnie's house—and her in it!"

Cudn Hope said, "Li'l Beulah had to watch whilst Miss Winnie went flyin' off to Kingdom Come. Next thang she knew—"

"Next thang she knew, the cyclone was liftin' the bridge right up from over her, like it was a piece a-paper." Mama, who had come to sit by me on the davenport, put her hand on mine and kept it there while Cudn Agnes finished the story. "But nary a hair on that chile's head got tetched. The good Lord spared her. And when she was seventeen, God called her to China as a missionary. Pore thang got over thar and died of the smallpox two months later."

But Cudn Hope got in the last word. "Us that knowed her," he said, "never doubted she saved some Chinamen first."

"I swannee to God," somebody breathed, and the room was quiet for a moment.

"Is that cyclone why the woods around here are full of uprooted pine stumps?" the Methodist preacher said finally.

Cudn Hope said naw, that happened around 1882. "We had a big wind and rainstorm one night and near all the pine trees blowed down. Peeler and Lovin Comp'ny put a sawmill in there and sawed'm up."

Papa told the preacher, "The stumps all point northeast to southwest. You can hunt coons in those woods at night and never need a compass."

It was after somebody brought in lemonade that they started on hit-by-the-train stories.

Mr. Gordy told how, back in aught-one or aught-two, Cold Sassy's first steam fire engine got hit crossing the tracks to the old Sanders Hotel fire. The engine was smashed and both horses killed, and a fire hook stabbed young Addis Morgan in the head and spilled his brains out.

"Next day they found one a-them horses' hoofs up past the depot," remembered old man Frazier. "It was already crawlin' with maggots."

"Oh, Lord, Will," whispered Mama, and got up and hurried toward the bathroom. Knowing Mama, I figured it was to vomit. In my mind I pictured that horse hoof. Then I pictured somebody finding my own foot at the water's edge on Blind Tillie Creek. About then Mr. Cratic Flournoy came out in the hall and noticed how pale I was, I reckon, and deliberately told one you could laugh at, about Mr. Farnam's brood sow getting picked up on the train's cowcatcher, and all it amounted to was the sow had a free ride to town. Wasn't hurt a bit. When somebody sent word to Mr. Farnam, why, he just walked into the depot and led her back home to her pigs.

Toddy Hughes lumbered in. Besides working at the foundry, he was a young stringer for the *Atlanta Constitution Tri-Weekly*. Said he wanted to write me up. Nobody in our family had ever been written up in the Atlanta papers. I was real excited, but Mama said he better wait till tomorrow. Oh, gosh, he might change his mind or forget about it. But he promised he'd be by right after breakfast.

And here came Mr. Tuttle, acting like he'd

personally saved me and like maybe I was his favorite young friend. After he inquired how I was, somebody asked him about the cow and mule that was killed yesterday. Then he told about one time ten or fifteen years ago when the southbound train ran over a bull yearling on a curve. "Two or three boxcars turned over and rolled down into the ravine. Spilled a mess of flour and sugar and I don't know what-all."

My daddy remembered riding his horse out there to see the wreck. "It looked like snow had fell down that embankment."

"When I ast the farmer how much he wanted for his dead yearlin'," said Mr. Tuttle, laughing, "he stood lookin' out at all that flour and stuff spilled broadcast down the bank and said, 'Tuttle?' he said, 'Tuttle, I'm willin' to strike off even, if you are. I think my bull got the best of it.' "

In the midst of the ladies' shrieky laughter and the men's guffaws and haws, Dr. Slaughter hurried in. "How you feelin', son?" he asked. "I just heard, Mary Willis. I been out in the country all day. I want to be sure Will's all right."

While he poked around on my stomach, felt my bones, and told Mama not to give me anything but liquids tonight, we heard a commotion at the door and Grandpa's voice boomed out from the veranda: "Gosh a'mighty! If'n I'd a-knowed y'all had made up a party for us, we'd a-got here sooner!"

16

I found out later that Grandpa and Miss Love knew about the train running over me. After Loomis spread the word all over town, Mr. Jimmy Dan Allsup had rushed into the hotel dining room to tell Grandpa, who was sitting at the little round table with Miss Love, eating a wedding supper of fried catfish and banana fritters.

Next day Mr. Allsup told French Gordy that Grandpa turned white as a sheet. Soon as he found out I was all right, though, he said they might as well finish supper. He'd have to pay for it anyway, and besides there wasn't anything at his house for Miss Love to cook. But Grandpa didn't let on to the crowd gathered at our house but what he thought they were all there to celebrate the wedding.

It's hard to believe how he carried that off.

It was like he didn't hear the silence that greeted them and didn't see Mama go pale or Aunt Loma flounce out of the parlor and down the hall, handling the baby so rough he woke up squalling. Grandpa walked in like it was the usual thing to go off and get a new young wife before your old wife is cold in the grave. Like it never dawned on him anybody would mind.

It's not easy for a pretty lady with her chin in the air to look flustered, but Miss Love did.

She was wearing a hand-embroidered blue dress, her brown hair in a big pompadour, and had on a little blue hat with white bird wings—the same hat Aunt Loma tried to buy that time. And as Grandpa pushed her forward, it was on her that all the eyes fastened. One by one the men stood up, the way you're supposed to when a lady comes in, but they looked uncertain what to say.

There was no uncertainty about Grandpa. "By golly, I'm shore glad to see you folks!" he said, ushering Miss Love toward the parlor door and ignoring me on the davenport in the hall. His blue eyes twinkled with excitement. First time I'd seen any life in him since Granny took sick.

Like there was no way in creation that anybody could know what he and Miss Love had been up to, Grandpa said, "We got a surprise for y'all." Standing in the double doorway to the parlor, his back to me, he put his right arm around Miss Love's shoulders and said, "We'd like to announce we done got married this evenin', over at Jefferson. Folks, meet the new Miz Enoch Rucker Blakeslee! Mary Willis? Where's Mary Willis?" Mama was right there, but he hollered like she was way at the back of the house. "Mary Willis, come kiss the bride. Loma?"

What else could a daughter do? Mama walked over and pecked Miss Love on the cheek. Loma stalked into the room, her face beet-red, and did the same. But they nor the bride said a word. Everybody else was quiet, too. Watching. All you could hear was the clock ticking and Mr. French's fork tapping his dessert plate. He and the other men were still standing, waiting for Miss Love to sit down.

"Where's the chi'ren?" Grandpa boomed out. "Y'all come kiss yore new granny." He turned to Miss Love and laughed. "Haw, I didn't think till now, but I done made you a granmaw!" To the company he said, "I reckon she's jest about the prettiest dang granmaw in Jackson County, ain't she, folks?" He looked around the room then. "Mary Toy, where you at, girl? Will Tweedy?"

"Cudn Temp took Mary Toy out to the country after the parade yesterday, Pa. And Will, h-he . . ." Mama started crying. With his arm around her, my daddy told Grandpa what happened on the train trestle.

"Good gosh a'mighty!" Grandpa turned toward me, his face beaming. "Now ain't thet jest like you, Will Tweedy! Always a-doin' something different. Well, son, I reckon if'n you jest got to git ran over by a train, how you done it was the best way." Ambling out of the parlor, he came over to me, grinning, and touched my shoulder.

I was starving all of a sudden. I sat up and said I was ready for a piece of pie.

"Dr. Slaughter wants you just to have liquids, Will," Mama said anxiously. "He said not give you any solid food tonight."

"Doggit, let'm have his pie," ordered Grandpa, slapping me on the back. "If'n a boy wants a piece a-pie, he cain't be all thet bad off. Come on, Will Tweedy, let's go git us some."

I do believe he forgot all about Miss Love.

As we went toward the kitchen, I looked back and saw that Cudn Hope had offered her the green velvet rocker and everybody was sitting down again.

Grandpa, laughing as if the triumph over the train had been as much his as mine, grabbed what was left of a chocolate pie from the dining room table and pushed me through the door into the kitchen. When the door swung to, it shut out everybody in the house but us.

I could hear voices in the parlor, but not what they said, and I could tell that nobody was saying a whole lot. Miss Love must have felt like a cat cornered by a pack of dogs. At the time nobody knew what a cat she could be when cornered. From what I heard tell later, though, she tried to be real nice that night.

While I served out the pie and poured me some sweetmilk from the pitcher on the table, Grandpa slipped into our company room closet for you-know-what. Then, seated across from me at the kitchen table, his face flushed with whiskey and pride, he said, "Tell me about it, son."

And I did. On the davenport in yonder I hadn't even wanted to think about what happened on the trestle, but with Grandpa I didn't feel like that. I told him how I was tired of being in mourning and got mad at Papa and slipped off, how grand it felt up there on the trestle, how awful it was when the engine commenced chasing me. I told him about the cinders hitting my back, the smell of hot creosote, and the huge roar as the train straddled the rails above me. "I felt like somebody was stabbing my eardrums. It was like I'd gone crazy, Grandpa. Like I was drownin' in sound."

Grandpa heard me out, his blue eyes intent. I even told him about "this mill girl I know at school" who was picking blackberries near the trestle and helped me off the tracks. "And you should of seen ole Loomis, Grandpa, sprintin' onto the trestle to get the dog. Loomis knew another train was comin', and went and got him anyhow! . . . Grandpa, uh, I cain't eat my pie." Couldn't even stand to look at it. Pushed it away, and the milk, too. But Grandpa didn't notice.

I knew he was real excited, because he kept scratching his head fast. But he didn't act like I'd been snatched from hell or go on about a maggotty horse hoof on the railroad tracks or how I had to pray God to use the life He had so mercifully spared. Grandpa reached across the table and put his hand on my arm, just for a second, then poked me in the ribs and said, "By George, gittin' ran over by a train must a-been some experience!" He acted like it was something to remember instead of something to forget.

With the way he took it so casual, and the relief of getting it told, I felt like I'd been stuck back together. But one thing worried me. "Grandpa, you think I'm alive tonight cause it was God's will?"

"Naw, you livin' cause you had the good sense to fall down 'twixt them tracks."

"Maybe God gave me the idea."

"You can believe thet, son, if'n you think it was God's idea for you to be up on thet there trestle in the first place. What God give you was a brain. Hit's His will for you to use it— p'tickler when a train's comin'.'"

Resting my chin in my hand, I thought about that while Grandpa finished up his pie. I felt awful tired. "Sir, do you think it was God's will for Bluford Jackson to get lockjaw and die?"

Grandpa spoke kindly. "The Lord don't make firecrackers, son. Hit's jest too bad pore

Blu didn't be more careful when he was shootin'm off."

"You don't think God wills any of the things that happen to us?"

"Maybe. Maybe not. Who knows?"

"Mama and Papa think He does."

Grandpa licked some meringue off his fork while he pondered. Finally he said, "Life bullies us, son, but God don't. He had good reasons for fixin' it where if'n you git too sick or too hurt to live, why, you can die, same as a sick chicken. I've knowed a few really sick chickens to git well, and lots a-folks git well thet nobody ever thought to see out a-bed agin cept in a coffin. Still and all, common sense tells you this much: everwhat makes a wheel run over a track will make it run over a boy if'n he's in the way. If'n you'd a-got kilt, it'd mean you jest didn't move fast enough, like a rabbit that gits caught by a hound dog. You think God favors the dog over the rabbit, son?"

I shook my head.

"I don't neither. When it comes to prayin', we got it all over the other animals, but we ain't no different when it comes to livin' and dyin'. If'n you give God the credit when somebody don't die, you go'n blame Him

when they do die? Call it His will? Ever noticed we git well all the time and don't die but
once't? Thet has to mean God always wants
us to live if'n we can. Hit ain't never His *will*
for us to die—cept in the big sense. In the
sense He was smart enough not to make life
eternal on this here earth, with people and
bees and elephants and dogs piled up in
squirmin' mounds like Loma's dang cats
tryin' to keep warm in the wintertime. Does
all this make any sense, Will Tweedy?"

"Yessir, Grandpa." I wanted to go lay
down. But I also wanted some more answers.
"Grandpa, uh, why you think Jesus said ast
the Lord for anything you want and you'll get
it? 'Ast and it shall be given,' the Bible says.
But it ain't so." I felt blasphemous even to
think it, much less say it out loud.

Grandpa was silent a long time. "Maybe
Jesus was talkin' in His sleep, son, or folks
heard Him wrong. Or maybe them disciples
tryin' to start a church thought everbody
would join up if'n they said Jesus Christ
would give the Garden a-Eden to anybody
believed He was the son a-God and like
thet." Grandpa laughed. Gosh, I'd get a
whipping if Papa knew what was going on
with the Word in his kitchen. "All I know,"

he added, "is thet folks pray for food and still go hungry, and Adam and Eve ain't in thet garden a-theirs no more, and yore granny ain't in hers, and I ain't got no son a-my own to carry on the name and hep me run the store when I'm old. Like you say, you don't git things jest by astin'. Well, I'm a-go'n study on this some more. Jesus must a-meant something else, not what it sounds like."

"Grandpa, I think maybe I better go back in yonder and lay down."

"Yeah, you better. But I got one more thang to say. They's a heap more to God's will than death, disappoint-ment, and like thet. Hit's God's will for us to be good and do good, love one another, be forgivin'. . . ." He laughed. "I reckon I ain't very forgivin', son. I can forgive a fool, but I ain't inner-rested in coddlin' hypocrites. Well anyhow, folks who think God's will jest has to do with sufferin' and dyin', they done missed the whole point."

I stood up, weaving a little. That brought Grandpa out of his sermon. "Gosh a'mighty, pore Miss Love! You reckon they've et her up alive in there?" He leaped to his feet and burst through the swinging door to the dining room.

We got back to the parlor just in time to hear my daddy, in a strained and formal voice, making polite conversation by telling Mrs. Love Simpson Blakeslee what was coming along in our garden in the way of vegetables.

You could tell that Miss Love and Papa both were mighty glad to see Grandpa. Everybody else was, too. It's not easy to keep up a conversation with somebody you'd rather not even be speaking to.

Miss Love stood up and moved toward us, and all the men rose, polite but stiff.

"Well, folks," said Grandpa, taking aholt of her elbow, "I reckon we best mosey on home now. Hit's been a long fancy day."

Miss Love looked at me. "How are you feeling now, Will?"

"Pretty good, ma'am."

"Fore we go," said Grandpa, "I'd like all y'all to join me and my wife in a word a-prayer."

You can't hardly refuse a man that.

In stony silence they all bowed their heads, where they stood or sat. With his right arm around Miss Love and his left arm stub laid across my shoulder and me facing the two of them, Grandpa prayed.

I didn't close my eyes. I was too busy watching faces—Mama's and Papa's and Aunt Loma's and, of course, Miss Love's. Clasping her hands together, she closed those gray-blue eyes and ducked her head down and all I could see then was the big mass of wavy brown hair and the little blue hat. I noticed for the first time that her hair had a lot of gray sprinkled through it.

After what Grandpa had been saying to me in the kitchen, I should of been prepared for what he said to God in the parlor: "Lord above, afore this gatherin' assembled, I ast You to bless the memory of Miss Mattie Lou."

Everybody gasped. Nobody expected him to bring *her* up.

Grandpa didn't seem to hear the gasps. "Please God, forgive me all the ways I ain't done right by her. Thou knowest what she meant to me and our chi'ren, Mary Willis and Loma," he continued, "and to Will Tweedy and li'l Mary Toy." There was a pause, his face working like he might not could go on, but he did. "And now I ast yore blessin' on this here girl I married today." Miss Love raised her head and stared up at Grandpa, mouth agape. I do think his were the only eyes in the room still shut. "Lord, hep me be good to her. You know I need Miss Love. Hep her to need me likewise. And give her the grace to unner-stand thet if'n they's aught to respect in me, it's because a-thet one in the grave out yonder, what all she learnt me."

Tears were flowing down Miss Love's cheeks. I never before saw anything so beautiful as the way she reached up and put her left hand over the big bony hand that clasped her right shoulder. Grandpa opened his eyes then and looked a long time into hers—till finally, like he'd just remembered God and the other people in the room, he bowed his head again. "And last, bless my daughters and their fam'lies. Specially Will Tweedy, who as You know didn't git kilt today. We're mighty proud to still have him." His voice broke. My own throat swelled and ached. Even with all Grandpa had said in the kitchen, I half expected him to thank God for sparing me, but he didn't. Somebody in the room started sniffling. I couldn't tell who, but I knew it wasn't Aunt Loma.

Grandpa had made the Lord seem so real, I wouldn't of been surprised if he'd said good night to Him. But after a long pause he just said a-men.

It was a strange thing happened then. My mama went up to her pa and kissed him and, crying, hugged Miss Love, who, crying, hugged her back. My daddy kissed Miss Love on the cheek and then shook hands with Grandpa. Uncle Camp naturally did the same thing. So did Mr. French Gordy, Granny's stepbrother. After that all the friends and neighbors filed by—it was still more like a funeral than a wedding party—and shook hands with Grandpa, and either hugged Miss Love or clasped her hand.

I saw Mama whispering to Aunt Loma. Mama believed you had to be nice even to a rat if it was a guest in your home. But Loma shook her off and stalked past Miss Love and Grandpa to join Uncle Camp, who had taken Campbell Junior out on the porch. She didn't even make a polite show of wishing them well. Didn't say good night, even. But I couldn't tell that Grandpa noticed or cared.

In the back of my mind I'd been thinking I had saved him and Miss Love from the gossipers. I mean I figured everybody would be talking about me getting run over by the train instead of about them eloping. That just shows how swell-headed I was, and how I underestimated Grandpa. If I had deliberately planned on nearly getting myself killed just to help him out, it would of been a waste of time.

Grandpa was equal to anything.

17

That night in a dream I stood on the tracks at the edge of Blind Tillie Trestle. Lightfoot Mc-Lendon was way out at the middle, over the deepest part of the gorge. Her hair, white-gold in the sunlight, hung loose down to her hips. She looked like a doll out there, and her voice echoed as she kept calling my name. "Come on, Will! It's so pretty up here? . . . Don't be skeerdy!" I put one foot on the trestle, then pulled back. "Will?" she called. "Will?" Then, oh gosh, she unbuttoned her shirtwaist, let it drop to the rail, and stretched her arms toward the sky. "Come on, Will," she teased, and went to swaying.

Later, remembering the dream, I thought about a porcelain lady with no head or arms that I saw one time in a shop in Atlanta. All she had on was a cloth, draped around her hips, and I could hardly take my eyes off of her. In the dream I could hardly take my eyes off of Lightfoot, swaying out there on the trestle. Then I saw the train loom up behind her. It made no sound, and Lightfoot didn't see it coming. I tried to yell, but like the train I had no voice. I wanted to save her, but my legs wouldn't move.

Swaying her hips, she all of a sudden dropped her skirt and was stepping out of it when the engine hit and exploded her into a thousand pieces. They fell in a slow shower to the creek below.

She shattered without any blood, as if she'd died without ever living.

I screamed. . . .

"Will! What's the matter, sugar?" Mama was shaking me awake.

I told her I dreamed the train hit somebody. I didn't say it was a naked mill girl.

I had another nightmare that night. I was running for my life, the train nipping at my heels, but I was winning the race! The end of the trestle was only a few feet away, and I was like a wind-up tin man with four legs spinning. This time, boy howdy, I was go'n make it! Then Loma appeared on the trestle, barring my way, flapping her arms at me like a farm wife trying to keep a goat out of the garden. "Move!" I shouted. "Get out a-my way!"

"Call me Aint Loma and I'll let you by!" she yelled in a high, child voice.

"I won't! Move!"

"Say Aint Loma!" With every flap of her arms, her body swelled, till she and the train were the same size, and me caught between.

"You ain't my aunt! MOVE!"

Struggling out of the dream, I heard myself babbling sounds that made no sense. Gosh a'mighty, if only I'd had time to grab Loma and push her off into the gorge or under the train wheels! I was so mad it took me a minute to see that I was safe and alone in my room at home. In the next instant, a time out of my childhood flashed before me: the day Loma turned twelve. It put light on what had long been a dark puzzlement.

Up till that birthday we were like a sister and a little brother. She'd get mad and hit me if I crossed her or sassed her, and I'd do meany things to her, like tripping her up or putting sugar in her salt cellar. Still and all, we got along about like you'd expect till, on the day she was twelve (I was just six), she ordered me in a growny tone to start calling her Aint Loma. "Say it. Call me Aint Loma." She raised her fist over my head.

"Silly, you ain't my aunt."

"I am so, too. Ast Sister." Sitting smug in the porch swing, she cut herself another piece of chocolate birthday cake.

"I want some, Loma." I held out my hands.

"If you say Aint Loma and ast me nice."

Jerking her braids, I ran upstairs to my room and slammed the door. Later, coming out, I nearly stepped on my lead soldiers, which Grandpa had ordered for me from London, England. They were in a pile by the door. All broken.

I never forgot the pitiful sight of those dead soldiers, some without heads or arms, some with legs missing, and rifles bent or snapped in two. But I had forgotten why Aunt Loma did it.

After the dream I remembered everything: how I cried till suppertime about the soldiers but still wouldn't say Aint Loma. How she taunted me, singsonging, "Crybaby, come let your Aint Loma hold you."

"I'm go'n tell Mama on you!" I yelled.

"You do and I'll say you done it. And who you think she'll believe, smarty crybaby?

She's seen you get mad and tear up things before."

I spat in Loma's face.

She told Mama on me for spitting at her. I said she broke my lead soldiers. She said I did it. Mama believed her instead of me, and Papa whipped me good. That night when she tucked me in, Mama said, "Will, sugar, try to be a better boy tomorrow. Hear?"

"Yes'm. But tell Loma to quit sayin' she's my aunt. She says I got to call her Aunt Loma."

"We'll talk about it tomorrow, son. Go to sleep now."

You need to understand that in Cold Sassy when the word "aunt" is followed by a name, it's pronounced *aint,* as in Aint Loma or Aint Carrie. We also say *dubya* for the letter "w," *sump'm* for something, *idn'* for isn't, *dudn'* for doesn't, *raig'n* for reckon, *chim'ly* for chimney, *wrench* for rinse, *sut* for soot, as in train or chim'ly sut, and *like* for lack, as in "Do you like much of bein' th'ew?" Well, I know that how we speak is part of what we are. I sure don't want Cold Sassy folks to sound like a bunch of Yankees. But I don't want us to sound ignorant, either, and pronunciations like *sump'm* and *id'n* sound ignorant. So I'm trying to remember not to use such—except right now to tell how Loma became Aint Loma.

The morning after our fuss about it, Mama sat me down for a talking-to. "Now, sugarfoot, you got to get something straight," she began. "Loma is my sister, which makes her your aunt. And it's high time you started callin' her that. She's twelve now, a young lady."

"Then how come she's still goin' barefooted?"

"Well, she cain't go barefooted anymore. And you got to start showin' her proper respect. You hear? Take in that lip and answer me."

"Yes'm."

"Look at me when you answer me."

"Yes'm."

"Now if I hear of you and your Aint Loma fussin' about this again, you go'n get another whippin'. You understand?"

"Yes'm."

Loma was at our house as much as at her own, I reckon, and for a long time after Mama laid down the law I didn't call her anything. But because Mama and Papa and Grandpa and Granny started speaking of her to me as "your Aint Loma," I gradually thought of that as her name, and after the awful first time, saying it wasn't much harder than saying doodly-squat or Peter Rabbit. By time Mary Toy was old enough to talk, Loma was Aint Loma to both of us. And though I finally forgot *why* she broke my soldiers—until the nightmare—I never forgot or forgave her for doing it.

When Miss Love came into my life, Aunt Loma was still my prime hate, and getting even with her was still my prime goal.

Mama thought hating folks was sinful. She could make allowances for anybody. When I'd get to fussing about Aunt Loma, she'd say, "Your Aunt Loma means well, son. I know she's hateful sometimes, but she's got a good heart."

Good heart, my foot. Aunt Loma's heart was down on a level with Mr. Angus Tuttle's, and he had caused me more whippings than I could count. Us boys were always trying to get back at him. Just for instance, one day we sneaked into his barn, just fooling around, and chanced to see a gallon of the yellow paint that he put on the handles of all his farm tools so if somebody showed up with a yellow-handled hoe, everybody would know it was stolen from Mr. Tuttle.

Well, it was real cold the day we went in there, and his barn was full of mules, horses, and cows brought in from his farm; share-cropper tenants being bad to steal, if you live in town, it's the custom to bring in all your animals, wagons, and farm tools for the winter. What we did, and it was my idea, we dipped every horse, mule, and cow tail in that yellow paint. When one flipped, good gosh it sent a spray of yellow all over the dern animal, the stalls, the hayracks, everything. Then we got the idea to paint all the hoofs yellow, too, and the cows' horns, and we caught a rooster that was up on the rafters and painted his beak and toenails.

You never saw anybody mad as Mr. Tuttle when he got home, and he never doubted who'd done it. That night Mama didn't just ask me to be a better boy; she insisted on it.

If I had told her just how much I hated Mr. Tuttle, she wouldn't of believed it. But compared to the way I felt about Aunt Loma, he was like a favorite uncle.

There were a few other people I couldn't stand, like Hosie Roach, the mill boy in my class at school. Most mill children went to school just two or three years, then dropped out to work at the spindles. If they were too little to reach the spindles, they stood on boxes. Children caught playing on the job got a whipping from the supervisor. I didn't like to think about that. I didn't like to think about mill children at all, and never had to as long as the mill ran its own school. Then a few years back, though the *Cold Sassy Weekly* ran editorials against "allowing cotton mill folks to mix and mingle with the children of our fair city," the school board voted to close the mill school and let the lintheads come to ours. Papa was one of the board members in favor. If he'd had to sit next to Hosie, I bet you he'd of thought twice.

Hosie was still not through high school, even though he was twenty-one. He'd work a few months in the mill, then come to classes a few months. Sometimes he worked at night after being at school in the day. So he hadn't been promoted regular, despite he was right smart for a mill boy. Our superintendent kept trying to get him to quit school, but Hosie vowed he was go'n graduate if it took him till he was thirty years old.

We were always fighting at recess. I really hated him, and the feeling was mutual. But compared to Aunt Loma, Hosie Roach seemed like a best friend.

Then there was Grandpa Tweedy, my daddy's daddy out in Banks County. He talked hard times morning, noon, and night. Called himself a farmer, but you never saw him behind a plow or driving a team. Lazy, great goodness. Like the lilies of the field in the Bible, he toiled not, neither did he spend his own money. He was always asking Papa to help him out. All he ever did was sit on the porch and swat flies, and like I said, even had him a pet hen to peck them up.

When Papa left the farm at sixteen to go work for Grandpa Blakeslee, he made twenty dollars a month and had to send half of it home to pay the field hand who took his place. That was the custom. But even after Papa married at nineteen, making forty dollars a month, he still had to send Grandpa Tweedy ten of it till the day he was twenty-one. My mother never said she didn't like her father-in-law, but I could tell she didn't, and that may of been why.

What started me hating him, he wouldn't let me fish on Sunday. Said it was a sin. I remember I put out some set hooks late one Saturday, thinking if I caught a fish, it wouldn't be a sin to take him off the hook next morning. End his suffering, you know. Early Sunday I ran down to the river and one of the lines was just a-jiggling! But when I ran up the hill and asked Grandpa's permission to get my fish off the hook, he said, "Hit'll still be thar t'morrer, Lord willin'. The Lord ain't willin', it'll be gone. Now git in the house and study yore catechism till time to leave for preachin'."

Of course the fish was gone Monday morning. But I got back at Grandpa Tweedy. I'd noticed a big hornet's nest in the privy, just under the tin roof, so I bided my time behind a tree till I saw him go in there. Giving him just long enough to get settled good, I let fly a rock and it hit that tin roof like a gunshot. Grandpa burst out of there in a cloud of hornets, trying to swat and hold his pants up at the same time. He knew I'd done it. "Will Tweedy, I'll git you, boy!" he yelled. "I'll git you!"

I just couldn't hardly stand him. One time when he was fussing about tenants stealing out of his woodpile, I watched while he drilled holes in several sticks of stovewood, filled the holes with gunpowder, sealed them over with candlewax, and put them on top of the woodpile. "What if somebody gets kilt?" I asked him.

I was just a little bitty boy, so I believed him when he said, "Ain't go'n hurt nobody. Hit'll jest scare the livin' daylights out of'm."

Next morning at breakfast we heard a big WHOMP, BOOM from the tenant shack. A few minutes later, the cook rushed in and said, "Mist' Tweedy, one them white-trash chillun's hand done got tore up, po li'l lamb, an' dey stove's ruint."

Grandpa saucered his coffee and took a big slurp before he spoke. His voice was hard. "Well, then I reckon they won't steal no more a-my f'ar wood."

You can see why I despised Grandpa Tweedy and didn't have a dab of respect for him. But compared to Aunt Loma, he was King Arthur and I was a Knight of the Round Table.

Lying there in the dark, thinking about Aunt Loma, I got really mad. She could of at least pretended to be glad I'd escaped from the jaws of death on that trestle. It wouldn't of hurt her. But she hadn't said one word, and then flounced off without so much as a good night to Grandpa and Miss Love.

I wondered would she meet her match in
Miss Love. Or would Miss Love do like
Mama and kowtow to Loma for the sake of
peace in the family?

18

It's not to my credit that the next morning I
forgot all about telling Lightfoot we'd pick
blackberries.

I couldn't of gone. I had to wait for Toddy
Hughes to come by and interview me for the
Atlanta newspaper. Also, I felt awful tired,
and Dr. Slaughter had said I better stay quiet
and not get hot. Mama would have a fit if I
tried to go off somewhere. She wouldn't even
let me milk that day. Got Loomis to do it.

There wasn't any way to let Lightfoot
know, but I should of at least remembered.

I guess what messed me up was so many
folks coming to call, from right after breakfast on. If they weren't asking me about getting run over by the train, they were asking
Mama about Grandpa and Miss Love.

I was on the front veranda with young
Toddy Hughes about ten o'clock when Mr.

Son Black rode up bareback on his red mare mule. He had unhitched her from the plow and she still had on her collar, the traces draped over her neck. Wearing an old felt hat and dirty overalls, Son sat sideways, slumped, with one leg crossed over the mule's shoulder and the other hanging loose. He looked so seedy I wondered what Miss Love, or even Aunt Loma, had ever seen in him.

"Whoa, Lucy," he said to the mule, then kicked her halfway up our walk and asked where my granddaddy was. He sounded mad. "I want to see him. He ain't come in yet at the store."

"That ain't surprisin', Son," Toddy Hughes said with a leery grin, "bein' as yesterd'y was Mr. Blakeslee's weddin' day. Or ain't you heard?"

Son spat. "I heard."

"Well, and I just guess they slept late," Toddy called as the mule turned away and trotted down the walk.

"Mr. Hughes!" snapped Mama, who came out on the porch in time to hear that.

Toddy stood up quick, blushing, and said, "Sorry, ma'am. Sorry. Well, I'll mosey along. Got to go write this up and put it on the telegraph to Atlanta. I, uh, reckon they'll use it right away, Will. The paper ain't likely to of had anything like bein' run over by a train and lived to tell it before. Uh, be seein' you, ma'am." He tipped his straw hat to Mama. Looked like he couldn't get away fast enough.

He was gone before I remembered I was going to tell him about Lightfoot McLendon running out on the trestle to help me off and about Loomis saving my dog. Likely they wouldn't of put Loomis in the paper, him being colored, but I meant to ask Toddy to try.

It's no credit to me that I was sort of glad he rushed off before I could tell him about Lightfoot. I didn't want to hear what Pink and Lee Roy and them would say about me and her if they saw her name in the paper. Also, it would take Mama and Papa a month to convince folks that, no, I wasn't at the trestle with a mill girl. She just happened to be picking berries nearby.

Aunt Loma spent most of that morning at our house, fussing about Miss Love and jerking the baby around like it was all his fault that his grandpa had disgraced the family. She kept saying, "I'm go'n get even with Love Simpson if it's the last thing I ever do."

* * *

Despite everybody acting so nice the night before, nobody went to call on Grandpa and Miss Love—at least nobody that I heard of. Even the few who weren't mad for Granny's sake likely didn't know what to say, under the circumstances, and nobody was going to risk criticism by paying a formal call or taking a wedding present. Not even those who had hugged her the night before would do that.

I wondered if the newlyweds had anything to eat. I knew Miss Love could make coffee, but after boarding so many years, she might not know how to cook anything else. "You go'n send them some dinner?" I asked Mama. "I could carry it up there."

She said, "You got to rest, like Dr. Slaughter told you. And I'll say it right now, Will: you are not to go runnin' up there all the time like you used to. We don't owe Love Simpson any favors. And you can see your granddaddy at the store. You understand?"

I understood, all right.

But Grandpa didn't.

He never appeared at the store at all that day, or at our house, either. When he didn't even come by for his whiskey, I and Papa and Mama must of each thought Miss Love didn't object to a man's having a little toddy at home. But then real early Saturday morning he stopped in as usual before work, like he still didn't have a closet of his own, and came out of the company room scratching his head and hitching up his trousers with his arm stub, the way he always did when he was excited or upset. Right in front of Mama, he said, "Will Tweedy, git on up home, son, and see can you hep Miss Love any. She's a-tearin' the place apart! Scourin' floors, washin' win-ders and curtains, and scrubbin' furniture like they's cooties or bedbugs in ever piece. She had me workin' all day yesterd'y."

"You, Pa? Housework? Shah!" Mama didn't believe it.

"Yes'm. Sunup to bedtime." A sheepish look came on his face. Pulling at his bushy beard, he announced, "Mary Willis, you and Loma got to come go th'ew yore ma's thangs."

Mama didn't answer.

"I ain't never see sech a one for cleanin' house as Miss Love." He spoke with a pride that he tried to hide. "You got time to hep her any, Mary Willis?"

"No, Pa, I haven't," she said. "Queenie and I are cannin' soup vegetables today. We got to, or lose everything, one." I was surprised she spoke up to him. She never had before. "And," she added firmly, "I'm countin' on Will to pick the vegetables."

Grandpa was a little taken back. "Well," he said. "All right. But send him on up soon as he gits th'ew."

My mama was really something when she got mad. Blue eyes blazing, hands on hips, she watched her daddy go down the walk and cross the railroad tracks. "Tearin' into that house like it was hers!" she muttered.

I thought Grandpa had prayed away all the town's hard feelings, and maybe he really had. But that was Thursday night and this was early Saturday morning, and he'd just showed he didn't know pea-turkey about how grown daughters feel when a young stepmother is brought into the family, or how they feel about being told to clear out their mama's personal belongings to make room for the new wife's things.

I saw what was going through Mama's mind like she was in the funny paper with a balloon coming out of her head:

It's enough he up and married like he did, said the balloon. *It's enough they neither one, Pa nor Love, went anywhere the day after the weddin' and now everybody's sniggerin' about it. But to find out Miss Love cain't wait a minute to take over Ma's house is too much and then some.*

Even I could see that for the bride to start fall cleaning the day after the wedding, in the middle of the hottest summer on record, was the same as announcing to the world that the first Mrs. Blakeslee was sloven and her house too dirty to live in—and that the Blakeslee daughters hadn't cared enough for their poor bereaved papa to keep it clean for him.

Mama and Aunt Loma always did think Grandpa should of hired a cook for Granny. Aunt Loma said as much to her daddy one time, but he just laughed. "Last buyin' trip I took," he said, "a New York feller got to talkin' bout Southern ladies rockin' on the porch at five o'clock ever evenin'. He called it a waste of woman power. Thet's the only time I ever seen eye to eye with a Yankee. Anyhow, Loma, yore ma had a long sight rather be a-workin' than a-settin'."

I was fixing to ask Mama what I was to do —I mean, was I to mind Grandpa or her— when she said in a spitting voice, "Will, pick everything that's ready and then make haste on up to your grandpa's."

She was scared she had gone too far in crossing him. And she was mad at herself for giving in.

I never in my life stripped a garden so fast, and my feet raced each other past the depot and the Cold Sassy tree and the nine houses between Grandpa's house and ours. I was about even with the Tate house when I caught the first muffled sounds of "Ta-Ra-Ra-Boom-de-Ay" on Granny's piano.

Miss Effie Belle's 102-year-old brother was sitting on their front porch, his square, moldy, splotched face unsmiling and vacant. I knew he couldn't hear Miss Love's music, not without his ear trumpet. But Miss Effie Belle could. Eighty-nine, and skin and bones like a mummy, she stood listening at her open front door, hands on hips and very grim of face.

Miss Effie Belle had a grim face any time, punctuated by a big pink wart that stuck out from the side of her upper lip like the feeler of a bee. She being the kind that put down newspapers so old Mr. Tate wouldn't track in dirt on her floors, you can imagine that she wasn't taking kindly to Miss Love's music. She would be thinking that when you've married somebody else's husband, if you play on her pi-ana it ought to be a contrite hymn that starts, "Lord, my sins be as scarlet" or "Too shamed to lift my head, Lord, too stained to hope for Heaven." Miss Effie Belle would call Miss Love awful to be playing dance-hall music.

I reckon the bride thought that with the parlor windows shut, nobody could hear it. That did dull the loudness, but not the joy and bam with which she played. The music really wasn't fittin', under the circumstances of Granny being dead and all, but it sounded mighty fine.

I didn't know whether to knock or just go on in, like I used to when Granny was alive. I knocked. But of course Miss Love couldn't hear me over the racket, so I tiptoed into the hall. Just then she went to singing, for gosh sake. "Ta-ra-ra-BOOM-de-ay! Ta-ra-ra-BOOM-de-ay!" I stood listening to the deep, rich goodtimes voice. Without a pause after the last "BOOM-de-ay," she burst into a chorus of "I'm Only a Bird in a Gilded Cage" and then sang "It'll be a HOT time, in the OLD town, to-ni-ight!"

I sure would of missed something if that train had of killed me!

I stepped over the parlor rug, which was in the hall, rolled up like a long log. Nearby was

a pile of dusty ragged sheets that Granny had
kept draped over the upholstered parlor furniture. Following the song to the parlor, as if
Miss Love was a Pied Piper, I stopped at the
door in pure amazement.

The room, pounding with music, was so
bright with sunlight it might near put my eyes
out. It had always been dark and cool in
there. I'd never seen the rich red velour on
the loveseat and sidechairs or on what
Granny called "my gentleman's and lady's
chairs." Of course the sheets weren't on the
furniture when Granny had lain in state in
there, but even then, because of her being
dead and all, the blinds were closed and the
draperies drawn.

Today, despite the windows were closed,
Miss Love had opened the shutters wide.
And the dark heavy draperies weren't just
pushed apart; they were down and laid across
a chair, like a sweaty dress after Sunday
morning preachin'.

The good smell of wet wood rose from the
floor, still damp after being scrubbed.
Granny's big upright grand piano had been
pulled way out, at an angle to the wall, and I
saw Miss Love's new gold wedding band on
the piano top beside a rag and a square of

beeswax in a saucer. I guess she had been about to polish the rosewood but sat down to play instead. The rug being out and the draperies down, the piano sounded tinny and alive.

Miss Love had started playing "All Hail the Power of Jesus' Name" with a strong marching beat and lots of walking bass. She still hadn't seen me, though I had a good side view of her. I stood by the door while she finished the hymn and ran through choruses of "Maple Leaf Rag," "Georgia Blues," and "Good Ole Summertime," which she hummed, then played again, singing the words. After that she bammed out "Meet Me in St. Louis, Louis," as if her purpose in life was to play loud enough for old man Tate to hear through the shut windows.

I don't know what I was most flabbergasted at, the bright sun in the parlor (already fading the furniture, I was sure) or the bing-bang music (which I knew she would quit playing as soon as she saw me) or Miss Love herself, seated on the round stool, legs apart, long skirt hiked up above her knees (to be cooler, I reckon), and her heels and toes rocking the way I imagined a piano player's would in a cabaret.

Maybe it was her clothes. I had never seen Miss Love when she wasn't dolled up like one of those M. Rich & Bros. fashion advertisements in the Atlanta newspapers. Working at the store or playing for preachin' on Sunday at the Methodist Episcopal Church, South, she wore perfume and a hat, and her hair fixed fancy, and was always corseted and gusseted or whatever it was ladies did to shape their hips and bosoms.

But today she looked like a girl instead of a lady.

Her heavy brown hair was bound up and covered with a kerchief made out of a rag— actually a piece of Granny's old white outing nightgown. Mama always wore loose housework dresses at home, but Miss Love had on an old pink afternoon dress with white eyelet embroidery and a low-cut neckline. If she'd of bent down in that dress, her bosoms would of looked like two puppies trying to climb over a fence. Whenever her hands hit bass and treble chords at the same time, the bodice stretched tight across her bust, and on fast pieces, the jiggle was something to see! I tried not to stare, but I couldn't exactly help it.

With all that and her rollicking songs, I was on fire. My bare left foot patted to beat the band while she was singing "Yes, Sir, That's My Baby." Then she repeated the last line real slow and soft, except this time she sang, "Yes, sir, it's my baby . . . yes, sir, this house is . . . my baby . . . now-ow . . ." She ended with a slow, subdued flourish of treble chords and finally one soft single bass note, like a Graphophone winding down.

"Boy howdy, Miss Love!" I exclaimed.

Surprised, she swung toward me on the piano stool, clutching her low dress front with one hand and flipping down the long pink skirt with the other.

"Will Tweedy!" she exclaimed, the way a child caught with his hand in the cookie jar might say "Mama!"

"I, uh, knocked, but you didn't hear me," I said. She blushed. I reckon she was embarrassed at being caught with her knees showing, or being caught so happy when her husband's real wife wasn't yet cold in the grave.

"What can I do for you?" she asked, as if this was the store and I was a lady come in to order an Easter hat.

"Uh, Grandpa said you could use some hep," I offered, hitching my overalls and scratching my left heel with my right big toe.

"I hadn't expected your mama could spare you."

"Grandpa told her to send me up here."

"That man! I never saw anybody get away like he did this morning." She laughed gaily, her hand still clutching the low dress front.

"I reckon he was scairt somebody would see him doin' housework," said I, grinning. "He don't know doodly-squat about cleanin', you know. The one that always hepped Granny was me. Uh, excuse me, ma'am," I said lamely. "I shouldn't of mentioned my grandmother."

Waving a hand in protest, Miss Love got up from the piano stool. She looked a little flustered, as if trying to decide what to say and how to say it. "Look here, Will. Miss Mattie Lou was nicer to me than anybody else in Cold Sassy. Even if she weren't all around me in this house, I'd never forget her. So please don't think I expect to take her place. I'm—well, I'm just going to try to look after your grandfather."

"Yes'm."

We talked a little about me on the train trestle. She asked if I felt all right and I said yes'm. Then she went to get a gold bar pin for her dress front, to make the neck higher, and

I went out to the porch for a drink of well water. On the way back up the hall, I chanced to look in Grandpa's room and saw that the bed in there wasn't made up.

Mama wouldn't ever start anything else without she made up the beds first.

Miss Love had raised the parlor windows by time I got back. "First," she said cheerfully, "I'd like you to shake these dusty draperies outside. I want to make new ones, soon as I can get around to it; the room needs brightening. But these will do for now."

How was Granny going to stay all around Miss Love if she got new parlor draperies?

Next I hefted the rolled-up parlor rug over my right shoulder and started out to hang it on the line. "When you get through beating it, leave it out in the sun a while," she said.

"Uh, won't it fade in the sun? Mama always says sun will fade a rug." It didn't matter to me personally, but I knew what Mama and Cold Sassy would say if Miss Love ruined Granny's things.

It got her dander up, my saying that. "The rug is moldy, mildewed, and full of moths, Will," she snapped. "That's what happens when a room stays shut up. The sun may fade it a little, but at least it won't smell musty."

To my mind she was same as saying that Granny was a dirty housekeeper. I lacked the nerve to explain about Grandpa not hiring help. As if reading my mind, Miss Love came over and patted my arm. "I didn't mean to be passing judgment, Will. When a woman gets sick, the house gets sick, too."

She was in the dining room when I came in from beating the rug. "I'd like you to take down the curtains in here," she said, "and put them out to burn. They're rotten. Then please sweep the walls and the ceiling in here, and when the dust settles, we'll wash the windows and the floor. But first, Will, take the coat rack and the little pine desk out of the hall into the parlor. I've already washed and waxed them."

Toting the desk into the parlor, I saw that Miss Love had laid the big Toy family Bible on Granny's loveseat. Seeing it, I longed for Granny. It sounds crazy, but I still found it hard to believe she was gone, and half expected that her death wasn't really written down in the Bible.

It was there, all right, in Grandpa's bold handwriting: *Died June 14, 1906.*

And below it, there was a new line. In a fine ladylike hand it said, *Enoch Rucker*

Blakeslee married Love Honour Simpson in Jefferson, Georgia, July 5, 1906.

Gosh, Mama would sure be mad! This was the Toy Bible, not the Blakeslee Bible. To my knowing there wasn't any Blakeslee Bible. And I had heard Mama tell Aunt Loma right after the funeral, "I'm go'n bring Ma's Bible over here, if Pa don't mind."

I wondered if Grandpa knew Miss Love had put her name in it.

All the walls in Granny's house were horizontal pine boards, painted to look like plaster. I swept those in the dining room, like I was told to. When I came out, Miss Love was down on her hands and knees, scrubbing the hall floor, and humming like it was the most fun she'd ever had in her whole life.

She had just fired up the stove and put the kettle on when Grandpa walked in to eat dinner. Not a blessed thing fixed! He always was one to want a big meal in the middle of the day, and he told Miss Love so.

You never saw the like of how she took it. Instead of getting her dander up like Loma would, or being upset and apologizing the way Mama would, Miss Love, just calm and cool as you please and with a happy smile on her face, said, "Goodness, Mr. Blakeslee, cleaning this wonderful house made me forget all about time!" Her eyes were glowing. "Look, I'll cook you a real good supper. But for now, we can have the apple pie left from yesterday, sir, with a big hunk of that rat cheese from the store on it, and some cool milk. Is that all right?"

I expected him to explode. Instead he just went out on the back porch, poured some water from the bucket into the gray enamel basin on the shelf, washed up, came on in, sat down at the table, and said the blessing over the pie and milk. He didn't fuss at all, and didn't seem to notice she wasn't wearing the gold wedding band, which was still on the piano. She'd told me the ring was a little big and kept slipping off when her hands were in the soapy wash water.

While I bolted down my pie, Grandpa blurted out that Son Black had come in the store that morning. "He says you and him had a unner-standin'. He's talkin' bout breach a-promise. He got any call to think you was go'n marry him?"

Miss Love looked startled. "If he did, it was all in his own head. He talked about us getting married, but I always just passed it off as a joke."

"Thet's all I need to know," said Grandpa, finishing up his pie. "Miss Love, you think you could trim my hair some?" He tried to smooth it down with his hand, but it was too thick and bushy to mind anything but scissors.

"I'd love to trim your hair, Mr. B." There in the kitchen she danced around, studying his face this way and that, and finally burst out, "Mr. Blakeslee, you don't know how long I've wanted to see what's under that shelf of a mustache and that old gray beard!"

He jerked his arm across his face. "I didn't say cut my beard off, woman. I said cut my hair. I reckon the beard could use a li'l trimmin', but thet's all, hear. I ain't fond a-shavin'."

She didn't give up. "With a close haircut and a thin mustache and no beard, sir, you'd look—distinguished! Can I? Oh, please, Mr. Blakeslee?"

"I don't think so. I ain't seen my face in so long I mightn't know me."

"Wouldn't nobody know you, Grandpa," said I, pitching a hunk of cheese in the air so it dropped into my mouth. "Cain't you just see my daddy and Uncle Camp and Cudn

Hope if you walked in the store shaved? They'd take you for a stranger and sell you a mule collar or something."

The idea really appealed to him. "By dang, Will Tweedy, you right. They wouldn't know me from Adam!"

"But you won't look like somebody who needs a mule collar," Miss Love protested. "You'll look like a judge who's come in for fine tobacco. All right, Mr. B.?" She was real excited. "Can I? Please?"

"By George, yes!" he said, slapping his knee. "If'n you can fix a lady's hair to go with them fancy hats, Miss Love, I reckon you ain't go'n make me look no worse'n I already do. Will Tweedy, go git the strop and my Wade and Butcher razor. Hit used to be my daddy's," he told her. "And, son, find them hair-cuttin' scissors yore granny always used. They's somewhere on my bureau."

Miss Love cut off most of the thick gray beard with the scissors, after which Grandpa wrapped a steaming towel around his face to soften the stubble. He shaved kind of awkward, nicking his face in several places. Then Miss Love trimmed the mustache into a pencil-thin line and cropped his hair down from a mane to short as mine.

Boy howdy, I couldn't believe what a difference! His hair and mustache being dark, he looked years younger without the gray beard. His face was lean and handsome. He looked like a fine gentleman.

Later, considering who arrived on the train that same evening, I couldn't help thinking how glad I was that Miss Love got Grandpa changed from a bushy-headed, bushy-faced old country man to somebody she could be proud to stand beside and introduce as her husband.

19

Grandpa couldn't stop looking at himself in the mirror. Preening like a rooster, he kept saying things like "I do recollect seein' thet feller somewheres before. Ain't he a buster though!"

Miss Love was so excited she hugged him.

I could tell the hug surprised her as much as it did Grandpa, who looked like he didn't know whether to hug her back or not, which he didn't. But he seemed mighty pleased, and didn't object when she said, "Mr. B., don't go back to the store wearing that same tobacco-stained shirt, or you won't fool a soul."

Grandpa generally wore just two shirts a week, and Saturday wasn't his day to change. But he went to his room and came out buttoning a clean one. Then as he pulled up his suspenders, he said, real formal, "I'm much obliged to you, Miz Rucker Blakeslee."

He hardly ever thanked anybody for anything. Gratitude embarrassed him. I guess the words popped out because he was so pleased to see how good he looked after all these years.

While he dusted off his hat, Miss Love said, "You'd really look spiffy in a new cut of suit, Mr. Blakeslee."

"Cain't afford no new suit," he said gruffly.

"I'll make you one."

"Thet'd be a dang waste a-time. I wouldn't live to wear it out. Will Tweedy, you think they'll know me at the store?"

"No, sir! Specially if you walk in kind of sideways, so they won't see your arm off."

He looked at the clock on the mantelpiece. "I better git on back. Camp'll go to sleep if'n I ain't there." He set his hat at a jaunty angle and raised his hand good-bye. Reminded me of a little boy going off by himself for the first time.

We stood watching as he walked across the tracks, a new sort of strut in his long stride. "Boy howdy, Miss Love," said I, still amazed at the change. "If I was at the store and Grandpa walked in, I wouldn't know him. I might think I'd seen him somewhere, but I wouldn't know him."

She turned toward me, beaming. "He likes it, Will Tweedy! And isn't your grandfather a handsome man! You and him—I mean you and he—you look a lot alike, Will. I never realized it before."

"Granny always said so."

"It's the mouth and the shape of the jaw, and—" She put her hand on my shoulder, turned me toward her, and studied my face. Blushing, I bent my head. "No, look at me, Will. It's also your eyes, big like his. And your brows are arched like his."

Soon as Miss Love went to the kitchen, I went hunting for the painted mirror that usually hung over the marble-top table in the front hall—the mirror Aunt Loma and Mama both wanted. I found it laid across a table in the parlor. Bending over the glass, I stared around Saint Cecilia at the organ and all the painted angels and flower garlands to see if something of Grandpa would stare back at me.

Well, gosh, yes. Now that I had finally seen his face, I could say I did look like him. A lot like him. When I grinned at myself, the lower lip turned up at the corners, just like Grandpa's. His mouth was like a boy's anyhow, except looser. I preened a while, this way and that. If I looked like Grandpa, and Miss Love thought he was handsome, then that meant I was handsome, too.

Lee Roy and them might not think so, but Miss Love did.

I combed my hair down with my fingers, squeezed a red sore place on my chin, and examined my upper lip to see if my mustache was any more ready to be shaved than yesterday. Hearing Miss Love coming, I sort of waved good-bye to myself and straightened up. She said, "Will, bring those pasteboard boxes in off the back porch to the company room, and I'll tell you what to do next."

When I came in with the boxes, I asked, "Ma'am, what you want me to do with'm?" I couldn't see her over the high stack I carried, but I knew she was in there. I could hear her opening drawers.

"I want you to pack up everything in this bureau," she said evenly. "And the things in the wardrobe, too."

"Everything?" I dropped the boxes. They fell with a thick dull clatter. I couldn't believe it. Without so much as a by-your-leave from Mama or Aunt Loma, Miss Love was planning on getting rid of Granny's belongings!

"Yes, everything. Mostly it's stuff that was packed away—old quilts and things your grandmother obviously wasn't using but I suppose hated to get rid of. The clothes she was wearing are all in Mr. Blakeslee's room. He wants everything in there to stay the way she had it."

I couldn't think what to say to that. So I asked, "Where we go'n put what's in here, Miss Love?"

"I want you to take it home. Your mother and Loma can go through it and throw stuff out or give it away. I need the space for my things, you see. It's—uh, this will be my room." She blushed.

It slowly dawned on me that it already was her room. Several of her dresses hung on wall nails, and also her nightgown, and she had pushed back a blue thousand-eye tray on the princess dresser to make room for a shoebox full of her combs and ribbons and doodads. Why, she had already brought over her things from the Crabtrees'! Two big trunks sat in front of the fireplace.

Looking around, I noticed a small poster tacked on the wall, advertising a women's suffrage speech in Baltimore in 1888. It said:

The Subject: Throw Off the Yoke of Oppressor Man!
Miss Hannah Lee, The Long-Tongued Orator
Will Emit Impassioned Yawps at Borough Hall
7 O'Clock Monday Night!
The Belva E. Lockwood Quartette
Will Furnish Discord!
Come One, Come All
And Bring Your Chewing Gum!

I didn't want to offend Miss Love, but I thought that was the silliest thing I ever read. Seeing I was trying to keep a straight face, she giggled. "Go on. Laugh. Your grandpa did. I laugh myself, every time I look at it. That's why I put it up."

"I thought you wanted women to get the vote, Miss Love."

"I do. Oh, I do. But that doesn't mean I can't laugh."

" 'The long-tongued orator will emit impassioned yawps,' " I read. "Haw, I sure would of liked to hear that! Was she chewin' chewin' gum while she talked?"

Miss Love laughed. "I doubt it, Will, but I wasn't there. I found that poster on the sidewalk later. For a long time I tried to figure it out. I didn't know whether Miss Hannah Lee thought the suffrage movement was getting too grim and made this up to poke fun at herself and the rest of us, or whether some printer did it as an insult. I just know that every time I start taking life too seriously, I can look at that silly poster and get my sense of humor back."

Laughing merrily, she started out the door, then turned and asked, "Did you ever hear of Belva E. Lockwood, Will?"

"No'm. Was she that lady scientist over in France? Well, no, I see she was a singer." I nodded toward the poster.

"More than a singer. She ran for president that year."

"Of what?"

"The United States. I campaigned for her.

She was a lawyer in Washington, and I thought she had a lot of sense."

Miss Love left the room. I read the poster again, then looked around at her clothes and at the bed. Maybe Miss Love and Grandpa were sleeping in here out of respect for the dead. I mean, maybe they were trying to show respect by not using the bed where the dead had died. But then I remembered that the big bed Granny and Grandpa shared wasn't made up. That must mean Grandpa slept in there last night. Maybe on his wedding night, too.

Who ever heard of a married lady wanting to pretend she was still an old maid—even to having a room to herself? Was this her idea of "throwing off the yoke of oppressor man"?

Well, her sleeping like an old maid did prove one thing: she and Grandpa hadn't been sweet on each other before Granny died. I couldn't wait to go home and tell Mama.

"See?" I'd say. "They weren't courtin' on the sly or anything like that. The fact Miss Love is usin' the comp'ny room proves it. They just got married so she could stay there and keep house."

Aw, I couldn't say that to Mama.

For one thing, it wouldn't help. She'd get another headache trying to decide all over again what Miss Love wanted out of her daddy. If she didn't intend to have babies, what had made her willing to marry an old man? She wouldn't do it just to keep house for him.

Also, Mama would worry that somebody else might find out about the sleeping arrangement and start sniggering the way they did about Mr. and Mrs. Abernathy, who hadn't slept in the same room for thirty years. The Abernathys each claimed the other one snored, but nobody believed that was the real reason.

As I wiped the sweat off my face and picked up a pasteboard box, I knew I couldn't mention such to Mama anyway—about the beds, I mean. In her mind, I didn't know what went on in bedrooms.

Which I didn't. Not exactly. When I was little I asked Papa one day where babies came from and he said ask him again when I was ten and he'd tell me. As soon as we sat down to breakfast on my tenth birthday, I said, "Well, Papa, I'm ten!"

He said, "Yes, I know, son. Happy birthday!"

I waited for him to explain about babies, but he just kept eating. On his second cup of coffee I said, "Papa, you said when I got ten, you'd tell me where babies come from. Remember? You said—"

Mama blushed and picked up little Mary Toy, who was four, and took her out. Papa blushed and said, "Well, uh, let's see, son. It's kind of like the way hens lay eggs and then biddies hatch out of the eggs." He stood up and wiped his mouth on his napkin.

"But what about the rooster? Don't he have something to do with it? Bluford says the rooster does something when he lights on a hen. What—"

"I got to get down to the store, Will." It didn't dawn on me till after he left that I still didn't know any more about ladies having babies than I did yesterday when I was just nine.

Filling one of Miss Love's boxes, I remembered one time Smiley said his folks were gone off and he'd get his little sister to go down to the barn with us. He wanted to show me what "it" was like. I was twelve. His sister was only five and wouldn't know what it was all about, he said. But just the idea scared me so bad I made up that Papa had told me to build a shelf on the back porch for Mama's flower-potting stuff.

By then I understood how it was with roosters and hens, of course, and cows and dogs and cats. And because of all the smutty stories I'd heard, I had a pretty good guess about people. I certainly knew that getting married meant you were supposed to sleep in the same bed, and that the bed had a lot to do with having babies. When Aunt Loma got married, she and Camp didn't have but one bed. Still and all, I used to look at her and wonder if they had done "it." The day I found out she was in the family way, I finally knew for sure they had.

Well, it looked like Miss Love and Grandpa weren't aiming to do it or anything else—have a baby or sleep in the same bed, either one.

I could hear Miss Love in the kitchen, getting Grandpa's good supper started. I emptied a bureau drawer full of ragged, baby-stained old quilts into a big box. In the next drawer was a stack of baby clothes, ironed and done up nice, like for the next birthing. Why come Granny hadn't given all that to Mama when I was born—or when Mama was expecting the baby that died or when Mary

Toy came? Or at least why didn't she give the clothes to Aunt Loma? By time Campbell Junior came along, Granny surely wasn't still hoping to have another baby herself.

I kind of wished the little gowns and lacy caps could stay here in the bureau. With a new young wife, Grandpa might still get him a boy. But this was Miss Love's bed in here, and his bed was in yonder, so I knew it wasn't ever going to happen. Anyway I, Will Tweedy, was his boy. And I was certain that's the way Mama and them wanted it to stay.

I reckon I did, too, I'm ashamed to say.

Miss Love brought me some sweetmilk just as I emptied one of the small top drawers into a box. It was full of old brass keys, old receipts, yellowed letters tied in bundles, hairpins, tintypes, and at least a dozen pairs of gold-rimmed spectacles with bent or missing rims, and some with the glass missing. I pointed out Grandpa's medal from the Confederate Veterans' Reunion in 1875. Miss Love picked it out of the pile. "I suppose we should put this in a drawer in his room. But take the rest of it home, Will."

Her face was flushed with heat, and the pink dress was so soaked that it stuck to her skin in the back. She had the same cardboard fan in her hand that I'd fanned Granny with when she lay dying. Miss Love fanned hard, and BIRDSONG'S FUNERAL PARLOR became a blur. "I'm so hot, Will. And I'm tired. I think I'll go lie down a while."

"Yes'm, you look like you could use a rest." I gulped down the sweetmilk. "Most ladies take a nap after dinner."

"Take what?" Miss Love hadn't heard a word I said.

"A nap, ma'am."

"I have never napped in my life."

"Mama says a nap makes her feel better."

"How could I feel any better?" she asked, laughing. "Anyway, I'm not planning to sleep. I'm just going to lie down a minute."

"Yes'm." I drained the glass. My thumb accidentally touched her forefinger as I handed it back. "Thank you, ma'am."

Miss Love had hardly sat down on the daybed in the hall before she hopped up and said maybe we ought to bring the parlor rug in out of the sun. We did, and then she decided we should place the parlor furniture. I saw right off that she didn't plan on putting anything back just like Granny had it.

"I want this over here, this over there," said Miss Love, pointing first to the loveseat, then the marble-top table. After I moved them, she got at one end of the piano to help shove. When the furniture was all changed around, she asked, smiling and fanning, if I thought my mother and Loma would like it.

"You think Grandpa will?" It was just as well not to say about Mama and Aunt Loma.

"Men think they don't like changes, but they can get used to anything. Besides, I think furniture likes to be moved. Wouldn't you say so?" I thought that sounded foolish, till I saw she was just teasing.

"I reckon." Grinning, I glanced around the room. It did look nice. "Want me to hang the pictures back up, Miss Love?"

"Well, uh, I'm going to let you take those to your mother and Loma. All except the round print of the three horses' heads over there. I want it. Did you know it's part of a big battle scene? I saw the whole picture once, in a book. Look at those flaring nostrils and wild eyes, Will!" She held the picture up to show me, as if I hadn't been seeing it all my life, then traced her finger over the profile of the biggest horse. "I rode a lot when I was out in Texas. I haven't seen any ladies riding in Cold Sassy except Mrs. Sheffield."

"That's because she's the only one that does."

Miss Love fanned some more. "Golly Pete, Will, it's so hot!"

Later I couldn't of told you to save my neck why I asked her what I did then. I was thinking with my mouth, not my brain. But after she took off the dusty head rag, her brown hair came tumbling down around her flushed face, and she was so pretty that I couldn't for the life of me figure out why in the heck she would marry an old man.

Anyhow, I said it: "How come you married my grandpa?"

The question blurted out like a pitcher's fast ball, and I knew right off that I had over-stepped.

20

Blushing, I stammered out that it was none of my business and please forget I asked.

Miss Love blushed, too. Didn't say a word. She fanned fast for a minute, then sank down in Granny's big rocker, the high-back one with apples and pears carved on it. I knew she must be furious.

But as it turned out, she was busting to talk. I think if I was a frog she'd of talked to me just the same, once I got her started with that smart-aleck question. Twisting her hair into a topknot and fastening it with three big tortoise-shell pins, she said, "Sit down, Will." I sat. "Partly I married your grandfather to have a family." Oh, Lord, that's what Mama was scared of. But Miss Love didn't mean babies. "I don't think of myself as a stepmother to Mary Willis and Loma, of course. But I hope they'll come to regard me as—well, like a sister. I want so much to belong in this family. I want kinfolks."

"You ain't got any?"

"My mother died when I was twelve. Cousin Lottie raised me, and she died last year. She was eighty-five. I'm my own last living relative, so to speak."

Gosh. It would be awful not to have folks. "Your daddy, what about him?"

A hard look came on her face. "I have no living relative." Then, taking a deep breath, she said, "My father was a drunkard. I decided a long time ago to pretend he never existed. But enough about my people. Will,

I'm aware that I've given Cold Sassy plenty to gossip about this week, and I know your mother and Loma are upset. I wish I could apologize but . . . I don't know how to approach them."

I didn't know either, so I didn't answer.

"I hate being talked about. I hate feeling disliked. I hate it that your folks are embarrassed." I wondered if she knew *scandalized* was more the word for it. "But Mr. Blakeslee thinks the talk will die down if I don't feed it. He says just keep my mouth shut."

And get Aunt Loma to shut hers, I thought. "Yes'm, he's right. He gets away with a lot that way. And if he don't want to hear about something, he just changes the subject or makes a joke."

She smiled. "Yes, I've seen that happen at the store. People will be arguing politics or complaining about the weather and he'll say, 'What time will the sun set this evenin'?' or, 'I been tryin' to remember when was the Battle of Chickamauga.' But I'm not answering your question, Will. I married him because—"

"You ain't got to answer, Miss Love." I fumbled with the rusty wire on the back of the horse picture, twisting it back in place. "I shouldn't of ast that."

"But I want to tell you. Usually people who don't approve of what you do never wonder or care why you did it. I appreciate your wanting to know."

"Ma'am, I didn't say I disapprove. It ain't my place to say."

"But of course you disapprove." She was rubbing sweat off her face and neck with the dusty head rag. It left a grimy smear down one cheek. She took a long breath, like before diving into a swimming hole. "So I am going to tell you how it happened. I went back to the store last Wednesday after the parade. Nobody else was there. The store was closed, of course, but Miss Pauline was anxious to get her hat, so I was going to finish it. Then your grandfather walked in. He came right over to the millinery table and asked if I would marry him." She blushed. "Said it would be a marriage in name only. I'd just be his housekeeper. He made it clear he didn't love me or anything, and of course I didn't love him. 'But I always liked havin' you around the store,' he said, 'and I figger you like me all right, bein' as you ain't quit or nothin'.' You know how he talks."

"Yes'm."

"And he said he liked my coffee. I reminded him it was Mrs. Crabtree's coffee. Mr. Blakeslee was coming to work every morning without breakfast, Will, and I got worried about him and asked Mrs. Crabtree if I could take him some coffee. I got him to eat store cheese and crackers with it."

"Yes'm. I heard."

"You did? How?"

"Well'm, Papa told us. He knew Mama was worryin' about Grandpa not eatin' breakfast. He was glad you'd thunk it up."

It didn't seem polite to tell her what Miss Effie Belle Tate said, namely, that every old maid and widow woman in town had been bidin' her time, tryin' to wait a decent period after the funeral before invitin' Rucker to Sunday dinner. "But wouldn't you know Love Simpson got to him first with a quart jar a-coffee!"

Miss Love was talking on. ". . . so it would just be a business arrangement. I was to cook and clean up and wash. In exchange he would deed the house over to me. He said that seemed fair enough. Will, I decided he had to be joking, so I joked back. I said, 'Now, Mr. Blakeslee, that sounds fine, but you'd have to deed over the furniture, too. After you pass on, what good would the house do me without a bed to sleep in?' He said, 'Gosh a'mighty, woman, you're astin' too much.' I laughed and said, 'Take it or leave it, Mr. Blakeslee.'"

Miss Love said she was still just carrying on. "It didn't seem appropriate to be joking like that, Will, Miss Mattie Lou being so recently dead. But I didn't know how else to handle it."

After pondering a minute, Grandpa had agreed to give her the furniture with the house. "Thet way, when I die they won't be no big fuss bout who's to have what."

"Will, that's when I realized he really meant to marry me," said Miss Love. "I was flabbergasted. I told him, 'I'll have to pray about it, Mr. Blakeslee. I've never made an important decision in my life without praying about it.' 'Well, kneel down,' he said. 'Let's go to prayin'.' He had one knee bent toward the floor when I said, 'Don't rush me, Mr. Blakeslee—me or God, either.'"

Miss Love put her hands up to her cheeks and closed her eyes for a minute, then talked on. "I couldn't believe this. Two years ago I— I almost married somebody, Will. When things didn't work out, I felt that God was trying to tell me I shouldn't ever marry. But

—well, if I was just to be a housekeeper, that would be the same as not marrying, except I would have a home. On the other hand, it was a proposal that blasphemed holy matrimony. I sat there not saying a word, my mind a jumble. I guess Mr. Blakeslee thought I wasn't sold on the idea, because he put some more icing on the cake. Said, 'Well, and I'll set aside a little cash money for you in my will, Miss Love. Say two hundred dollars.' "

"Grandpa must of been mighty lonesome, or else mighty anxious to get the house cleaned up," said I. "It ain't like him to pay that much for anything."

"Well, he made it plain he had offered as much as he was going to. He also made it plain that the store and all his other property would go to your mother and Loma."

Oh, boy, I couldn't wait to tell Mama. I grinned. "Well, it ain't hard to figure out you said yes."

"I told him I couldn't possibly give him an answer, just like that. He said if I needed a while to think it over, I could let him know next day."

All of a sudden Miss Love hopped up like she'd sat on a pin, plopped herself down on the piano stool, and went to playing chords. I thought she'd gone loose in the head. But I soon saw she was playing music to go along with what she was saying, like at a picture show. Glancing over her shoulder at me, she slowly walked two fingers of her right hand up and down the keyboard. "This is me thinking," she said, nodding toward the two fingers. "Trying to sort out all Mr. Blakeslee said. . . . Now this is me talking." Accompanied by a *plink-a-plink* up above middle C, she quoted her answer: " 'What's the rush, Mr. Blakeslee? We'd have to wait a year anyway.' "

With bass notes and a deep voice, Miss Love became Grandpa: " 'I ain't talkin' bout no year. I'm talkin' bout t'morrer, Miss Love. Marryin' t'morrer. I got to go on and git married or hire me a housekeeper, one.' " Gosh, she sounded just like him. Even looked like him, using her tongue like a wad of tobacco being switched from one cheek to the other.

"I said,"—*three stiff, prissy notes*—" 'It's not proper, Mr. Blakeslee. It's not even right.' " *A pause, then sad chords.* " 'Sir, Miss Mattie Lou has been dead only three weeks.' What he said then sent chills down my spine, Will." *Heavy bass notes followed by harsh discords.* "He said—"

"She's dead as she'll ever be"?

Bam! "That's it exactly. How did you know?"

"That's what he said to Mama and Aunt Loma and me."

Miss Love had been as stunned as we were. "I told him he hadn't had time for her to die in his heart or his mind and I was afraid he'd regret rushing into something like this. 'Well,' he said"—*discords in the bass*—" 'I ain't go'n spend the rest a-my life sweepin' and arnin' shirts. And I ain't go'n move in on Mary Willis and them—or Loma, either. Loma's got too many cats and talks ugly, and Mary Willis would worry me to death. She fusses over me like a old hen. Besides, I don't want to be no burden on'm.' He said marrying was the only solution he'd been able to come up with, and I and one other woman in town were the only ones he thought he could stand to have around the house."

I wondered who the other lady was.

Miss Love wiped her sweaty hands on her dress, closed her eyes, clasped her fingers tight around her knees, and stopped talking, like she'd forgot I was there. But then her long black lashes fluttered open, and in a soft, sad voice she continued, "I was so shocked, I could hardly take in anything he said."

Her hands went straying around the keyboard, found "Abide With Me," and played a few lines, real quiet. "I remember Mr. Blakeslee said I could keep being a Methodist. 'Go ever Sunday,' he said, 'but don't ast me to go, not to the Methodist or Baptist or any of'm. I'm done with it. I went to preachin' with Miss Mattie Lou for jest one reason. Hit made her happy. But thet don't matter now, and I'm tired a-preachers. They talk tithin' all the time' " —*sharp, stingy single notes*—" 'and say thangs like if a man sins, God's go'n punish him by takin' his wife or his son or his bizness.' " *Discords in the bass, and fire in Miss Love's eyes, just like Grandpa's.* " 'I'm tired of'm tryin' to scare folks to Heaven with all thet hellfire and damnation. I want to hear bout the lovin', forgivin' God thet Jesus preached. But all you git at Christian churches is Old Testa-ment vengeance: watch out and be good or the Lord will smite you down.' "

Lost in thought, Miss Love played a chorus of "Faith of Our Fathers, Living Still." Then she said, "I told your grandfather that the church was very important to me. He said,

'Well, you go on by yoreself, jest like you been a-doin'.'" Thinking how pretty her hands were, despite they were red from scrubbing floors, I watched her fingers move dreamy up and down the keyboard. "Mr. Blakeslee said he never told your grandmother how he felt about the church. 'Hit would a-hurt her feelin's, same as sayin' I didn't like her daddy or her roses.'"

She twirled around on the piano stool, facing me, and I saw her eyes were glistening with tears. Wiping them in a quick motion with the back of her hand, she smiled. "He must have loved your grandmother very much."

"Yes'm, he did."

"Well, he went on to say he'd lived fifty-nine years by other people's rules—'but from now on, I'm a-go'n do what I dang want to. Startin' with marryin' you, Miss Love, if'n you'll have me. I'll deed over the house and furniture when we go to the courthouse to git married, and I'll write a new will. But when I'm th'ew with thet, don't try to tell me what to do or make me over. If'n the way I want to live don't suit you, then don't marry me.'

"I said, 'Well, I don't suppose what you do

or don't do would affect me the way it might a real wife.'

" 'Thet's the way I look on it,' " he said.

For several minutes I didn't say anything, and Miss Love didn't, either. Finally she spoke. "I'd quit praying for a husband two years ago, Will. But I've prayed all my life for a home of my own—and for this." She patted the sounding board of the piano. Defensive, she added, "It was going to be me or somebody else. He said so. Folks will talk, I know, but. . . . You ask why did I marry him? Yes, for a house! Can you imagine what this means to me, Will Tweedy? All my life I've lived in rented upstairs rooms with ugly rented furniture. Cousin Lottie used to say we were so poor that we didn't have a pot to throw out the window, and we didn't. We had to move every time the rent was overdue."

"But when you went to work—"

"Milliners make room money, Will. Not house money."

"Yes'm, I s'pose so."

"But after it seemed to be God's will that I never marry, I gave up hope of ever having a home. . . . Does it sound so awful, Will, to marry for worldy goods?"

"No'm. It don't to me. Maybe to some folks."

"The Lord answers prayers in strange ways."

I nodded to show I understood. Then, stretching, I tried to figure some way to lighten up the conversation. "Too bad you didn't hold out a little longer. Grandpa and God might of give you a ridin' horse, too."

She laughed. "If I'd tried to get everything I ever wanted, Will, I'd have asked for a diamond necklace and a motorcar and—"

"Yes'm but he might of married that other lady."

Miss Love smiled, but it was a weak smile. The steam had gone clean out of her. "Will, do you think they'll let me in? Your family?"

I didn't know how to say what she wouldn't want to hear. So I said, "There's just one thing I cain't figure, ma'am. Why didn't you get married long time ago? A lady pretty as you, I bet the Lord didn't have no trouble givin' you chances. For instance, why didn't you marry Mr. Son Black? He's got a nice house."

Miss Love stood up, so I did, too. She said, "I knew God didn't want me to marry a man like him. He talks tough but inside he's just a little bitty boy, scared of his mama. And any-how, it's her house." She was silent a minute, then laughed and made a joke. "Reading King Arthur is what made me an old maid, Will. I kept holding out for a hero, a knight in shining armor. I really thought some rich, ex-citing man would come riding up on a white horse and rescue me from being poor and unhappy. After I fell in love with the man in Texas. . . . Well, he was rich and had a white horse, but he was no knight. And neither is Son Black. He couldn't qualify as the hero in a cheap novel."

Glad to be on a new subject, I said, "I been readin' a novel, Miss Love, one called *Damaged Goods*. I got it hid in the barn. Papa would have a fit, but it's got a good moral lesson. I think books like that are good for a boy if he has the right mind. You want to borrow it when I get through?"

She didn't laugh at me. "Well, uh, maybe." She sighed. "Do you know what I'm talking about, Will?"

"Yes'm. Maybe."

"I'm saying that after I missed the love boat, I wasn't going to settle for a raft—meaning somebody like Son Black. But I'm glad to settle for a man I can respect, and a family I'm proud to be part of. I think Mr. Blakeslee is probably the only completely honest man I've ever known. He drinks a little, but"—she hesitated—"not like my father. Whiskey isn't important to Mr. Blakeslee."

"No'm. I think Grandpa mostly takes that one drink to prove he's got a right to." And maybe, I thought, he married you to prove the same thing.

Miss Love looked at her hands. "My nails are a sight from all that scouring," she said, taking a long file off the mantelpiece and smoothing a frayed thumbnail. Then, meeting my eyes, she sighed and said, "Now, Will, have I answered your question?"

"Yes'm, thank you, ma'am. I understand." I was so flattered, the way she'd poured out her heart. "Miss Love, why don't you go lay down now? You look wore out."

"Never say *lay*, Will." She was teasing. "I will not lay. But I think I may *lie* for a while. I really am tired." Walking slowly to the hall, where there was a little breeze, she stretched out on the daybed and went to filing her nails.

I went to her bedroom and started filling up the boxes. I was pulling moldy old-timey dresses and frayed coats and hats of Granny's out of the wardrobe when I chanced to look out the front window and saw a well-dressed stranger pass by on the dirt sidewalk.

Hung over his right arm was a fancy saddle with silver trim that gleamed so bright in the sun, it just about put my eyes out. That saddle wasn't like anything you'd ever think to see in Cold Sassy, then or now. Neither was the man.

And suddenly he paused and looked toward Grandpa's house.

21

I had seen pictures of cowboys in books and magazines, and this fellow didn't exactly look like a cowboy. I mean, he wasn't dirty, didn't have on spurs or cowhide chaps or a red bandanna around his neck, and didn't carry a lasso. He looked like he'd just had a bath and a shave, and he was wearing an expensive black suit. But he was a cowboy, all right. I knew by the high-heeled, tooled-leather boots, the big white felt hat, and the pistol in a holster on his hip. When a Cold Sassy man carries a pistol, he straps it across his chest under his shirt and you don't see it.

The main thing, though, was that tooled-leather Western saddle he toted, which like I said was ornamented with silver. The stranger held it careless, as if it weighed no more than a rooster, though even to a horse it would of been heavy as lead.

What I could hardly believe was the man himself. His legs were so long it seemed like they swung from his waist. His body was long, too, and his arms and hands, and even his craggy, sun-browned face. He must of been six feet three at least and walked with a different gait altogether from the men in Cold Sassy.

After pausing and squinting hard in my direction, the stranger walked on. I rushed to the front door to get a better look. I watched as he stopped little Timmy Hopkins, who was rolling a hoop in the street. They talked a minute, Timmy pointed toward Grandpa's house, and the stranger, shifting the saddle to his other arm, came back.

"Miss Love!" I called softly. "Come 'ere, quick!"

I pointed down the street as she came up beside me. "Lord, it's hot," she mumbled sleepily, rubbing the small of her back. "Will, what are you staring at?"

"Look at that feller."

Her gaze focused where my finger was pointing. "Oh, my God in Heaven!" she gasped. Both hands flew to her mouth. "Oh, Lord, what can I do?" She ran back a few steps into the hall, whirled around. Her face had gone so white, the freckles stood out like tiny brown poky dots. "Don't let him in, Will!"

But even as she said it, she bent down to wipe the sweat off her face with her skirt, then tried to smooth her hair. "Oh, Lord, he mustn't see me like this! Will, say I'm not home."

But the man was already up the steps and, before she could escape, had either heard or seen her. Without so much as a knock or a by-your-leave, he stalked through the door, brushing past me, eased the saddle to the floor, and, seeing nothing but her, moved down the hall toward Miss Love.

She stood there like she'd gone numb, her hands on her mouth. When he got to her, they just stood staring at one another. He took off the big hat, real slow, his eyes never leaving hers, dropped it on the daybed, and took her hands and kissed them. Then he put his arms around her and kissed her, right on the mouth! Kissed her like he was starved and she was something to eat.

I never in my life dreamed of a kiss being like that. It sure wasn't that time I kissed Mary Riley St. John behind the door at Oralee McGibboney's party, and it sure wasn't like that when Papa kissed Mama good-bye after breakfast. Mama was usually still eating, so he'd bend down and wait while she wiped her mouth, then smack her one, and that's all there was to it.

Well, this man kissing Miss Love, he didn't just kiss her. He kept on kissing her. A string of kisses a mile long melted together as his lips brushed her ears, her neck, her arms, her hair, and then got back to her mouth again. And Miss Love was kissing him back, no doubt about it. I didn't know what to do. I stood on one foot, then the other, and if I'd had a third foot, I'd of shifted to it. For sure I was in the way and I ought to slip on out. But I was pinned to the sight.

Oh, gosh, what if Grandpa walked in! Like it was me that was guilty, I glanced through the open door, half-expecting to see him. Who I saw instead was Miss Effie Belle Tate from next door, hurrying up the walk with a frosted coconut cake!

I first thought she was bringing it to Miss Love as a welcome-to-the-bride present. But in her hurry to get over there, Miss Effie Belle had forgot to change out of her bedroom shoes, so I knew right off she hadn't planned a social call. What happened, I guessed, was that Miss Effie Belle saw the tall stranger walk into Grandpa's house with the saddle and, as an excuse to get a good look at him, had grabbed up the cake she just frosted.

Bursting out onto the veranda, I met her at the top step. "Sure is a hot day, ain't it, Miss Effie Belle?" I talked loud as I could. She wasn't deaf or anything, like her brother, but I was hoping if Miss Love had any ears left, she would hear me and run sit down prim and proper in the parlor. If the stranger sat clear over on the other side of the room, they could make like they'd just been talking.

As Miss Effie Belle marched toward the doorway, I kind of stepped in front of her and yelled, "Did you see that tall feller that's come callin', Miss Effie Belle? Ain't he a buster! Uh, I think he's her lawyer or somebody." I had my voice aimed halfway at the coconut cake and halfway into the hall. "Miss

Love would have more time to set a spell if you'd come back later, Miss Effie Belle."

"Oh, shut up, Will," she said. But she stopped at the door, chewed on her bottom lip like she was thinking, and then seemed to change her mind about barging in. The way the big pink wart on her upper lip quivered, I couldn't tell if she had seen them kissing or just lost her nerve. At any rate, she turned on her heel, nearly losing a bedroom slipper, and without a word and without so much as handing me the coconut cake—though I reached for it—she marched down the steps and took her cake back home.

I sure hated that. And her forgetting to give it to me made me think for sure she'd seen the kissing.

About time I got back in the house, Miss Love came to herself and opened her eyes, and the fireworks started!

The stranger just laughed when she tried to push him away. Didn't back off till she scratched his neck with claw fingers. "You ain't changed a bit, Love." He rubbed his neck, but he was still laughing.

"You ain't either, you devil!" she screamed, bursting into tears. That was the first time I ever heard her say *ain't*. "Why did you c-come here? Get out of m-m-my house!"

"Your house?" He looked around the front hall, took in all the signs of cleaning, ambled over and peered into the parlor, and put on an exaggerated mock expression of being impressed. "Millinery sure must pay good in Georgia." He strolled toward her.

She backed back. "You put your hands on me again, Clayton McAllister, I'll gouge your eyes out! I'll kill you!" She grabbed the long nail file off the daybed.

He laughed again, but not with his whole face, I noticed. "That's what I like about you, tiger," he drawled. "You got spirit. But if you kill me, honey, you'll be killin' the man that's gonna take you out of this hick town. Love, I come to get you!"

She stared at him, dumfounded. "Get me? What're you talking about?"

"If you'd opened my letters stead of sendin'm back, you wouldn't be so surprised. Lord knows I've written you enough."

Whatever Miss Love felt when he was kissing her sure had evaporated. The gold pin was undone and she hadn't even noticed— though I expect he had, standing where he could look right down that low-cut pink dress.

I knew I ought to leave. "Miss Love," I said, "I got to get on home and milk the cow."

She exploded like a fireworks rocket. "Don't you dare, Will Tweedy! You leave me alone here with him and nobody in this town will ever speak to me again!"

"Go 'long home, boy," said Clayton McAllister, as if he'd known I was there all the time. "It won't matter if nobody here speaks to her again, cause she won't be livin' here no more."

Miss Love swung around, her hands clenched, face red, those gray-blue eyes hard as steel, and the fanciest gosh dern words coming out of that big mouth you ever heard. She didn't yell. She spat words. I can't remember all she said, but Mr. McAllister got the message that she had made the mistake of loving him once and she sure wouldn't ever make that mistake again, and why did he think she would run off to Texas with him, for heaven's sake.

He wasn't laughing now. "You don't know what you talkin' bout." He was mad. "I'm astin' you to marry me, not run off with me."

"You asked me once before, if I remember correctly." She blazed away like a six-shooter, hitting him with words. "And off I went to Baltimore, all dreamy-eyed, to sew my trousseau. Cousin Lottie and I were finishing up the wedding dress when your letter came. It just about killed me, Clayton McAllister." (Gosh, that must of been how she found out he'd eloped with her best friend!) Miss Love sat down on the daybed. "Oh, how I've hated you!"

"I deserve it, Love." He looked miserable. "But I've come to tell you, I'll make it up to you if you'll let me."

She stood up and said, "Well, that's settled. So good-bye."

He took a long breath and pointed at the saddle. "I had that made for you, remember? It's been in the tack room all this time. Nobody's used it. I want you to have it."

"I don't want it. I don't want anything of yours—especially not a saddle that was an engagement present, for heaven's sake! Take it back to Texas."

"Love, I've brung it back to be your engagement present agin. Cain't you understand?" (Gosh, that must mean Miss Love's best friend had died.)

Her lips were trembling like she might cry. She sank down on the daybed again. "Lord,

Clayt, you don't have a grain of sense. You write me I'm not good enough for you, and now two years later you—"

"I didn't say that, damnit!"

"Don't you curse at me. Whatever it was you said, that's what you meant." She didn't look about to cry now. She looked mad. "How a philanderer like you could sit in judgment on me, I'll never understand!"

"I felt like you were—like you'd been pretending to be something you weren't. That's why I got so mad at you. How pride could of made me hurt an angel like you—" He moved toward her. There was the same look on his face as on Grandpa's when Granny's hand went limp in his. But there was hope, too. "Love," he whispered, "you're the only woman I could ever marry. You know that." (Gosh, then he'd never eloped with Miss Love's best friend! Loma must of made that up.) "There's been other women in my life," he admitted, "but nobody I wanted to marry but you."

"Ha. What you mean is that the pickings are slim in Texas. You've given up on finding somebody decent out there. Well, if the only white women you know are married ladies or white trash, or both, that's your worry, not mine. Get you a Mexican wife. Get you a squaw. Or spend the winter in town again. Remember my friend Edna Mae? She wrote me they've sent in another milliner from Baltimore."

"But I want you, Love. Only you. And you still care for me. I can tell. Please, Love, forgive me."

I do think that for a moment Miss Love yearned toward him. Then all of a sudden she laughed out loud. "Clayton McAllister, what's there to forgive? Will, you've heard all this. Do you see anything to forgive?"

All this time I was standing in the darkest, out-of-the-way corner I could find. I thought they'd both forgot I was there. "I don't know'm," I mumbled.

"Well, there's not. You did me a favor, Clayt. If you had even pretended to be a forgiving Christian gentleman, I'd now be the lonely wife of a rich, stuck-up philanderer. Meaning you, God help me. Because that's all you were when we met and that's all you were when you asked for the ring back, and that's all you are now. Edna Mae wrote me all about you and that married woman you've been—"

He was real mad. "Whatever Edna Mae said, it ain't true."

"But I believe her. You wanted to marry me in the first place, Clayt, because I wouldn't . . . I was just a challenge. You always did want anything you couldn't get. Then when I told you what you didn't want to hear, you—" She stopped, biting her lip. "Well, so here you are again, all the way from Texas. I guess your pride's hurt because I wouldn't read your letters, much less answer them. It's a helpless feeling to get letters back unopened, isn't it, Clayton? I know. In case you don't remember, I wrote you after you asked me to send back the ring. I poured out my heart in that letter. When it came back in the mail, I opened it and read it. Lord, I was glad you never knew how I had groveled at your feet!"

"Love, I'm grovelin' at yours now. Please, listen to me."

Ignoring him, she said brightly, "I just had another thought. Maybe that married lady friend is what has brought you back to me. Is she after your money, Clayt? Is she talking about divorcing her husband? She's got you scared, hasn't she? You'd rather marry somebody like me than a divorced person, and if

you can take me to Texas, she'll be off your
back. Is that it?"

Mr. McAllister was furious. "Love, will you
shut up? I've come back for just one reason. *I
love you.*" He reached to touch her arm. She
jerked away. Her hands were shaking. She
hid them in her skirt.

"I've changed, Love. God knows it."

"Well, I don't. So you just pick up that saddle and ride it out of here. I don't want it. It's
tainted."

"You're comin' with me, Love Simpson.
You still love me and you know it." It looked
like he was fixing to grab her for another ten-
minute kiss. Gosh, I didn't think I could
watch that again. And had she forgot all
about Grandpa? Why didn't she just tell Mr.
Cowboy she was already married?

Right then she came out with it. Almost
laughing as she looked up at him, she said
sweet and easy, "If you were the last man on
earth, Mr. Clayton McAllister, I wouldn't go
a mile with you. Even if I was free to."

"What do you mean?"

She held the back of her left hand up to his
face and wiggled the fourth finger. Then I
guess she remembered her wedding band was
still on top of the piano. She tapped the fin-

ger. "I've got a wedding ring goes on this." A sound on the porch made her look toward the front door. "And I do believe," she said, cool and calm as you please, though I bet her knees were shaking, "I do believe here comes my husband now!"

Of course somebody must of gone to the store and told Grandpa there was a tall stranger with a silver-trimmed saddle up at his house. And something about the way it was said had made him hot-foot it home, else why would he leave the store on a busy Saturday?

When I saw him walk in with that clean-shaved face, close-cut dark hair, and thin mustache, my first thought was to wonder if it was really Grandpa. My second thought was to be proud of him, especially for Miss Love's sake. My third thought was that Miss Effie Belle—unless she took Grandpa for another stranger calling on Miss Love—must of run out and told him about the kissing.

Gosh, in that case he might bust Mr. McAllister's head wide open!

22

I didn't know then whether Miss Effie Belle had got to Grandpa or not. But I found out later that white-haired old Mr. Boop had. Papa told us that night how Mr. Boop ran over from the hotel to say a feller wearin' a Stetson hat and cowboy boots had come in on the train from Lula.

"Where's Rucker at?" Mr. Boop asked, picking up a can of pipe tobacco and handing Grandpa the money.

"You talkin' to him, Amos." Grandpa grinned and ran his hand over his smooth-shaved face. Papa and them laughed out loud as Mr. Boop stared. "Hit's me all right, Amos. See?" Grandpa held up that left arm and dangled the knotted sleeve in his face.

"Well, I be-dog. Ain't you a sight! I was just a-wonderin' how Rucker could a-hired a new man and I ain't heard bout it. Well, I want to tell you bout this here stranger, Rucker. He come in the ho-tel totin' a fine brown and white cowhide grip and the fanciest dang saddle you ever seen. Silver dohickies all over it. The feller said he needed to shave and git a bath but might not be stayin' for the night."

"What's his bizness here?" Grandpa asked, real interested.

"Didn't state his bizness. But pretty soon he come back to the ho-tel dest. He was cleaned up, slicked down, and wearin' a nice black suit—and still carryin' that dad-gum saddle. You know what he ast, Rucker? Ast where did Miss Love Simpson board at, or would she be at work." After letting that soak in on Grandpa, Mr. Boop said, "I pointed the way to yore house, Rucker, but I didn't bother tellin' him she'd got marrit. Didn't seem to me it was any of his bizness. But I thought you ought to know that a tooled-leather saddle orny-mented with Mexican silver is headin' up North Main toward yore house."

"Is thet so," said Grandpa. According to Papa, he didn't even look up.

"This man's so good-lookin', Rucker, I bet he has to use tar soap to keep the ladies from lassoin' him!"

"Is thet so," said Grandpa.

"You goin' down there, Rucker?"

"I ain't got time right now. I reckon Miss

Love knows how to make a stranger welcome."

Mr. Boop having felt Grandpa's right fist
on his jaw one time, he was probably hoping
a good fight would come out of the situation.

But I wasn't hoping it when Grandpa saun-
tered through the front door of his house. I
couldn't think of anything worse for an old
man than getting beat up by his wife's former
fee-ance. Maybe Grandpa wasn't in a fighting
mood that day, or maybe he took one look at
Mr. McAllister and figured discretion was the
better part of valor, as the saying goes. He
not only didn't pitch Mr. McAllister out, he
shook hands nice as you please, saying where
you from and why don't we go set down in
the parlor.

"Miss Love, see if'n they's some a-Miss
Mattie Lou's scup'non nectar in the pantry,
hear," said Grandpa, taking the rocking chair
and motioning Mr. McAllister to Granny's
gentleman's chair. "Fix us a drink with thet,
Miss Love."

After she went to the kitchen, Grandpa
winked at Mr. McAllister and said, "Sorry I
ain't got no locust beer to offer you. My son-
in-law, he makes it by the barrelful. Ever had
locust beer?"

"Never cared for it much," said Mr. McAllister. "The other'll be fine, Mr.—uh, what's your name, sir?"

"Blakeslee. E. R. Blakeslee."

"Clayton McAllister, sir."

They stood up and shook hands again, like they'd just met, and went on talking.

Miss Love was gone a good while. When she finally brought in a tray with the pale gold drinks, she had on lots of perfume and a clean yellow dress with a high neck, and her hair was fixed nice. She looked real fresh and pretty.

Grandpa was just the friendliest host you ever saw. He asked how long was the train trip from Texas, spoke of the drought, and discussed the difference between Texas barbecue and the Georgia kind. Then they got to talking hard times, but I couldn't listen for wondering if Miss Love was thinking about Mr. McAllister kissing her. If she was, she didn't let on. But that's what I was thinking about. If God had sent this man all the way from Texas to barge in and tempt her, she sure had been found wanting.

From there I got to thinking about predestination. The Southern Presbyterians believe that what is to be is to be and you can't do a thing about it. I mean, they think that from the day you're born, God knows everything that's going to happen to you. Preordains it, the preacher keeps saying. It hasn't ever made any sense to me to try so hard, or even to pray for something, if God is either going to make it happen despite all your prayers and all you do or don't do, or else make it not happen despite everything. For instance, suppose Mr. McAllister hadn't got mad and called off the wedding, and Miss Love had married him despite his reputation for philandering. Would that mean God preordained them to marry no matter what? Or would it just mean Miss Love wanted to marry him no matter what? I sure wished I could ask Papa how to fit predestination into this puzzle.

Well, suppose the Lord wanted Miss Love to marry Mr. McAllister, hoping she could save him from his sinning ways, and suppose she *had* married him, but then he just kept right on chasing women? Could she ever again have counted on God to steer her right?

It's a pity God ever let Miss Love out of Baltimore. If she'd never met up with Mr. McAllister, she wouldn't of had to get that nasty letter from him so God could show her He didn't approve of the match, and Granny wouldn't of had to die so God would find Miss Love a house. When I tried to make sense out of all that, it seemed like the Bible was right. The Lord does work in mysterious ways His wonders to perform.

Grandpa had gone to talking politics. He was telling Mr. McAllister about the winter morning when Brother Belie Jones's wife fired up her stove and shut the oven door, not knowing her cat was asleep in there. "By the time Miz Jones opened the oven and found Essie, the dang cat was cooked. Later Miz Jones come down to the store jest a-cryin'. Said, 'Pore Essie. She must a-slept right th'ew. Else why wouldn't I of heard her holler?' Sometimes I think us folks in the South are jest like pore Essie. We sleepin' right th'ew them unfair freight rates, for instance, when we ought to be hollerin' all the way to Washington."

Mr. McAllister laughed. Miss Love laughed, too, but uneasy—like at the circus when the man puts his head in the tiger's mouth and you giggle when what you want to do is cover your eyes.

The husband and the fee-ance really liked

COLD SASSY TREE 261

each other, I could tell. Grandpa even asked
Mr. McAllister to take pot luck and stay to
supper. Practically insisted. "We don't git
folks from Texas here ever day," he said in his
best hospitality voice.

Knowing what I knew and not knowing
what if anything Grandpa knew, all this funning and politeness gave me the creeps. Lord
knows what it was doing to Miss Love, who
had hardly said a word since Grandpa walked
in. But the invitation brought the Texan back
to the situation at hand. "Thank you, sir, but
I got to catch the train to Atlanta. I better get
on back to the ho-tel and pick up my grip."

He stood up, and Grandpa and Miss Love
stood up, and I did, and there was an awkward minute till Grandpa said, "Well, I wisht
you'd stay on, sir. We could put you up for
the night."

That must of give Miss Love a start. Picking up the big white hat off the daybed, she
handed it to Mr. McAllister and said, nervous
as a witch, "He was just leaving when you
came, Mr. Blakeslee. He's got business in Atlanta."

The long tall man flipped his hand in the
general direction of the saddle laying on the
floor. He said, kind of casual, "This here be-

longs to your wife, Mr. Blakeslee. I come by
to bring it to her—bein' as I was in the vicin-
ity, so to speak."

"You shouldn't have gone to all that trouble, Mr. McAllister," said Miss Love, real formal. "I don't have a horse. You take it on
back to Texas."

"Naw," he said. "If you don't want it, Miss
Love—I mean Miz Blakeslee—why, sell it.
And it wasn't no trouble, you bein' such a
friend of the fam'ly while you were out in
Texas. The saddle was a good excuse to drop
by. And, uh"—he actually winked at her—"if
you and Mr. Blakeslee ever get out my way,
y'all be sure and look me up. I'd like to feed
Mr. Blakeslee some Texas barbecue."

Ignoring the invite, Miss Love said, "It's
been nice to see you again, Mr. McAllister."
She looked up at him like he was no more to
her now than some ten-year-old boy come in
for penny candy at the store. Then she placed
her trembling hand on Grandpa's good arm,
smiling up at him like he was made out of
money and honey both. Boy howdy, you
wouldn't guess that fifty minutes ago she had
been kissing this other man!

Grandpa walked the Texan out to the

street, clapped him on the shoulder, good-natured like, and pointed directions to town.

It wasn't till my grandfather came back in the house that he really looked at the saddle. Going over where it lay on the floor, he hooked it up with the toe of one high-top shoe to see it better. "Miss Love, I think—"

"Mr. Blakeslee, I was once engaged to marry Mr. McAllister. He had that saddle made for me. It was his engagement present." She was talking fast, like if she slowed down she might lose her nerve. She told Grandpa in a small pinched voice that what Mr. McAllister really came for was to get her to marry him.

Then Miss Love flung herself face down on the daybed and went to crying. "I-hate-him-I-hate-him-I-hate-him!" She beat her fist on the thin mattress in time to the I-hate-hims.

"She sure told him off, Grandpa," said I, trying to be helpful. "You should of heard her."

Grandpa didn't answer. Just stood there, looking down at the fancy saddle.

"I was a f-fool, Mr. Blakeslee." Her words were muffled sobs. Now it's coming, I thought. She's going to tell Grandpa about the kissing. Instead, she said, "How I ever th-

thought I wanted to m-m-marry him, I don't know. I was such a fool. And old enough to know b-better. . . ."

Grandpa sighed and sat down by her on the daybed. "Best fool knows he's a fool, Miss Love. I don't know a soul who couldn't see a fool jest by lookin' in the glass. I been one myself, once't or twice't. So hesh up now. Cryin' ain't go'n do no good." Grandpa just couldn't hardly stand to watch a woman cry.

Well, plainly Miss Love wasn't a big enough fool to mention getting kissed. But thinking to kind of warn her, in case she didn't know that somebody besides me may have seen the peep show, I butted into the silence.

"I thought y'all were go'n have a coconut cake for supper, Grandpa. Miss Effie Belle came over with one just now."

Miss Love shot to a sitting position, her hands covering her mouth and the whites of her eyes showing. "Miss Effie Belle? She came over here?"

"Yes'm. I reckon she wanted to get a good look at Mr. McAllister. But I went out on the porch and told her y'all were talkin' bizness and maybe it'd be best if she came callin' to-morrow."

"Oh, Lord." Miss Love moaned.

"She forgot to hand me the cake."

Miss Love wasn't interested in the cake. "Did she . . . uh, did she see Mr. McAllister?" I could tell she was really worried and dying to find out what else I knew. Importance swelled me up inside.

At that point Grandpa held up his right hand like a policeman. "Y'all shet up. Lemme think a minute. Hear?"

Well, Miss Love and I shut up, and Grandpa commenced pacing the floor. I couldn't take my eyes off of him. From the neck down he was the same old Grandpa Blakeslee; from the neck up he was a distinguished, smooth-faced stranger who looked kind of familiar. After while he slowed down to bite off a plug of tobacco and move it into his cheek. Then he paced some more. Finally he stopped in front of the saddle, shoving it with his foot.

Just to look at Grandpa, most people wouldn't know he was upset. But I could tell. All the time he was pacing, his shoulders kept twitching forward, one or the other or both— a sure sign—and every minute or two he stopped to scratch his head hard and fast.

When he finally spoke, what he said was

"Miss Love, you want to marry Mr. McAllister?"

Why would he ask a thing like that when she was already married and also had just finished saying how much she hated the man?

She was as surprised as I was. Too surprised even to answer. Just sat on the daybed staring at Grandpa with wide-open eyes and a wide-open mouth.

"Cause if'n you do, or if'n you have a mind to after you git over bein' so mad at him, why, we could git this'n annulled. Folks in Cold Sassy will have a good time talkin', but if you go on off to Texas, why, you won't have to put up with nothin' on account of it. So you want to marry him or don't you?"

23

Miss Love rose to her feet, looking just about as stunned as old Cholly Smith did after he sold the family home place and heard the new owner had found a bag of gold coins behind a square of crumbling plaster in the dining room.

Walking slowly toward the back door, she

stood looking out for a long time, twisting her hands and saying nothing. Finally she turned and spoke, sounding like a wrung-out dish-rag. "Mr. Blakeslee," she said, her eyes cast down, "I don't want an annulment. If I weren't married to you, I still wouldn't marry him."

He went over close and she looked him square in the face. "I reckon you done an-swered my question," he said.

But then Miss Love's hands were on her mouth again. "Oh, Lord! Maybe you were trying to say—maybe what you mean is that you, sir, want an annulment. I don't blame you. I've embarrassed you before the wh-whole t-town." Big new tears streaked down her cheeks. "You want me to l-leave, don't you, Mr. Blakeslee?"

"God A'mighty, why would I want thet?" I could see him thinking he would have to hire him a housekeeper if she left. "If'n it was in my mind to ast you to leave, thet's what I would a-said, Miss Love. So in which case the subject is closed. Now what bout thet there saddle?"

"I don't w-want it." Trying to stop crying, she snuffled and blew her nose.

"Well, now," said Grandpa. Sitting down,

he lifted the saddle onto his knee and looked close at the silver and the tooling. "Hit shore is a handsome thang."

"I don't care." She glanced at Granny's clock on the mantelpiece. "Will, I want you to run up to the hotel with it. If he's not there, take it to the depot."

"Now let's think about this a minute, Miss Love," said Grandpa, motioning me to wait.

"I don't want it."

"Thet ain't the point. A man with a bad conscience, and stubborn enough to lug something this heavy all the way from Texas, he ain't a-go'n lug it back home. You send it up to the ho-tel, why, he'll have to bring it back down here. Miss Effie Belle's neck will break off, tryin' to keep up with all the back and forths. Besides, Mr. McAllister might miss his train." He grinned. "You keep it. Then thet will be the end a-thet and you won't need no more truck with him."

Miss Love was speechless.

Thinking to get in a lick for her, I said, "Gosh, Grandpa, what good is a saddle without a horse? Haw, I can just see Miss Love sittin' up on that fancy gee-gaw on your old mule."

"Haw, yeah, old Jack'd pure die from em-

barrass-ment," said Grandpa, laughing for
the first time since Mr. McAllister left. "But I
cain't afford no hoss. Miss Love, I reckon
you'll jest have to hang up thet saddle for a
orna-ment."

She didn't answer. Just kept snuffling.

Grandpa was pacing around nervous,
scratching his head hard and fast again. "Shet
up, hear?" he finally said to Miss Love. "One
thang I cain't stand is a cryin' woman."

That made her cry worse.

All of a sudden Grandpa slapped his leg,
excited. "Y'all, I jest recollected a letter I got
from Cudn Jake, not long fore Miss Mattie
Lou died. You know Cudn Jake, son."

"I ain't sure, Grandpa."

"Well, maybe you too young to remember
the last time he come to Cold Sassy." He
turned to Miss Love. "Jake lives jest this
side a-Cornelia. Raises Thoroughbred racehosses." She looked up from her crying, curious to know what Grandpa was driving at.
"Jake's near bout gone broke on them
racehosses. Not from bettin'. He's got too
much sense to bet. He jest cain't find much of
a market for'm right now. Anyhow, he offered to give me a three-year-old if'n I'd
come git him. Said the hoss had been broke

to a halter and thet's all, but if I had a mind
to fool with it I could have her for nothin'.
Said it would save him feedin' thet big mouth
another winter. At the time, the last thang I
wanted was a dang racehoss. But . . . Miss
Love, you want her?"

"I, uh, I never thought to want a racehorse,
Mr. Blakeslee, but—"

"Think you could train him?"

"Didn't you say it was a her?"

"I don't recollect. Same difference. A gelding, maybe. Point is, could you train it to thet
there saddle? I cain't pay nobody to train it,
but Will Tweedy here could hep you. So you
want a free hoss or don't you? If'n ole Jake
ain't got shet of it already."

"Yes. Yes, I do want it! Oh, I do!" Miss
Love was up and practically hopping, she was
so excited.

"Then what say we let Will Tweedy go git
him?" Grandpa looked at me and winked.
"Son, what's today? Sarady?"

"Yessir."

"Well, early Monday mornin' I want you to
hitch old Jack to my buggy and go git thet
hoss. Maybe you could carry the Predmore
boy along for comp'ny."

It was my turn to be hopping now. You'd of

thought I'd been in jail for three weeks instead of in mourning. Boy howdy! Then I had
another idea, which I didn't waste time pre-
senting. "How about if I borrow Grandpa
Tweedy's covered wagon, sir, and us boys go
campin' in the mountains. We could go by
Cudn Jake's on the way home. Can I? Please,
sir?"

"Shore, if'n Mr. Tweedy can spare the mule
team and yore folks say so. But it cain't be no
long campin' trip."

"Sir?"

"Yore daddy's go'n be leavin' for New York
City in two or three weeks. I don't recollect
the exact date, but I don't want yore mama
stayin' by herself whilst he's gone. I shore
wish she'd change her mind and go on with
him. Miss Mattie Lou would want her to.
Hit'd do her good, and hit's jest a dang
shame to waste a free boat ticket."

I was so excited I hardly noticed when Miss
Love left the room. "We'll just camp a few
days," I told Grandpa.

"Them mountains is the best place in the
world to be in the hot summertime," he said.
"I jest hope yore mother and them see fit to
let you go."

"Yessir, I do, too." But I wasn't worried.

With Grandpa practically ordering me to go, there wasn't any real question about it.

"Miss Love?" he called. "I'm a-goin' on back to the store now. Will Tweedy, you come on with me. I got a sack a-groceries I need delivered."

I'd of liked to stay and talk with Miss Love. I wanted her to know I wouldn't tell on her. Miss Effie Belle would, of course. But I wouldn't.

We were halfway to town when Grandpa said sternly, as if I was leaving for Cornelia in a few minutes, "Now you be careful with thet hoss, Will Tweedy."

"I will, sir."

"Tie him up good to the back of the wagon and don't let them fool boys try to ride it or git to cuttin' up with him or anythang. Or you, either."

"Oh, no, sir."

"Likely he's skittish and high-strung. Most racehosses are. If I know Cudn Jake, thet free hoss may have more wrong with it than havin' to eat. How-some-ever, Miss Love needs something to take her mind off of Mr. Texas. Hope she can ride good as she says she can."

"I think Miss Love can do just about anything, Grandpa." I was thinking if she can marry you like she did, and turn you into a judge with just a shave and a haircut, and tell off a man like Mr. McAllister, then I reckon she can train a horse.

Grandpa didn't mention the Texan again that day. In his mind, Mr. McAllister was dead as he'd ever be.

Well, he wasn't dead to me. Even walking along beside Grandpa, I kept remembering the kissing. I figured Miss Effie Belle couldn't have helped seeing—but hey, with her coming out of the bright sunshine, maybe she couldn't see down the hall! I'd like to of comforted Miss Love with that possibility. It wasn't going to be easy for her to cook a nice supper for Grandpa when her reputation depended on the eyesight of a mean old lady with a lip wart and the loyalty of a fourteen-year-old boy who had never been known to keep his mouth shut.

Also, she must still be either hating Mr. McAllister like poison or else loving his eyes out and having second thoughts about not getting annulled. I wanted to tell her that I for one hoped she'd stay in the family.

24

I really juned around when I got home that evening. I needed to lay in a store of good feelings as well as stovewood before asking permission to go camping.

At supper I was trying to think how to bring up the subject, when Papa did it for me. "Mary Willis, your daddy wants Will to go to Cornelia next week," he began. "Cudn Jake has offered him a horse if he'll send for it. And Mr. Blakeslee said maybe Will and the boys should go campin' for a few days first." Mama looked dumfounded. "I know it's mighty soon after your ma's passin', hon, but I think myself the trip would do the boy good. Get his mind off of that train trestle."

Looking tired and kind of forlorn, she said, "Well, if you think folks will under-stand. . . ."

Boy howdy! "Mama," I said, "a trip would do you good, too. Why don't you go on to New York with Papa?"

She ignored me. "Hoyt, why does Pa want a horse? He's got Big Jack. What does he need a horse for?" Then, sarcastic, "I guess it's Love that wants the horse. Ridin' in a buggy behind a mule ain't good enough for her. Will, were you down there today when that man from Texas brought her a silver saddle?"

"Yes'm." I reached for a biscuit. "But it ain't exactly a silver saddle, Mama."

"I heard it was a silver saddle. It's all over town about that saddle."

"Yes'm, but it's only trimmed with silver."

Her blue eyes flashing, Mama plonked down her fork and looked across the table at Papa. "Don't she care at all if folks talk? Hadn't she done enough already, without acceptin' an expensive gift like that from a man with a reputation so bad it rides ahead of him?"

"Mr. McAllister didn't give her the saddle, Mama," I said airily. "It was already hers. He just brung it to her. She didn't even want it, and told him so."

"I wish you'd quit takin' up for that woman," said Mama.

"Now, hon, Will's not—"

"It was Grandpa thought she ought to keep the saddle," said I. "Grandpa liked Mr. McAllister, Mama. Even ast him to stay to supper, and spend the night, too."

"Aw, shah!"

Not knowing what if anything Grandpa had told when he got back to the store, I was getting uneasy about shading the situation. It occurred to me to change the subject. "Papa, I bet y'all didn't reck-anize Grandpa when he came in without his beard and all."

Papa grinned and took another helping of potato salad. "Mary Willis, you ain't seen him yet, have you, hon?"

"No. But I heard." She spoke bitter.

"I took him for a stranger. Camp did, too. Camp just kept sittin' there on the counter swingin' his legs, and Mr. Blakeslee fine'ly yelled, 'Git down from there, boy, and find something to do!' I knew then it was him, but I couldn't hardly believe it! Mary Willis, you got you a young daddy. Miss Love shaved ten years off of him, gettin' rid of that long whitey beard and that mane of bushy hair."

"Is that so?" My mother didn't smile. "Well, Pa looked just fine to me the way he was. Seems like if Love Simpson cain't get him talked about one way, she does it another. Everybody will say she didn't want people thinkin' he's old enough to be her daddy. But he is."

We ate a while in silence. Then my mother said, real sarcastic, "Hoyt, y'all might as well put up a sign down at the store. Announce the widower is givin' his new bride a race-horse for a weddin' present."

"Now, hon, you know it's not like that." Papa reached over and patted her hand, but she didn't notice.

"Oh, Hoyt, however will it all end?" She pressed her napkin to her quivering mouth. "Ma would spin in her grave. . . ."

I had never in my life heard my mother speak out so bitter about anything or anybody. She was the one always took up for the preacher when folks complained about a dull sermon, and she always talked kind about old Mr. Tate if somebody laughed about him liking sugar in his buttermilk. Remembering how Mama had laid on her bed crying just two days ago, so scared Miss Love would get willed the store, I wondered if she could stand it when she found out Pa's house was already deeded over. Or if, Lord help us, she heard about Miss Love kissing Mr. McAllister.

I wanted to tell her the store was to be hers and Loma's. Instead, I found myself saying, in a small voice, "If it'll make you feel better, Mama, I'll give up the campin' trip."

"No, go on," she said. "Go on. Get it over

with. You've been whinin' around about it ever since Ma passed." She started crying. "But, son, t-try not to have too good a time."

"I'll wear my black armband all the way, Mama," I said, eager to comfort her, but she left the table and ran upstairs. "Papa?" I asked. "What's the matter with Mama? It ain't like her to be so hard on folks."

"I think she's mad at your granny, son," he said, folding his napkin. He looked like he had a stomachache.

"Mad at Granny?"

"For dyin', Will. Mama never made a decision in her life without thinkin' would her mother approve of it or not. Ever since she passed, it's been like Mama's lost holt of the reins. Like she's bein' pulled along by a team she cain't control. And she don't see any sense a-tall in your granddaddy marryin' like he did. She don't know Miss Love, Will. Not like I do—from working with her. She's a nice lady and Mr. Blakeslee needs lookin' after. But Mama cain't see that yet."

I was so excited about the camping trip that I didn't worry as much about Miss Love as she deserved. But I did run up there for a few minutes that night, after I was sure it was too

late for Miss Effie Belle to come tell on her.
Miss Effie Belle didn't have a telephone, so
she couldn't call, and she hadn't left home by
herself after dark since she was eighty-five
and stumbled on a tree root coming in from
Wednesday night prayer meeting. So her not
appearing at our house didn't mean yes or no
about what she had seen. Just in case, I
wanted to make sure Miss Love knew she
could count on me. I'd cross my heart and
hope to die before I'd tell on her to anybody.

I found her in the kitchen, washing up the
supper dishes. Her eyes were still red from
crying, she looked awful tired, and I didn't
quite know how to get out what she needed
to hear. "Where's Grandpa at?" I asked.

"Out at the barn, feeding the mule. He got
in late, so I managed to get up a pretty good
supper for him," she said. "Salmon croquettes, and slaw, and, uh. . . ." Forgetting
what she was talking about, she just stood
there with her hands in the dishwater. "I—I
don't know how I let it happen," she said all
of a sudden.

"You were just so surprised," said I, being
helpful.

"Surprised? I guess I was. Will Tweedy, I
swear I hardly knew what was happening. It

was like being in a dream where you can't move."

"Miss Love, you can, uh, count on me." My words stumbled around. "Uh, I mean, uh, I know you couldn't hep what happened. He just overpowered you." She stared at me, saying nothing. "And, uh, I mean I ain't go'n tell Grandpa or Papa or anybody how Mr. McAllister and you—well, uh, you know."

I felt like a plumb fool, but Miss Love guessed what I was driving at. Blushing, she patted my arm and thanked me for being her friend. I felt so noble and generous.

"Don't you worry, now. If Miss Effie Belle says anything around town, I'll tell everybody it wasn't like that at all. I'll say it was just a brotherly kiss. And besides, I'll say, you really told Mr. McAllister off afterwards."

That got Miss Love nervous. "Don't, Will. Don't say anything at all. This is for grown folks. Anything you say might just make it worse."

I felt like a fool. Where Miss Love had been talking to me like I was a man, now she had cut me back down to size. "You go'n tell Grandpa?" I asked in a small voice.

"I don't know. I don't think I can face him if he f-finds out." And she burst into tears.

She soon got aholt of herself, though, and went back to washing dishes. Holding a plate in midair, she looked at me kindly, smiling that big wide smile as if this was no bigger problem than getting the stove hot enough to fry the croquettes. "Don't worry about me, Will. I've been taking care of myself a long time. I just don't want to embarrass your grandfather, or the family any more than they're already embarrassed." She flushed. "I mean they're embarrassed enough over us marrying so quickly, without . . . Well, we'll all survive." She straightened up.

"Yes'm. I reckon."

She saw that I didn't know what to say next. "Thank you, Will, for not wanting to be the one who spreads gossip. It shows you've got real character. I do hate gossipers." And with that, she kissed me on the cheek.

I practically danced home, thinking about her having confidence in me and about that little peck. By time I got to bed that night I was making like it was a kiss full on the mouth. From there I got to imagining what it would be like to kiss her the way Mr. McAllister did it, with kisses that ran together like a string of pearls.

That sure beat thinking about getting run

over by a train, but I went too far with it. In the dark, alone in my bed, I tried sucking a knuckle of my finger and pretending it was her mouth. When I got so hot and squirmy I couldn't stand it, I tiptoed downstairs to pour me some sweetmilk.

With the glass still half full in my hand, I set my mind on Lightfoot McLendon, wondering if she would let me kiss her like that— the way Mr. Texas did it. But in no time at all I had my arms around Miss Love again.

It seemed so evil, I felt sick.

If it's true what the Bible says—that lusting in your heart after another man's wife is the same as if you actually did what you're thinking about—then I was guiltier than Mr. McAllister. When he was kissing Miss Love, he didn't know she was married. But I for sure knew, and it was my own grandfather's wife I was hankering after, which seemed like an awful sin. I was soon trembling with remorse as well as lust.

I purely made myself get out paper and a pencil and put my mind on the camping trip. Well, we'd take our shotguns, of course, to shoot game with. And fishing tackle. And a wood ax. Baseball and bat and gloves.

Matches . . . flour, of course. Sugar and salt. A big iron skillet, some lard . . .

There isn't anything like planning a camping trip to get your mind off of what it shouldn't be on.

Miss Effie Belle appeared next morning, just as we were fixing to walk out the door to go to Sunday school. "I would of come last night, but Bubba was feelin' po'ly," she began, all excited. "Well, I hate to be the bearer of evil, but I know y'all had a heap rather hear it from me than somebody else." And then with her pink lip wart quivering and her skin-and-bones face lit up like a Christmas tree, she proceeded to tell what the tall stranger had done besides bring Miss Love a saddle. "And her just two days past vowin' to cleave only unto Rucker! I swanny to God, these modrun women are something else." Her voice was shaking so bad that she had to stop a minute to breathe. Then she said, "Well, Mary Willis, I reckon now your daddy will ship her back to Baltimore. Pore man, look what bein' lonesome got him into."

After Miss Effie Belle hurried off to Sunday school, Mama and Papa lit into me. Did I see the kissing? Well, why hadn't I come straight home and told them? Did Grandpa know? Did Miss Love know Miss Effie Belle saw it? Sounding just like Aunt Loma, Mama said, "Her conduct proves it, Hoyt. That Woman ain't fit to be a servant in Pa's house, much less married to him."

Naturally Mama stayed home. Said she had a headache. Probably she did. But mostly she was too mortified to face the congregation. Papa would of stayed with her, except he had to take up collection.

It was just an awful day.

Miss Effie Belle's words flew from mouth to mouth in every churchyard in Cold Sassy. Then after folks talked about Miss Love cleavin' to somebody besides Grandpa, they had to speculate about her church affiliation. Her having married a Baptist, Cold Sassy naturally expected her to show up there that morning. The Baptists considered themselves above the rest of us. Most of them, including Aunt Loma, thought Miss Love would join their congregation with Grandpa "for the same reason she married him—to come up in the world." It must of been a relief to the Baptists when she didn't appear, because nobody knew whether to treat her like a grave robber or just a repentant sinner.

Since the Presbyterians weren't involved, there was no suspense at our preachin' service. Just pity for the shamed family.

The ones in a pickle were the Methodists. Most had thought Miss Love would go over to the Baptists right away or else hide at home, one. Well, she not only appeared at the Methodist Episcopal Church, South, but she wore a black dress, like she was in mourning for the one whose death had been her good fortune—and, as usual, sat down at the piano soon as she came in.

Miss Effie Belle stopped by after preachin' to tell us about it. "That Woman ain't got no respect for nobody. Wearin' mournin', for heaven's sake, and—"

Just the thought of it made Mama mad, but she tried to be fair. "It'd look a heap worse if she'd worn red," she said.

"Humph. Anyhow, we fixed her. Nobody sang. Well, Cratic and Agnes did. You know how they are. Them two were singin' by theirselves, though, I can tell you. Like we'd agreed to it ahead of time, the rest of us kept our mouths shut."

Aunt Loma came up our walk with Uncle Camp and the baby in time to hear that. "Did Love get the message?" she asked, hateful.

"By the second verse her face was red as the songbook," Miss Effie Belle said proudly. "Still, the nerve of That Woman ain't got no limits. She played all eight verses, right down to the a-men. But the preacher made certain sure she didn't get to do it agin."

"He ast her to leave?" asked Loma.

"No. He just didn't announce no more songs. Miss Love was still sittin' at the pi-ana waitin' for the next page number when he started his sermon. It fine'ly dawned on her he wasn't go'n let her play agin, and she jumped up and flounced out. Well, I better git on home and see about Bubba." Like an afterthought, she added, "Rucker didn't come to church with her, you know. I reckon he was shamed to. When I left this mornin', I seen him settin' on that big rock in Miss Mattie Lou's rose garden. Repentin' of his hasty puddin', I don't doubt."

25

I met Pink early Monday morning in front of Clark's Drug Store to wait for Mr. Lias Foster, the rural mailman, who would be coming from Commerce in his buggy. "He's a talker," I warned. "If he cain't think of anything else, he'll say, 'Git yore foot away from thet aigg basket fore you bust them aiggs.' " We both laughed.

"What's he takin' eggs to country people for?"

"He ain't. They give him eggs for stamps. He puts stamps on their letters and then trades out the eggs at Grandpa's store or at Williford, Burns, and Rice in Commerce."

Mr. Lias made three buggy trips a week, delivering letters, newspapers, and Sears, Roebuck packages in Banks County. Out one day and back the next. The rural post offices were mostly in farmhouses, my Grandpa Tweedy's place being one of them.

We waited for Mr. Lias at the drug store because Cold Sassy's post office was in there, a big pigeonhole desk over where the telephone central switchboard used to be. They had moved the switchboard to Miss Lucille's house so that she could operate it nights as well as days. When Mr. Lias arrived, we followed him inside. Five or six old men were already sitting around in there, talking crops and fussing about the gov'ment in Washington while they cut one another's hair. A colored man named Henry had started a white barbershop in Cold Sassy a few years back, but these old fellers liked the drug store better. Folks coming in for their mail would stop and talk a while.

"Hey, Will, where y'all goin'?" Mr. Tom Rainwater asked me.

"Out to Banks County, Mr. Tom. My Grandpa Tweedy's got a big blue North Ca'lina wagon, and we go'n borrow it and go campin'."

The ride started off as a high ole time, us laughing loud and cutting up behind Mr. Lias as the buggy racked out of Cold Sassy. Old T.R. trotted ahead or dropped behind or went dashing off across worn-out fields grown up in broom sedge. Pink and I talked about camping plans till the clip-clopping of the horses made him sleepy. Mr. Lias, contrary to his usual nature, said next to nothing. So I was left to myself.

I sat staring at his lean old hulk in the front seat and at the hind ends of the dappled-gray horses. I hardly noticed when one of the horses raised his tail and plopped in rhythm with the clip-clop. I didn't see the red dust that coated sassafras bushes and wild flowers by the roadside. I hardly noticed the blackberries that glistened among the brambles. All I saw was Bluford Jackson in his grave.

The camping trip had been Blu's idea. We were talking about it that morning we climbed up the water tower to throw down lighted firecrackers and scare people—the day Blu got the firecracker burn that gave him lockjaw.

Though I liked Pink just fine, I couldn't help thinking that if Blu hadn't of died, it would be him going out to Banks County with me this hot July morning. I wondered had he rotted down to bones yet. How long did it take? And what about Granny? Despite the fine hardwood casket, might she have worms in her already?

Lord help me.

I tried to think about Lightfoot McLendon's hair shining white in the sun, but that just set me to worrying about whether she went to Blind Tillie Trestle on Saturday, expecting me to be there like I said I would. Dern, why hadn't I tried some way to get word to her?

Right about then, Mr. Lias looked over his shoulder at me and asked how did my folks take it when they found out Mr. Blakeslee done got marrit.

"They took it all right." I knew whatever I said would be written down in his mind to deliver with the mail.

"The milliner is a handsome lady, you can say thet for her."

"Yessir. How's Miss Ora, Mr. Lias?"

"Tol'able. Jest tol'able. She ain't never really got over her pleurisy." He flopped the reins. "I been thinkin' lately on Sal, my first wife. How she ruint my life."

"Ruint your life, sir?" I grabbed his words like they were a rope to hang on to.

Mr. Lias clucked his cheek sideways and flipped the reins till the horses picked up their trot. Then he waved at two old country ladies sitting on their front steps picking through a little girl's hair for cooties. They waved back and stared after us. I thought Mr. Lias would go on telling about his wife then, but his tongue had already burned out. He just sat there, flopping the reins every now and again or slapping at a fly or fanning his leathery face with his straw hat. We passed a chain gang of Negro convicts grading the road. They had to step into the ditch to let us pass. Then he spoke.

"I knowed hit were a mis-take, soon as me and Sal got marrit. She warn't like any woman I ever seen before. A purty thang, but when it come to washin' or cookin', if she'd a-moved any slower she'd a-been goin' backwards. Everthang happened to her was contrary to nature. If she'd a-drownded, I'd a-gone upstream to look for her. And she said sech dang-fool thangs. When she was in the fam'ly way, her ma got worrit bout Sal was losin' weight. You know what Sal said? She said, 'Ma, I cain't see I've lost any. But course I ain't looked under my feet yet, haw.' She thought thet was cute talk. I told her she sounded like a idjit. 'For God's dang sake, Sal, shet up fore some jedge commits you to Milledgeville.' "

Another silence. Clip-clop, clip-clop, slap, flop, fan. Reins jiggling, horses snorting and pooting, buggy rocking and creaking, steel wheel rims hitting rocks, a caw-caw from a crow somewhere, T.R. way off in the woods, barking at something.

Another mile and Mr. Lias's gravelly old voice said, "I was pitchin' hay one mornin', Sal up thar on the wagon seat a-holdin' the reins, when here come Mr. James Henry's bull. A mean'un. Charged me, and got me down right by the wagon. My wife, she had two good wood axes up thar beside her, but she didn't do one dang thang to hep me."

He spat. After we passed the Antioch Baptist Church, I couldn't stand watching him think any longer. I poked him on the shoulder. "How'd you get away from the bull, Mr. Lias?"

"Huh? Why, I gouged his eyes out," he said, matter of fact. "Reached up and grabbed a horn with one hand and gouged with the other'n. Then I quick rolled under the wagon out'n his way. I would a-kilt thet bull if I could of. Dang thang run off a-bellerin' and a-bleedin' and a-bumpin' into haystacks and fences. Thet very next week, I found out my wife been runnin' round on me for five year with a sorry low-down good-fer-nothin' cropper on Mr. James Henry's place. I don't doubt a minute but he let thet bull out and sicked him on me."

Silence. The horses picked their way around a hole in the road. Mr. Lias spat again. "One night I got my gun and follered Sal straight to his house. Busted the door down and caught'm together, and had the dang hammer pulled back to shoot'm both when it dawned on me they warn't worth killin', neither one of'm. Eased the hammer back and lowered my gun and plain walked off. I went to live in Cold Sassy with my brother's fam'ly and got the mail route."

"What about Miss Sal?"

"Died. Got bit by a cottonmouth at a church picnic. Vengeance is mine, saith the Lord. Good riddance, saith I, and the next year I marrit a spinster lady over in Commerce with a nice house. Miss Ora. She's three inches taller'n me and six year older, but she tells me a dozen times a day how much she loves me."

By then I was barely listening. From the minute Mr. Lias mentioned Miss Sal carrying on with another man, I went to thinking about Miss Love carrying on with Mr. McAllister.

If Grandpa hadn't heard about the kissing yet, he was the only one in Cold Sassy still left to tell.

Gosh, what if he found out before we left for the mountains? If he decided to send Miss Love back to Baltimore, he sure as heck wouldn't want me to go on to Cornelia for any racehorse.

The buggy rolled between gullied slopes of red clay. Then we passed the gristmill built by my great-grandfather Tweedy around 1850 on the Hudson River, and rattled through the cool of the covered bridge he built across the river to join his land together. I wondered how a man smart enough to do all that could of had a son lazy as my Grandpa Tweedy, who couldn't even get around to treating his cows for hollow horn or when they got maggots under the skin.

One time I asked Papa didn't he think his daddy was lazy, leaving all the work to field hands or sorry no-count tenants and croppers. Papa said, "Your granddaddy's just fresh out of hope, son, like most farmers in Georgia these days."

I wished I could of known Grandpa Tweedy's daddy, but he died of the typhoid in 1867. He was too old to go fight in the War of the Sixties, but they made him a general in the local militia. General Tweedy, he was called. By time I came along, most everybody in Banks County thought General Tweedy had been a high monkity-monk in the Army of the Confederacy instead of just in the home guard. And I never heard any Tweedy, not even my own daddy, try to correct the impression.

* * *

Mr. Lias turned his team off the highway into the rutty lane that led up to the old home place. It, too, was built by General Tweedy, out of hand-hewed logs and hand-sawed and hand-planed boards, and had portholes in the upper story for shooting Indians.

I poked Pink awake. "Someday I'm go'n farm this land," I bragged, gesturing in every direction. "Papa's go'n buy it and let me farm it."

Mr. Lias spoke up. "Everbody always figgered you'd go in the store with Mr. Blakeslee, Will."

"Well, I ain't. I like farmin'. All there is to store work is watchin' out for rice weevils and rotten potatoes, and keepin' the rats out of the seed corn." I was feeling real smart-aleck. "But on a farm it's always something to worry about or be excited about. Foot-and-mouth disease, weevils, too much rain, too little rain, hired hands goin' off in the night with half your tools. . . . I'm a gambler, I reckon, because the way I see it, farmin' is one big dice game."

"You talkin' like a dang fool, Will," said Mr. Lias. "Ain't nothin' excitin' bout a dang weevil, or plantin' fer seventeen-cent cotton and then cotton goes down to twelve cent cause everbody overplanted. I'm glad to be out of it. Ever now and agin you make enough to cover the mortgage and taxes and pay off the store thet give you credit. But even when it's a good fall, you might's well count on it, Will: fore the year's out yore mule's go'n die or yore barn burn down."

I wasn't discouraged. "I've heard farmers talk like that all my life, Mr. Lias. But, see, I aim to study agriculture over at the University and learn better ways. For instance, I ain't go'n buy corn from a store to feed my livestock. I'm go'n grow my own corn. And cotton ain't go'n be my only cash crop."

"Well, if it ain't, boy, you cain't git no lien from the store. And if'n you don't git no lien, you cain't buy no seed and guano. Well, *you* could, I reckon. Bein' who you are. Yore granddaddy'll give you good terms, and he ain't go'n charge you double when you send a nigger to town to git sugar and coffee on credit."

I didn't like him suggesting Grandpa overcharged, but I let that go by. Naturally Grandpa would give me favorable terms. But it was better farming methods I counted on to turn a profit. "I'll learn how to plan ahead," I said.

"See can you learn how to plan ahead for rain or drought, son. Do thet and they'll give you a prize over at thet Ag College." Mr. Lias clucked his team up to a trot. "Hope you don't never have to find out what it's like, bein' pore. But ain't no farmer in Georgie seen thet prosperity Mr. Henry W. New-South Grady used to write about in them Atlanta newspapers. When I was farmin', I'd go in town and them bankers and store men treated me like white trash. Since I got this here job carryin' the mail, I git some respect."

As we rode past the old barn, weathered gray and leaning into a clump of hollyhocks and daisies, I pointed toward the shed. "Our wagon's in there, Pink. It's got a cover that flares up four or five feet, front and back. My great-grandfather brought his whole family down to Georgia in it, even his old daddy. His daddy was a blacksmith with four forges, till he crippled his arm, and a missionary to the Indians besides."

"Gosh," said Pink, impressed.

"I knowed yore great-grandpa when I was a boy," said Mr. Lias. "General Tweedy was his name. He shore was a fine old man."

When we turned into the swept yard, I noticed for the first time how rundown the place looked. Almost like white trash lived there. Grandpa Tweedy wasn't white trash. He owned his land. But, like all farmers, he had to contend with high taxes, high freight rates, and land so worn out that he might spend more for guano than he could get for his cotton crop. Still and all, he got better terms at the store than most, on account of my daddy, and Papa helped out some with cash money. Times weren't as hard for him as they could be.

Grandpa Tweedy was sitting on the porch swatting flies. His pet hen, a White Leghorn, clucked with excitement every time the swatter came down. I guess I saw him through Pink's eyes that morning, because I was embarrassed all of a sudden, how seedy Grandpa Tweedy looked in ragged overalls, his beard so long and scraggly.

While Mr. Lias walked to the back of the buggy to get out the mail, Pink and I went up on the porch. Before we could even say howdy, Grandpa Tweedy hollered to Miz Jones to put on two extry plates for dinner.

"Besides for Mr. Lias?" she called from inside the house.

"Yes'm," he yelled back. "Will's here, and another boy." Then he thundered his gravelly voice at me. "Will, answer me. 'What is God?'"

Without batting an eye I quoted from the Shorter Catechism in my best Sunday school voice: " 'God is a Spirit, Infinite, Eternal and Unchangeable.' "

Grandpa Tweedy had been drilling me on the catechism all my life. "Now, tell me. 'What is a lie?' " He picked up his swatter off the floor, killed a fly on his arm as he said the word *lie,* and flipped the fly off for the chicken.

" 'A lie is an abomination in the sight of God and . . .' uh, 'and a . . .' "

"And a what, boy?"

I knew the answer. I was just debating whether to give it or act smart and show off before Pink. I decided to act smart. " 'A lie is an abomination in the sight of God,' " I repeated, " 'and a very present help in time of trouble!' Ain't that right, Pink?"

Before Grandpa could bless me out for being sacrilegious, I told him about getting run over by the train. He said, "Thar you go, son, temptin' the Almighty Hisself."

Then I stated my business, namely, that Papa wanted him to let me use Big Red and

Satan and the covered wagon. "Some of us boys are go'n go campin'."

Grandpa banged on the arm of his rocking chair. "What you arter be doin' instead, you arter be studyin' the catechism and the Bible. Ain't thet right, Lias? You ever see sech a smart-aleck boy?"

Coming up the porch steps, Mr. Lias grinned and said I was smart-aleck, all right. "But he ain't a bad boy, Mr. Tweedy."

"Then he must a-changed here lately."

Real respectful, I asked, "Is it all right for us to take the team and the wagon, sir? Papa said you might could spare'm."

"I need them mules." It was like he'd forgot Papa was the one that bought Big Red and Satan in the first place. "I need them and the wagon, both. You know good'n' well we use thet wagon ever fourth Sunday to go to Hebron for preachin'."

"We'll be back long fore time for Hebron, Grandpa."

"Well, anyhow, hit ain't all right with me. What y'all go'n go campin' for? Why cain't you jest lay out in some a-them woods around Cold Sassy a few days, or come out here?"

"Time for dinner, y'all," Mrs. Jones called

from the door. "How you do, Will? Who's your young friend?"

She was a huge fat woman, Grandpa Tweedy's third wife, and I liked her. The reason she was still Mrs. Jones, Grandpa had called her that all the time they were courting —her being a widow woman—and after they got married he was too lazy to bother changing her name. Granny Blakeslee used to laugh about that, and she thought it worth mentioning that Mrs. Jones had kicked Mr. Jones after he was dead. Of course, Mrs. Jones hadn't known he was dead. She just thought he was snoring again. Doc said the snore was the breath going out for the last time.

As we started in to dinner, Grandpa Tweedy walked over to the edge of the porch and picked up a conch shell off the banister rail. "I ordered this'n from Savannah," he told Pink, and blew a loud blast. "Thet's to call the hands to dinner," he explained.

We had just sat down to the table when a rumble of colored men's voices suddenly drifted in from the kitchen. It was the field hands, coming in to eat. "Miz Jones, reach back of you and shet the kitchen door," said Grandpa Tweedy. "Now, Willy. Hit jest makes me nervous, the idee a-you takin' off in thet big wagon. And shore as sin, if it ain't here we'll need it."

I knew he meant somebody might die. The covered wagon was the hearse for anybody who needed one in that part of Banks County. General Tweedy had taken his last ride in it nearly forty years before, to the Hebron graveyard. His widow, Arminda, my great-grandmother, had gone in it to the same place just a year ago, and also when she died the first time.

Before Grandpa Tweedy could say any more about the wagon, Mr. Lias said, "Y'all heard bout Will's other granddaddy gittin' marrit last week?"

"Is thet a fact," said Grandpa, helping his plate. "Seems like it wadn't more'n a week or two ago, Lias, you come in with a message from Hoyt sayin' Miss Mattie Lou had died. Rucker shore acks fast."

Mrs. Jones wanted to know who was the bride, who married them, and all about it. Then she asked, "Will, is they any more room in Mr. Blakeslee's cemetery plot? Besides for him, I mean? You reckon they's room for this Miss Love in there with him and Miss Mattie Lou?"

"Yes'm," I said, embarrassed. "I think so."

Grandpa Tweedy grinned. "Miz Jones worries bout where I'm go'n put her down when the time comes, son. Hit bein' the custom, I got to be buried twixt yore daddy's mama, Will, and Miss Flo. But Miz Jones don't want to be put at our feet, which is the only other space left."

"That's all right, Mr. Tweedy, I fine'ly figgered out a plan," she said, laughing merrily. "Want to hear?"

He looked up, suspicious. "Say it."

"I've decided I want to be put down settin' up. Settin' in a rockin' cheer with a whole choc'late cake in my lap and a silver fork to eat it with. And naturally it's go'n take a heap a-room, me bein' a fairly large woman."

"Ain't no way to bury somebody settin' up in no rockin' cheer."

"Lemme finish now. Since they ain't that much room in yore lot, I just think I'll set beside Mr. Jones through eternity. I'm go'n ast the fam'ly when we go to Hebron next fourth Sunday."

It really made Grandpa Tweedy mad. He didn't say another word the whole meal, not even when the cook and Mrs. Jones were clearing the table. But a gleam came in his eye while he was spooning a mound of whip cream on his blackberry cobbler, and he started telling about when he was a boy and went to the mountains with his daddy, General Tweedy. "We was ridin' horseback, buyin' up cattle. Camped up there in the Blue Ridge for a week or more, gittin' maybe two-three cows from one farmer and six or seven from another. We drove home thirty-five head, just me and him. Son, you ain't never seen anythang pretty as them big blue Georgie mountains!"

The upshot of this remembering was that my grandfather not only went with us to the pasture and watched us catch Big Red and Satan, but got two of his field hands to come help us load the wagon bed with corn, oats, and hay. And all he said as we hitched up was "Y'all be good now. And come Sunday, find you a Presbyterian church to go to. You hear me?" I turned the team into the road, T.R. riding high on the seat between me and Pink.

"Y'all take good care them mules, Will!" Grandpa Tweedy hollered after us. "They's a matched pair and I'll be in a fix if'n anythang happens to'm! Be careful, hear."

"Yessir," I called back as the team broke into a trot. "Don't worry, Grandpa, I know all about handlin' mules!"

26

Eight years after our camping trip, I still can't believe how good I told that tale about Aunt Loma nursing a pig, not to mention the one about sticking a pin in her rubber busts.

Five of us boys went to the mountains: Pink, Lee Roy, Smiley, myself, and—at the last minute—Dunson McCall. His daddy, the school superintendent, had a two-horse farm near town and bought a lot of seed and fertilizer at the store, so Papa thought it would be "a nice thing to do" to invite Dunson along.

Dunse kept his nose in a book all the time and couldn't hit a baseball if you hung it on a string in front of his bat. And as the saying goes, he was a lost ball in high weeds when it came to hunting and fishing. But he was all right. We didn't mind having him.

Grandpa Blakeslee's house was on our way out of Cold Sassy. As we rolled past it, Smiley snickered and said, "How you like your new two-timin' grandma, Will?"

I raised the whip and said shut up. "If you got to talk like that, you just get out and go on back home. You and anybody else that thinks she's any of their business." I glared at the whole bunch of them.

By time we got out in the country, we were having a high old time, whooping, talking loud, and all like that. If we saw a creakity wagon up ahead full of country folks going to town, I'd cluck the mules to a smart trot and we'd all wave as we passed them. We knew the big blue-painted covered wagon was something to stare at, and five boys off for the mountains were something to envy.

I began to forget all about Miss Love and what Cold Sassy must be saying about her kissing another man two days after promising to cleave only unto Grandpa. I even forgot to hope she knew it was Miss Effie Belle that told on her and not me.

Our mothers had packed baskets of food to keep us going. Fried chicken and boiled ham, baked sweet potatoes, peach pickles, big buttermilk biscuits, cookies, cakes, apples, boiled eggs, I don't know what all. We traveled thirty miles that first day and never stopped eating. About two o'clock the second day, just past the little town of Clayton in the foothills of the Blue Ridge Mountains, we took an old logging road into the woods and picked out a site near a little branch. While I fed and watered the mules and staked them out under some trees, the other fellers made camp. We didn't know whose land it was, of course. Just so you didn't set the woods afire and weren't Gypsies, nobody minded. You didn't have to ask.

Though we counted on getting plenty of fish and wild game, we had a wooden grub box full of staples. Smoked ham, bacon, a bucket of salt mackerel, flour, cornmeal, grits, raw sweet potatoes, lard, coffee, a tin of butter, some store bread, and a can of beaten biscuits that Dunse's mama made.

That night we put the box out under a tree to make more room for us to sleep in the wagon. I'd barely closed my eyes good when T.R. went to growling and the mules commenced raring up and squealing. Boy howdy, we scrambled out quick to grab those mules. If they'd pulled up their stakes and run away, I'd never of heard the last of it from Grandpa Tweedy.

What happened, two great big black bears

had busted into our grub box. We could see them in the moonlight, eating the ham and those raw sweet potatoes, breaking open cans, scattering coffee and meal—having just the best time you ever saw. Acted like we weren't even there.

Smiley got his gun and was fixing to take aim when I stopped him. "How you think we go'n hold the mules if you go to shootin'? These ain't huntin' mules." He raised the gun anyhow. "I'm tellin' you, Smiley! I rather be hungry than walk home!"

You talk about hungry, there's nothing like knowing your grub is off somewhere digesting in a bear to make you feel starved to death. At daybreak we scavenged in the wreckage of the box, but what hadn't been eaten was mashed into the wet pine needles. All we found was a little damp flour in the bottom of a busted can.

In the gloomy, misty, gray morning we grazed on blackberries. That was breakfast. We had blackberries again for dinner. Supper was a boiled goose that Smiley shot on a nearby pond after the sun came out. We had to skin him to get the feathers off, and he was tough, great goodness, despite we boiled him and boiled him and boiled him. But he made a meal, and we thought to skim the goose grease off the top of the water. Used it next morning to fry a few middling-size trout.

We ate blackberries off and on all that second morning, which was cold and damp and overcast. I managed to shoot a dove and a rabbit—not much for five boys—and at noon we roasted them on a spit over the fire. We'd just finished eating when the rain that had threatened all morning blew in over the mountains in heavy black thunderheads. We barely had time to string up some canvas over the mules before the storm hit.

Safe in the wagon, we had a fine time for a while, tussling in the hay and talking about girls and all. But as the day wore on with no let-up of rain, we started getting hungry and cold and miserable. We got even more miserable when Lee Roy noticed that Smiley had left our box of shotgun shells out under a tree. Wet shells meant the end of hunting anything except blackberries and dry wood, which we hadn't thought to collect any real supply of.

I was really mad at Smiley. Bluford Jackson wouldn't of been careless about the shotgun shells or the grub box, either. And he'd of thought to gather piles of wood when we first

got there, instead of keeping just enough
ahead for the next campfire. I groaned. My
throat swelled and ached. Bluford Jackson
was six feet under, and the camping trip he
planned was deader than him.

Trying to put some life in the party, so to
speak, I sat up and said, "Dunse, I don't think
you've heard how my Uncle Johnny hung a
cow by mistake."

"Aw, shut up, Will," said Lee Roy.
"Dunse's heard it. We all done heard it. A
million times." He found a blanket and
started pulling hay over himself for warmth
as the sky got darker. We sat some more,
watching the rain drip off the back canvas.
When it started down in sheets, I said, "Why
don't I tell about Raw Head and Bloody
Bones?"

"How about shut up, Will?" said Smiley.
"We get tired of your damn stories."

"Don't you cuss me, dernit!"

"Well, shut up then."

There wasn't room in the wagon for a fight.
"One time my daddy saw his ancestor who'd
been dead a hundred years," I said, stubborn.
There was a slight stir of interest.

Pink thought I meant Papa saw his ancestor's ghost.

"Naw, I mean he saw his actual great-great-dead-granddaddy. He was in a brick crypt in a old church graveyard up in North Ca'lina. When Papa and a cousin of his went over to check on the crypt, so much ivy had grown in through the cracks, you couldn't tell if the vines were holding the bricks together or pushing them apart. So they went in, and there was their great-great granddaddy. The coffin had rotted to pieces and his bones were just layin' there. Papa said the skull had a hatchet cut on the forehead."

"Goll-ee," Pink whispered.

"That ain't all. A little-girl skeleton was in the crypt, too, in a coffin with a glass top. Her bones were just so white and pretty—"

"How'd your daddy know it was a girl?" asked Smiley, suspicioning I had made up more of it than I really had.

"The bones had on a little white poky-dot dress that hadn't all rotted yet, that's how."

The drumming of rain on the canvas was easing up, which was a good thing; it had started to drip through on us. But I hardly noticed. Like an actor whose audience has stood up to clap, I didn't want to quit. And now I knew what bait to use.

I said, "I've told y'all bout Great-Granmaw

Tweedy dyin' twice. The first time, you remember, she jumped out of the coffin just fore they were fixin' to nail the lid. The second time she stayed dead. But what I thought might inner-rest y'all right now, she rode to the Hebron cemetery both times in this very wagon." I knocked on the side of it. The hollow wooden sound like to busted Pink and Lee Roy clear out of the hay.

"Did you see her die, Will—either time?" Dunse asked in a hushed voice.

"Naw. But last summer they'd just pulled the sheet over her head when me and my fam'ly got out home. And I went in there where she was at."

Smiley gasped. "I wouldn't a-gone in there," he admitted.

"Me neither," said Dunse. "I never been that close to a dead person."

"A old colored woman was sittin' with the body. She said, 'Want to see yo granny, boy?' I shook my head, but she said, 'Miss Mindy ain' gwine hurt you,' and she pulled that sheet back. Granmaw was propped up on pillows. What little hair she had was damp and standin' out like a scairt cat's. Her mouth had dropped open and her eyes stared straight at me. I could a-kilt that nigger woman, showin' off like that, tryin' to scare me. I backed out of that room, I tell you.

"Miz Jones and Mama laid Granmaw out. Fixed her mouth shut with a handkerchief tied under her chin and over her head. Papa hepped my uncles finish makin' the coffin, and soon as the preacher came, we ate dinner quick and set out for Hebron, it bein' a hot day and her not embalmed or anything. And like I said, they carried her to the graveyard in this very wagon here. Used those same mules out yonder, Big Red and Satan. All the way to Hebron, Mary Toy complained about us havin' to miss the Ringling Brothers Circus over in Athens. Every time we had to walk up a hill to save the horses, she'd say why couldn't Granmaw have died last week."

It gave us the creeps, sitting there in that hearse. It was pitch-black dark before the rain finally drizzled away and the moon came out. Wispy clouds scurried across the sky like little ghosts.

I said maybe there was enough dry wood under the wagon to build a fire with.

The fire warmed us some, after we finally got it going, but it didn't cheer anybody up. "I wish we had some good old hot buttered arsh potatoes," said Lee Roy.

Every now and again somebody would say, "I ain't scared a-no old dead woman." Or, "Is all that so, Will?" Once Pink went shush and whispered, "Y'all hear that? . . . I thought I heard something. Over by the wagon . . ."

"Just the wind," I said airily, holding a twig in the fire till it got red hot on the end, like a long cigar. I waved it in circles a while, thinking what I could tell next. Pink got up off his log and turned his back to the fire. As we sat listening to the katydids, singing loud as they came out into the wetness, the moon lit up a layer of fog below us.

Blu Jackson is dead, I thought bitterly. Granny Blakeslee is dead. And reckon what has happened by now with Grandpa and Miss Love? I wanted to go home.

Dunse was like-minded. "I'm sick of this dern campout." He groaned. "I'm hungry and I'm cold." Huddled in a blanket, he kicked at a log on the fire. It sent up sparks. The flaring of light made big shadows dance on the wet gray canvas of the hearse.

Suddenly it didn't make any sense at all to stay on here till next week, when all we had to do was leave. I said as much, and the faces lit by the campfire grinned with relief. So it was decided. We would set out for Cudn Jake's place early in the morning and get Miss Love's racehorse.

Not a one of the boys would sleep in or under the wagon that night, despite the ground was wet as heck. I had counted on that. I was going to have a bed of hay all to myself. But as I put one foot up on the axle to climb in, I decided I might as well stay out with the fellers instead.

That night Bluford Jackson came to me in a dream. He didn't look dead but said he was. Said he was damaged goods in the worst way. He wanted me to tell Emma Lee Crutchfield to let him sit by her at preachin' next Sunday and please to save a space for him in her family pew.

"How big a space do you take now, Blu? Same as before, or just a inch or two?"

He didn't answer that. Just said he'd need Sunday clothes, and would I find him some and leave them in the crotch of the maple tree in his backyard.

"What you need clothes for, Blu? If you went to church naked as a jaybird, nobody'd know it."

"Ain't that the least you can do for me,

Will, considerin' it was your firecrackers?"
That made me mad, but he kept talking.
"Will, I got lots of time now. If you want to
be a doctor, when you get to medical school
you can make room for me in your seat and
I'll hep you with your lessons and all."

"I'm not go'n be a doctor. You the one was
go'n be a doctor. I'm go'n farm. I cain't live
your life for you, Blu." Then I woke up,
frightened, and shivering from the cold.

I didn't tell my dream to the fellers, but
weeks later I told it to Grandpa Blakeslee. I
said, "Grandpa, it was like Blu didn't believe
he was dead. Like he don't know what bein'
dead means, for gosh sake."

Grandpa studied on it a minute and said,
"I think it's you thet don't believe he's dead,
son. I think it's you thet don't know what
bein' dead means. But who does? Only them
as has passed on."

Cudn Rachel was almost as big and fat as
Mrs. Jones, and said she could spot hungry
boys a mile away. She and Cudn Jake had
already eaten, but her cook made us some big
graham biscuits and fried half a ham, looked
like, and a bunch of eggs, and put a gallon of
milk on the table. The cook, having heard

about our bears, said this blessing: "Lawd, hep us an' feed us, an' keep our en'mies from us, cause some'll come upon us, an' take our rations from us. A-men."

We ate it all.

Miss Love's horse turned out to be a tall, prancy black gelding with a star on his forehead. With him tied behind the wagon on a lead rope, head held proud and high, we felt mighty fancy on the down-go to Cold Sassy, and we made mighty good time. The mules knew they were headed home.

We did lots of talking about whether or not Miss Love could train him. And then for the first time since we left Cold Sassy, the boys got to talking about her and Grandpa. Smiley started it. He said his mother thought Miss Love must have money and that's why Mr. Blakeslee married her. "My grandmother always did think the reason Mr. Blakeslee married Miss Mattie Lou was cause her daddy owned all that land."

That really made me mad. "Shut up!"

"Miss Mattie Lou was a old maid, wasn't she? Why would anybody marry a old maid cept for land or money?"

"I said shut up!" I yelled.

"Yeah, shut up, Smiley," said Dunse. "It ain't right to talk like that about the dead."

But they couldn't let go of the subject. And the more they got my goat, the worse things they said, especially about Miss Love. Things like "Hey, Will, how long you think they been sweet on one another?" and "You reckon Miss Love's too old to have babies?"

"They ain't plannin' to have babies," I burst out, furious. "Grandpa and Miss Love have a business arrange-ment."

"What you mean by that?" Lee Roy asked with a smirk.

"I mean Miss Love is sleepin' in the comp'ny room," I said. "She's just livin' down there to keep house."

"I don't believe it."

"Well, it's so."

"Says who?"

"Says her. She told me."

"Haw! Since when have ladies started sayin' such as that to a boy? Shoot-dog."

Then Smiley crowded close up behind the driver's seat to talk ugly about the rich-lookin' stranger from Texas. "I heard he tore her clothes half off fore he got done kissin' her."

"Well, he didn't!" I was really mad now. "And I ought to know. I was there."

The boys took to making up jokes then, saying things you wouldn't want said about your grandpa's wife even if you hated her. I decided to change the subject. I swear I didn't know when I opened my mouth that I would say what I said, but it changed the subject all right:

"Y'all want to hear about Aunt Loma nursin' a pig?"

"You mean Campbell Junior?" asked Pink Predmore.

"I ain't talkin' bout the baby." We had started down a steep hill. "Slow down, Big Red. Whoa, Satan! Lee Roy, push hard on the brake post! The wagon's go'n run over the team!" Careening downhill, bumping over rocks and dried mud holes, we like to shook apart before we got the dern wagon under control.

"Did you say Miss Loma nursed a pig?" Pink asked as soon as he was able.

"You mean she put a pig up to her tits and let it suck?" asked Smiley.

"If Miss Loma did that, she must be crazy," said Dunse. "Anyhow, Will, how would you know it?"

I didn't, of course. One time I overheard Mama and Aunt Loma talking about a distant cousin over in Athens that did it to keep her milk going while her baby was in the hospital, but I just made up that it was Aunt Loma.

"Well, you know Campbell Junior was born little," I began, thinking fast. "I mean he didn't weigh more'n a fryin-size chicken. Born early."

"Funny, I don't recollect him ever bein' little bitty," said Lee Roy.

"Well, he was. To keep him warm they had to put him in a pasteboard box with hot water bottles wrapped in towels all around him." That part was true. You just couldn't get Aunt Loma's house warm in winter. The rest I made up as I went along. "He was too weak to suck good, so Mama showed Aunt Loma how to milk herself and they gave it to him with a eyedropper. But seems like she never really had full bags. Not enough milk to feed a jaybird. And the baby bein' such a sorry sucker, they were scairt she'd go dry."

We were moving up a hill now, the mules straining forward. I flipped their rumps with the whip.

"Get to the pig," fat Lee Roy said impatiently. "Tell us bout the pig."

"Well, my daddy fine'ly got on the telephone and rung up a hospital doctor over in Athens and ast what to do. It was the doctor said get a pig."

"Naw!" The boys said naw like there was just one voice for the four of them.

"Yeah! The doc said a pig would really get her milk goin'."

"I don't believe any lady would nurse a pig," said Dunse. "Not even your Aunt Loma."

"You can believe it or not, it's so," said I, and at the moment I half-believed it myself. "They sent me out to Grandpa Tweedy's in the buggy to get one. His Poland China sow had just whelped a new litter. I got the runtiest and took it home in a box. Mama bathed it and wrapped it up in a blue blanket and took it in to Aunt Loma. Mama couldn't stand the sight, that little pig gruntin' and pushin', but I heard her tell Papa that Loma said it felt real good. You know how if a cow ain't stripped proper she gets a swollen bag and sore tits? Well, Aunt Loma had been hurtin' a lot, besides worryin' bout the baby starvin' to death. She nursed that pig a week or more, I don't remember how long."

"If the pig was nursin' her," asked Pink, doubting, "what was happenin' to Campbell Junior?"

I thought fast. "The way it worked," I said, "Aunt Loma would let the baby nurse her a few minutes. Then she'd milk herself into a bottle. Then while Mama went to work feedin' Campbell Junior with a eyedropper, Granny would wrap the pig up and take it in to Aunt Loma, to get her stripped good. After that, I or Mary Toy, one, had to take the pig and feed it some cow's milk with a baby bottle so it wouldn't starve to death. We had a three-ring circus goin' there for a while."

"What happened to the pig?" asked Lee Roy as we crested a hill.

"Granny cooked him."

"Taste all right?"

"Nobody could eat him," said I. "But from then on Campbell Junior got fatter and fatter, and it's all on account of Aunt Loma havin' so much milk from gettin' started good with that pig."

"How come nobody's heard all this till now?" Pink said after while. He had laid down back there in the hay. "I cain't figure you knowin' something that good, Will, and keepin' it to yourself."

"Papa said I couldn't go fishin' for a year if I told it," I lied. "Which reminds me, don't *y'all* tell it, or what I said about Miss Love and Grandpa, either." All of a sudden I was real worried about what Miss Love would think if she heard it, but they all crossed their hearts and hoped to die.

It was really something to make up an outlandish story like that. I thought up another one right off, but needing a little time to work it out, all I said was, "Maybe I'll tell y'all about Aunt Loma and the rubber busts."

"The rubber what?" asked Smiley.

"Aunt Loma's rubber bust set that she bought for her weddin'. But y'all got to promise not to repeat it."

They like to fell out of the wagon promising, but I said let's wait till we stop to eat. Right off, Lee Roy commenced saying how hungry he was, though it was only ten o'clock.

"Me, too," said Dunse. "I'm starved. Wonder what Miss Rachel put in the basket?"

We soon saw an old wagon road that led up to a lonesome chimney and on to a shady creek. As we turned off the highway, I said, "I'll tell y'all just one fact that's important to the story. Until Campbell Junior was on the way, Aunt Loma was flat as a battercake, so to speak. Before she got married, Grandpa used to say he never could find a towel; Loma was always makin' herself a bosom or a bustle, one."

First we had to tend to the mules and Miss Love's racehorse. Then while Dunse pulled out Cudn Rachel's basket, I got shet of my clothes and jumped in the creek. I was hot, for one thing, and also I'd been remembering a floating trick Blu Jackson told me about last fall. He said you won't sink if you stretch your arms out on the water like Jesus Christ crucified, or like ten minutes to two on a clock. Well, it worked, by gosh. I felt like I was on a mattress. When I made my body straight and stiff, even my toes rose out of the water.

"Bet cain't any of y'all float this good!" I yelled. They all took off their clothes, waded in, and laid down on the water, but their feet and legs sank straight down as usual.

It made Smiley mad. "You just layin' in shallows, Will. You ain't floatin'."

"I am, too. It's deep here. Come feel." And he did, whooshing his arm under my back to make sure. I rocked like a boat, my toes still sticking out of the water.

"You ain't never floated like that before," said Pink, still suspicious.

I tried making a pillow out of my hands, putting them under the back of my head, and that worked even better. Closing my eyes, I could of gone to sleep if the boys hadn't pounced on me and sent me under.

Without bothering to put on clothes, we opened up Cudn Rachel's picnic and ate, sitting on the mossy creek bank with our feet cooling in the water. When I finished, I lay back, feet still in the water, and said, "Now I'm go'n tell about Aunt Loma and the rubber busts!

"Well, when Aunt Loma was go'n get married," I began, "she ordered her this rubber bust set from Sears and Roebuck, but she couldn't get'm blowed up. It was nearly time for the weddin' and she couldn't get the bicycle pump to work, so she ast me to do it." I sat up, splashing my feet in the cool water. "Said she'd pay me a dollar. Also said she'd kill me if I told anybody."

"Specially us, haw!" said Pink, raising on one elbow to chuck a rock at a hickernut tree.

"Well, so I blowed'm up. But then I took a needle and stuck this little bitty hole in the left bust. It went *pssssssssssst* all through the weddin' and Aunt Loma had a flat by the last I-do! You never in your life saw a bride as mad as her, or one holdin' her bouquet as high up."

"She yell at you, Will?" Pink asked, grinning.

"She couldn't. The preacher was still marryin' them. But boy howdy, she shot me a look! She was so mad that when Uncle Camp had trouble pushin' the ring on her finger, she jerked her hand away and put it on herself. Uncle Camp is sort of a mouse, you know. When Aunt Loma fusses, he looks pitiful and says, 'I'm sorry, Loma Baby.' After they were man and wife, I heard him whisper, 'Loma Baby, what did I do?' "

We all guffawed and hawed.

"As you can imagine," I added, "I stayed out of the way till they got on the train to Tallulah Falls."

I didn't say so to the boys, but Aunt Loma thought Camp had made reservations at a nice honeymoon hotel, whereas he planned on staying with his aunt. He said they could go see the falls just as good from her house as from the hotel, and a whole lot cheaper. It turned out his aunt was a widow woman with ten children, living in a nasty, rundown old cabin on a turkey farm where you couldn't get to the privy without stepping in turkey mess. Aunt Loma stayed ten minutes and, holding her nose, said she was taking the next train home.

Before they left town, though, she dressed up in her first-day outfit and got a street photographer to snap a honeymoon picture of her and Camp smiling at each other in front of the biggest hotel in Tallulah Falls. But when the picture finally came in the mail, it wasn't her and Uncle Camp. It was another couple.

Getting mixed up by the photographer seemed to be the last straw. Aunt Loma was not only mad at Camp, she was furious at Granny and Grandpa for not forbidding the marriage. And now that she was stuck with it, she was mad at Mama for having married so much better than her. Despite Camp had grown up in a tenant shack, she thought he knew what was meant by coming up in the world. Now she knew he didn't.

27

We rolled into Cold Sassy about five o'clock that Saturday evening. As we neared my house, I said real solemn, "Now if y'all tell about the pig or the bust set, I'll catch heck." As if it was a casual afterthought, I added, "And don't tell your folks about Miss Love stayin' in the comp'ny room at Grandpa's house. Because if you do—" I glared at Pink on the seat beside me, holding the brake post, and then at the others lolling back there in the hay. "Because if you do," I repeated, and they knew I meant it, "I'll make up something and tell it on y'all, if you know what I mean." They hoped to die first.

With my threat hanging over their heads, I trusted them all the time we unhitched and tended the mules, turning them out into Papa's pasture for the night.

I trusted them while Queenie praised and patted the black gelding, which Mama wouldn't even look at. Mama hovered around, asking why did we come back so soon and how was Cudn Rachel and them, did we have a good time and stay cool, were we warm enough at night, and did we have enough to eat. But she didn't ask one thing about the gelding.

I still trusted the boys when we all marched down to Grandpa's house, proudly leading the prancy horse to Miss Love, and helped her put him in a stall. When we were leaving she took my hand and said, "Will, he's just beautiful. Mr. Beautiful, that's what I'll name him. Thank you so much. Thank you."

All the time we were unloading the covered wagon, I believed the boys wouldn't tell on me. I still believed it while I took a bath. But about time I sat down to eat, it came to me with a sinking feeling that probably everything I'd said was being repeated right now all over town.

I wasn't too worried about Aunt Loma. Those were whacking good stories, if I do say so myself. And everybody would know they were made up. I'd made up things before. Anyhow, it would be worth a whipping to see Aunt Loma's face after she heard.

What made my stomach sink was knowing I had betrayed Miss Love. Folks would already be sniggering about those separate rooms. It was a strange thing to me that the same people who condemned her on her wedding day for taking advantage of an old man's loneliness would be condemning her now, just ten days later, for denying Grandpa his rights.

We were hardly through supper before here came Miss Sarah Gordy, saying I ought to be ashamed. Mr. French being Granny's stepbrother, his wife felt like they were kin and had a right to speak up in the family. After blessing me out, she took Mama in the house to tell her in private what all Mrs. Snodgrass said Smiley said I said. As they came out, Mama was nodding in agreement. "You're absolutely right, Miss Sarah. This time Will has gone too far."

After Mrs. Gordy left, Mama made me go to my room while she told Papa what Miss Sarah said Mrs. Snodgrass said Smiley said I said. Mama's furious voice drifted up from the porch, and pretty soon Papa came to the bottom of the stairs and hollered for me to get down there. He was already taking off his belt when I came out my door.

After the whipping, Papa said, "Son, we go'n go out to the barn, you and me. I think it's time I told you a few things."

Boy howdy, at last. But it was just another lecture about respecting ladies. "It's not fittin' to make jokes about a woman's—uh, womanhood," Papa began, looking stern. "If you got to show off before a bunch of boys by makin' up tales about a woman's—" He sputtered, unable to say the word. "Well, if you got to make up a story, Will, for heaven's sake don't pin it on anybody that anybody knows."

All in all, I came out about even on Aunt Loma that night. One beating and one lecture was about right for two good stories that would be told for a long time by old men playing checkers under the Cold Sassy tree at the depot. If Aunt Loma was mad, which she would be, that suited me just fine.

The next day at Sunday dinner, Papa had hardly finished serving the baked hen when my mother said, real pleasant, "I wonder who played the piano for the Methodists today."

"Miss Effie Belle," said Aunt Loma. Picking a curly red hair out of her sweet potato sooflay, she dropped it daintily to the floor. "They say there were lots of wrong notes and she played pretty slow, but they got by. Will, start the gravy. Don't just let it sit there."

Scared Aunt Loma might switch from Miss Effie Belle's piano playing to my camping trip, I asked, "Why didn't Miss Love play?"

"She wasn't there. That's one reason."

Aunt Loma sounded like she'd just been weaned on a lemon.

Mama said maybe Love went to the Baptist church with Grandpa.

"If they came, I didn't see'm. Did you see'm, Camp?"

I said maybe Miss Love is sick.

"She's sick, all right," answered Aunt Loma, talking around a bite of chicken. "After two years of showin' off at the piano, your Miss Love has found out the Methodists can do without her. A committee of ladies went callin' on her last week, Will, to let our new Miz Blakeslee know that a married woman is expected to behave herself."

"It wasn't like that," protested Papa. "The ladies just—"

"—told her they didn't need her to play for preachin' anymore," Aunt Loma said, looking smug. "She tried to act like it didn't matter, but I bet after they left she threw things and cried her eyes out."

"Loma, you listen here—" Papa said sternly.

"Don't worry so, Brother Hoyt. What we're sayin' is in the bosom of the family." She looked straight at me then. "Unless Will here decides to tell it on his next campin' trip."

Just by the way Papa jabbed his spoon in the sugar dish, I knew something was coming. But he stirred his coffee good and put the spoon down before exploding. "I don't know why you're so happy about all that, Loma. Your pa sure ain't. Now I want you and Mary Willis both to hush up talkin' about her."

"You cain't make the whole town hush up, Brother Hoyt."

"Well, y'all don't have to join in. What's done is done, and we go'n live with it and be nice." I knew and they knew he was saying we got to remember which side our bread is buttered on down at the store, and who is buttering it.

"Brother Hoyt's right, Loma Baby," Uncle Camp said boldly. "We need to—"

"Oh, shut up, Camp, and pass my coffee cup to Sister. I just want a half a cup, Sister. Brother Hoyt, Love is the one you ought to say hush to. After her tirade down at the store last week, how can you think it's just me and Sister keepin' the town talkin'? It's mostly her."

"Your daddy don't see it that way," said Papa. "He says Miss Love's bein' tarred and feathered for what ain't nobody's business

but his and hers." I was dying to ask what
Miss Love said at the store, but I didn't dare.

Nobody spoke the rest of the meal except
to say the gravy sure is good and please pass
the muscadine jelly.

Mainly to get out of Aunt Loma's way before she could catch me alone and fuss about
the rubber busts and all, I hurried to the pasture right after dinner. Papa wanted me to
get the team and the wagon back to Banks
County. Just as I was backing the mules into
place on either side of the wagon tongue,
here came trouble in the form of Grandpa
Blakeslee.

Seeing him with short hair, and without
that big droopy mustache and bushy gray
beard, I was surprised all over again. I swear
my granddaddy didn't look more'n eight or
ten years older than my daddy.

It was the expression on his face that made
me uneasy, and the sharp edge on his voice.
"You fixin' to take thet rig back out to the
country?" he asked.

"Yessir." I kept my eyes on the strap I was
buckling. The leather was still damp from
yesterday's mule sweat.

Grandpa didn't speak again for a minute.
Then he said, "Yore daddy says you go'n stop

by Temp's place on the way back and see
Mary Toy."

"Yessir."

While I hooked the traces, Grandpa asked
did my mother change her mind yet about
going to New York.

"No, sir. Not as I know of. . . . Move
over, Red!"

As I fastened the last strap, out there in the
hot sun with the mules snorting and stomping
and twitching off green flies, he finally said it.
"Will Tweedy, I'm plumb shamed a-you."

I didn't have to ask why. I just stood there
wondering who told him what I said about
Miss Love taking over the company room. I
even wondered how it was phrased to him.
"Grandpa, I was just tryin' to—"

"I ain't inner-rested in what you was
a-tryin' to do. What you done was bad
enough. You done made a laughin' stock out
a-Loma agin."

Loma?

Grandpa was mad about what I told on
Aunt Loma?

"Now she does bring a lot on herself," he
was saying. "Loma's so hateful sometimes
I'm sorry to have to claim her. But you don't
make her no nicer by outsmartin' her ever

few days or makin' fun of her. Them stories
you told ain't so, and ain't fittin' to be told on
no lady. Loma may be hateful, but she lives
decent and you ain't a-go'n talk bout her like
thet no more." He spat his tobacco juice
close to Big Red's front hoofs. "You hear
me?"

"Yessir." I felt about as low as O.K. Dun-
bar crawling home drunk at midnight. I
couldn't honestly say I was sorry, but I hung
my head.

I figured Grandpa would turn then and
stalk off, but he didn't. After ordering me in
no uncertain terms to apologize to Aunt
Loma, he put his arm around my shoulders.
"I sure want to hear bout thet campin' trip,"
he said with a rough tenderness in his voice. I
felt like the sun had just come out.

"We had us a swell time, Grandpa!" There
wasn't any use saying otherwise. It's bad
enough to be miserable on a camping trip
without telling the world. Lighthearted now, I
put one foot on the wagon axle, whistled for
T.R., and swung myself to the driver's seat.
The dog jumped up there beside me, landing
so hard—*zomp!*—he liked to knocked me
over.

"Old T.R. knows you better be gittin' on

if'n you go'n be home fore dark," said Grandpa. Then, squinting up at me, he went to talking like I had all day long. "We held church up at the house this mornin'.""

"Sir?"

"I was the preacher, Miss Love was the pi-ana player, and the both of us made up the congregation. Hit was a real nice service." He enjoyed seeing I was confused. "Wish you'd a-been there, son. We sang us some hymns, after which I talked to the Lord a while, tellin' Him bout the week, and I then preached a sermon. Tell you the truth, I think I upset Miss Love."

"Sir?"

"I didn't have no words thought out, you know, so I jest commenced sayin' thangs I been a-thinkin' on lately—bout the Virgin Birth and Resurrection and all like thet. I said don't any a-them thangs matter. Well, Miss Love like to had a fit. Said she warn't raised to think like thet. I said I warn't nei-ther, but thet didn't keep me from thinkin', and I ast her do Methodists interrupt and ar-gue with the preacher or do they sit and listen to what he's got to say."

"Gosh, Grandpa. You mean you don't think Jesus rose from the dead?"

"I'm a-sayin' thet did He or didn't He ain't important, son. What's important is thet when the spirit a-Jesus Christ come down on them disciples later, they quit settin' round a-moanin' and a-tremblin', and got to work. They warn't scairt no more, and the words they spoke had fire in'm. Compared to a miracle like thet, Jesus rollin' back a dang rock and flyin' off to Heaven ain't nothin'.'"

"What did Miss Love say to that, Grandpa?" I was real excited.

"Nothin'. I didn't let her interrupt me agin. I said thet same miracle is still a-happenin', right here in Cold Sassy, in July of nineteen aught-six. A crippled person or a invalid, or the meanest thief or the most despairin' misfit, why, if'n he can ketch aholt of the spirit of Jesus Christ, he can quit bein' scairt and be like risin' up from the dead. Once his soul gits cured, no matter what his body's like, why, he can start a new life. Well, next I preached bout the Virgin Birth. To my thinkin', the birth ain't the dang miracle. Hit's the fact thet a boy like Jesus was born to a mama who could leave Him be. Well, and then I talked to Miss Love bout Eternal Life. As you know, son, jest believin' we go'n live

forever in the next world don't make it so—
or not so."

I felt awful. "Grandpa, you don't think
Granny's gone to Heaven? She ain't Up
There waitin' on us to come?"

"I like to think so, son. If'n they is a
Heaven, she's Up There, I know thet," he
said softly. Then he laughed and slapped his
hand on Satan's rump. "Ain't but one way to
find out if she is or ain't, though. And I'm not
thet curious." He sighed, spat, and said,
"Havin' faith means it's all right either way,
son. 'The Lord is my shepherd' means I trust
Him. Whatever happens in this life or the
next, and even if they ain't a life after this'n,
God planned it. So why wouldn't it be all
right?" He looked dead serious, then all of a
sudden laughed again. "You know, if'n I was
a real preacher, Will Tweedy, wouldn't nobody come to my church."

"I would, Grandpa."

"Well, I ain't shore bout Miss Love. She
was expectin' the Lord to strike me down this
mornin'. When I finished preachin', she
brought in some lemonade and pound cake
and I said it was the best Lord's Supper I ever
et, and she didn't like my sayin' thet one bit.
Said it was blasphemy. When I wanted to sing

some barbershop harmony, she called it sacrilegious, bein' Sunday, but fine'ly I got her
goin' on the pi-ana and we had us a real good
time. Ever church ought to do thet—give
God a good time stead of po-mouthin' and
always be astin' Him to save us from temptation and sufferin' and death. If'n you live,
Will Tweedy, you go'n be tempted, and you
go'n suffer, and you go'n die. Ain't no way
out of it. But with the Lord's hep, you can
stand up to temptation, and live th'ew the
bad times, and look Death in the eye. You
remember what I say, son."

"Yessir. But I'd still like to hear you explain Jesus sayin' ast God for something and
you'll get it. One time I prayed for a million
dollars, to test Him, and didn't get one
dime."

"Thet was jest wishin'. Hit warn't prayin'."

T.R. had long since jumped down to chase
something, and the mules were restless, but I
liked being with Grandpa like this, just him
and me. I didn't want him to quit talking.
"Did Miss Love think it up? I mean havin'
preachin' at home?"

"Naw, son. I did. I—well, I expect you

heard bout them Methodist ladies comin' to see her last week?"

"Yessir."

"Figgered you would." His tone was hard. "Miss Love was the maddest white woman you ever saw bout thet. She come down to the store a hour or so later and blessed out the whole dang town. Then yesterd'y she got a unsigned letter in the mail. Well, it warn't a letter, jest a old newspaper clippin' bout fallen women. Hit said thangs like 'A female by one transgression forfeits her place in society forever.' Miss Love cried all night last night."

Poor Miss Love.

"This mornin' she put on her Sunday clothes, but then she got to cryin' and carryin' on agin. I said to her, 'Miss Love, why'n't you stay home?' She said, 'I can't. They'll know I care.' So I put it to her plain. 'Miss Love, what *good's* it go'n do, mad as you are? If'n don't nobody speak to you or sit by you, you jest go'n be mad all over agin. We got a piana. Let's have preachin' right here. Jest you and me.'

"Well, son, we had a heap better time than the dang Methodists, I gol-gar'ntee you. I unner-stand Miss Effie Belle played for them

today. She's worse'n yore granny for losin'
the place." Grinning, he smoothed his pencil
mustache with one finger. "I made dang
shore Miss Effie Belle got a earful when she
got home. I said, 'The Lord loves a joyful
noise, Miss Love, and here comes Miss Effie
Belle up her walk. I want you to play "Ta-Ra-
Ra-Boom-de-Ay" and rattle the rafters! Then
she can tell it all over town how we dese-
crated the Sabbath.' And, son, Miss Love was
mad enough to do it! The sound like to
knocked Miss Effie Belle over. . . . Well, I
reckon you really had best git started."

I bet Miss Love's bosom really bounced
while she rattled the rafters. I wondered if
Grandpa noticed. Naw, he wouldn't.

"Miss Love's already a plumb fool bout
thet hoss, son," he said then. "Come up
home t'morrer sometime, hear, and see can
you hep her with him."

"Yessir," I said, but I wasn't happy about it.
I didn't know if I could face her.

As the wagon rolled into the street, I
thought how Granny would have enjoyed
their preachin' service. If it could of been the
three of them, I mean. Granny used to strike
as many wrong keys on the piano as Miss Effie Belle. And she'd sing while she played,

holding on to each note with her voice till she could find the next one with her fingers. As far as I know, she and Grandpa never sang together, just the two of them. But whenever Miss Love came for a family dinner, Grandpa would ask her to play hymns, and we'd all sing, and nobody enjoyed it more than Granny.

One thing I knew as the mules pulled out into South Main, I was not going to apologize to Aunt Loma. I'd just have to owe her one.

Turning onto the Banks County road, I was thinking what a difference a week can make. Before we went to the mountains, I felt sure Miss Love would tell me everything that happened while I was gone. I even planned to ask her did Grandpa find out about her kissing Mr. McAllister. But now I didn't think she'd ever tell me anything personal again. Even if she did, I wouldn't know what to say to her, or what not to say, or how not to say it, because now she wouldn't trust me.

"Giddy-up there!" I yelled, reaching for the whip. "I ain't got all day, dern you. Git up, Red! Git up, Satan!"

As we rattled toward the Banks County line, what really puzzled me was how come Grandpa blessed me out about Aunt Loma but didn't say pea-turkey about my discussing him and Miss Love with a bunch of snotty boys. Gosh, it must be he hadn't heard! Folks would snigger behind Grandpa's back but not many would dare repeat it to his face. They knew that hard fist.

I didn't find out till night that Miss Love sleeping in the company room just wasn't news anymore. While us boys were up in the mountains getting our food snatched by bears and cooking our goose and all, she had announced it herself!

28

"I'm beginnin' to hate her with a passion," Mama said, and I hadn't a doubt who she was talking about.

Papa was still down at the church, making up his treasurer's report, so it was just Mama and me out there on the veranda in the dark, trying to get cool. I was bone tired. Not from walking the ten miles from Grandpa Tweedy's farm. That wasn't anything. It was from the camping trip. It had finally caught up with me. At the Sunday night preachin', my eyelids had been like heavy little windows flipping open and shut.

With me sitting in the swing and Mama in the tall porch rocker, she launched into a tirade about desecration of the Sabbath. "That Woman and your granddaddy were singin' dance songs at churchtime this mornin', Will. Miss Effie Belle heard them. Anybody who don't know or care if it's Sunday has to be common as pigs' tracks."

"Grandpa ain't common, Mama." I didn't dare say Miss Love wasn't common.

"It ain't him. It's her. He never did such a thing when Ma was alive, and you know it."

"Grandpa said they were havin' church," I told her. "Just him and her, Mama, in the parlor. He prayed and preached a sermon and they sang hymns and all."

"Aw, shah. You call 'Ta-Ra-Ra-Boom-de-Ay' a hymn?"

"That was after, Mama. They had church first."

Her chair stopped rocking. "How you know so much?"

"He told me all about it." I slapped at a mosquito, and the chains at the top of the swing jangled.

Mama rocked fast for a minute, then

stopped dead. "Speakin' of common, did he tell you about Miss Love havin' a fuss with Miz Predmore down at the store last week?"

"Well'm, he mentioned it in passin'."

And so she told me. I knew she hoped it would make me quit taking up for Miss Love Simpson. "Miz Predmore was on the Methodist committee about the piano playin'," Mama began. "After they called on her, Miz Predmore stopped by Pa's store and was pickin' out some piece goods when here came Miss Love, hair done up fancy and dressed to the nines in a red dress and a straw hat with big red flowers on it." Mama's fan was just a-goin'. "Imagine, wearin' a red dress in public when the fam'ly's in mournin'."

Folks had criticized Miss Love the week before for wearing black as if she was grieving for Granny. Now she was awful to wear red.

As Mrs. Predmore told it to Mama and she told it to me that night on the veranda, Miss Love had flounced into the store like she owned it. She came in smiling big at two farmers who wanted Papa to extend credit for a new mule, and then greeted Mr. Cratic Flournoy, who was complaining of indigestion. Just as Camp walked in, carrying a glass of water clouded with baking soda for Mr.

Flournoy, Miss Love spied Mrs. Predmore back near the millinery table, looking through bolts of cloth.

"Good morning, Mrs. Predmore!" she called, smiling her big wide-mouth smile as if Mrs. P. was her best friend and like she hadn't seen her in a week. Naturally Mrs. P. didn't speak or smile back. Fixing her mouth like saying prune, she just went on studying the piece goods.

But Mr. Flournoy, always the gentleman, lifted his glass of soda water in greeting and, as Mrs. Predmore reported later, "spoke to that hussy like she was a queen or something. Hitched up his pants over that big belly and practically bowed to her. Said, 'Mornin', Miz Blakeslee. How's the bride?' "

"Fine, sir. But, uh, I have decided not to use Mr. Blakeslee's name, Mr. Flournoy," said the bride, speaking pleasant but formal, and loud enough to be heard in the piece-goods department. "Of course that is now my legal title, but for personal reasons I prefer to be addressed in the usual way." While Mr. Flournoy and everybody else, including Grandpa, stared at her, she flashed them all a great big nervous smile.

Grandpa was standing behind the counter,

his one hand resting on the cast-iron string holder. Miss Love turned to him and said in a flirty voice, "Mr. Blakeslee, don't you agree it's not appropriate for me to be called Mrs. Blakeslee?"

A funny look came on Grandpa's face. Everybody could tell he was surprised. But he just shrugged his shoulders and laughed. "If you say so, Miss Love." Then he changed the subject. "I reckon you need some hep with yore millinery stuff. Camp, go git some a-them clean pasteboard boxes for our Miss Simpson here."

There wasn't much conversation in the store while Miss Love gathered up her hat-making gee-gaws. The way she threw things in the boxes, though, it began to dawn on everybody that, underneath the smile, Miss Love was boiling mad. Mrs. Predmore knew why, of course. The others could only guess.

When Miss Love and Uncle Camp went out to load boxes in the buggy, Mrs. P. put in her two cents' worth about a wife not using her husband's name. She thought Grandpa would welcome her opinion, but he just laughed. Acted like the whole thing was a big joke. "I look at it like this, Thelma," he was saying when Miss Love came back in. "Long as she cooks good and ain't aggravatin', I don't really care what she calls herself. Ain't thet how you see it, Hoyt?"

Papa was embarrassed and didn't know what to say. Miss Love didn't seem to notice. ("Too brazen to even blush," Mrs. Predmore told Mama.)

But a storm was brewing inside Miss Love. I figured later she was mad not only about the church piano stool being jerked out from under her, but about her whole life: having a drunkard for a daddy, getting jilted by Mr. McAllister, and being looked on in Cold Sassy as a Yankee outsider.

Still and all, she might not of gone as far as she went if Mrs. Predmore hadn't stalked over to Grandpa and let out exactly what she thought of him and her, both.

"Mr. Blakeslee, y'all ain't got no respect for the fam'ly or for this community, either one. It ain't decent, marryin' the way y'all done, with Miss Mattie Lou just barely dead."

It was like the smile on Grandpa's face dropped right off on the floor. "Don't you bring up Miss Mattie Lou, Thelma." He banged his fist on the counter. "And don't preach at me, or Miss Love, either."

Miss Love said, "For your information, Miss Thelma, we aren't indecently married. We aren't married at all." Giving her time to gasp, she added, "Except legally."

"Now ladies, now ladies . . ." sputtered Mr. Flournoy.

Miss Love didn't even hear him. With her chin in the air, she said, "I keep house for Mr. Blakeslee, and that's all. In case you don't get my meaning, I'll say it plain: I'm sleeping in Mrs. Blakeslee's company room. It is not my plan to take her name or her place, except to cook and wash for Mr. Blakeslee and keep the—"

"Shet up, Miss Love!" ordered Grandpa.

She blazed out, "Don't you ever say shut up to me!"

"Hit ain't nobody else's bizness!" He was furious.

"I'll hush when everybody quits talking about me. And that won't happen till there's nothing else anybody can wonder about. Now, Miss Thelma?" She drew a deep breath and spoke like her words were sorghum syrup. "Be sure and repeat everything I've said. Tell it all over town. But do try to keep the facts straight."

During all this, the two farmers pretended

to be looking at some hardware and Mr. Flournoy kept waving his hands and saying, "Now ladies . . . now ladies . . ." And Mrs. P. kept dumping insults like she was emptying slop jars: "Love Simpson, you don't make no more sense than a chicken with its head cut off. If you're just comp'ny, like you say, and don't even want Mr. Blakeslee's name, how come you bothered to get married? I hear that up where you come from, lots of white servants stay with the fam'ly they work for."

Grandpa banged his fist again and yelled, "Thelma, you git outer my store!"

"I'm gettin'!" she shouted. "And I ain't comin' back, neither!"

Miss Love called, "Miss Thelma, let me say one thing more—"

"I ain't listenin'. It's trashy talk."

"Don't you want to know what I'll get out of this arrangement?" Her voice was impudent, but Papa told Mama she looked tired and her lips trembled. Papa said he felt sorry for her right then. As Mrs. P. paused near the door, Miss Love said, "Wait a minute and I'll tell you."

"Shet up, Miss Love!" Grandpa demanded again.

"I know what you gettin'," Mrs. Predmore retorted. "You savin' yourself from goin' single file all your life and havin' Miss on your tombstone. But bein' a wife in name only, and not even usin' the name . . . Well, you really still just a old maid, ain't you?"

"He has deeded me the house," said Miss Love.

It took a few seconds for that to soak in. Mrs. Predmore put one foot out the door and said, "Well, call you Miz Greedy! First you grab Miss Mattie Lou's husband, then you grab property that should rightly be Loma's and Mary Willis's!"

Miss Love didn't answer as Mrs. P. marched out.

I need to say that for a long time Miss Love never answered those who called her Miz Blakeslee. Some folks who hadn't planned on speaking to her at all started saying, for meanness, "G'mornin', Miz Blakeslee!" But the only ones she spoke back to were the few who called her Miss Love or—for meanness—Miss Simpson.

Pink Predmore told me that what really burned his mother up was the way Mr. Blakeslee got to laughing. She heard him say, "Doggit, Miss Love, I'd shore hate for you to

git mad at me. Wouldn't you, Hoyt?"
Grandpa didn't give Papa time to answer before he added, "In case Thelma don't pass
the word around, Miss Love, maybe you better git up at the next ladies' missionary society meetin' and say it agin. Or take out a personal advertisement in the *Cold Sassy
Weekly*."

"The word will get around," Miss Love
said, bitter.

After Pink's mother left the store, she went
across the street to Clark's to get her mail,
and was just coming out when Miss Love
swept from the store with the last of her
boxes and climbed into the buggy. As Mrs.
Predmore put it, "She clucked at that silly
mule like he was a horse, and drove off like
that old buggy was a gold coach."

Miss Effie Belle was in her yard hanging
out clothes when Miss Love got home. She
told it around, with great satisfaction, that
"That Woman was just a-cryin' all the time
she unloaded the buggy. And late that night I
seen Rucker pacin' the brick walk in Mattie
Lou's rose garden. The lamp in Miss Love's
room went off around midnight, but Rucker
was still out there in that garden, walkin' back
and forth, forth and back. I could see him by

the moon. Pore Rucker, I reckon he was so upset after Mattie Lou died, he didn't hardly know what he was doin', marryin' That Woman. So I can forgive him. But not her. She could a-had the decency to refuse his proposition. Instead, she latched aholt. A grievin' man just ain't no match for a schemin' woman. Specially a pretty one."

29

I agreed with Mama: there was just no excuse for the way Miss Love acted. No nice lady would pick a fuss in public like that, much less tell anybody and everybody her personal business. What on earth got into her?

Somehow it brought to mind the time I helped Smiley Snodgrass blow up a hen with a bicycle pump. We like to died laughing, watching that bloated chicken wobble around like a dern balloon. It's far-fetched to compare that to Miss Love blowing up Cold Sassy, but I'm saying it's one thing to embarrass a hen and another thing entirely to embarrass a family and a whole town.

Neither Mama nor I said much for a while.

Just sat there on the porch in the dark, waiting for Papa. While the tree frogs croaked
and the porch swing creaked, it came to me
that there might not of been a fuss at the
store if I'd told what Miss Love said the day I
helped her clean up. Gosh, I'd felt so set-up
and proud, her confiding in me like I could be
counted on to keep my mouth shut, and all
the time she must of been hoping I'd scatter
her words broadcast like turnip seed.

Probably Miss Love thought Mama and
them would take her right on into the family
if they knew she wasn't a real wife and that all
she'd ever get out of Grandpa was the house
and furniture—not the store, not the farm
lands or his other houses or the railroad stock
and the cottonseed oil company stock.

Of course it could be she just needed to
talk to somebody who was kind and understanding. If not me, who? Miss Love didn't
have one close friend in Cold Sassy and no
doubt was lonesome, being used to working
around people at the store.

But tell the truth, she'd been lonesome
ever since she hit town. Cold Sassy took pride
in being hospitable to outsiders, so Miss Love
had always got her share of invites. But she
was still an outsider and acted like one. De-

spite being friendly and lively, like Grandpa she had always held a part of herself back. Closemouthed, they called her.

So it just didn't make any sense at all for Miss Love to tell me about the arrangement unless she hoped I'd go home and set Mama and Aunt Loma straight—and through Aunt Loma, the whole town. If I was right about that, I'd sure let her down.

But now that Miss Love had declared war on Cold Sassy, where did that put me? Right smack in the middle that's where—between Grandpa on the one side and Mama and Cold Sassy on the other. I knew I still wanted to be her friend. Lord knows she needed one. And I couldn't help liking her. But I hated taking her part against Mama and them.

Papa was right. The family would just have to let bygones be bygones, and be nice no matter what.

That night Miss Love declared war on the family, too. She fired the opening shots at Aunt Loma.

Mama and I were still out there on the porch, waiting for Papa, when here came Loma and Camp—her carrying the baby, him carrying Granny's big mirror with Saint

Cecilia painted on it. Boy, was Aunt Loma mad!

They had gone up to Grandpa's house straight from Sunday night preachin' at the Baptist church. "To pay a friendly Christian call, Sister. I was go'n try and show Pa that we weren't holdin' hard feelin's," said Loma. "Quit that, Campbell Junior." He was fretting and grabbing at her face.

"But Mr. Blakeslee warn't to home," Uncle Camp put in as Aunt Loma plunked herself down in a porch rocker, unbuttoned the shirtwaist of her mourning dress, and let the baby nurse.

"Love said Pa had gone to the store to make up his order," said Loma. "Workin' on Sunday, Sister! He never did that when Ma was alive."

"He sure didn't." Mama was disgusted.

"Well, after Love lit a lamp in the parlor, we all sat down. She took Campbell Junior and played with him a while, but then we just sat there. Sister, if Miss Love isn't a Yankee, she sure acts like one. You know the way they can sit for hours and nobody say a word? Drives you crazy. Finally I said isn't it a hot night and Camp said how much we could use some rain. Then I ast if she'd found out what

was wrong with the horse Will brought her. I
mean, you know, why would Cudn Jake give
him away like that? Instead of answerin', she
ast would we like some refreshments.

"With her gone to the kitchen, we could
take a good look at the parlor. Sister, you
wouldn't believe how she's changed things
around. 'You sure have changed things
around,' I said when she came in with lemonade and pound cake. But I spoke real nice,
didn't I, Camp? I did tell her she better close
the blinds every mornin' and keep the sheets
on the loveseat and all. I reminded her about
sun fadin' things."

"What'd she say?"

"She said she likes mornin' sun and doesn't
intend to close the blinds at all. I ast her was
that all right with Pa, her lettin' the sun fade
Ma's things. She said she hadn't ast him."

Camp's voice spoke up in the darkness.
"She shore does make a good pound cake, I'll
say that for her. Loma Baby, I wish you'd
make me some pound cake."

Loma Baby ignored him. "Then she offered to show us her room. She picked up the
lamp and started across the hall, but I said,
'I'd like to see Ma's room, first.' 'All right,'
Love said, 'but all I've done in there is sweep

and dust. Your father wants it to stay just like Miss Mattie Lou had it.' "

"Maybe you hadn't ought to dust even," Camp told her. "Where somebody has died is a sacred place. Even the dust is sacred."

Miss Love had laughed at him! Said, "Camp, that's the silliest thing you ever said. Dust is dirt. There's no such thing as sacred dirt, for heaven's sake."

"The nerve," said Mama, "talkin' like that to Camp."

Shifting Campbell Junior to her other side, Loma said softly, "Well, we went in there, and Sister, it looked like Ma was still livin' in that room. Their weddin' picture on the wall over the bed, you know, and Ma's hair not even combed out of the brush, and her glasses still on her Bible on the night stand. . . . Love hasn't even thrown out that dried-up old rose in the bud vase. I hate dead flowers. I said, 'Love, you could at least throw out that old rose,' but she didn't answer me. Well, then I saw Ma's blue beads in the pin tray on the dresser."

"The weddin' beads that Pa gave her," Mama said, her voice choking a little. "We should of buried her in them. You know, Loma, I never saw Ma without them till the funeral. Did you? I'd sure like to have those beads."

"I already got'm, Sister," Aunt Loma said with an I-bid-first tone in her voice, and pulled them out of her pocket. "I told Love I wanted those beads and she said to ast Pa. Said she couldn't give permission. That really made me mad. 'I don't need your permission,' I told her, and I just prissed over and got them. 'Just tell Pa I have them.'

" 'You tell him,' Miss Love snapped, high and mighty, and hurried back up the hall to light the way to the company room.

"Sister, you ought to see what she's done to the comp'ny room." Aunt Loma was jealous, I could tell. Listening to her, I felt jealous myself—for Granny's sake, I mean. Granny used to talk about fixing things nice but never had the time or the money, either one. Loma said the board walls in there were painted a bright yellow, and everything else was white: mantelpiece, door and window frames, iron bed, night stand, dresser, wardrobe, wicker chair—all white. There were ruffledy yellow and brown checked curtains at the windows and the same cloth was on the ceiling, glued up there like wallpaper.

Mama hooted. "Cloth on the ceiling? Who ever heard of paperin' with cloth!"

"I have to admit, it looks right nice," said Loma. "I ast her did Pa do all the paintin'. She said, 'Where would he find the time? I painted it myself.' Said she liked to paint. 'That's man's work,' I told her. I couldn't hep it; I said, 'Love Simpson, you remind me of a crowin' hen.' Well, anyhow, Sister, she's put Ma's tulip quilt on her bed. And she's got that little yellow, orange, and brown plaited rug beside the bed—the one Grandmother Toy made. And Ma's 'Yard of Yellow Roses' picture is hangin' over the mantelpiece. I told her, 'I want that picture. Miss Pearl Lozier copied it for Ma and I want it.' "

"What did she say?"

"She didn't answer, so I just let it go. I'll ast Pa for it later. I tried to remember that I was down there to be nice, pay a Christian call. So I inquired politely about the tintypes and photographs on the dresser. Who they were, I mean. One was her mother, and one was an old lady who raised her. A cousin, I think. At least she hadn't put out a picture of her Union Army daddy for Pa to have to look at. Well, Sister, then I spied a stirrup under the bed! I figured the silver saddle must be under there! But just as I bent down to look, Love said, 'Let's go back to the parlor where we can sit down.' Going across the hall with the lamp, she said, 'I have no family at all now. They're all dead.' "

Mama blew out a breath. "Well, that's a relief."

Back in the parlor with nobody talking, Loma had had time to consider the situation. "The more I thought about it," she told us, "the madder I got. I mean the way she has just taken over. All of a sudden I said to her, 'Love Simpson, I cain't hep sayin' you sure got your nerve, movin' Ma's rooms around like this.' Camp said, 'Loma's right, Miss Love.' You know what Love said to him, Sister? She said, 'Campbell Williams, it's not your place to tell me anything.' I said he had more right to speak out in the fam'ly than she did. She said, 'Not in my house.' I said maybe it was her house, but it was still Pa's home. Boy, that shut her up."

Then Aunt Loma told Miss Love there were some things she wanted. "Things of Ma's. I don't mean old clothes and letters and ragged quilts like you sent over. I mean—" She almost lost her nerve, she told us, but had barged on. "I'm talkin' about things like the piano. I want the piano."

If she had said she wanted the whole house, I bet Miss Love wouldn't of been more shocked. "Why in the world would you want the piano, Loma? You don't play!"

"That don't keep me from wantin' it. Every house needs a piano."

"Well, you can't have it. I'm sorry."

"I'll ast Pa for it. He'll give it to me. He gives me anything I want."

"Go on, ask him! It won't do you any good." Miss Love was trembling, she was so mad. But she calmed down some and said, nice enough, "But maybe there's something else you want, Loma. Anything I can't use, you're welcome to it."

There was a silence till Uncle Camp spoke up. "She wants that mirror," he said timid, pointing behind the loveseat where "Saint Cecilia at the Organ" had been leaned against the wall.

"Shut up, Camp," Loma said. "I'm not go'n ast her for anything. I'll ast Pa."

"He'll just tell you to ask me," said Miss Love. It was too bad she hadn't made it clear that day at the store that Grandpa deeded her the furniture, too. She proceeded to make it clear to Aunt Loma now. "Maybe you don't know I own everything in this house."

Aunt Loma said she stood up so fast that the rocking chair nearly turned over backwards. Camp stood up, too, and so did Miss Love. "I ast her, 'Have you got that in writin', Love Simpson?'"

Miss Love said coldly, "Are you telling me your father would go back on his word?" Then she went over and pulled out the Saint Cecilia mirror. "Here, Camp, take this. I hate it. But, Loma, over my dead body you'll get the piano!"

And that's how the second Mrs. Blakeslee, alias Love Simpson, declared war on the family.

30

The next morning I was sitting in Miss Love's kitchen, eating hot apple pie and cheese and hoping she wouldn't pick a fuss with me like she had with everybody else. If she did, or if she got to raving on about Cold Sassy treating her bad, I was go'n say, "Ma'am, I just remembered. Papa told me to paint the iron fence today. I better get on home." If she brought up that mess about keeping her maiden name, I'd say, "I reckon you got a right to, Miss Love. But it's foolish if you care a hoot about Cold Sassy acceptin' you as Grandpa's wife—or his housekeeper, either one."

I didn't get a chance to see if my nerve would hold up to my indignation, because she was just nice as you please. Besides that big piece of pie, she fixed me a glass of lemonade and some for herself, and sat down to talk. She asked right off how was the camping trip, which made me uneasy, I tell you.

"We had a swell time," I said. Taking a big slurp of lemonade, I changed the subject. "You sure make good lemonade, Miss Love."

"Well, I've got plenty. Help yourself."

"One time I ast Queenie why she drinks tea out of a quart Mason jar instead of a glass, and you know what she said? Said, 'Mr. Will, dat fust glassful always be's de bestis, so I makes it jes' big as I can.'" I laughed the way white folks always do when they tell something funny a colored person said.

Miss Love laughed, too. Then she said,

"But of course you know the real truth about that, Will."

"What you mean?" My pie fork paused in midair on its way to my mouth.

"I mean colored cooks know white people don't want them using their dishes and things. That's why they all drink out of jars and eat out of old plates or pie pans."

"Ma'am?"

"Well, does Queenie use the same plates as the family?"

"Course not, Miss Love. It ain't the custom."

"And what's Queenie's joke about that?"

The color rose to my face. Clearly Miss Love didn't understand. Despite she wasn't exactly a Yankee, she was from way north of Cold Sassy. Before I could change the subject, she said, "Queenie uses an old knife and fork at your house, too, doesn't she, Will? And always washes them and her pan and her jar last—just before the dog and cat dishes? That's the custom, isn't it?"

"Queenie doesn't care what she eats out of, Miss Love. No more'n she cares if pot licker runs off of the turnip salad and soaks her biscuits, or if the cream gravy gets all over her mashed sweet potatoes. She likes usin' a pan. It holds more'n a plate." Being an outsider, Miss Love couldn't understand that Queenie really just didn't care. *Yankee,* I thought, burning. *Yankee, Yankee* . . .

It was a hot day, but there came a chill in the air as I finished my pie. Miss Love chopped up two big carrots and put them in her apron pocket, along with some shriveled little yellow apples out of Granny's bowl on the work table. Then she reached into Granny's old brown crock for some sugar lumps.

She tossed me one.

I wasn't a child. She couldn't make up to me with a dern sugar lump. "I'll save it for the horse," I mumbled, dropping it in a pocket of my overalls.

Miss Love took a green print sunbonnet of Granny's from a nail in the kitchen and we headed for the barn. Old T.R. sprang up from under Granny's boxwood, where he'd been cooling off, and ran ahead of us to chase Granny's dominecker hens out of the path. I didn't say a word all the way to the barn.

"Look, there he is!" Miss Love pointed to the gelding. He was cropping grass in the back pasture not far from Grandpa's mule. Mr. Beautiful raised his head and stared at us, and Miss Love squeezed my arm. "He's just so handsome, Will—that shiny black coat, and the white blaze on his forehead! And look how he holds his head!" I don't think she even noticed she had touched me, but the pit of my stomach might near flipped over.

Looking toward us, the horse sniffed the wind, started walking, then quickly picked up his gait to a fast trot. As he got near the barn, he shied at a rock in the grass, stumbled, rared up, and raced away, tail arched high. But he was soon back, nickering and snorting as he pranced sideways toward the pasture gate we were leaning on. Then he shot off again like an arrow.

Miss Love put her hands to her mouth, as if she couldn't believe him. She said softly, "That's got to be the fastest horse in Cold Sassy. Maybe the fastest in Georgia . . ."

"Yes'm." Pride rose up in me for being the one that had brought him to her.

Every time the gelding came near, Miss Love held out a piece of carrot. Finally he stopped, walked slowly toward her, stopped again, came closer, and, glistening with sweat, stretched his neck to get the carrot. His breathing was hard. "Come here, Mr. Beautiful, I won't hurt you. Here, baby," she murmured, holding out an apple.

"Boy howdy, I cain't hardly wait to see that fancy Texas saddle on him!" I said. She blushed, as if she thought the saddle might remind me how she'd kissed Clayton McAllister. I blushed, too, because it did remind me of that. I said quickly, "Ma'am, I hope you ain't forgot. That horse ain't broke to anything but a halter. You won't try to ride him any time soon, will you?"

"I wish I dared. But no, I'm still just making friends. Here, boy," she called, walking along the fence.

"A big horse like him, he could kill you."

She met my eyes with her gray-blue ones and the long dark lashes didn't even flutter. She said, "Mr. McAllister taught me all about training horses, Will. It's done in definite stages. I helped him train the mare that was" —she hesitated—"the mare that was to be mine after we married. The one the saddle was made for."

Yeah, I thought, and I bet you kissed Mr. McAllister between every sugar lump and apple, and hugged him every time the mare did what you wanted her to. I hated Mr. McAllister.

I wished Miss Love would touch me again.

She didn't. It was the horse she kept touching. She rubbed his ears and his neck, talking soft and holding tight to the halter. Soon as she let him go, he was off again across the pasture.

We watched him a few minutes, then walked back toward the house. We were about even with Granny's flower pit when I stopped and asked the question that had been on my mind ever since I got there. "Does Grandpa know . . . I mean did anybody tell him about, uh, about the way Mr. McAllister, uh—"

There was an empty minute before she came right out with it. "Kissed me?" Her face was hidden under the bonnet, so I don't know if she blushed. But I did. "As a matter of fact, Will, somebody did tell Mr. Blakeslee."

"It wasn't me, Miss Love, I swear. Must of been Miss Effie Belle."

"Maybe she did. I don't know. But I told him first."

"You?" I couldn't believe any lady was that dumb. I said I bet he'd already heard.

She waved a honeybee away from her face. "No. This was on Saturday night after Mr. McAllister was here. And if he had heard, he'd have said so as soon as he got home. Your grandfather is a very direct man, Will."

"Yes'm, he is."

"Still, I kept thinking what if he does know. I got nervous as a witch, wondering. But all he talked about at supper was the horse. Which stall it could have, which day you might get back with it, things like that. And he asked what did I know about breaking a horse. I could see he didn't know one thing about it himself."

"When did you tell him, Miss Love? About —you know."

"At one o'clock Sunday morning. We both went to bed early, but I just tossed and turned. I was so nervous I thought I'd scream. Finally I decided my only hope was to be honest and tell him myself, before you . . . I mean before Miss Effie Belle did, or somebody else."

"You called him out of bed? He don't like—"

"I just went to his door. It was open—for the breeze, you know. I stood there holding my lamp and called, 'Mr. Blakeslee?' He said, 'What you want? What's wrong?' So I told him how Mr. McAllister had barged in and was kissing me before I knew what was happening—and that Miss Effie Belle probably saw it. I said I'd pack up and leave as soon as it got light."

I kicked my bare foot at a bunch of tall grass. I had a glimmer of something I didn't like. Sounding bolder than I felt, I said, "Why'd you offer to leave, Miss Love? I thought you were hopin' if you were honest about it, he'd let you stay."

"Well, yes, Will." A wry little smile lit her face. "But I guess I thought I should at least offer to leave."

"Did you cry, ma'am?"

I think she sensed what I was driving at. Hesitating, she admitted she cried a little.

"What'd Grandpa say?"

"Nothing, for a minute. Then he told me to go to bed. 'Mr. McAllister's on the train to Texas, Miss Love, so that's the end of it. Effie Belle or no Effie Belle.' Then he raised up on his elbow and said, 'Now if'n you want to see me mad, Miss Love, jest let me git up for breakfast and you ain't made me no yeast bread like I ast you to.' "

We both laughed, ambling on toward the house. She said, "Tell the truth, I had forgotten all about making that bread. I was . . . well, it had been an awful day, as you know,

Will, and I was worn out. But I went to the kitchen and got at it."

"In the middle of the night?"

"Yes. The oven was still warm from supper, so I mixed the dough and set it in there to rise. About three o'clock I got up to knead it, and at five I fired up the stove. I had the bread baked and toast ready when Mr. Blakeslee came in to breakfast."

I had to admire any lady that anxious to please.

Well, in all of that talking, Miss Love hadn't mentioned me gossiping about her on the camping trip, or her being taken off of the Methodist piano stool, or how she told off Pink Predmore's mama down at the store. She hadn't spoken Aunt Loma's name, much less Saint Cecilia's. But she'd told me the one thing I needed to hear if I was to keep coming up here: that Grandpa knew about her kissing Mr. McAllister. As long as I was wondering whether he knew or didn't, I'd of been worrying about what he might do to Miss Love when and if he found out, and how she would act toward me if she thought I was the one had told him.

On the back porch, she picked up the tin

dipper that floated in the well bucket and started to drink.

"Here, I'll draw you some fresh, Miss Love," I said, emptying the bucket into the wash pan. With the well right up by the porch, I only had to lean over to let the bucket down. When I heard it splash, I turned the crank to draw it up and, feeling that I was being what Aunt Loma called gallant, offered Miss Love the first cool drink.

"Why, thank you, Will." She drank from the dipper, then poured her leavings on a pot of begonias. "And thank you for being my friend."

Gosh, Miss Love sure knew how to make a boy feel like a man. Dipping up some water, I was careful to put my mouth where hers had been. I watched her over the rim of tin.

She hesitated as if trying to think of something to say, then asked, "Tell me, Will, uh, don't you think your mother will go on to New York City after all?"

"No'm. She ain't go'n go," I said as we left the porch and entered the cool hall. "She planned big on it all spring, you know. But not since Granny died."

"Are you very sure she won't change her mind? It would do her good to get away from here." Miss Love really cared about Mama, I could tell.

"Yes'm, I'm certain sure. Papa keeps tryin' to talk her into it, but she won't change her mind. She says it wouldn't be fittin'. Uh, I expect you been plenty times, ain't you, Miss Love? New York ain't all that far from Baltimore."

"I went just once. When I was a little girl." She smiled kind of wistful.

I reckon Miss Love was pure starved for company, because when we got to the front veranda, she sat down in the swing, patted the cushion beside her, and said come sit a while. "You went to New York with your daddy one time, didn't you, Will?"

"Yes'm, when I was seven, and I sure was glad to get back home. I'd heard about damn-yankees all my life, and up there I was in a city just full of'm."

Miss Love really laughed.

"I been on lots of other trips with Papa," I bragged. "When I was ten, he took me to Atlanta just to ride a new street-car line to College Park and back. Another time we went to Atlanta to hear President Roosevelt. The speaking was in a place called Piedmont Park. Afterwards we took a street car to Davison-

Paxon-Stokes Company, and then went to M. Rich and Brothers. You ever been in that store, Miss Love?"

"Oh, yes. They have very fashionable clothes."

"Yes'm. Well, while we stood outside lookin' at their show window, a man dressed up in a Sunday suit came out and greeted us. Then he opened the door wide, bowed to Papa with a big flourish, and said, 'Enter, sir! The store is yours!' It was Mr. Rich himself. Later I ast Papa why didn't he and Grandpa dress nice like that to go to work, and do like that. Bow, I mean, and open the door and say, 'Enter, sir, the store is yours.' Papa said, 'Cause if we did, Cold Sassy would think we were off in the head.'"

Miss Love was very entertained. "I guess you've been lots of places with your grandpa, too," she said, rubbing a chain link on the swing with her finger.

"No'm. He took me and Mary Toy to Maysville one time in the buggy to visit Aunt Fody, his youngest sister. The year he went to the Homer Celebration he took me, and since we were already halfway to Cornelia, we went on to see Aunt Clyde, his oldest sister. But Grandpa don't really like to go places.

Last time he went to Atlanta was to General John B. Gordon's funeral, and that was two or three years ago. General Gordon was a Confederate general, you know."

"Well, your grandfather is so full of fun, I expect he has a grand time when he goes to New York for the store."

"I don't know'm. He ain't been since before you moved here. He feels about it like me; they got too many Yankees in New York. He said one time he'd just soon go to the bad place. That's why Papa's always the one goes on the buyin' trips."

I didn't find out till next morning that Miss Love wasn't just passing the time of day talking about New York City. She'd had an idea. An idea that just about tore our family to pieces.

31

With no inkling of what was to come, I left there on top of the world. I just had to do something, for gosh sake. So I decided to go apologize to Aunt Loma like Grandpa told me to. Not that I was regretting those titty stories. I was just in the mood to enjoy hearing Aunt Loma fuss and fume.

Every now and again she didn't react like I thought she would—for instance, that time she got Papa to make me paint her dining room. After I finished, I caught about ten of her cats, dipped their feet in the can of gold paint, and chased them around in the empty room. Boy howdy, the floor in there looked like a dern leopard skin! I expected Aunt Loma would be furious, but she said what a darlin' idea. Thought I'd done it to please her.

Well, she wouldn't be clapping her hands about the *psssssssssssst* and pig stories, which by now would be coming at her from every direction. She'd like folks saying what a bad boy I was, and how dirty-mouthed, but it would get her goat when they asked, "Loma, did you really nurse a pig?"

Her not fussing at me yesterday at Sunday dinner didn't mean she hadn't heard. She was just too busy low-rating Miss Love to fool with me. And last night she was too upset over not getting the piano.

And now as I came up on her back porch, Aunt Loma was the maddest white woman you ever saw. Her face was red. Her blue eyes spat fire. Her fists were clenched and her voice harsh. "I'm so mad I could die, Will!" That was her greeting. Boy howdy, I thought. But it wasn't me she was mad at. She said, "Come look what Camp's done now!"

Jerking up Campbell Junior from the kitchen floor, where he sat sucking a greasy chicken bone, Aunt Loma marched ahead of me to the parlor and pointed at the mantel-piece, gleaming with a new coat of hard shiny white enamel paint. "Just look!" she exploded.

"What's wrong, Aunt Loma? I think it's a big improvement."

"Go look. You'll see."

I looked and I saw. Without wiping off the mantelpiece at all, Uncle Camp had painted around a tin matchbox and right over a cockroach, a pencil stub, and a shirt button.

Trying not to laugh, I said, "Why didn't you make him get it up before the paint dried? Ain't nothin' harder than enamel paint."

"I only just noticed it, that's why."

"It's go'n be a job to scrape it off."

"I don't want it scraped off. I want Camp to be reminded how dumb he is every time he comes in this parlor. Will, I cain't bear to think I'm married to somebody that stupid."

"He ain't that stupid," I said, trying to make her feel better.

"Then he just don't care, and that's worse."

"Maybe he did it on purpose."

"You're crazy. He wouldn't have the nerve."

"Maybe he ain't got any nerve when you get to fussin' at him, Aunt Loma. But that don't mean he couldn't do this on purpose."

Her face flushed. She knew I was calling her bossy. "You know good'n'well if I didn't keep after him, he wouldn't ever do a blessed thing."

"Yeah, but that don't mean he likes bein' pushed around. And maybe for once he's showin' it. I feel right proud of him, Aunt Loma. Maybe you ought to be, too."

"Well, aren't you smart! I guess you got that notion from Miss Love Simpson Blakeslee. I'll thank her to keep her mouth shut, especially to you."

"Ain't nobody ever said nothin' out loud bout you henpeckin' Uncle Camp, Aunt Loma. It don't take much brains to notice, though. If you treated a colored cook like you do him, she'd quit."

"Colored folks got more sense than Camp. Lord, Will, I had to show him the roach before he knew what I was mad about."

I would of laid a bet that when she got on him about it, Camp had looked down at the floor instead of at the mantelpiece. I bet he said, "I'm sorry, Loma Baby. I'm sorry."

I hated how he was and how she treated him.

"Grandpa said I had to apologize about those stories I told on you, Aunt Loma. So I'm apologizin'."

"Pa told you to?"

"Yeah, he did."

She looked real pleased. "Well, now! I never thought he'd take up for me against you, Will."

"He was mad as heck about it, tell you the truth. So I'm sorry. And soon as you finish bawlin' me out, I got to go."

She set the baby down on a plaited cotton rug by the fireplace and spoke sternly. "All right, I'll bawl you out: How dare you say I nursed a pig!" Then she giggled. "Will, you're awful. You ought to be ashamed. But my land, I haven't enjoyed anything this much since I left LaGrange College. It's almost like playin' the lead in a theatrical. Campbell Junior, come out of the fireplace! Get him, Will. He'll turn black before our eyes if he gets into that chimney sut."

I picked the fat baby up and swung him around. He squealed with pleasure. "You're your mama's little piggy, ain't you, Campbell Junior?" I held him high above my head and he squealed again. "So part of what I told wasn't no pig tale." Aunt Loma laughed. It was like we were having a party. I put Campbell Junior on my shoulder and rode him around, then tossed him up.

"Will, I've decided. . . . Will, are you listenin'? Put the baby down and listen to me."

"I'm listenin'." I tossed him one more time and put him back on the floor.

"I've decided you ought to be a writer, Will. Those stories you told on me, they're outlandish, but they'd be so easy to act out. Those and all the other stories you tell. Will, I want you to write plays." She said it as solemn as if she was a queen knighting me with words.

I couldn't hide how pleased I was. I grinned from ear to ear. Still and all, why couldn't Aunt Loma just be nice and compliment me and let it go at that without saying what I had to be. Long as I could remember, she'd been trying to direct me like I was one of her dad-gum Christmas pageants.

It gave me some satisfaction to say "But I'm go'n be a farmer. You know that, Aunt Loma, unless you ain't ever listened to me talk. I'm go'n go to the Ag College over at the University. Papa's aimin' to buy Grandpa Tweedy's farm, and I'm go'n farm it."

"Anybody can be a farmer," she said, flipping away my dream. "We cain't let a talent like yours go to waste, Will, and I want you to start by putting down those stories you made up about me. Do it right away, before you forget them." She blushed a little. "I don't mean I think you could sell'm. They're too—well, most editors would call them vulgar. But they'll do fine for writing practice."

If I had pos-i-*tive*-ly decided to be a writer and at that moment had picked up a pencil to get started, I'd of put it down. I just couldn't stand her telling me what to do. "I don't like to write stories," I said stubbornly. "I just like tellin' stories. But ain't nobody go'n make me do either one. Specially not you, Loma Blakeslee Williams."

Campbell Junior was crawling from her to me and back from me to her, but Aunt Loma didn't even notice him. All of a sudden she stood up and started singing, "Here comes the bride, dog bite her hide." We had sung it like that when we were children. Then she *dum-dummed* the rest of the wedding march. I didn't guess what she was doing till she made like she was adjusting a veil and mouthed I do and all, and then went *pssssssssssssst.* Her eyes rolled with mock alarm and her hands quickly hid one side of her chest. Then she doubled up laughing. I was laughing, too. Campbell Junior must of thought we were a couple of hyenas.

"How in the . . . world . . . did you think up such a . . . thing as a . . . *rubber bust*!" She couldn't talk for ha-ha-ing and hee-hee-ing.

I was shocked that Aunt Loma had come right out and said *bust* in mixed company, but that just made it funnier. Between guffaws and gasps we moaned and clutched our stomachs. The poor baby sat staring at us, then dropped his chicken bone and commenced squalling. To her credit, Aunt Loma picked him up, sat down in the rocker, and unbuttoned her dress for him. I always watched close when she did that, hoping she'd be careless, but she never was. Like all the other nursing ladies in Cold Sassy, Aunt Loma would turn sideways to her audience or else cover herself with the baby, and also drape a clean diaper over herself.

I got up to go, but she told me to wait till she could put Campbell Junior down for his nap. She hummed the wedding march while she rocked him, only sometimes she had to press her lips together to keep from laughing out loud. "Is there any such a thing, Will?"

"As what?"

"As . . . well, you know. If there is, I sure wish I'd heard about it in time for my weddin'!" And we both died laughing again. Except it was quiet laughing, so as not to distract the baby from nursing. In a few minutes she sat him up and he let out a loud belch.

"I really got to go, Aunt Loma."

"Oh, you can wait another minute. I got something for you." She laid Campbell Junior down on the rug by the fireplace, a clean diaper under his fat face, and he was asleep by time she came back downstairs, carrying a thick book.

"I made this before Campbell Junior was born." She flipped open the book, which had cloth-covered cardboard covers and blank pages inside. "I was go'n copy all my poems and plays in it. But as you know I never have a minute to call my own now." Her voice a little hard, she nodded toward the sleeping baby. "So I want you to have it, Will."

This was the nearest Aunt Loma had come to being nice since I was a little bitty boy, and I liked it, despite I also felt like she was trying to railroad me. When I hesitated, she held the book out to me. "You must write something in it every day." She nodded to cement her words. "Write down the stories you make up. Write poems and plays. Write down things that happen, and surprising things you see or hear about. Listen when people talk, and put their words down just like they speak. If you go'n be a writer, you got to practice, that's all there is to it. My professors preached that to me all the time at LaGrange College." Aunt Loma never missed a chance to mention LaGrange College, where she had studied elocution and expression.

"Well . . ." I took the book and flipped through the blank pages, then handed it back. "But I done told you, I ain't go'n be no writer. You be one."

"Fat chance," she said, bitter. "Camp won't ever be able to afford a cook. Not while he's workin' for Pa. And I cain't write without hep. I know that now. So you just do what I

say, Will. Quit arguin'. Here, read this."
Opening it to the first page, she forced the
book into my hands again. "Look at this."

At the top of the page, in fancy printing, it
said LOMA BLAKESLEE WILLIAMS, HER BOOK. Under that it said PRESENTED TO HOYT WILLIS
TWEEDY, JULY 1906. "Do like I say, Will. And
when you get famous, don't forget to mention
it was your Aunt Loma that pushed you toward your destiny."

Bossy, same old bossy, I thought. But I was
touched. And all of a sudden those empty
pages were like the si-rene call I'd heard
when I looked up at Blind Tillie Trestle and
wanted to see how it was up there. I knew I
wouldn't write any dang poetry or plays. But
right that minute I got the notion I'd like to
keep a journal.

It's been eight years since Loma gave me
that book, and not long ago I read through all
I wrote down on its blank pages. That's why I
can remember so much that happened to
Miss Love and Grandpa, and what went on in
the family and the town, and what people
said and how they said it, and how I felt when
it was happening. Reading my notes in the
journal brings it all back.

* * *

I never knew before that Aunt Loma could be fun to be with—that, like Grandpa and me, she preferred three-legged chickens to the usual kind. What really surprised me was finding out I liked her. At least, that day I did. She was Grandpa all over again. She was hardheaded like him, wanted her own way like him, and had a sense of fun to match his. But of course she was mean and vindictive in a way Grandpa wasn't. At least that's what I thought right then.

Not till the next morning, when the matter of the trip to New York came to a head, did I suspect he had a mean streak that put Loma's in the shade.

32

I was still laughing in my mind at supper that night, like if Aunt Loma was there beside me going *pssssssssssssst.*

Then Mama asked about the trip to New York City. "What day is it you are leaving, Hoyt?" In her black cotton dress she looked like warmed-over despair.

"Two weeks from today, hon." As Mama

cut a bite of roast beef, looking pitiful, Papa
reached across the table and put his hand on
her hand that held the knife. "Mary Willis,
hon, come with me. It'd be . . . well, like a
second honeymoon."

She blushed, but looked him straight in the
eye. "I wish I could, Hoyt. It sure hasn't been
any honeymoon around here for a long
time." She bit her lip, I guess to keep from
saying anything against Grandpa or Miss
Love that would upset my daddy. Then she
kind of jerked, like people do at church trying
to shake themselves awake. "You know I
cain't go, Hoyt. It would scandalize the
town."

Thinking with my mouth again, I said,
"Mama, how could Cold Sassy be any more
scandalized than it is already?"

Oh, for gosh sake, why did I have to say
that?

But Papa took it up. "I say the same thing,
Mary Willis. Please, hon, come with me,
hear."

It seemed like Mama was weakening.

"Granny would want you to," I urged.
"Not long before she took sick, she told me
how happy she was about you gettin' this nice
trip."

"Did she really say that, Will?" Quick tears came to Mama's eyes.

What Granny had also said, so wistful, was how she used to dream of going to New York with Grandpa, but he never saw why she wanted to. Granny said he always talked like it was just a long, tiring, boring time. Besides, he couldn't afford to pay her way and his, too.

"I couldn't get ready in two weeks," Mama was saying. "All those clothes I made back in the spring, they wouldn't do now. I'd need mournin' clothes. All I got for nice is two black dresses."

"That's all you need," said Papa, getting excited. "There's so many people up in New York, you could wear the same dress every day and nobody'd notice."

"Well, I'd notice and the hotel clerk."

"Listen, hon, I could buy you a readymade dress or two after we get up there. Get'm wholesale."

All of a sudden, Mama's face went from looking like nine miles of bad road to like somebody had left her a million dollars. "Oh, Hoyt, do you really think it would be all right?" she asked anxiously. "People wouldn't talk?"

"They might," he admitted, drinking the

last of his buttermilk. "But Lord, Mary Willis, everybody knows what you been through lately. And it ain't like we'd be havin' a good time or anything. Still and all, there's enough to see and do up there to make goin' worthwhile. Ain't it, Will? You were so little when you and me went, though, maybe you don't remember much."

"I remember a lot, Papa."

"And Mary Toy's taken care of," he reminded Mama. "So all you got to do is get ready. Please say you'll come with me, hon."

Mama hesitated, then all of a sudden smiled and, clasping her hands together, raised them and touched her thumbs to her forehead—a way she had of showing when she was happy. "I've decided! I'm go'n go, Hoyt! I'm go'n go!"

My daddy jumped up out of his chair, came around the table with his arms outstretched, grabbed Mama out of her chair, and kissed her hard. It wasn't like Mr. McAllister kissing Miss Love, but it wasn't the usual peck, either.

As we left the table, Mama asked him, "Hoyt, what do you think about—uh, do you reckon I could ast Miss Love to make me a new black hat? I don't want you to be shamed of me."

"Sure, ast her," said Papa. "Like I keep tellin' you and Loma, she's a nice lady. I know Miss Love, see. She'd be proud to hep you get off. And it might heal things over in the fam'ly."

I joined in. "Miss Love said just today how it would do you good to take the trip."

Mama looked surprised, but was too happy to say *aw shah.*

Next morning at breakfast she was down-right ecstatic. "I didn't sleep a wink, Hoyt! Just laid there turnin' over and over in my mind what I'll pack and what all I got to do. My tail will be in the wind from now till we leave, I know that. First thing, I got to write Temp a postcard and be sure it's all right for Mary Toy to stay on till we get back."

"Maybe we could go see Mary Toy next Sunday," said Papa, sopping up sorghum syrup with his biscuit. "I miss my baby."

"I do, too, but I'm not sure we have time. Besides all the gettin' ready, I got to can some vegetables. If I don't, we'll lose too much. Goodness gracious, two weeks from now I may be too tired to go!" But despite Mama had a lot to worry about, there was a smile on her plain face and a light in her blue eyes that we hadn't seen in weeks.

Right after Papa left for the store, here came Grandpa Blakeslee.

As usual, he headed straight for the company room. His snort must of been pretty strong, judging by the redness of his face when he came out, calling, "Mary Willis? Mary Willis! Where you at? I got something to say."

Mama hurried down the stair steps, wearing a bright smile and carrying her nicest petticoats and nightgowns to hang out for airing. I knew she could hardly wait to tell Grandpa the good news. But before she got a word out, he said, "Mary Willis, since you cain't go to New York with Hoyt, I done decided to go myself. And I'm a-go'n take Miss Love. Ain't no use lettin' thet other free boat ticket go to waste."

Mama looked like a farmer seeing his barn burst into flames. While she stood there trying not to believe her ears, Grandpa said, "Miss Love thinks she can be a big hep in New York. She's go'n pick out the housewares and dress goods, and the ladies' ready-to-wear and all like thet."

"What, Pa?"

He raised his voice. "I said Miss Love thinks she can pick out what ladies want to buy better than a man can. Makes sense, her bein' fashionable and all. Anyhow, Mary Willis, I know Hoyt's go'n be glad not to go. He's been mighty worried bout leavin' you here by yoreself, grievin' for yore ma."

My mother didn't say a word. Just stood there staring at him, and then turned and took her petticoats back upstairs.

I followed Grandpa out the door. Before I could speak, though, he scratched his head hard and fast, like a dog scratching fleas, and said, "I ain't lookin' forward to New York, son, but Cold Sassy's been a-givin' Miss Love a hard time. I figger the trip'll take her mind off a-all thet mess."

"But Mama was—"

"I cain't live with thangs in sech a stew."

He was walking away when I said, "But Grandpa, Miss Love's got the horse. She's so excited about the horse. She don't even care what folks say anymore."

"Thet's what I thought, too, Will Tweedy." He stopped and looked at me. "But last night Miss Love was jest all to pieces. She got to cryin' agin bout thet fuss she had with Miz Predmore while you was gone, son, and said maybe she ought of went on to Texas so I could git some peace. And then it come to her all a-sudden thet her and me could go to New York on them boat passes. Git away for a spell. Now as you know, I ain't much on New York City. But I knowed yore ma warn't go'n change her mind and yore daddy had jest soon not go 'thout her. So when Miss Love kept a-beggin' me, I . . . well, I jest cain't stand to see no woman carry on like thet. I said we'd go if'n she could go cheap and not plan to stay at no fancy ho-tel."

Grandpa plopped his hat on and stalked off before I could tell him that Mama was the one crying now.

It was all my fault. Miss Love had questioned me, trying to make certain sure Mama wasn't going before she put on her act for Grandpa. Well, I'd go tell her how it was, that's what I'd do. She was so kind and understanding, I was sure she wouldn't stand in the way of Mama going.

I was right.

When I got there, Miss Love was in the kitchen at the wash table, scouring pans. Her face was more freckledy than usual, I reckon from being out with the horse, and she'd pulled her hair back in a tight knot. She didn't look pretty. I blurted it right out, how just last night Mama decided to go to New York with Papa after all, "only now Grandpa says you and him are go'n go."

She looked stunned. Her hands were sudsy from the dishwater but she didn't rinse or dry them before plonking herself down at the kitchen table. Her wet fists clenched and a hard look came on her face as the disappointment sunk in. Then she calmed down and said sweetly, "Will, I feel terrible about this. Your mother must go, by all means. She needs to get away. Anyhow, it's her trip."

"I was sure you'd say that, Miss Love, once you knew how it was!" I could hardly wait to run home and tell Mama. When I was halfway out the door, Miss Love asked me what Grandpa said when he found out that Mama had decided to go.

"He don't know yet. Mama didn't tell him."

She seemed surprised. Giving a long sigh, she said, "Then I'll tell him at dinner. This was all his idea, you know. He said Mary Willis definitely wasn't going and it was a pity to waste a free boat ticket. You know how frugal

he is. Well, he'll certainly want your mother
to have the trip."

It struck me how different her explanation
of how it came about was from what Grandpa
said. I guess she was just too proud to admit
to me how it had got to her, the way Cold
Sassy was treating her. The important thing,
Miss Love wanted to do right by Mama, just
like I knew she would.

There's no way she could of guessed that
Mama would say, "No, let Love go on to New
York. Let her have a good time. It don't mat-
ter about me." Miss Love was just sorry as
could be when neither Papa nor I nor Aunt
Loma could talk Mama into going.

Aunt Loma was really furious about it.
Soon as she heard—Camp told her when he
came home to dinner that day—she rushed
over home and ran upstairs, where Mama
was crying in her room. Speaking so loud I
could hear her from the downstairs hall,
Loma said, "Sister, you cain't let Love Simpson go off like that with Pa! You know
good'n'well she'll hope to come back with
more than the latest in housewares and dress
goods."

Mama mumbled something into her pillow.

"She'll try to get you-know-what, that's

what I'm talkin' about. Pa won't pay for two rooms at the hotel and Love knows it. She's prob'ly been tryin' ever since their weddin' day to get him into her bed. This is her chance!"

"Loma, hush up!" cried Mama.

"I mean just what I'm sayin'. And, Sister, if That Woman has a baby, you know good'n'well she'll get her hooks on a whole lot more of Pa's money than she bargained with him for. Sister, you got to go to New York!"

"Well, I'm not. I don't even want to go now. I don't even feel like goin'."

Still and all, if Aunt Loma had kept her mouth shut, Mama might of had her trip. She didn't have a gnat's chance after Loma stormed into the store and gave her daddy down the country, blessing him out right in front of Papa, Uncle Camp, me, and two customers.

Grandpa let her rave till she shouted, "Pa, Love Simpson has earned the disrespect of everybody in town. And now she's go'n get everything she can out of you, startin' with New York City! But you, Pa, you're too blind to see!"

Grandpa held up his hand like a policeman

—to stop her or slap her, I couldn't tell which —and shouted, "Good gosh a'mighty, Loma, ain't none a-this any a-yore dang bizness! Now go on home and be-have!"

Then he turned to my daddy and said in a harsh voice, "Hoyt, I wisht I'd a-knowed last night thet Mary Willis done changed her mind. But now it's jest too late."

I didn't see why it was too late.

I bet Papa felt like crying, or like knocking Grandpa to Kingdom Come and back, and Loma with him. But all he said was, "It's all right, Mr. Blakeslee. I'm sure Mary Willis understands."

Furious, I went back to the storage room to finish ripping open a crate of canned Alaska salmon. A few minutes later Grandpa yelled, "Will Tweedy? You come here, boy!"

As I soon found out, anger at me had been festering in him ever since yesterday, and Aunt Loma's fit brought it to a head. Standing behind the counter, he spoke sternly as I came toward him. "Will Tweedy, ain't I always treated you special?"

"Yessir?"

"Then how come, if'n you aim to be a dang farmer stead a-comin' in the store with me, how come you told it to a dang fool like Lias

Foster? You ain't said pea-turkey to me bout it—you or yore daddy, either one. How you think it felt yesterd'y when I went to braggin' bout you takin' over the store some day and thet fool contradicted me? This here store's made a livin' for me and yore daddy, too, boy, and lots a-other folks. You think you go'n make a better livin' farmin'?"

"No, sir, that ain't it."

"Well, then maybe you think it's something noble to walk behind a dang plow and starve to death on five-cent cotton. Is thet it?"

I looked over at Papa, who was working on the ledger. His face was red as a beet, but he didn't put in a word for me. He was too upset about Mama losing her trip, I reckon, and anyhow he believed in a boy fighting his own battles. Without a word he went outside where the sacks of chicken grits were stacked against the show window and commenced talking to some old men sitting on the bench in the sun. I wished Papa had at least told me what Mr. Lias said I said. Later I found out he hadn't heard what Mr. Lias said I said.

The more Grandpa talked, the madder he got. "Why you want to be a no-count farmer?" he thundered.

"I ain't go'n be no-count, sir. I'm goin' to

the Ag College over at the University and study new methods. I'm go'n make farmin' pay."

"I reckon you think I'll give you cheap credit." He said it sarcastic.

"Yessir, I do." I looked him straight in the eye. "Ain't you always talked like I was the same as your own son?"

A proud grin came on his face and his tone softened. "At least you smart enough to know how to get around me. But doggit, Will Tweedy, I thought you liked store work."

"I like bein' here with you, Grandpa. You and Papa." I couldn't hardly stand it, seeing him let down. "But I'd rather work outdoors, sir. I like makin' things grow. Raisin' animals, gettin' up plants."

I didn't tell him that the reason I first started liking farm work was because I could make fifty cents a day hoeing cotton and fifty cents a hundred pounds picking it, whereas at the store I never even got a thank-you. What I did there was just expected. "Store work ain't excitin', Grandpa. But farmin' is just one great big old dice game. Else why would so many men stay in it, times like these?"

"What else can a farmer do cept farm?

And heck fire, boy, you think they ain't no gamble to runnin' a store?"

"Yessir, some. But not much."

"You think it don't matter if'n I order something thet don't sell? Hit ain't gamblin' if'n I order ten ladies' dresses from New York and find out I could a-sold twenty-five? Answer me thet."

"Well, sir, but farmin's for bigger stakes, Grandpa. A readymade dress or a can of salmon ain't near as big as a bale of cotton or a cow."

That made him laugh. Slapping his knee, he picked up the wholesale order form and I started back to the storage room. Then, with his pencil poised over the form, Grandpa looked up over his reading glasses and asked, "Son, why ain't you said nothin' bout this up to now?"

"I'm always talkin' bout farmin', Grandpa," I said boldly. "Maybe you just ain't been listenin'."

"Well, but you ain't talked bout not comin' in the store."

All of a sudden I didn't feel bold at all. "I reckon I was scared to," I mumbled. "Scared I wouldn't be your boy anymore, Grandpa."

He flushed, and in a gruff voice said, "You

ain't old enough to know what in ding-dong you go'n want to do two-three year from now, Will Tweedy. Here I'm willin' to give you a chance in life and you say you don't want it. Gosh a'mighty, how I used to wish some-body'd give me a hand up. I had to make it all on my own, and it's a hard road, son. Well, time you git th'ew high school, you go'n be glad you got a job waitin' for you here at the store. In the meanwhile, don't be talkin' our bizness to Lias Foster."

Grandpa hadn't heard a word I said. He'd put the whole thing down to my being young and foolish and talking big. Like I hadn't said a word, he was still offering me the store, just like Aunt Loma offered me her blank book. Neither one of them cared what I wanted to be. Well, when the time came and somebody had to give in—him, her, or me—it sure dern wasn't going to be me.

Later I wondered if Miss Love had guessed how the fuss about the New York trip would turn out. Because despite she acted so willing to step aside after I told her the situation that morning, and despite it seemed like she took it for granted Mama and Papa would be the ones to go, when I went up there later that

day to clean the stable, she had some gray
and white striped taffeta cloth spread out on
Granny's dining table and was pinning pattern pieces on it.

The pattern envelope said in big letters:
TRAVELING DRESS.

She couldn't of known then that her trip
was still on, since Grandpa had been too busy
to come home to dinner that day and just ate
sardines and crackers at the store. So who
would of told her she was still going?

It really made me mad.

Still and all, when Miss Love looked at me
and said how sweet I was to come clean out
the stable for her, I felt almost as glad she
was going as I was sorry that Mama wasn't.
Cold Sassy really had been awful about her
kissing Mr. McAllister.

No telling what they'd say about her going
off to New York unchaperoned with a man
she claimed she wasn't really married to. But
at least she'd be away from the gossip for a
while.

Grandpa had sense enough to know what
folks were saying. It was like he'd married
Miss Love in the first place as a practical joke
and couldn't understand why nobody bragged
on him for thinking it up; and now he was

furious because Cold Sassy was saying Miss Love stole Mama's trip to New York.

By next morning Grandpa had found a way to thumb his nose at the whole dang town, so pious and hypocritical: he started giving out invites to Sunday morning preachin' at his house.

When Mr. Predmore came in for pipe tobacco, for instance, Grandpa smiled big and friendly and said, "We havin' preachin' and communion agin at my house come Sunday. Miss Love and me, I mean. We'd be mighty proud to have you and yore fam'ly join us." Knowing he was being taunted, Mr. Predmore didn't answer. "Won't cost you a red cent," Grandpa called after him as he stalked out. "We don't pass no dang collection plate."

Uncle Lige whispered to Papa, "Thet in iteself would be a miracle—hearin' a sermon 'thout havin' to pay for it." Cudn Hope laughed, but Papa looked like he'd just heard heresy incarnate.

Showing off for customers, Uncle Lige kept making jokes about miracles, and Grandpa joked back. "Who knows, Lige, might be we'll even turn water into wine, haw! If'n we do, I'll save you some." Then, waving his arm to include several customers in the store, Grandpa called out like a dern circus barker, "Come one, come all y'all! Be glad to have you. We ain't havin' Sunday school, jest singin' and prayin' and preachin'. Miss Love's go'n make ten pound cakes to take care a-the communion crowd." Whacking a slab of cheese off the round for Thurman Osgood, the dwarf, Grandpa wrapped it and said as he handed down the package, "Join us Sunday mornin', son. We go'n have us a good time."

The church people of Cold Sassy, Georgia, didn't look at Sunday morning as the time to have a good time. As Grandpa expected and intended, they took it like he was making fun of religion, or like he was asking folks to come to a house of ill repute and call it church. People said it looked like Mr. Blakeslee just wanted to make everybody mad. Which he did.

Mr. Flournoy said he and his wife would come, but most folks either acted like they didn't hear the invite or else huffed out of the store without buying a thing.

Finally Papa dared to say "Mr. Blakeslee, folks are mad about you makin' fun of the

Lord's Day. What if they quit buyin' from us?"

Grandpa just laughed. "Ain't go'n happen. You think anybody's go'n hitch up and ride a buggy all the way to Commerce just for twenty pounds a-sugar or a dime's worth a-nails at Hardman Hardware or Williford, Burns, and Rice? Naw, Hoyt. Hit's easy to git mad, but it takes time to go over to Commerce."

What my daddy didn't see was that Grandpa was madder than anybody else in Cold Sassy. Grandpa had thought marrying Miss Love was a cheap way to get a white housekeeper and not be a burden on his daughters, but now the town had changed her from a nice pleasant milliner into a Mad Hatter who cried all the time.

33

Grandpa didn't preach the sermon at his second home church service. He asked Queenie's husband, Loomis, to do it.

Despite all the invites, the congregation didn't swell much that day. Only Mr. and

Mrs. Cratic Flournoy came—probably because they liked Miss Love, but also because they liked to sing and couldn't bear the thought of trying to drag through another hymn with Miss Effie Belle feeling her way over the piano. But they claimed later they went to remind Cold Sassy in general and the Methodists in particular that God loves sinners and forgives them, "and we ought to, too."

Cold Sassy thought Grandpa had really stepped out of bounds, asking a Negro preacher to give the sermon. Old Loomis had preached many a one in the white kitchens of Cold Sassy. If he was bringing in stovewood and noticed a silver spoon that was tarnished, he'd say, "You know, white folks, 'ligion be jes lak dis here silver. You got to keep it polish reg'lar or it don' shine, naw suh."

Every June during the time of our school exhibition, the graduating class gave orations and dialogues on Friday night. Then on Saturday night the colored would make money for their church by putting on a show for us white folks. First they'd have a Negro minstrel, then a Negro sermon by Loomis, all dressed up in his dingy white vest, black pants, jim-swing black tailcoat, and beaver hat. Later, after the spirituals, Loomis and old Uncle Lem would put on a debate, all in fun. Old Lem always took the "nigitive" and Loomis the "infirmity." I remember one time the evening ended with Loomis saying, "You know, white folks, when a man cast his bread pon de waters, it gwine come back buttered toast, praise Jesus." Passing his hat, he joked, "Tonight, I repersents de waters. So cast yo bread on me an' de good Lawd gwine bless yo gingerosity." Everybody laughed—and Loomis made some extra money.

But everybody knows there's a difference between a colored preacher preaching in a white kitchen or at the Negro entertainments and the same man preaching in a white parlor. Nobody blamed Loomis. He worked at the store, so he had to do what he was told. But Cold Sassy felt like Grandpa was slapping the town in the face, all over again, and nobody doubted Miss Love had put him up to it.

The Flournoys told it all over town, what Loomis said at the end of his parlor sermon. "Mr. Rucker, sir? Miss Love? Y'all scuse me fer sayin' so, but y'all white peoples knows better'n to ack lak dis. De Lawd God wonts peace mongst His peoples. He say git on back to yo own church an' quit dis here foolish-ment."

I, for one, had a lot rather been hearing Loomis up at Grandpa's house than listening to the Presbyterian preacher saying what's go'n happen to you if you dance, play cards, or spend your money on "adorn-ments," like fur coats. There wasn't a fur coat in Cold Sassy, but any time he talked about sin he brought up fur coats.

Mama and I weren't really listening that morning, though. We were worrying about my daddy. He had stayed home, and he wasn't sick.

Papa had been trying his best to cheer Mama up ever since the Tuesday before, when, as Aunt Loma put it, "Miss Love grabbed Sister's ticket to New York." Wednesday at breakfast he even offered to take Mama to Atlanta for the day, but she said, "Hoyt Tweedy, I'm not bout to be disre-spectful of the dead for just a li'l old seventy-mile trip."

The next night he actually stayed home with her instead of going to the Presbytery meeting. That worried Mama. She said, "Hoyt, you haven't missed a meetin' since you had the flu ten years ago. What will people think?"

He touched her cheek, real tender, and said, "I'm tired, Mary Willis. I thought maybe you and me could go to bed early tonight."

"Aw, shah, Hoyt," she said impatiently. But then she put her arms around his neck and her head on his shoulder and cried.

Friday morning Papa had taken the train to Atlanta. "Business," he explained, but wouldn't say any more. When he got home late that evening, he was all smiles. After breakfast Saturday morning, when Mama wiped her mouth for him to kiss her good-bye, he kissed her twice and then came back and kissed her twice again.

I wasn't the only one wondering what he was up to. Queenie said, "Lawd Jesus, Mr. Will, yo pa he ack lak he got a dimon ring in his pocket!"

Queenie fried a chicken and cooked up a mess of vegetables for dinner that day, but I don't think Papa knew what he was eating. He talked a mile a minute the whole meal. He was so chock full of news, Mama nor I could get in a word. "Oh, by the way, Will," he said, forking a drumstick onto his plate. "A mill girl came in the store today to buy some black goods for a dress. Said her daddy died. She ast if I knew you."

My heart thumped hard. "Did she say her name?"

"No. But she was a pretty little thing, and clean."

"Tow-headed?"

"Ain't they all tow-headed?" Papa swished buttermilk in his mouth. I could tell he was watching me. Town people thought you couldn't be too careful when it was a question of your children hobnobbing with mill folks.

"It may have been the girl that hepped me off the trestle. You know, after the train ran over me," I said casually. "She's in my grade at school. Mama, can I have the chicken head?"

"Don't you always?" She suspicioned me, too.

"Well," said my daddy, "the girl ast me to tell you that her and her aunt are go'n take her daddy back home to the mountains for buryin'."

"On the train?"

He shrugged. "I reckon."

Queenie was clearing the table. Papa put out a hand to stop her as she reached for the chicken platter. "Mary Willis," he said to Mama, "just look at that platter!"

Was it dirty or something? Mama looked. Queenie looked. I looked. Near as I could tell, it was just a wing, a back, and a gizzard, laying lonely on the platter. "That's all we have left over," Papa complained. "Queenie, from now on if you fry a pullet this small, fry two."

"Yassuh, Mr. Hoyt!" To Queenie, that just meant more for her to take home. But Papa saw it as his providing a bounteous table.

I did admire his style that day. Some might think what difference did it make, who would know? Well, Queenie knew. And she would tell Loomis and her cousin Sissyretta and all her friends who did yard work or cooked in white kitchens or took in washing or nursed white children. Naturally they would all tell their white folks, and two days from now, everybody in town would know Mr. Hoyt Tweedy could afford more food than he needed.

Papa had always been looked up to in Cold Sassy as a good man with a flair for good living. You wouldn't say he put on airs or pretended to be what he wasn't, but unlike Grandpa Blakeslee, he liked seeming well-off and "modrun." Unlike Mama, he didn't worry about folks thinking bad of him, but he always made sure they thought well of him.

When Papa went back to the store after dinner, he was whistling.

It wasn't till Sunday morning that Mama got really worried about him. After working till Saturday midnight at the store, he always bathed before he went to bed so he could sleep later on Sunday, and normally he was barely up in time to eat breakfast and get to Sunday school. But this Sabbath morning he was already dressed when I went out to milk the cow. I could hear him singing and whistling clear to the barn.

At breakfast, Mama said, "My, you feel good this mornin', don't you, Hoyt?" And she smiled at him across the breakfast table. She looked real pretty in a new black and white striped wrapper, and instead of having her hair pulled back in a plain knot, she had done it up for church in a pompadour.

You can imagine the shock when we got downstairs in our Sunday clothes, ready for Sunday school, and Papa said he wasn't go'n go.

It didn't make any sense. He was wearing his suit and had his Bible in his hand, but there he stood, saying he had to stay home. I noticed his hand shook a little, and his eyes sparkled.

We couldn't of been more dumfounded. Papa was a deacon. Papa was clerk of the session. Papa was church treasurer. Papa couldn't just not go, for gosh sake. While Mama stared at him with her mouth open, I offered to stay home with him.

"You will not," he said sternly. "Y'all go on now. Make haste, or you'll be late." He walked nervously to the door, looked up and down the street, then practically pushed us out onto the porch. When I looked back, he had sat down in the swing and opened his Bible.

Mama was all to pieces as we went down the walk. "Will, do you think he's gone crazy?" she whispered, her face pale.

After Sunday school, folks naturally asked where was Mr. Tweedy. Looking confused and flustered, which she was, Mama said weakly, "He seems to be ailin'." I opened my mouth to say he looked all right to me, but she poked me in the ribs.

When we got to our pew, Mama let me know what her real fear was. "I bet your daddy's up there with Pa and them," she whispered from behind the palm-frond fan she was fluttering like a house afire. I shrugged, which was supposed to mean that couldn't be it.

Tell the truth, that possibility was uppermost in my own mind, even though I couldn't believe it. Papa was anxious to please Grandpa, but not anxious enough to desecrate the Sabbath by singing songs like "Bird in a Gilded Cage" or "Waltz Me Around Again, Willie." Certainly not "Ta-Ra-Ra-Boom-de-Ay."

As the Presbyterian preacher commenced his sermon, I was puzzled by the behavior of Mr. French Gordy, who sat with Miss Sarah in front of us, smelling of soap as usual. He kept turning around during the sermon to grin at us, yet when church finally let out, he rushed past and didn't even wait for his wife, much less stop to ask Mama what my daddy was sick with.

Everybody else did, however. Mama looked embarrassed and upset as she said over and over, "I don't know. I just don't know what's wrong with Mr. Tweedy."

In a minute here Mr. French came back, his ruddy face beaming, and took my mother's arm. "Mary Willis, how I wish your ma was alive to see this miracle! You and Will come outside and look!" When she hesitated, kind of dazed, he pushed her toward the church's big open door. I ran ahead to go see.

If Santy Claus had been out there with his sleigh and his reindeer that hot Sunday morning, it wouldn't of been any more surprising than the sight of Papa grinning like a chessy cat from the driver's seat of a big shiny red Cadillac car! He was wearing a cap and goggles, and his Sunday suit just barely showed under a long linen coat.

The automobile had a black canvas roof, slotted rubber tires, and a brass horn, and was shimmying and shaking and backfiring to beat the band.

"Papa!" I yelled, forgetting I wasn't supposed to holler in the churchyard. Everybody else had forgot, too. I was the first to reach the motorcar, but the congregation quickly crowded around. "Mama!" I called, looking toward the church steps. "Come on!"

Mama stood there on Mr. French's arm like she was looking at a man with a tail. She was pure transfixed, mouth gaping, eyes shining. There must of been thirty or forty people crowded around, and they got quiet just from the sight of her. "Well, I declare. I declare,

Hoyt, don't you beat all!" she said finally, and
then, "Well, I swan. Won't Mary Toy have a
fit!"

There wasn't a Presbyterian in Cold Sassy
who wasn't proud for Mama at that moment.
Something good had finally happened to Miss
Mary Willis.

I opened a back door, jumped in, bounced
on the seat, and started asking Papa questions. With all the engine racket, he couldn't
hear a word I said. He was busy shaking
hands with all the men, anyhow, and getting
slapped on the back and being asked for a
ride.

Boy howdy, that was some morning.

I'm not sure Mama ever would of made it
to the Cadillac if Papa hadn't climbed out
and gone to get her. The crowd parted like
the Red Sea as he led her to his shaking red
chariot. Picking up a new linen coat off the
front seat, he held it out grandly for her to
put on, then draped a big dust veil over her
hat and face, and handed her in. When she
turned toward the congregation and waved,
everybody smiled and clapped.

About then the motor conked out. Papa
was so excited he like to never got it started
again. He cranked, then showed me how, and

I cranked, but nothing happened. "Let me check the directions," he said, reaching in his pocket to take out a little booklet.

It said he had forgot to use the gas feed.

Away we went at last. But we went away lots slower than if we'd had the horse and buggy. Papa hadn't practiced his driving but for a few minutes before church let out, so he wasn't all that sure he could remember where the foot brake was or how much gas to feed. Also, every time he saw a buggy or wagon coming, he had to stop the car and shut off the motor so the horses wouldn't bolt. It was a slow progress till we were out in the country.

As we got to going faster, a grand cloud of dust rose behind us and folks ran out of their houses to watch us go by. Every time we hit a bump or just missed a squawking chicken we'd laugh like children. Boy howdy, what a day! Mama yelled over the racket, "Hoyt, I just cain't believe it! When did you buy it? Can we afford it? Where did you have it hid? Does Pa know about it?"

I kept begging him to let me drive. "Naw!" he yelled. "I better learn how first myself, Will!"

Coming back into town, we passed

Grandpa's house just as he and Miss Love came out on the front veranda with the Flournoys. Big Loomis, who naturally took his communion cake in the kitchen, was just coming around the house from the back door as Papa honked the brass horn and we all waved.

They were too dumfounded to wave back, I reckon, or maybe didn't recognize anybody but me, on account of the linen coats and Mama's veil and Papa's goggles. Papa didn't stop or so much as slow up. It was grand, the way we raced by!

"Oh, won't she be jealous!" Mama crowed when we got home. There was no doubt who was meant by *she*.

I felt real satisfied. I knew Miss Love would love to have a motorcar, probably more than my mother wanted to go to New York City. So now they were just about even.

Which was what my daddy had in mind.

If you'd paid him to do it, Papa couldn't of stood up to Grandpa and argued to get Mama the trip. But he had the nerve to ride by Grandpa's house and not stop.

34

Mama put dinner on the table that day while Papa rode Queenie around the block. After we ate, I started clearing out the barn shed for a garage, but couldn't make much headway for folks dropping by to see the automobile. They admired the shiny red paint, blew the horn, tried out the seats, and of course asked to ride. Some were jealous, I could tell. There is a price to pay for having the first something in town. But Lee Roy, Smiley, Pink, and Dunse McCall were as excited as if it was their folks' car. They asked me all kinds of questions: What's the choke for, and lemme see the toolbox, and how do you start it, and how do you stop it, and how fast will it go.

It helped feelings a lot when, by the next Sunday, Papa and I had practiced enough to take passengers out. Aunt Loma bid first, her and Uncle Camp. Papa took Aunt Carrie home after dinner, then let me drive Pink and them around the block by myself. Later we went and got Miss Effie Belle. Poor old Mr. Bubba, he wanted to go so bad, but Miss Effie Belle thought the excitement would be too much for anybody 102. I think that meant she was scared he might wet his pants.

Papa offered to ride Grandpa around, but Grandpa wouldn't even get in. "A car is a fool dangerous contraption. Worse'n a bicycle," he said. "I speck Miss Love would like to go, though."

Instead of asking her, Papa said, "I just remembered, Mr. Blakeslee, I told Mary Willis I'd be back by now." And we drove off. It was so pointed that I felt embarrassed for Miss Love's sake—but pleased for Mama's.

The next morning I hitched up Big Jack to the buggy and took Grandpa and Miss Love and a mountain of grips to the depot. They would go to Savannah by train and get a boat there for New York City. Standing in the shade of the Cold Sassy tree, I watched their train pull out, then drove Jack home, turned him into the pasture with Miss Love's horse, filled their feed boxes and the watering trough, fed the chickens, and got the Toy family Bible off the desk in the hall like Mama told me to. She had asked Grandpa for it and he'd said shore you can have it, come git it. But Mama thought it best to wait till they left for New York.

I hoped it would be years before she

looked in that Bible and saw how Miss Love had written herself into the family.

I may have said already that on Wednesdays all the stores in Cold Sassy closed for the day at noon. On Wednesday that week, we left in the Cadillac right after dinner to drive out to Cudn Temp's and bring Mary Toy home. The trip was up one hill and down another on humpback roads, two feet deep in dust all the way. Papa worried about dark thunderheads in the distance. Lord knows we needed rain. But if the road got wet, we'd soon be two feet deep in red mud instead of dust. The clouds passed off, though, and we had only one puncture, and everybody at Cudn Temp's like to had a fit about the motorcar. Mary Toy just couldn't believe it was really ours.

The purple had faded out of her hair, but it was still a right peculiar shade of red.

We got home too late for prayer meeting, so after supper the four of us just sat out on the veranda together in the cool dark. Mary Toy was curled up in Papa's lap in the swing, and Mama sat content beside them. Sprawled on the top step, I leaned against a turned post and listened to the swing's slow creaking. It felt like we were a real family again. "I'm

424 OLIVE ANN BURNS

glad you home, Mary Toy," I said, and meant it.

"Will's tired of gatherin' eggs," Mama teased.

"But maybe Mary Toy's forgot how," said Papa, tickling her ribs.

"I ain't, either. Cudn Temp's got a heap of layin' hens. Guess what was in one of the nests, Mama? A great big black snake!"

"Lord hep us!" Mama shrieked.

"He was sound asleep," Mary Toy said. "Just nice as he could be. Me and Sara Christine, we—"

"Sara Christine and I," Mama corrected, but I could tell her mind was on the snake, not the grammar.

"We petted him."

"No!"

"Yes'm, and I put him in my apron and went and showed him to Cudn Temp."

"Lord hep us!"

For a while all you could hear was crickets cricketing and the swing creaking . . . back and forth, back and forth. Mary Toy said sleepily, "Mama, what am I s'pose to call Miss Love? Do I call her Granny?"

"Say Miss Love, just like you been doin'." Mama's voice was hard. "She's not your grandmother by any stretch of the imagination. She's only your grandpa's wife, and there's a big difference."

On Sunday, which was the first Sunday in August, we drove the Cadillac to the Presbyterian church out at Hebron for the annual reunion and dinner on the grounds. Grandpa Tweedy and Mrs. Jones were there, of course, and we took them to ride.

The next Wednesday, Papa took the whole day off and we went to Comer and back, which he thought had never been done before in one day.

If the Cadillac had been a circus elephant, it couldn't of done a better job of taking Mama's and Cold Sassy's mind off of Grandpa Blakeslee and Miss Love.

35

The car was all Cold Sassy talked about, and all we talked about in the family. You'd think Grandpa and Miss Love had just disappeared, instead of being off in New York enjoying Mama's trip. Then Miss Love's picture postcards of Coney Island and Ellis Island started coming.

Most folks who take a trip send postcards. Usually they write, "Having wonderful time wish you were here," or "How are you fine I hope," or maybe just their name. What Miss Love did, she wrote every lady and schoolgirl in Cold Sassy about something special she'd found for her at the wholesale house.

Miss Vada Goosby was so pleased, she came down to show Mama her postcard. It said, "I've picked out the nicest pattern for you and some lovely crêpe de Chine that is just your best color! I can't wait for you to see it!"

Mrs. Boozer—Miss Alice Ann, not Miss Catherine—came in the store for some flour and sugar one day and told Papa she'd never got mail from as far away as New York City before. She was showing the card to everybody. Miss Love had written her about "a stylish cloak that is inexpensive but will look elegant on you."

Mrs. Flournoy reported that Miss Love had ordered a whole outfit with her in mind.

Loma's card said, "Your father wants to pay for a lovely dress I picked out for you! I can't wait to see if I guessed right on the size!

You'll be the grandest lady in town next summer!"

Aunt Loma hooted. "Pa wants to pay for me a dress? That'll be the day. And why next summer? Why not now? Well, I'll believe it when I see it."

She half-believed she had a free dress, though, when here came a card to Mama saying Grandpa was buying her a black grosgrain coat. "It will look really ritzy when you ride to church in the new Cadillac this fall!" wrote Miss Love. "I've found all the materials to make a hat to go with it, too!"

Mary Toy heard only that Grandpa had "a surprise" for her, but Miss Love wrote other girls about a dress or pattern or a bolt of poky-dot material or some such. She knew this would make them start pestering their mamas as to when Miss Love would be back and when would the wholesale house ship the orders.

Mama and Aunt Loma grudgingly admired the postcard salesmanship. Papa was beside himself about it. I heard him tell Cudn Hope that the postcards were "a stroke of genius." With just a one-cent stamp apiece, Miss Love had let every lady and girl in Cold Sassy know she had been thought about way up in New

York City. Papa said, "When word gets out that the shipment is in, it's go'n look like we're havin' the women's missionary meetin' down here."

I got a postcard. It said, "Your grandfather and I thank you from the bottom of our hearts for all you are doing at our house. I hope Mr. Beautiful is behaving. Yours, Miss Love."

I kissed Yours and then I kissed Miss Love—the words, I mean. But I felt let down. Everybody else in the family could look forward to presents from New York, but it seemed like I was doing all the work for just a thank-you.

Tell the truth, I wasn't doing near what I'd meant to, because when I wasn't busy at the store or hurrying through chores at home, I was out driving with Papa, either practicing or going somewhere, or else washing and polishing the Cadillac. It got a layer of dust every time we drove around the block.

Smiley and Pink and them worked on it about as much as I did. Lots of times Mama came out there to the barn shed and sat on the milking stool just to watch us. It was like she couldn't believe we really had a motorcar unless she could go to ride or sit and look at it, one.

Tell the truth, we none of us could quite believe it.

One morning I was just fixing to run up to Grandpa's and lead Miss Love's horse around some when here came fat Lee Roy Sleep, saying the Gypsy caravans were going through town.

The Gypsies always came in August—telling fortunes, selling lace, tarring barn roofs, trading horses and mules. It was a sight to see —the bright-painted wagons with little curtained windows, and the horses decorated with tassels and silver beads. Cold Sassy always turned out to watch. By time Lee Roy and I got downtown, the caravans had reached the public well near my granddaddy's store. Several Gypsy men were on horseback, riding ahead of or behind their wagons or leading strings of mules and horses. I still remember a pretty, olive-skinned girl I saw that day, riding on a big gray stallion behind a heavy-set man who was dusky black. At the well he reined in and the girl slid off to drink from the flowing pipe. Getting up my nerve, I walked over to her and asked politely, "Where are y'all from?"

She looked scared and mumbled in a foreign accent, "I do not know." Before she could say anything else or even get her a drink, the man spoke short to her in another language and jerked her back up on the horse, and they rode off to rejoin the caravans. When I told Papa about it, he said he wouldn't trust anybody who didn't know where they came from.

I still think about the Gypsy girl sometimes. Then as now, you hardly ever saw any olive-skinned people in Cold Sassy. And boy howdy, she was pretty.

I also still think about another girl I saw that day. Lightfoot McLendon. Not more than an hour after the Gypsies passed through town, I saw Lightfoot walking the railroad tracks toward Mill Town.

I was driving the Cadillac, taking some corn and squash and tomatoes to old Mr. Slocum, who was laid up with a bad back. The car made a swell racket, and if I went slow, folks who heard me coming had plenty time to run out on the porch and watch me drive by. They'd wave, and I'd honk the horn.

I recognized Lightfoot even when she was

way up ahead. But gosh, she was changed. I'd always thought of her as bounding along like a young mountain goat, but now she looked like any other mill hand. Shoulders slumped, head down, hair pulled back tight and plain. She turned as the auto came up behind her, and I saw that her face was thin and pale against the black of her mourning dress.

Braking quick, I stopped beside the tracks and blew the horn at her. "Lightfoot!" I called. "Come 'ere a minute!"

She shaded her eyes against the sun. "Will? Thet you?"

"Come look-a-here at my automobile!"

She came running across the railroad ditch to the road and, like a wilted pot plant that just got watered, smiled up at me with the purest pleasure on her face. "Law, is this here yore'n?"

"Well, it's—ours. My daddy bought it."

"I ain't never been this close to a motorcar afore." She ran her hand over the red paint of the hood. "Don't it feel shiny! Kin I set in the seat fer jest a minute, Will?"

"Better'n that. I'll ride you down the road a piece. Hop in." As she stepped up on the running board, I nodded toward the basket of corn and tomatoes in the back seat. "I'm takin' those to a old man who lives over on the other side of the cemetery."

I wished I could give her the vegetables. It would kind of make up for that bucket of blackberries she lost. But her pride was in my way. It would be the same as saying I knew that nothing grew good in the hard-packed clay behind the mill houses, and that mill hands didn't have plows to cultivate the soil deep or money for guano.

Well, it was something, at least, to give Lightfoot her first ride in a car.

I tried to make conversation, but had to yell over the car racket, and she had such a thin voice I couldn't hear a word she said. Just before turning left at the corner house where Miss Alice Ann Boozer and Mr. Homer lived, I stopped to let her out—then had an idea. "I'm go'n turn up this street," I said, "but if you ain't in a hurry, we could drive into the cemetery and sit and talk a while."

Without waiting for an answer, I turned the corner and drove through the cemetery gates and down the narrow wagon road that wound around old graves and old trees. I didn't once think to wonder if Miss Alice Ann or Mr. Homer or anybody had seen me turn into the graveyard with a mill girl in the front seat.

From habit, I headed for the Toy burial plot. After I cut off the motor it was really quiet in there, and cool under the trees. Lightfoot said, "Jest listen to them birds sangin'. Hit shore is a pretty place, Will. And so peaceful."

"Well, it seems peaceful when I look at old graves like those." I pointed toward the moldy headstones of people I never knew, some of them born a hundred and fifty years ago or more in Scotland or Ireland or New Hope, Pennsylvania. "But, Lightfoot, I feel like I'm go'n suffocate when I think about Granny Blakeslee or my friend Bluford Jackson, layin' down there in the dark."

An uneasy look came on her face and she sighed a long sigh. "My daddy passed, Will."

"Yeah, Papa told me. Said you came in the store."

The silence hung heavy over us as I tried to think of something to say. Lightfoot kept rubbing the brass horn with her right thumb. Finally she looked at me kind of shy-like and asked if I'd been in any fights lately. "I seen you fightin' lots a-times at school. You're a good skull-knocker, Will."

I blushed under the compliment. "Well, I ain't had time for it lately," I said. "Anyhow,

I mostly fight to keep from gettin' called a sissy. And it's a way to get my share of whippin's at school. If you don't get whippin's, they call you teacher's pet."

She laughed. "Ain't nobody go'n call you a sissy or teacher's pet, either one, Will."

"Well, I reckon. But I mostly fight for fun, like my grandfather does. If I feel like sayin' to somebody I bet I can lick you, I say it and we square off and all the boys crowd around, rootin' for one or the other of us, and everybody has a good time." I paused and added, "But it's a real fight when I'm tryin' to beat up Hosie Roach."

She rubbed the brass horn some more, and then said, without looking at me, "Why come you hate Hosie, Will?"

"I don't know. He's—well, snobby and smart-aleck. Always got a chip on his shoulder. And he's dirty."

She said real low, "He ain't got no bathtub like you."

I hated feeling ashamed for having a bathtub. "You seen Hosie this summer, Lightfoot?"

She blushed. "Ever day. He works same shift in the mill as me. Will, you'd like Hosie if'n you knowed him better. He's real smart—

like you. Everbody at the mill thinks he's go'n amount to something some day. I mean, you know, get a job thet ain't at the mill."

"Yeah. Maybe."

Feeling around for something better than Hosie to talk about, I showed her how the gears worked, and the choke, and then thought to ask if she saw the covered wagons that came through Cold Sassy last week.

"Yeah. I went out on the highway to watch them pass. I 'as thinkin' it might be folks I knew from White County. But turned out they 'as from way up in the mountains. My folks is from the hills, not the mountains."

Silence. A breeze rustled the leaves overhead and cooled us some. Then Lightfoot said she came through Cold Sassy one time when she was little bitty. "They 'as ten or twelve fam'lies in our wagon train, takin' thangs south to sell in Washin'ton, Georgie. Quilts and arsh potatoes, you know, and them blue mountain cabbages, and apples and chinquapins and home-twist t'bacca. All like thet."

I grinned. "And moonshine?"

She grinned back. "Yeah, I reckon. I remember we stopped in Cold Sassy on the way back home. Went in a store and bought a cast-arn stove, and some piece goods and sugar and coffee. Might be it 'as yore grandpa's store. I always remembered Cold Sassy cause it 'as sech a funny name."

"It ain't funny if you know how it came about. You ever noticed that great big sassafras tree, Lightfoot? The one over by the depot?"

She nodded.

"Everybody calls it the Cold Sassy tree. Back a hundred years ago it was a big sassafras grove there, and the wagoners goin' through said that was the coldest spot between the mountains and Augusta. They all knew what was meant if somebody said let's camp at them cold sassy trees. By time settlers got to comin' in, Cold Sassy was its natural name."

"Hit still sounds funny, Will. Leastways to me it does," said Lightfoot.

"Lots of other folks think that. There's talk about changin' it to something prosperous-soundin', the way Harmony Grove was changed to Commerce a few years ago. Don't you think Commerce is a awful improvement over a pretty name like Harmony Grove?"

More silence, except for birds twittering and a dog barking somewhere. I felt uncom-

fortable. Aunt Loma's right, I thought.
Southerners can't just sit and not say anything. I said, "My granny's great-granddaddy
led a wagon train here from North Ca'lina.
They were the first settlers."

"Had he heired the land?"

"Maybe, I don't know. I think he had a
land grant for fightin' in the Revolution."

"Where I come from, most folks jest tuck it
up. Their land, I mean. Maybe thet's what
yore folks done."

Time lagged again till Lightfoot asked
would anybody mind if she looked around
some.

"Naw, course not." Jumping down, I ran
around and helped her out, like she was Cin-
derella stepping out of a coach. I showed her
Granny's unmarked grave. "The tombstone
ain't come yet," I explained, embarrassed.
"Grandpa ordered one from Sears, Roebuck,
but it ain't come yet." Then I took her over to
the Sheffield plot. Being as Mr. Sheffield
owned the cotton mill, I thought she might
like to see where some of his money went.
"I'm go'n show you two big fancy headstones
for men who weren't dead when they were
buried," I said gaily.

"They warn't dead?" She was horrified, the

way I'd felt when Granny told me about it. Stopping before a huge marble tombstone carved like a scroll, I said, "See? 'Daniel Bohannan Sheffield.' He was the Sheffields' only son."

"He got buried alive?"

"Naw, course not. Ain't nobody under there. Granny said Mr. Dan married a rich Jew lady in New York and was go'n bring her home to meet the fam'ly, but Miz Sheffield wrote him not to come. Said anybody who'd marry a Yankee or a Jew was the same as dead—specially if it was a Yankee Jew. Turned out the bride's family shut the door on her, too, but I don't know if they buried her. Anyhow, Mr. and Miz Sheffield put up this tombstone. See, it don't give a date. Just says 'Died in a foreign land.'"

"He still livin'?" Lightfoot looked around like she thought Mr. Dan might be standing behind her.

"Who knows? They don't talk about him. Now let me show you the other one. See that big carved marble angel over yonder?" As we walked toward it, I told her about Mrs. Sheffield's youngest brother. "Granny said he was around my age when the Yankee army came through. Just fourteen or fifteen. The Laceys lived on a big plantation, and they sent this boy down the Savannah River one dark night in a rowboat with a trunk full of money and silver and jewels—all like that. If he made it to Savannah, he was s'posed to buy passage on a ship to England and wait out the War over there. Which he did. But when it was over, he didn't come home. Granny said after Mr. Sheffield started the mill and they could afford it, Miz Sheffield hired her a lawyer over in England, and he found out her brother had squandered everything. He was workin' as a chim'ly sweep. Wanted to come home."

"Well, I reckon Miz Sheffield bought him passage."

"Naw. She buried him. See? 'Royal Garnet Lacey, Gone But Not Forgotten.' "

I plucked a leaf from the oak tree we were standing under and tore it in little bits while Lightfoot studied the gravestone. "Maybe he did die over in England," she said finally. "If Miz Sheffield said he 'as dead, he must a-been."

"Naw, he wasn't. Granny said he kept writin' letters for years." I laughed, but Lightfoot didn't. She stood for the longest kind of time, staring from one to the other of the expensive tombstones for live men. Then running her hand over the carved angel, she said, "I shore wisht I could get one a-them angels for Pa." She looked up at me, and I noticed for the first time the lavender-blue circles under her eyes.

I felt embarrassed, her wishing for such. Finally I mumbled, "Did you . . . uh, where's he buried at, Lightfoot?"

"Back home. Me and my aunt tuck him back to the hills on the train. I knowed he warn't go'n rest easy in no grave down here." With that, Lightfoot sank down on the empty grave of Mr. Royal Garnet Lacey, put her head against the angel's stomach, and cried and cried.

I didn't know what to do. I patted her shoulder and said I was sorry her pa died, but that just made her cry worse. She sobbed out that he 'as lucky to be dead; now he didn't have to work all day after coughin' all night, and didn't have to worry bout gittin' enough vittles.

"Was he . . . uh, did he have the TB, Lightfoot? Like your mama?"

She didn't answer. Just sat there and cried some more. Finally she wiped her eyes on the skirt of her black dress, trying hard to get aholt of herself. When she could talk, she said softly, "I think maybe Pa did have the TB. Pneumony's what kilt him, though. Hit come on him sudden like. He 'as deader'n Hell a day later." I hadn't ever before heard a girl say Hell, but she didn't even notice she'd said it. "I wanted to git a doctor, but my aunt, she said he 'as too fur gone. Said we didn' have no money to waste on no doctor when it couldn't do no good. . . . Oh, Will, I wisht I'd a-stayed with my sister after the funeral. Buster axed me to. Thet's her husband. I said thankee, but I ain't a-go'n be beholden to nobody. Buster said I'd earn my keep if'n I holped him in the fields."

"Why'n't you stay, then?"

"I didn't like the way Buster looked at me when he said I could holp him in the fields."

She picked up a stick and talked on, almost like I wasn't there. "Anyways, I wanted to come back here and go to school. Amount to something. We 'as halfway back to Cold Sassy on the train when my aunt she said, 'Now, Lightfoot, with yore pa dead 'n' all, I cain't keep you no more less'n you go in the mill full time an' pay yore part. Fast as you larn thangs, you'll be a-workin' both sides of the aisle in no time.' Will, I begged her and begged her, 'Please'm, let me git one more year a-schoolin'.' But she said her chi'ren got two year apiece in school, and it ain't holped them a bit in the mill. Said if they'd a-been borned with books for brains, they'd be makin' bottom wages jest the same."

Over near Granny's grave a jaybird screeched. I stood drawing lines in the dirt with my big toe, saying nothing. Then all of a sudden Lightfoot hit Mr. Royal Garnet Lacey's marble angel hard as she could with her stick! Her eyes narrowed. "Here's somebody ain't even dead yet," she said, poking out her bottom lip, "and I bet his headstone cost more money than I or my people will ever see in our whole lives. Hit ain't fair!"

"No, it ain't, Lightfoot." I wanted to tell her about Blu Jackson dying so unfair young, but she started crying again. "Please, Lightfoot. Cryin' ain't go'n help. Hush up now."

"I don' want to hesh up. I'm a-go'n cry the r-r-rest a-my l-life. . . ."

"Look, I'll carry you home. In the car. Come on, Lightfoot. Quit cryin' and I'll ride you home." I caught her wrist and pulled her up.

And then I kissed her.

I swear I hadn't once thought of doing such

a thing, and I'm sure she hadn't, either. But before you could say doodly-squat, my arms had circled her and she had flung her arms around my neck, and I could feel her wet cheek against mine. For what seemed like ages I just held her, thinking nothing but the purest thoughts, my heart aching for her, so poor and miserable and lonesome. And then I don't know what happened, I was kissing Lightfoot! Just like Mr. McAllister kissed Miss Love. On her mouth, her cheeks, her closed eyes, her neck . . . She kept saying, "No, Will, no, no, no, no . . ." But she didn't push me away.

My breath came in trembling gasps, and hers did, too. I felt dizzy. I was on fire. I pressed her against Mr. Royal Garnet Lacey's angel and wrapped my arms tight around her waist.

Just then God spoke out loud in the voice of Miss Alice Ann. "Will Tweedy, you ought to be ashamed!" said God. I looked up and there He stood in a pink and white poky-dot dress, pointing His plump forefinger at us.

Lightfoot put her arm across her face just like Eve in the garden when God saw her nakedness.

"You, girl, I don't know who you are,"

shouted God, "but I can tell you're from Mill
Town. Now you just git on home. Will's a
good boy from a nice fam'ly. You ain't got no
right to come to town like this and corrupt
him." God was indignant as all get-out.
"Soon as I see y'all ride in here, I thought to
myself they ain't up to no good. Will, I just
hate to think what your daddy's go'n say."

"It ain't like you see it, Miss Alice Ann! We
didn't mean to—"

"I got eyes, ain't I?" God retorted. "Your
trouble, Will, you ain't got no shame! Imagine, actin' like that right in sight of your poor
granny's grave!"

36

While I was staring at Miss Alice Ann, my
mouth open like a dummy, Lightfoot disappeared. Evaporated. Just like she had at the
depot that day she helped me off the train
trestle. She must of run across the cemetery
and gone out through the woods at the back.

Then while I had my back turned, trying to
crank up the Cadillac, Miss Alice Ann disappeared, too—I reckon to go spread the word.

I felt sick.

I took the vegetables to Mr. Slocum, and when I got back home, parked the car under the barn shed and sneaked up to the loft. I wanted to think about kissing Lightfoot Mc-Lendon before I had to think about a whipping. I wanted to remember my arms tight around her. I wanted to feel her lips on mine, her hands on my back, her breath coming in trembly gasps at my ear. Closing my eyes, I groaned and sank down in the hay.

Now I knew why Miss Love couldn't stop Mr. McAllister when he was kissing her, despite how bad she hated him. She had lost her senses. Well, I'd lost mine, too, and I wanted to stay that way. I wanted to keep aholt of all the feelings that kept passing over me in waves.

But I was also scareder and more ashamed than I had ever been in my life.

There was no point in worrying about Lightfoot. Nobody would go tell her aunt on her. Even if Miss Alice Ann knew where she lived, she wouldn't think a mill girl was worth the trouble. It was my sins that were as scarlet, not Lightfoot's.

I hated it that folks would talk about me. I knew now how Miss Love must feel. Lord, what would Mama say? I wished I was dead. I also wished Grandpa was home from New York. I could explain it to him, how I didn't mean to do wrong. But how could I explain to Papa or Mama? For that matter, how could I explain a thing like that to Pink and Smiley and them? They wouldn't believe it just happened, that I didn't plan it when I turned in those cemetery gates. They wouldn't understand or care that Lightfoot was crying and I only meant to comfort her. They'd just haw and guffaw and ask how it felt and did she kiss with her mouth open. She didn't, but they'd never believe it. They'd make the whole thing dirty.

All of a sudden I couldn't stand the suspense any longer—the waiting for Miss Alice Ann to get to Mama. I decided to go tell her myself, the way Miss Love told Grandpa before he could hear it from Miss Effie Belle Tate—or me.

There's no use going into all that followed. Telling on myself saved my pride somehow, but it didn't ease the punishment. I got my whipping from Papa, and my shaming from Mama to the point I tried to duck out of sight whenever I heard her coming. But what hurt,

Papa decided I couldn't drive the Cadillac for two months.

He was really mad.

After the way I'd done bad and brought shame on the family, I deserved the whipping. But two months out from under the steering wheel was six weeks too much. Compared to being punished for kissing a mill girl, being in mourning for Granny had been like a picnic up at Tallulah Falls.

It occurred to me that mine and Mary Toy's punishments never had been equal. Whenever I misbehaved, Mama told Papa and he wore me out with the razor strop. But when occasionally Mama said to whip Mary Toy, why that was something else entirely. Taking a rolled-up newspaper, he would jerk her up to her room, and from downstairs we'd hear him speak harsh. "Now, young lady, bend over that bed!" Mama would cringe, hearing the blows fall. What she didn't know was that Papa would whisper to Mary Toy to start hollering, and then commence swatting the mattress instead of her. Mary Toy told me about it one time.

If I thought about Mama, that seemed like a good joke, but if I thought about me, it made me mad. I realized Papa was strict and hard on me because a boy had to amount to something, whereas Mary Toy didn't, being a girl. But just the same it made me mad.

I didn't go anywhere the next day except up to Grandpa's to feed and water the horse and mule and Granny's chickens. But the following day there was no way out of it; I had to help at the store.

It seems like everybody I saw took up for me, even Miss Effie Belle. She lectured me good, right there in the store, but it was about mill people. "Stay away from them folks, son. They all sorry and no-count and good for nothin'. You ain't a bad boy, Will. You was just led astray."

After she went out, Uncle Lige put his arm around my shoulders and said, "Natcherly you go'n sow some wild oats, boy. We all done it. But right now you jest a mite young. Wait till you old enough to be careful and not git caught."

Later Aunt Loma came in, carrying Campbell Junior, and patted my shoulder like she was forgiving me for doing evil. "Now, Will," she whispered, "be sure and write down about you and that mill girl."

Gosh, I wouldn't of written that down then for anything!

I left for dinner early. I didn't want to walk home with Papa. But as I hurried to cross the street just before reaching the depot, the old men playing checkers on a barrelhead under the Cold Sassy tree winked and grinned at me.

It's to my credit that when Smiley and them talked dirty about it and old men sniggered and spoke of wild oats, I felt even more ashamed than when I'd told Mama and then had to listen while she repeated it to Papa.

It's not to my credit that ever since Mr. McAllister came to town, I'd had a deep-down itch to kiss somebody the way he did it and see how it felt and all. I think I had Miss Love in mind, but I knew that would never happen. If I hadn't watched Mr. McAllister, I wouldn't even know about kissing like that. I might of put my arm around Lightfoot till she stopped crying, but probably I wouldn't of kissed her at all.

She was not a bad girl, or common, either, and I hated it that she would think I didn't respect her. She'd know I wouldn't kiss any girl from a nice town family the way I kissed her.

*   *   *

When Grandpa and Miss Love left for New York City, nobody knew how long they would be gone. "Hit jest depends," Grandpa had said when Papa asked. "But I gol-gar'ntee you I ain't a-go'n stay a day more'n I have to. I can stand them Yankees jest so long fore my arm goes to hurtin'."

They had been away for nearly two weeks ("Doin' no tellin' what," as Aunt Loma put it) when on August 13th Papa got a telegram that said: ARRIVING 11:40 A.M. AUG 16 E.R. BLAKESLEE. I tell you, on the morning of August 16th, we were all mighty excited.

I naturally got up early to go groom Miss Love's horse and see if everything was all right up there.

I don't know whether it was Mama's idea or Papa's, but it was decided to invite the travelers to dinner. Maybe what did it was Miss Love's postcard promises, but bygones almost seemed to be bygones as Mama and Queenie bustled about, fixing a Sunday dinner despite it was only Thursday.

Papa ordered ice from Athens for the lemonade. Mama put out the goblets and good china and good silver, and invited Aunt Loma and Uncle Camp and also Aunt Carrie, who was back from visiting her cousin in Athens.

Aunt Carrie, remember, was the one who read poetry, studied Latin and Greek, talked cultured, believed in human excrement, and put mourning dye on Mary Toy's hair for Granny's funeral.

It really pleased me, seeing places set for Grandpa and Miss Love. She hadn't eaten at our house since before Granny took sick, and Grandpa hadn't been there for a meal since they got married. If Mama was letting Miss Love in the house, maybe she'd let her in the family, too.

Papa came home to get the Cadillac and drive it to the depot. "I know Mr. Blakeslee won't ride in it," he said as he left the house, "but I can bring Miss Love and their grips."

Right after he left, Mama looked up from peeling peaches and said, "Will, I just thought. Maybe you better go take the Toy Bible out of the parlor. Uh, let me think. Well, put it on my dresser upstairs."

I did as I was told. Laying it on the dresser, I felt a wave of grief for Granny, wishing she could be here today, with us eating on the good china and all. On an impulse I turned to where her life was recorded.

Gosh, no wonder Mama wanted me to hide that Bible! She had nearly wore out the page erasing *Enoch Rucker Blakeslee married Love Honour Simpson on July 5, 1906.*

Hearing the brass horn just a-honking, we all rushed out. There was Grandpa in the front seat by Papa; he was the one honking the horn! Miss Love was in the back, squeezed in between two mountains of grips, boxes, and hatboxes and boy howdy dressed fit to kill in a new fall outfit. She was probably hotter'n heck, but by dern she sure was fashionable.

Grandpa was so taken with the automobile he hardly noticed anybody except me. Stepping off the running board, he slapped me on the shoulder and said, "Gosh a'mighty Peter Rabbit, Will Tweedy, these here artermobiles is something else and then some!"

"Sir? I thought you liked mules better."

"Even a dummy can change his mind, son. I've rode ever dang artermobile in New York City. Stanley Steamers, Fords, Holsmans, Pierces, Buicks, Caddy-lacs, all of'm. Course Miss Love had to push me into the first car. Hit was a Franklin, and I'd jest soon been caught in the compress down yonder at the cotton gin. Scared me half to death. But you can git used to anythang." Catching Miss Love's eye, he grinned at her.

"Mr. Blakeslee held on like he thought that Franklin might fly," she said, teasing. "But next day he couldn't wait to try it again!" While everybody laughed, Mary Toy peeped out from behind Mama's skirt. "Why, Mary Toy!" said Miss Love. "You've come home!"

"Go kiss your grandpa, sugar," said Mama.

Grandpa bent down for the kiss, gave Mary Toy a penny and said how much she'd growed, then straightened up and slapped the hood of the Cadillac the way a horse-trader slaps the flank of a fine stallion. He said, "I done joined the dang twentieth century, folks! Gosh a'mighty, a motorcar is a marvel. A dang marvel! Hoyt, I shore am proud you got one!"

Queenie and Mama had dinner nearly ready to be served up, but Miss Love had brought some of the boxes in with her, and nothing would do Grandpa but to open them and pass out his presents. He had done so little gift-giving in his lifetime, he was like a child who's learned a new trick.

As Miss Love had promised, there was a black grosgrain coat for Mama, and for Loma a thin, expensive-looking white dress with big pastel flowers embroidered on it. Aunt Loma like to had a fit over that dress. While she danced around holding it up to her, Grandpa said proudly, "I got thet'n real cheap. Besides wholesale, it was marked down for end of season, which don't matter, cause what's end of season up North is jest right for August down South."

Mama and Papa both looked like they'd swallowed a straight pin. Mama said firmly, "Pa, have you forgot we're in mournin'? Loma cain't wear a white dress."

Miss Love defended herself. "Your pa was dead set on that dress. I figured—"

"A good-looker like Loma ought'n to wear black all the time," Grandpa interrupted. Aunt Loma's face prettied with pleasure at the compliment. "When you was little bitty, honey, yore ma was always makin' you flowerdy dresses."

"I figured it would keep till next summer," Miss Love put in real quick.

Aunt Loma's face fell a mile. "You did it on purpose, Love Simpson," she said, and burst out crying.

"Hesh up, Loma," Grandpa ordered.

Miss Love's face flushed. Closing her eyes for a second, she sighed, and then spoke like to a child. "Tell you what, Loma, I'll make you a big fashionable black hat with black ostrich plumes to wear this fall. Would you like that?" And Aunt Loma nodded through her tears.

There were presents all around. Derby hats for Papa and Uncle Camp, a little fur muff for Mary Toy that had a bunch of silk violets pinned on it, a book for Aunt Carrie, a beaded purse for Queenie—and for me a linen duster and driving cap with goggles, just like Papa's!

"Well, thet's it, folks," said Grandpa, real proud of himself. "Santy Claus is over. Now let's go eat some good Southern cookin'. Mary Willis, you ought to see what them folks in New York call fried chicken."

Nobody asked Miss Love to, but she explained about Yankee fried chicken. "They use only a little grease, and after the chicken pieces brown, they put water in the pan and let it steam."

"Another thang bout them Yankees," said Grandpa, heading for the dining room, "they never heard a-sweetmilk. When I ast for it, the waitress lady brought me some with *sugar* in it."

Papa said Lord make us thankful for these and all our blessin's for Christ sake a-men and started slicing the ham. Everybody was talking at once—except Mama. She was suspicioning, with funny-paper balloons hovering over her head. The first one said, *How come all those nice presents?* The next said, *Love's tryin' to buy a ticket into the fam'ly. But how'd she get him to spend so much?* The third balloon explained it: *He's sweet on her. They were together in that hotel in New York and now they feel guilty. They're hidin' guilt behind all that Santy Claus.*

But then Mama's mind came back to the fact she had dinner guests. She called Queenie to bring the hot rolls.

Papa kept trying to keep the talk away from New York, I guess thinking it would hurt Mama to have to listen to it. The whole time we ate, he was telling Grandpa about our motor trips. Described every puncture, every hill, every rut and gully.

"What I want to know," Grandpa said finally, turning to me, "did you do any a-the drivin', son?"

"Yessir. Drove all the way home from Comer."

He looked proud. "Hit shore is a wonder how young folks ketch on. Miss Love, now, she thinks she could drive a car." He grinned.

"But I don't know as I'd ride with her or any other lady." That got Miss Love's goat, I could tell.

When it was time for dessert, Miss Love got up to help Mama and them clear the table. But Mama said keep your seat. By not letting her help, she made it clear that Miss Love was comp'ny, not fam'ly.

Grandpa, noticing, got back at Mama right quick. "Why don't you tell what all we done in New York, Miss Love? I mean besides ride artermobiles."

Miss Love said sweetly (too sweetly), "Mary Willis, your daddy will try to say he didn't have a good time. But he had a real good time."

"I got to admit it, folks, it was a dang sight more fun with Miss Love than them times I went by myself."

"What all did you do?" asked Aunt Carrie. The flowers in her hair today were daisies.

Grandpa said, "You tell'm, Miss Love."

"Of course we were at the wholesale house most of the time. But we went to Coney Island one evening and walked on the beach. Another day we rode the ferry to Ellis Island, where they take in immigrants. And we visited a lot of churches and museums."

"I ain't talkin' bout them dang churches and museums when I say I had a good time, Miss Carrie," Grandpa said gaily. "What I liked was ridin' in them artermobiles and seein' them musical reviews and all like thet."

Miss Love shook her head at Grandpa like a mother trying to shush a child in public, but he chose not to notice. He didn't see the shocked looks that Mama and Papa exchanged, either.

Aunt Carrie said, "Did you hear that, Mary Willis? They went to a musical! How nice! Tell me, Rucker, did you see any theatricals? Any Shakespeare plays?"

"Naw, Miss Carrie, we didn't see no Shakespeare. But we seen a stage play. The main actress shore was a looker."

Aunt Loma came to life. "What was her name, Pa?"

"What was her name, Miss Love? Aw, it don't matter who she was. Well, and we went to a dance place. Miss Love, tell about us at thet dance place."

Miss Love, real flustered, said, "Why don't you tell about the big new department store we went in, Mr. Blakeslee?"

But Aunt Carrie was excited about the dance place. "Did you dance, Rucker?"

"You know I cain't dance, Miss Carrie." He laughed and slapped his knee. "I jest watched. Miss Love done the dancin'."

Aunt Loma looked interested. Mama's and Papa's faces turned fiery red. And Miss Love just about died as Aunt Carrie said, "Rucker, is it the style in New York these days for a lady to dance by herself?"

"Naw. At the dance hall they got extry men to dance with unescorted ladies. Miss Love kept astin' me to let's dance, so I give one a-them men a quarter to be her partner. She's a crackerjack dancer," Grandpa bragged. "I want her to learn me how."

Aunt Carrie didn't feel the chill in the air, and neither did Grandpa. "Did I ever tell you, Rucker," she asked him, "about the time another young lady and myself got caught dancing? It was when I was a student in Athens. We were just having fun, singing popular tunes, but the songs were not of the type approved by Madame Joubert. And then we started dancing. Of course somebody told on us and here came Madame. Oh, my, it was an awful scene. Papa gave Madame my mother's piano for her school and she let me stay, but I was restricted for the longest kind of time. The other young lady went home in disgrace and was turned out of her church. Oh, my, I don't like to remember all that. You were the smart one, Love. Always do your dancing out of town. . . . Thank you, Queenie," she said as the cook put dessert in front of her—coconut cake and fresh peaches.

Nobody said a word. Finally Aunt Carrie spoke again. "One should be allowed to dance if one wishes to. And read Greek poetry, and make use of human excrement for the beautification of God's earth." She spoke with a stiff dignity. It was the first time she'd ever let on that she knew Cold Sassy laughed at her behind her back, and that it bothered her.

I knew Mama and them were shocked at Aunt Carrie, but she made sense to me. Long as you didn't hurt anybody, why shouldn't you dance if you liked dancing, and marry again if you needed looking after, and go fishing or wear a flowerdy dress if it might lift your grief a little?

Yes, and hold and kiss a lonely mill girl.

37

An uneasy silence followed Aunt Carrie's little speech. Then Grandpa yelled toward the kitchen, "Queenie? Queenie!"

She came to the dining room with a clean vegetable bowl in one hand and a drying cloth in the other. "Yassuh, Mr. Rucker?"

"This here's the best coconut cake you ever made." He took another bite. "I want you to give Miss Love the receipt."

"I ain't made dat cake, Mr. Rucker. Miss Mary Willis made dat cake."

"Well, it shore is good, Mary Willis. I want Miss Love to make me one."

Mama picked up her dessert spoon. Her voice iced over as she said, "It's Ma's receipt, Pa."

"Well, copy it down, hear?" Grandpa pulled a cigar out of his shirt pocket, bit it, and spat the tip on the floor.

Taking a sip of lemonade, Mama looked right at Miss Love. "It's in that old brown shoebox in the pantry with all Ma's other receipts. Unless you threw the box out."

I could tell that Miss Love didn't remember any brown shoebox. There was a silence while Grandpa struck a match on the sole of his shoe, put it to the cigar, and changed the subject. "Y'all ain't even noticed my see-gar. In New York, Miss Love kept tellin' me to try one. Said it's more modrun than plug tobacco and I'd like it better. I ain't smoked enough yet to know, but a see-gar shore is tasty to chew. One thang bout smokin', you don't have to spit so dang much." He looked over at Miss Love and winked. I mean, he actually winked!

Plain as day, there was something new between the two of them. Winking is not something an old man does at a lady who only keeps house for him. They were excited, almost like two children with a secret. I couldn't figure it out. I stole a glance at Mama and I could tell she noticed, too. I didn't know if she was wondering just how good a time they'd had in New York City or worrying what folks would say if Grandpa told it at the store about Miss Love dancing.

As usual, Papa finished his dessert first and tilted his chair back on its hind legs. When everybody else was through, he let the chair down and said, "Well, Camp, I reckon you and me better get on back to the store."

"Yessir."

Mama folded her napkin carefully. "Don't you think you'd better chauffeur our comp'ny home first, Hoyt?" I reckon she was too nervous to want them there all day.

Papa laughed. "Law, I forgot. Y'all ready, Mr. Blakeslee?"

"Let Will Tweedy drive us," said Grandpa. "I want to see is he any good at it."

Papa hesitated. He looked at Mama. I looked down at the peach juice in my empty compote.

"What's the matter?" asked Grandpa. "He ain't hit a horse or run th'ew somebody's parlor, is he?"

"Uh, no, sir, nothin' like that," said my daddy. Then he took a deep breath and told me to drive Grandpa home but then come straight back. "You hear? Straight back!"

"Yessir."

"He cain't come right straight back," said Grandpa. "I want him to hep us git our thangs in."

"Well, soon as you can, Will," Papa said sternly.

"Yessir."

Mary Toy wanted to go, too, but Mama said no. "With all the baggage, honey, there's

not room. Now kiss Grandpa bye and thank
him for your present."

She didn't tell her to thank Miss Love, I
noticed, and I didn't much blame her.
Grandpa had rubbed in their good time a little too much.

Papa turned the crank for me. Just before
the engine caught up, Miss Love leaned forward and whispered, "Will, your grandfather
has saved the best surprise just for you!"

Grandpa opened his mouth to say something, but the motor drowned him out, so he
shook Papa's hand and yelled above the
racket, "I'll be down terreckly, Hoyt!"

"Mighty glad y'all are back, sir!" yelled
Papa. "The store ain't the same with you
gone!"

"Proud to hear it, Hoyt!" Grandpa yelled
back. "Giddy-up now, son, let's see does it
know gee from haw with you a-holdin' the
reins. Hit run fine for yore daddy."

Soon as I shut off the motor in front of
their house, Miss Love spoke up in an excited
whisper. "Tell Will what you've done, Mr.
B.!"

Like he was about to bust from holding
back the news, Grandpa's whispered, "I done
bought me a dang artermobile, Will Tweedy!

A Pierce!" Blue eyes dancing, he reached in his vest pocket and pulled out an advertising leaflet, covered with drawings of cars, and pointed to a black open sedan.

With him waving the paper about, I couldn't get a good look. But I saw good enough to be flabbergasted. "Boy howdy, Grandpa!"

"Sh-h-h, don't holler." Smoothing his thin mustache with thumb and forefinger, Grandpa grinned big. "Hit's a secret. Ain't tellin' nobody but you till it comes in on the train." Stepping to the ground, he opened the car door for Miss Love and reached for his grip, which was beside her on the back seat.

"Boy howdy, Grandpa!" I whispered, coming around the car.

He put the grip down and handed me the advertising leaflet. "See it? Thet'n right there. Thet's the one I bought. They sendin' it in a few weeks. When it's on the way, they go'n telegraph me which train to meet."

Grandpa and Miss Love stood there watching me read what it said under the picture: "PIERCE, 8 h.p., Geo. N. Pierce Co., Buffalo, N.Y. Price $900, without top; seats 4 persons, doors in back only; single, water-cooled cylinder; jump spark ignition, planetary transmission, 3 speeds; wt. 1,250 pounds."

Gosh, Grandpa had spent $900?

"We seen a Ford thet was jest half as much," he whispered. "Thet's the one I wanted. But it was a two-seater, and Miss Love said we got to have room to take folks to ride or we ain't go'n sell any. I saved by not buyin' one a-them canvas tops—hit costs extry—and they give me a dealer's discount, besides."

Seeing my puzzlement, Miss Love whispered, "Your grandfather's got his name on two dealerships: Pierce and Cadillac! What do you think of that?"

"You mean we go'n sell cars?"

Miss Love shushed me.

"Thet's jest what she means," whispered Grandpa. "We go'n sell artermobiles. Come on, y'all, let's go in the house. Talkin' like this is a-gittin' me hoarse."

"We go'n get rich or go broke, Grandpa?" I whispered.

"Get rich!" Miss Love said as we marched up the walk, her carrying hatboxes and us loaded with grips.

"No tellin'," Grandpa admitted. "One or th'other, for shore. . . . Howdy, Miss Effie

Belle!" he called to what looked like a shadow just inside the Tates' front door.

"Howdy, Rucker," she called back, but didn't speak to Miss Love and didn't ask if they'd had a good time.

Soon as we were inside the house I said it'd be a miracle if we could sell more than one or two cars in Cold Sassy.

Grandpa laughed. "Thet's jest exackly what I told Miss Love, son. I said, 'How many folks is a-go'n shell out for a artermobile when they got a horse and buggy in the barn?' But Miss Love thinks she's figgered out the receipt for success in the motorcar business. And by dang, maybe she has!"

"Tell him what all you plan, Mr. B." We were still standing there in the front hall, so excited we hadn't even set down the boxes and grips. Miss Love was looking up at Grandpa like he was just the smartest man in the world.

"Well, I'm go'n keep my Pierce parked in front a-the store, and I want yore daddy to bring the Caddy-lac down there. Hit might not sell no cars, but it'll git folks here from Ila and Lula, and Pocatellago and Comer and Homer and Pendergrass. And after they git th'ew lookin' at them cars, they go'n come on in the store and buy fertilizer spreaders and chewin' tobacco and thangs."

"But it's the cars they'll go home talking about," said Miss Love. "Then first one and then another will buy one!"

They were chock full of ideas. Miss Love was planning a window display of linen dusters, dust veils, and driving caps with goggles. She'd already ordered some of those. Soon as they sold some cars, she was going to order sirens, hill holders, auto robes—"wind, water, dust, and oil proof"—and chain pulls for getting out of mud or sand.

"We'll let people sit out front in the cars all they want to," said Miss Love. Then she looked at me. "Uh, you haven't said much, Will. What do you think?"

I didn't think Papa would be all that glad to have folks pulling out the choke and flooding his engine, or turning the switch key on and off and using up his battery, or blowing his horn from morning to night. Not to mention how dusty the Cadillac would get, sitting out there on North Main.

But I didn't say all that. Because what could Papa do about it if Grandpa said to?

I had the feeling that displaying the automobiles was Miss Love's idea, not Grandpa's.

No woman would understand how easy a machine can get out of fix. Well, for that matter, neither would my grandfather. He never did have any sense about machinery. Hitching up Big Jack to the buggy was about his limit. He hadn't the faintest idea how a motor worked. Didn't even understand a bicycle.

"What we standin' here holdin' all these grips for?" Grandpa said all of a sudden, laughing. "Let's unload first and talk second."

I followed Miss Love into the company room, set down her baggage, and went out to bring in the rest of it. As I came in again, she called to me from Grandpa's room. "We're back here, Will."

"Yeah, come on back, son," he echoed. "We ain't half th'ew talkin'."

"I need to get on home," I called, but after I put the grips down I went back there like he said to.

Miss Love was sitting on the blanket chest that Granny's angels had come out of. Grandpa had taken the cane-back rocking chair by Granny's side of the bed. "What we expect to do," said Miss Love, taking off her hat and fanning herself with it, "is make peo-

ple want what they don't know they want.
You call that salesmanship, Will."

"I call it hocus-pocus," said Grandpa,
laughing at her.

"You'll see, sir." Getting up, she rumpled
his hair so familiar it made me uncomfort-
able. "One way we'll make everybody want a
car, Will, we're going places. And we'll take
anybody out riding who wants to go. I'm sure
Cold Sassy is already jealous as can be about
your family taking all those nice trips. When
Mr. Blakeslee's car arrives, they just won't be
able to stand not having one."

Grandpa leaned forward in the rocking
chair. "Thet's where you come in, Will
Tweedy."

Granny's clock on the mantelpiece struck
the hour. "Can I talk about it later, Grandpa?
I got to get home like Papa said."

He didn't even hear me. "Son, when my
black se-dan comes in at the depot, you go'n
be the one to drive it to the store!"

"Me?"

"Besides that," said Miss Love, "you're going to teach us how to drive!"

"Me? Y'all?"

"That's right. If Mr. Blakeslee and I learn
to drive, between us and you and your daddy

there'll always be somebody around to demonstrate." She looked over at Grandpa. "Mr. Blakeslee, I just thought of something else! Let's offer free driving lessons! Once a man gets his hands on a steering wheel, he'd sell his wife and children, if need be, to get up the money to buy one!"

Just barely listening, I could feel my punishment for kissing Lightfoot closing in on me. I didn't think Papa would let me out of it, not even to please Grandpa. And I knew he wouldn't want any and everybody monkeying with his car or learning how to drive on it. "Giving lessons sounds good, Miss Love," I said finally. "But it ain't go'n work."

"Why not? The man in New York said it takes only a few minutes. You just show a person this and that and let him drive a few miles and then teach him how to patch an inner tube. That's all there is to it."

"Yes'm, but if you offer free lessons, every boy in town is go'n be sittin' around the store waitin' his turn, not to mention every man. And school's go'n start up again in a few weeks, Miss Love. I won't be at the store like I am now."

She thought for a minute. "Well, we could just have a drawing once a week. Yes, we'll have one every Saturday! Whoever gets drawn, we'll teach him to drive. Man or boy."

"Not ladies?" I grinned.

She looked surprised. "Yes, of course. Men, boys, ladies, girls."

I didn't say so, but I had my doubts about any lady being able to crank an engine or change a tire. If Miss Love managed to learn, I didn't think any gentleman customer would ride with her for a demonstration. I mean, for one thing she was a woman, and for another she was a woman who had married a widower when his wife wasn't hardly cold in the grave, got caught kissing another man, made a scene in public—and then dog if she hadn't gone off to New York City unchaperoned with a husband whose name she wouldn't use and whose bed she claimed not to be sleeping in. No man in Cold Sassy would dare ride in a car with Miss Love Simpson.

But nothing like that was worrying the two of them right then, and Grandpa had just about as many plans in his head as she did. Lowering his voice, he said, "Now, Will Tweedy, you ain't to tell a soul bout all this."

"Not even Papa?"

"Naw, not even him. I'm go'n tell him and everbody thet they's something big comin' in

on the train in two-three weeks. And I'm go'n
ast the town band and the Negro band both
to come to the depot thet mornin', ready to
play for a parade. But I ain't a-go'n say why.
And don't you, either."

"Sir, what if somebody asts me?"

"Say you shore wisht you knew."

"What if nobody comes to the depot,
Grandpa?"

"Soon as they telegraph me from New
York, we go'n drape a big banner acrost the
front of the store, tellin' what train to meet.
And I gar'ntee you, Will Tweedy, everbody in
Cold Sassy's go'n come, outer pure curiosity.
And they go'n foller thet Pierce artermobile
down to the store so they can see it up close.
They mightn't sign up to buy one thet day,
but like Miss Love says, they'll start to
wantin' one. Now what you think a-all thet,
son?"

What I thought was Papa would snatch me
bald-headed if he saw me driving without his
permission. And how could I get permission
if I couldn't tell him about Grandpa's surprise?

Also, I worried whether it was possible to
hop into a new automobile and drive it. What
if it choked down or went dead, the whole

town watching? "What if I cain't get the dern thing started?" I asked Grandpa. "Your Pierce ain't go'n start or run just like Papa's Cadillac, you know."

That didn't even give Grandpa pause. "I got a instruction book here in my grip, and you got plenty time to study it. You won't have no trouble, son. You'll drive jest dandy."

"Of course you will, Will," echoed Miss Love. She stood up. "Goodness, I'm hot. I need to get out of these clothes."

Racing my shadow home, I was almost too excited to think. I didn't know how I'd have time to go to school, give driving lessons, demonstrate cars, groom the Cadillac for Papa and the Pierce for Grandpa and the horse for Miss Love, and be Mama's colored boy and Grandpa's stockboy at the store. But I knew one thing: in a few weeks I would be at the wheel of a shiny black Pierce automobile, chauffeuring Miss Love and Grandpa and leading two bands and a parade of people down to the store.

If Papa didn't accept that Grandpa made me do it, why, I'd just take my whipping like a man.

38

"Thet woman shore has got her a head for bizness," Grandpa said a few days later. He nodded in the direction of the kitchen, where Miss Love was washing up pans while waiting for her pound cake to get done. He picked a snag of chicken from his front teeth, sucked between tongue and teeth to clear out the rest of it, and then started telling me who all he aimed to sell a artermobile to.

I figured Miss Love was the one who suggested names to him. I bet she'd already figured out who would buy which car and what color, just like she knew who would buy which dress she picked out at the wholesale house in New York City. What I couldn't figure was how she got away with it. Grandpa always was one to admire business sense, but he'd never been one to let somebody else tell him what to do.

The cake wasn't out of the oven good before I got a glimpse of how Miss Love could lead him by the halter.

She came to the dining room door drying her hands and said sweetly, "Mr. B., I know now isn't the time or place to be talking about this, but don't you think it would be nice if the privy was nearer the house? Loomis could dig a pit and move it for us. What do you think?"

"I think it would stink."

"I read about some new chemicals to use."

"Doggit, woman, you got us eatin' in the dang dinin' room weekdays as well as Sundays; now you talkin' bout movin' the privy. Fore I know it, you'll be astin' for a bathroom!" He yelled that last. "Ain't I got enough to worry bout, buyin' thet dang artermobile, 'thout you talkin' bout no dang bathroom?"

Her dander went up like a flag. "Mr. Blakeslee, did I even mention a bathroom? I did not. I said let's move the privy closer to the house."

He grumped and sputtered, and then grinned at her. "Doggit, woman, I never seen the likes a-you." But he said it nice, and then swatted her on the behind as she walked past him to go get a plate for the cake.

It wasn't crude or anything, the way Grandpa flipped her, but the teasing look on his face somehow reminded me they'd been to New York together without a chaperone. And Miss Love took the flip as special, I could tell. She did a little dance all the way back to the kitchen.

I thought to myself that anybody who could get Grandpa to buy a car would have a bathroom in no time, and maybe even electric lights and a telephone. And if already, right now, she was in the family way and it was a boy, she was likely to get more out of Grandpa than Mama could stand—and heir more, too.

Gosh, having a baby uncle would be even worse than having Loma for an aunt. And where would it leave me? If Grandpa could make a pet out of Loma when she was little bitty and then just about throw her away after I was born, he sure-dog could lose track of me if he finally got him a boy of his own. Grandpa never could dote on two people at once.

Miss Love brought in the hot pound cake on Granny's best china plate, holding it high over her head, and set it down in front of Grandpa with a grand flourish. She was smiling big. "I hope it's just the very best you ever ate, Mr. B.," she said, as if she'd forgot me and wanted him to have the whole dang cake. "It's an old receipt, sir, but I added a little of this and that. I do hope you like it. The man who owns Cold Sassy's first Pierce deserves to eat Cold Sassy's best cake. Don't you think so, Will?"

Grandpa told her to quit the foolishness and cut the cake. But he grinned as he said it, and looked at her like the very air she breathed was made out of sugar and spice.

I could tell he'd already forgot about her wanting the privy moved and maybe hoping for a bathroom. But I knew she hadn't forgot. Like a cat smelling a rat, I sensed she was going to drop a hint here and an idea there and a big head-swelling compliment yonder— one this week, another next—till before Grandpa knew what happened, he would de- cide one day that it shore would be nice not to have to go out to Egypt on a rainy night or a cold winter morning. I didn't know how she would actually pry the money out of him, but she'd figure a way, and somehow make him like it.

Mama was in for a lot of headaches.

In the meanwhile, I had found out that a spate of kissing lasts only just so long. Like religion and silverware, it needs polishing up regular or it don't shine.

By that I mean this. For a few days after

Lightfoot McLendon and I got caught in the cemetery, I could just think about kissing her and it was like we were still doing it. I could hear her little gasps and feel her arms around my neck, her body so thin and helpless against me, and as if it was happening right now, my eyes would go out of focus and I'd be breathing like I just made a home run. But the effect was wearing off fast.

And I knew Lightfoot would never kiss me again.

Still and all, when school started next week I could at least look at her and talk to her. I'd find some way to let her know she wasn't a cheap something in my eyes.

The day school started, I was so nervous I could hardly eat my breakfast. What if Lightfoot cut me down with a cold stare? What if she slapped me? But maybe—I dared to hope it—maybe her eyes would light up and she'd smile as if just seeing me was like mountain sunshine breaking through the gray mists of morning. I didn't believe for a minute that her aunt wouldn't let her come back to school. By the time I got there, all I could think about was finding a way to touch her hand or her arm without anybody seeing.

Lightfoot didn't come.

Hosie Roach hurried in just before the second bell. As usual, he was dirty and uncombed. Trying to sound casual, I managed to ask him at recess if Lightfoot McLendon had gone back to the mountains. He said, "Naw, she's a-workin' at the mill."

"She gettin' on all right?" I asked like you'd ask about somebody's grandmother, just being polite. But I made the mistake of blushing.

"What's it to you how she's a-gittin' on?"

"Gosh, Hosie, what's it to you? I just ast. I heard her daddy died and all and I'm just— astin'."

"Yeah, her daddy died. But that don't make it no town boy's bizness how she's gittin' on."

"Says who, linthead?" I snarled, and we went at it.

When Miss Bertha broke up the fight, for once she didn't send us to the principal for a whipping. Instead, she sent us next door to chop stovewood for old Mr. Billy Whisnant. Me first, then Hosie. Miss Bertha roomed upstairs at the Whisnants' house, so I figured Mr. Billy had put her up to it. Him being bent with rheumatism, he couldn't do work like that anymore himself.

Well, I fixed Mr. Billy. And when it was Hosie's turn with the ax I told him what I'd done and he laughed and did likewise. For three days straight, every time I or another boy misbehaved, we had to go over there and chop wood.

Then Mr. Billy chanced to take in an armload of it.

He came storming over to the schoolhouse, face red and fists clenched. Busting into Miss Bertha's Latin lesson, he yelled, "Doggit to heck, I ain't go'n let no more a-you dang boys cut no more a-my dang stovewood!"

What we'd done, haw, and like I say it was my idea, we had cut every stick exactly four inches too long for the Whisnants' kitchen stove.

Worrying about driving Grandpa's automobile soon put Mr. Billy out of my mind. It even put Lightfoot out of my mind.

When Grandpa found out why I wasn't driving the Cadillac anymore, he just brushed it off. "I ain't heard yore daddy say you cain't drive my Pierce."

"No, sir, but he don't know about that."

"And long as he don't, he cain't say don't drive it."

Miss Love didn't fold her hands while waiting for word from the Pierce Company. She
put up tomatoes and corn out of Granny's
garden, made cucumber pickles, sewed new
dining room curtains, made big black hats
with black plumes for Mama and Aunt Loma,
and got her horse broke to the bridle and bit.

It was Monday a week after school took in
before the telegram came. I don't know how
Miss Love managed it, but she got the telegraph operator to swear not to tell anybody
what it said, namely, that the Pierce would
arrive the following Saturday.

That would be a dandy day for it. Everybody came to town on Saturdays.

Miss Love made a banner out of white
sheeting and painted big capital letters on it
that said:

BLAKESLEE'S BIG SURPRISE

IS ON THE WAY

MEET THE 1:40 SATURDAY!

BANDS, PARADE, FREE GIFTS!

Grandpa had balked at free gifts, but Miss
Love said the wholesale house in New York
gave her a big boxful of sample thread, which
would do for the ladies, and he could order

stick candy and chewing gum to hand out to the men and children. Free gifts would get people into the store, she said.

Grandpa looked at her like she was just the smartest businessman in the world.

That night she and I went to the store and hung the banner out of a second-story window. Next morning everybody in Cold Sassy was talking about it—nobody more than Papa, Uncle Camp, Cudn Hope, and Uncle Lige, who were right put out with Grandpa for not letting them in on the secret. When Uncle Lige said so, Grandpa just grinned and said, "Hit's go'n be a grand fancy day. Y'all be sure and git to the depot on time."

Naturally, folks asked me what it was all about. A lie being an ever-present help in time of trouble, I just said, "Gosh, I wish I knew!"

Tuesday after school, walking through Grandpa's house on my way out back to clean the horse's stall, I saw Miss Love's New York traveling suit draped over the rocking chair in her room, airing out, and her linen duster and veil hung on a wall nail. She herself was in the dining room, pinning pattern pieces on a length of dark blue serge. She looked up at me and smiled. "I'm making Mr. Blakeslee a suit." Opening her scissors into a big V, she started cutting. "I want him to look modern and successful for the parade. It's good for business."

"Yes'm, I reckon."

I went down there again right after supper on Friday evening, before the big day. I was about to bust with excitement, and at home all I could say was "Wonder what Grandpa's plannin' tomorrow, Papa?" or, "I cain't wait to see what's comin' in on the train."

I had already eaten, but I sat down with them and had some blackberry jam and buttered biscuits while getting around to telling my idea. "You finished the suit, Miss Love?" I asked.

"All except hemming the pants."

"Grandpa?" I said then. "Why don't you get Papa to bring his Cadillac to the depot? You don't have to tell him about your Pierce. Just say be there."

Miss Love took it right up. "And Mary Willis and Loma and Camp could ride with him! We can squeeze in Mary Toy between you and me, Mr. Blakeslee, and it will be a nice family affair!"

"Gosh a'mighty, why didn't we think a-this

before, Miss Love? Two artermobiles is twice't as many as one!"

Tell the truth, the reason I wanted Papa to be in on it, I wouldn't have to worry so much. He might be mad about Grandpa making me break punishment, but if the dern thing wouldn't start, or broke down halfway to the store, he and I together might could figure out the trouble.

39

If the governor of Georgia was coming in, he wouldn't of drawn a bigger crowd around the Cold Sassy tree at the depot than Grandpa's surprise. I saw lots of country people in mule-drawn wagons. The town was full of cotton-buyers and they came. And so did just about everybody who lived in Cold Sassy, white and colored.

Looking for Miss Love and Grandpa, I saw some mill people and wondered if Lightfoot was there. But if she was, I couldn't find her in the crowd, which well before train time had swelled bigger than for our Southern Independence Day Parade on the Glorious Fourth.

Papa soon drove up in the Cadillac, Mary Toy in Mama's lap, Loma and Camp in the back seat, all of them dressed to the nines and Aunt Loma waving to the crowd like she was the queen of England. Mary Toy was wearing her funeral outfit. Everybody knew that underneath Mama's linen duster she had on mourning clothes, but she looked smart and stylish all the same.

But where were Grandpa and Miss Love?

I was really getting worried when here he came without her. He had on his old black trousers and an old white shirt and string tie, and he was mad as heck. Motioning Papa to park the Cadillac, he stalked onto the loading platform where I was waiting. "Where's Miss Love at, sir?" I asked, anxious. "And why ain't you got on your new suit?"

"Cause I don't feel like puttin' on no airs," he said, ignoring my first question. "Miss Love, she can carry off sech, but I feel like a dang fool in them fancy clothes when I ain't goin' nowhere but downtown. . . . Howdy, Mr. Horace. Howdy, Miz Boswell, how y'all gittin' on?"

I tugged at his sleeve. "Sir, where's Miss Love? She's go'n be late for the train!"

"She ain't a-comin'."

"Ain't comin'?" I couldn't believe it.

"She said she couldn't sleep last night for thinkin' what folks are go'n say. Said they'd say she talked me into buyin' thet big artermobile."

"Gosh, Grandpa. Gosh."

I wanted to ask him more, but he was busy greeting folks. "Howdy, Jedge. Howdy, Miz Landrum. Y'all doin' all right? Well, if it ain't Cudn George! I heerd you got li'l Sara Ann married off." His mouth stretched like he was smiling, but he wasn't. Waving and nodding to folks in the crowd, not looking at me, he said, "I told her to good-gosh-a'mighty let'm talk. I said she had to come. She said it wouldn't hep sell artermobiles if she did. I said I didn't care. She said she did."

A farm boy called up to him, "Mr. Blakeslee?"

"Yeah, son, how's it goin' with yore ma?"

"She's gittin' better. What's yore surprise, sir? Air it a thang or a person?"

Grandpa grinned. "You'll see, son. You'll see." Then he muttered to me, "Dang woman wouldn't budge. Said she'd walk to the store with the crowd. I said I ain't a-go'n let you humble yoreself like thet, but she said she was sick and tarred a-bein' called names.'"

Poor Grandpa. All the fun had gone out of it for him. But Miss Love was right. If folks saw her perched high and mighty beside him in the back seat of a shiny motorcar, they'd call her snooty, or grave-snatcher. They'd recollect that all Miss Mattie Lou ever had to ride in was a buggy pulled by a mule—unless you counted Mr. Birdsong's glass-sided hearse pulled by fine black horses that she'd rode to the cemetery in.

"Thet woman is stubborn, great goodness!" Grandpa sputtered. I knew the real reason he didn't wear the new suit was he was mad at her. Also, I could smell he'd had a snort.

Just then Grandpa sighted the train. "Here she comes, folks!" he shouted, excited despite himself, and the crowd cheered. As Mr. Tuttle motioned everybody back from the tracks, the town band struck up "Waltz Me Around Again, Willie," and Grandpa called, "Hoyt, y'all git up here on the platform! Here she comes!"

As "Waltz Me Around Again" faded out, the Negro band took over, root-a-toot-tootin' and rat-a-tat-tattin' from their mule-drawn wagon. Every man played a different beat and a different tune, but the music meshed together into one big happy sound.

Loomis wasn't on the bandwagon. He was up on the loading platform with some other colored men, all of them grinning big and waving to friends, white and colored. It being their job to get the surprise out of the boxcar, they would be the first to see what it was.

"Where's Miss Love at, Mr. Blakeslee?" my daddy asked. It was like he just mouthed the words. You couldn't hear them. His question was lost in noise as the train engine screeched to a stop, brass bell ringing and steam belching over the rails. That's when Grandpa yelled into Papa's ear about the Pierce.

"You want me to drive it, sir?" Papa yelled, so excited he hopped from foot to foot.

"Naw, Will Tweedy's go'n drive."

"What'd you say, sir?"

"I said WILL TWEEDY! He's go'n DRIVE!"

I couldn't tell if Papa heard that or not. Like everybody else, he was watching Mr. Tuttle signal the engineer. Grandpa's boxcar stopped right where it was supposed to at the platform, and Mr. Tuttle helped Loomis open the big door. The crowd hushed as the big

Negro took a quick peep inside. He shouted, "Lawdy, Lawdy, Mr. Rucker! Ain't you de one! Bless Jesus, you done got yo'se'f a chariot!"

As the colored men rolled the automobile out and down the ramp to the ground, I pulled the Pierce instruction book out of the pocket of my new Sunday suit and handed it to my daddy. While he studied it, I put on my linen duster and the driving cap with goggles, and big Loomis flipped a towel over the black sedan like he was shining a millionaire's boots. He bowed as the crowd whistled and whooped.

Grandpa didn't waste any time. After helping Mary Toy into the back seat, he climbed in beside her and stood waving as the crowd cheered. Papa had opened up the hood. We looked good to see if it was much different from the Cadillac, then I jumped behind the steering wheel and Papa leaned in to help me locate the ignition switch, gas feed, choke, brakes, and all like that.

With men crowding around to congratulate him, Grandpa got up on the back seat, raised his hand for silence, and shouted for everybody to follow us down to the store. After the word *store,* Mr. Goosby took it on himself to hit the big drum—and kept hitting it every time Grandpa finished a sentence. "I want y'all to git a good look at this here artermobile, folks!"—BAM—"See how she works!"—BAM—"I ain't aimin' to have the only Pierce in town for long! I'm a-go'n sell all y'all one!" BAM!

Seeing the question mark on Papa's face, Grandpa reached down and shook my daddy's hand. "Thet's right, Hoyt! I got the Pierce dealership, and we go'n sell Caddy-lacs, too. Folks, a new day's a-dawnin' for Cold Sassy!"—BAM—"We go'n put ever man in town behind a dang artermobile wheel!" BAM!

The crowd clapped and whistled like they thought Grandpa was giving motorcars away. He raised his hand again. "Now, let's git on to the store! I got free thread for the ladies and lick-rish and peppermint sticks for all you chi'ren! Will Tweedy, son, start my dang artermobile!"—*Drum roll*—"Hoyt, start yore'n! Mary Willis? Loma? Y'all set? I'm ready to lead the dang parade!" BAM, BAM, BAM and another drum roll, and the bands struck up "Dixie."

I was scared to death the Pierce might not start. Turning the switch key, I pulled out the choke as Papa motioned big Loomis to turn the crank. The engine sputtered. He cranked again. The motor flipped over, sputtered, caught! The car shimmied and shook. Grandpa leaned forward and blew the horn, loud and long.

"Sit down, Grandpa! Here we go!" I yelled, and we were off. With drums beating, horn tooting, Mary Toy squealing, and Papa and them in the Cadillac right behind us, the crowd pushed forward toward Cold Sassy's new day dawnin'.

Except for me and Grandpa, I don't think a soul cared that Love Simpson wasn't in the party. But I expect a lot of folks noticed.

"You see her?" Grandpa asked, standing up to look as we chugged to a stop in front of the store. His eyes scanned the crowd. "I thought Miss Love would aw-ready be here, waitin'."

"I don't see her, sir," I said.

Mary Toy caught aholt of his knotted sleeve and tugged at it. "I saw her, sir, after you made your speech. She was goin' toward home. Why didn't Miss Love want to ride with us, Grandpa?"

He didn't answer.

In the store a few minutes later, Aunt

Loma said to me, real smug, "I reckon Pa wouldn't let Love horn in on his big day."

"It wasn't like that," I said. "Miss Love, she—she's sick this mornin'."

"Well, good for her!" said Aunt Loma, pleased. "That's poetic justice, considerin'."

I thought Miss Love would come in after while, but she didn't. And nobody seemed to mind she wasn't there, especially not Mama and Aunt Loma, who got busy giving out thread samples and candy and had a swell time.

The store did a big trade in everything but cars that day. Lots of folks said they'd sure like to own one, but it was after five o'clock before anybody actually talked business. The man who did was Mr. Sheffield, president of the mill. He rode up on his white Thoroughbred.

Those crowded around the two cars parted for Mr. Sheffield as he kicked his horse up to the Pierce. Folks white and colored watched, silent and curious, as the rich man dismounted, leaned in, examined the seats and the steering wheel, ran his hand over the horn, then tied up his horse and went in the store. I saw him motion to Grandpa.

Five minutes later he came out with my

daddy for a ride in the Cadillac. Then I took him out in the Pierce, with Grandpa in the back seat, shouting over the engine's putter that artermobiles is a dang marvel.

As Mr. Sheffield got back on his horse, he said he thought he'd rather have a Hanson touring car.

We all felt let down.

Just before dark, Grandpa told me to drive his car home and park it in the barn. Coming out to watch me crank up, he slapped his hand on the shimmying hood. "Be up home fore sunup, Will Tweedy!" he yelled. "You go'n learn me and her how to drive this here thang!"

"Tomorrow, sir? Tomorrow's Sunday!"

"Thet's right. Better tell Loomis to milk for you, son, cause we got to git a early start or we go'n run up on all them buggies and wagons comin' in for preachin'."

The sky was barely getting light and the birds just beginning to wake up and sing when I tiptoed downstairs in my Sunday suit and my new linen duster. Queenie hadn't even gotten there yet. After washing down a cold biscuit with some sweetmilk, I put on my driving cap and goggles and had just sneaked out the back door when Papa leaned out of his bedroom window upstairs. "Will?" he called softly.

Seen through my driving goggles, he looked dim in the halflight. "Sir?"

"Watch the time and don't be late gettin' back for Sunday school. You hear?"

"Yessir."

I ran all the way up to Grandpa's house.

Thirty minutes later we were on the Jefferson road, and it could of been Christmas, we were so excited.

There was no sign of leftover bad feelings between Grandpa and Miss Love. He had his new clothes on under his duster. Miss Love's gray fall suit barely showed under hers, and she wore the dust veil over her red hat. She said we looked like a fashion advertisement in the newspaper. But as the sun rose and the mist burned off, we really warmed up in our fashionable get-ups.

Grandpa was sitting up front with me to watch what I did. "Maybe we don't need the dang dusters!" he yelled, looking back at Miss Love.

Her answer was lost in the wind.

"What you say?" he yelled.

"I said somebody might see us!" she

shouted, leaning forward. "The man said part of selling cars is looking the part! Wearing the uniform! Remember?"

When we got to a long stretch of newly graded road, I shut off the engine, and the sudden silence sounded like noise. "Sit forward so you can see, Miss Love," I said, feeling important. "I'm go'n show y'all where the foot brake is, and the hand brake and gas feed and switch key." When I thought they understood it all, I got out to walk around the car and Grandpa moved over to the left side behind the wheel. Stepping onto the running board and seating myself, I said, "Now, sir you got to get all these dohickies set right or else she ain't go'n start up."

I knew he didn't have the faintest notion why he was doing any of it, but he said, real impatient, "You ain't got to tell me but once't, Will Tweedy. What's next?"

"Next you got to give the crank a few hard turns."

"You go do thet for me."

"Sir, you need the practice. Crankin' up is part of drivin'."

Miss Love had been watching closely, her arms on the back of the driver's seat. As

Grandpa stepped out, she said, "You forgot something, Mr. Blakeslee."

"I ain't forgot nothin'." He walked toward the front of the automobile.

"Yessir, you did, Grandpa," said I. "You didn't turn on the ignition."

"Gosh a'mighty, son, what's the ignition? You ain't mentioned thet'n."

"Yes, he did, sir," said Miss Love. "The ignition is what you turn on with the switch key."

"Well, doggit, whyn't you say so? Miss Love, reach over and turn the dang key."

She did. But as Grandpa bent to crank up the engine, she reached forward again and, with a chessy-cat grin at me, turned the switch back off! Naturally nothing happened when Grandpa cranked. Disgusted, he straightened up and bit off a plug of tobacco. "Hit must be outa gas-lene, Will Tweedy."

"Cain't be," said I, winking at Miss Love. "Come see if you set everything right, Grandpa." As he started toward us, head down in disgust, Miss Love quick reached forward and turned the key on. Grandpa leaned in, studied the board a minute, then said, "Will Tweedy? Everthang you told me to do, I done done. You see anythang I missed?"

"No, sir. I reckon you just ain't crankin' hard enough, Grandpa."

Soon as he turned his back, Miss Love shut off the switch again. We like to died, holding in laughter. Grandpa repeated his quick jerks of the crank, all for nothing. After he'd wore himself out up there, he kicked one of the front tires and said, "Giddy-up, you dang fool!"

Miss Love was laughing out loud now.

"Don't make fun a-me, woman!" yelled Grandpa. "Let's see you come have a try at it. You crank and I'll laugh."

As Miss Love sashayed to the front of the sedan, she looked back and winked at me, and I grinned and turned on the ignition. With one quick turn she had the engine putt-putting loud and pretty as you please. "It just needed a woman's touch!" she yelled sweetly. Grandpa swatted her behind as she went back to get in.

"I'm go'n shut it off now, Grandpa," I yelled. "You need to practice settin' all the dohickies, and I ain't sure you know how to crank it up yet. You get a knack for that by doin' it."

Glaring at me, Grandpa stalked back to the car, reached in, turned on the switch, pulled out the choke, spat, and went back to the front of the engine. Miss Love waited till he bent down to crank and then turned the key off again.

Crank, crank, *silence.* Crank, crank, *cuss.*

"Gosh a'mighty dang!" He raised up. "I never did like to do anythang I ain't done before!" Jerking off his linen duster and his cap and goggles, he threw them on the hood of the car and said he was a-go'n crank thet dang Pierce if'n it took all day. "Wisht I hadn't never heard the word artermobile."

The harder he cranked, the harder we laughed. Miss Love didn't see him coming toward us till he was nearly to the driver's seat. He caught her reaching for the switch key.

"I seen you! I seen what you done!" Grandpa shook his fist in her face and said, "Woman, if I ketch you doin' sech as thet again, you go'n walk home!"

I swear I don't know how she had the nerve, but she laughed in his face.

He walked backwards to the front of the auto, watching her, and then made her get out. This time when he cranked, the motor roared. "Now thet's more like!" yelled

Grandpa. With a satisfied grin, he flung his duster and goggles into the back seat, put on his cap at a jaunty angle, climbed in, and yelled over the racket, "Now then, I'm a'go'n drive this son-of-a-gun. How fast will she go, Will Tweedy? How do I start off? What do I do after we git to goin'?"

"Release the hand brake first, Grandpa!" I yelled over the engine noise. "Now, sir, feed a little gas. . . . Not much. Just a little bit till you get the hang of it. Go slow now! . . . Grandpa, don't wiggle the steerin' wheel so much!"

"Thet's what you done, son!"

"Only enough to keep it goin' straight."

"Thet don't make no sense a-tall."

We crawled along for a mile or two, Grandpa having the time of his life. Then we reached the crest of a hill—and the road plunged down on the other side like a roller coaster! I saw Grandpa swallow his tobacco chew as we picked up speed. "What do I do, son?" he yelled. "Whoa, doggit, whoa!" He tried to hold the steering wheel with his arm stub while turning off the switch key and moving every lever his hand could find. "Will Tweedy, stop the dang thang!"

"The brake! Use the brake, Grandpa!"

Faster and faster we went, Miss Love screaming and me yelling for the brake. At the foot of the hill, the road curved. With a wild turn of the steering wheel, Grandpa landed us in a shallow ditch.

Nobody was hurt, but it sure knocked the pride out of us, and it knocked the air out of the right front tire. It took me and Grandpa both to push the car onto the road, after which we just stood there looking at it. A crow called from a cornfield nearby. A fly buzzed around my ear. "We ought to brought Loomis along," I said, taking off the hot duster and my cap. "He could of just picked the car up and set it back on the road."

"If I'd a-had two good hands," said Grandpa, fuming, "I could a-kept it from happenin'."

I couldn't bring myself to remind Grandpa that he had two good feet, one of which should of found the brake.

While I patched the inner tube, Miss Love leaned against the hood of the car, looking like she might faint. Grandpa paced up and down scratching his head. Neither one watched what I was doing or tried to help me. Well, I'd teach them about inner tubes another day.

When I had the tire back on, I wiped my hands on a rag from the toolbox and said, "Now, Grandpa, you can crank her up again."

"Thet was my first and last time," he said, fishing in his pants pocket for his plug tobacco. "A artermobile ain't nothin' but a dang roller coaster. A mule's at least got sense of its own."

"Aw, Grandpa, come on." I tried to pull him toward the car. "It ain't hard, sir. You can learn."

"I'm shore I can, but I ain't a-goin' to. Anyhow, it's Miss Love's turn."

I motioned her toward the driver's seat, but she opened the back door and climbed in. "I think," she said in a weak voice, "that I'll wait my turn till later."

"Yes'm," I said, relieved. "It seems like maybe a good idea."

It looked like Miss Love was going to be a good driver. She wanted to practice without Grandpa in the car. The first time I took her out in the country, she just about sat on the brake and didn't go but two miles an hour, but she looked real stylish with her dust veil draped over Grandpa's driving cap and goggles, and she reeked of perfume. She said she always wore lots of perfume when she was nervous.

Two days later she speeded up considerable, and got brave enough to drive all the way home. We were in front of her house in no time, but instead of turning in, she kept right on going. "I want to drive to the store!" she yelled over the putt-putt. She was real excited. "I've been telling Mr. Blakeslee how easy driving is! I want him to see!"

It's just a pity that a bee got under Miss Love's dust veil about time she crept the car around the Confederate monument. I reckon it was the perfume did it. Probably the bee thought he'd found a flower. Then while Miss Love was slapping at him under her veil, the bee fell down the front of her dress! Got to crawling around on her bosom, I reckon, because she commenced screaming and hitting her chest, and the car went clean out of control! I grabbed for the wheel as Miss Love took her hands and feet off of everything and covered her eyes.

People screamed and ran, horses and mules screeched and rared. The Pierce bounced onto the curb of the monument, grazing the marble where it says OUR NOBLE

DEAD, then ambled across the street and bumped to a stop against the sycamore tree near the cast-iron watering trough in front of Grandpa's store. Miss Love didn't even notice when I cut off the ignition. She was still fighting the bee. As Grandpa and my daddy rushed out, followed by a bunch of customers, Miss Love screamed. "He bit me! He bit me! Somebody help! Get him out of here!"

"Will Tweedy, be-have yoreself!" yelled Grandpa as Miss Love leaped out of the car and ran in the store.

"I ain't done nothin', sir! She's got a bee down her dress!"

We rushed into the store. Uncle Lige motioned toward the storage room. "She run in thar!" Grandpa found her behind a stack of ninety-five-pound sacks of cow feed. Her veil and linen duster were on the floor beside the bee, which she had stomped to death, and Miss Love was buttoning her shirtwaist. Turning her back to us, she sobbed. "I g-got stung, Mr. Blakeslee."

He looked helpless, like he didn't know what to do, then commenced patting her shoulder. "Hit's all right, Miss Love," he whispered. "Hit's all right."

I couldn't help thinking that though Miss

Love could sass Mr. McAllister back to Texas and glare down a town full of folks sitting in judgment on her, with a bee in her bosom she was helpless as any lady I knew.

Finally she turned and faced Grandpa. Her cheeks were wet and she clutched her swelling breast with one hand, but she had control of her voice. "Mr. Blakeslee," she announced, "I'll not drive that or any car again. Ever."

"Now, Miss Love—"

"Sir, I mean it."

I couldn't hardly stand to see her give up. "You'll learn, Miss Love. It ain't like you go'n get a bee down you every time you drive."

She ignored that. "I guess we're alike, Mr. Blakeslee. I don't trust machinery. I don't understand how it works. I can talk to a horse and calm him down, but I can't talk to *that*!" She pointed in the general direction of the sycamore tree. "Oh, Mr. Blakeslee, I wanted a car so bad!" She started crying again. "How can we ever g-go m-motoring now!"

Grandpa, real agitated, looked over at me, where I stood leaning against a big wooden box. "Son," he said, "it 'pears to me like if thet dang Pierce ever sees the road agin, it's a-go'n have to be you at the wheel."

40

Any mule head could see that the automobiles wouldn't last long parked in front of the store—children jumping on the seats, men and big boys monkeying with the wires and knobs trying to see which did what. Papa was real upset about it. I finally told Grandpa we ought to make room for the cars in the buggy-and-wagon shed behind the store, but he dismissed the idea with a backward flip of his hand. "I ain't a-go'n do thet. Two elephants tied out yonder wouldn't draw customers to the store as good as them artermobiles."

That was the Lord's truth. Cold Sassy never had been a whirlpool of excitement. If the preacher's wife's petticoat showed, the ladies could make that last a week as something to talk about. We had our share of cotton-gin fires, epidemics, storms, and lawsuits, of course, but the only diversion we could count on was protracted meetings, recitals, ice cream socials, fish fries, and lectures—a doctor talking up his cure for cancer, an old man telling how he tracked a mammoth moose for nineteen days back in 1856, a young fellow talking about "Across Asia on a Bicycle." It's easy to see why not even the scarlet of the Cold Sassy tree in autumn could equal our big shiny automobiles as something to rave about, especially with the open invite to come sit in them and take a ride.

By the end of the week, though, even Grandpa was worried. "I reckon maybe you better move'm on to the back, Will Tweedy," he said. He was let down about it, I could tell, but he made sure nobody forgot the cars were back there. Any time he had an audience of customers, Grandpa would say what a dang marvel a artermobile is, and then light in talking about car-owners taking all-day trips together, sending delegations to the Georgia legislature to talk up better roads, and having auto races "uphill, downhill, cross-country, and hind-part-before."

While Grandpa did the talking, Papa and I did the driving people around. It was my job to give a driving lesson every Saturday after our drawing.

Miss Love did what the man in New York called "pushing the merchandise." For one thing, she wanted to order a lady mannequin for the store window and dress it up in a linen

duster and dust veil like one she saw at the
Cadillac agency in New York City. Grandpa
said, "Thet's jest fol-de-rol and foolish-ment.
Them big dolls cost too much to think about,
much less buy." But that wasn't the end of it.

Soon as the weather got cooler, Miss Love
turned herself into a big doll. Sat in the store
window nearly all day, wearing a veil, a
duster, and a frozen smile. She'd be a statue
till she had to scratch or something, then
come outside for a few minutes and talk to
folks about the latest in motorcar fashions.

Grandpa was really pleased, for Miss Love
in the store window was a sight to behold.
White folks and colored, too, stood in clumps
staring at her. If she chanced to bat her eyes
or yawn or shift a little in the chair, they'd
poke one another in the ribs and haw and
guffaw. Boys clowned and made faces trying
to make her laugh, but she looked straight
ahead and never even cracked a smile.

When Aunt Loma happened along, carrying the baby, she stared at Miss Love a minute, then flounced into the store and came
over where I stood putting bars of Octagon
soap on a shelf. "Love looks foolish," she
grumped.

Loma was jealous. The store window being

like a little stage and her having taken elocution, she considered herself the only person in Cold Sassy qualified to act like a dummy.

The county sheriff from over at Homer watched Miss Love a while and then went in and put down on a Pierce.

A country woman watched Miss Love and spent her egg money on a dust veil. Her husband was furious when he saw her draping the veil over her sunbonnet. Said you go git Mr. Blakeslee to give yore money back. But she wouldn't. Straightening up proud on her cut-off chair in the wagon, she said, "The same dust as gits on them fancy ladies in artermobiles gits on me when they go racin' by. I got jest as much right to look nice in a cloud a-dust as they do."

Late in September I drove Miss Love and Grandpa to the county fair over in Jefferson. Grandpa sold a car while Miss Love and I were on the Ferris wheel. Then he won the big prize at the rifle booth for three bull's eyes in a row. That really impressed Miss Love, and also the man who ran the booth. He wouldn't let Grandpa shoot again.

We had a swell time, just the three of us. I wrote down in my journal that night how pretty Miss Love looked. Her freckledy face was lit up with excitement all day, and seemed like Grandpa couldn't keep his eyes off of her.

I also wrote down that although he sat up front with me all the way to Jefferson—telling me when to slow down, when to speed up and, son, watch out for thet there bump in the road—coming home he sat with Miss Love, his right arm resting on the back of her seat.

Considering what happened soon after, it's interesting that I sensed it was worth noting in the journal how he sat with her on the trip home.

Early in October we had our first cold snap, and the next Monday, soon after I got to the store from school, Miss Love came in saying let's plan an overnight motoring trip for the weekend. "Weather permitting, of course. Wouldn't you like to take your family, Mr. Hoyt?"

Before Papa could answer, Grandpa said he'd rather take a day trip, get back to his own bed.

"That's a sign you're growing old, Mr. Blakeslee," she teased.

I could tell it made him mad. "Hit jest

don't suit me to go off now. Anyhow, what's the hurry?"

"The hurry is because we can't count on many more nice weekends." Miss Love's fingers went to drumming on the counter. "Once winter sets in, that's the end of any real motoring till spring. We can't travel when it's freezing cold."

"Thet's one way a artermobile ain't no different from a horse and buggy, Miss Love. So you ain't tellin' us nothin' we don't know."

"But I so wanted—" She looked up at Grandpa like a little girl who's been told she can't play with her new doll.

Papa butted in. "It's out of the question for us both to be gone on Sarady right now, Miss Love. Farmers are comin' in to pay up credit accounts and seed and fertilizer loans, and I'm run ragged with the automobile bizness. And—"

"And me and Lige are knee-deep in cotton, buyin' and warehousin' it," Grandpa argued. "So it'll have to be jest a Sunday ride or not a-tall, Miss Love."

"Well, of course. I understand, Mr. Blakeslee. I guess . . . I guess it just seemed so—" Her mouth trembled like she might cry, but

Grandpa didn't notice. He had got busy with a customer.

I tried to cheer her up. "If it's as cold next weekend as today, Miss Love, we cain't go anywhere anyhow."

On Friday it was still cold, with a strong wind. But Saturday turned off so warm you had to look at the reds and yellows and browns of the trees to remember how we'd shivered all week.

Papa thought it would be just as nice on Sunday, maybe better. "I'll get Mary Willis to fix enough food for all of us," he told Grandpa, "and we'll leave right after preachin'. Go out in the country and have a nice picnic together."

But Miss Love had a different idea. On my way home to milk, I met up with her and Mr. Beautiful, out for a late-evening canter. When she reined in, the horse prancing sideways and jerking the bit, she asked if I thought Papa and Mama would be willing to leave at daybreak. "That way we could go a long way."

"Yes'm, we could if Papa would miss Sunday school and preachin'. But he won't."

"Well, why don't we go then? Just you and Mr. Blakeslee and I."

Remembering the good time we'd had at the fair, I thought that was a swell idea. But I shook my head. "Papa ain't go'n let me miss, either, Miss Love."

The horse snorted, impatient. She patted his neck, spoke soft to him. "Whoa, baby. Whoa . . . You could ask him, Will."

"Ain't no use."

And that's what I thought. But when my daddy and I got back to the store—Saturday nights being one of our busiest times—Grandpa said, "Hoyt, I know how you and Mary Willis feel bout missin' preachin', but I'd like to leave early t'morrer mornin'."

Papa wanted to, I could tell, and not only just to please Grandpa. But he pushed Satan behind him. "Not this time, Mr. Blakeslee. Me bein' treasurer of the session, I got to be there t'morrer." He didn't mention Sin on Sunday, but I could feel the words hanging in the air.

About then old Mr. Billy Whisnant shuffled in and asked for a jar of lini-ment. "Hit shore heps my rheumatiz," he whined as Papa went to get it off the shelf. Mr. Billy looked around and saw me but didn't speak. He hadn't said pea-turkey to me, as a matter of fact, since I cut his wood too long.

But I wasn't studying him while Papa
wrapped up the liniment and made change. I
was thinking how lucky Miss Love and
Grandpa were, going to church at home. The
Flournoys having long since returned to the
Methodists, it was just the two of them. They
could run into the parlor, sing fast, pray
quick, and be on the road before the rest of
Cold Sassy got out its Sunday clothes.

I should explain that, though Grandpa
never mentioned their preachin' service anymore or invited anybody to come, Cold Sassy
knew the blasphemy was still going on. Miss
Effie Belle could hear them singing when she
got home from playing for the Methodists,
and what she heard wasn't "Holy Spirit, Truth
Divine."

After Mr. Billy shuffled out, Papa commenced toting up some figures, which meant
the subject of an all-day motor trip was
closed. But Grandpa didn't let it drop. "I respect yore position in the Presbytery, Hoyt,
but I'd be much obliged if Will Tweedy could
leave early to drive us." He laughed. "Miss
Love is threatenin' to drive us if'n the boy
cain't go." Not waiting for Papa to object,
Grandpa turned to me. "Son, if you ain't up
home by time we ready to eat, we'll save you

some breakfast. I don't want yore ma gittin' up early to feed you."

Next morning when I got to Grandpa's, Miss Love had already fried a chicken for our picnic and was serving up fried ham, grits, scrambled eggs, and hot biscuits. After breakfast she packed a basket: chicken, peach pickles, fresh tomatoes, butterbeans in a jar, the leftover biscuits, and half a pecan pie.

I hurried out to the barn to crank up. The birds were singing as if life depended on making noise, and I didn't care at all that the Pierce would drown out their songs. It was going to be just the three of us! A really swell day!

As we rode off, bundled in coats and lap robes, Miss Effie Belle Tate came out on her porch. She couldn't help seeing that Grandpa was in the back seat with Miss Love, but in case she didn't notice, he reached over my shoulder and blew the horn at her and waved.

Miss Effie Belle didn't wave back.

I wondered if he'd want to go by our house for his snort, but he didn't mention it.

The single-track dirt road had deep wagon ruts, and it like to jolted us to pieces. There were chuckholes, too, and whenever I hit one, the rebound just about tossed Grandpa and Miss Love out of the car. I could brace myself with the steering wheel, but they didn't grab anything except each other. Being scared they might pitch out, I started swerving around the holes. I'd yell, "Hold on!" and Grandpa would whoop and hold Miss Love tighter, and she'd shriek and giggle like a schoolgirl.

Looking back on that day, I'm reminded of a story Loomis told me about his uncle in Macon who chauffeured a bride and groom around the state on their wedding trip. Everywhere they went, he'd say to folks as a joke, "We's on our honeymoon!" Well, we were on our honeymoon that day. Me and Grandpa and Miss Love. I don't think we knew it then. At least, I didn't. But even before we got out of Cold Sassy good, I felt left out. We were going to be two and one on this trip. Not three.

One time when I stopped to let the motor cool off and said something funny, they not only didn't laugh, they didn't even hear me. At some point Grandpa asked did I think we ought to let the air out of the tires and put in some fresh. He was just showing off for Miss Love, trying to be funny. And I don't think he said anything else to me all morning.

If they laughed, they never thought to tell me what the joke was. When I glanced back as we rode along, usually they were looking at each other, not at the fall leaves or the distant blue mountains. If Grandpa weren't so old, I'd swear he was sweet on Miss Love, and vice versa. Just like at the fair, he couldn't keep his eyes off of her.

Good thing Papa's Cadillac wasn't back there in our dust. If Mama could of seen what I saw, it sure would of given her a headache.

We had the usual problems with punctures and the motor overheating, and though I tried to be careful, we scared our share of mules and horses. But it was another automobile that caused the accident.

We had eaten our picnic standing at a plank table in a country churchyard. They weren't having preachin' that Sunday, so we had the place all to ourselves. When we were stuffed full, we spread the lap robes on the ground and dozed in the warm sunshine a while—till Grandpa said he wanted to make it home by first dark so we better think about starting back. We had just got on the road again when a little two-seater black Ford pulled into the highway just ahead of us.

The driver blew his horn and the lady with

him waved at us. I blew our horn and we waved back. "The automobile book calls this the camaraderie of the road!" Miss Love shouted. She was having a grand time.

"Yes'm!" I shouted back.

We soon found out that camaraderie of the road really means eating somebody's dust. After we'd gone two or three miles behind the Ford, Miss Love tapped me on the shoulder and yelled, "Will, honey, stop a few minutes and let them get on ahead of us! I can't stand it."

So we stopped, waving good-bye as the Ford went on. A good while later we rounded a curve and there it was again, just ahead, laying on its side like a dead horse. Grandpa shouted, "Watch out, Will Tweedy! Stop, son!" Miss Love screamed. I braked. But not in time. To miss the Ford I had to cut the steering wheel sharp left and plunge the car into a creek—really just a little shallow branch. It had a good gravel bottom, so I drove through the water till I got around the wreck, then went up the slanted red-clay bank and got back to the road.

Grandpa had grabbed Miss Love hard when I swerved into the creek; he still had aholt of her when I looked back to see if they were all right. Her face was white as cotton and her voice shaky as she said, "We'd better see if those people are hurt."

The man and lady were already walking toward us. "We was hopin' y'all would come along soon," said the man. "I don't think our car is damaged, but I cain't right it by myself. I done tried."

"I'm Rucker Blakeslee, Caddy-lac and Pierce dealer from over at Cold Sassy," said Grandpa. "This here's my wife and my grandboy."

Introducing himself, the man shook hands with Grandpa and me. He was from Athens.

"What happened, mister?" I asked.

"See yonder?" he pointed to a deep narrow cut that ran across the road. "Creek must of swole up after the last rain. Thet washout th'owed my car clean out a-control."

Grandpa stared at the washout and then at the dead Ford. "Come on, Will Tweedy. Let's set up the artermobile." Us and the man made short work of it. Watching them drive off, I felt puffed up and proud to of helped somebody in trouble.

It's just too bad we didn't know about the leaking radiator before they left. I didn't see it till after Grandpa and Miss Love climbed in the back seat and I went around to crank up. The radiator must of hit a rock in the creek. "Lord hep us," I said.

"What's the matter?" asked Miss Love.

"Ma'am, we got a hole in the radiator."

"Well, plug it up," said Grandpa.

"It ain't that simple, sir."

"Will she crank?" he asked, getting out to come look.

"I reckon," said I. "But she'll get too hot if we run her without any water in the radiator. We might could find a mechanic in Athens, but I don't know if the car will make it to Athens."

Miss Love smiled at Grandpa. "Well, you said it, Mr. B. All we have to do is think up some way to plug the hole."

"We could cool the engine some by keepin' on pourin' water in the radiator," I said. "But I ain't even got a bucket."

An old colored woman was walking across a pasture toward us. Likely she was curious to know what happened, or maybe she just wanted to look at a motorcar up close. "Auntie?" I called.

"Yassuh?" She had on a blue striped head rag and a dirty faded old feed-sack dress that blew in the wind against her knobby legs. She walked awful slow.

"Make haste, we need some hep!" I yelled. I don't know what I thought she could do. Give us a bucket, maybe.

"Yassuh, I's comin'! But I cain't make no haste."

While we waited, Miss Love had an idea. "The water in the radiator gets very hot, doesn't it, Will?"

"Yes'm. It boils."

"Why don't we ask the colored lady for some grits? I think—"

Grandpa hooted. "You thet hungry, Miss Love? Ain't we still got some fried chicken?"

"Oh, I'm not hungry. Certainly not for grits." I noticed that a day in the sun and wind had reddened her face and multiplied her freckles. "I'm thinking we could plug the leak with grits, if the lady has some." She nodded toward the colored woman, who was nearly to the ditch that separated the unfenced pasture from the road. "If Will puts water in the radiator and starts the engine, and when it gets hot he dumps in some grits, wouldn't it make a big stiff lump and stop up the hole? What do you think, Mr. Blakeslee?"

Grandpa thought it was a really swell idea.

If she'd asked what I thought, I'd of said, "Well, maybe." But she didn't ask me.

When the Negro woman got to the ditch, I told her what we wanted.

"Chicken grits or reg'lar eatin' grits?" she asked.

"I think regular eating grits," Miss Love answered.

"Yas'm, but mought be dey's weev'ly."

"That don't matter," I said. "Can you spare us some?"

"Yassuh, sho can." I know she thought we were crazy.

Grandpa dug into his pocket and held out a dime. "Here you are, auntie."

Showing her bare mouth in a grin, the old woman spat snuff juice and put the dime in her pocket. "Son, I's gwine ax you to come up to de house wid me. My old feets, dey cain' make it back down heah agin today."

When I left the Negro shack, I was swinging a big old leaky enamel bucket with a cupful of grits in the bottom of it. I had paid the woman a nickel for the bucket.

Hurrying across the pasture, I saw Miss Love and Grandpa standing beside the car, just a-talking. When I was nearly to the big oak in the middle of the pasture, she turned away from him to climb back in the car. I was just fixing to holler that I got the grits when Grandpa put his hand on her arm and pulled her to him.

I didn't holler. I stood stock still and watched as Grandpa touched her cheek, then put his arms around her and kissed her long and hard—on the mouth! And Miss Love was kissing him back, no doubt about it. Same as if he'd been Mr. McAllister.

Not knowing what to do or say, I ducked behind the oak tree, feeling for the first time like Granny had been betrayed.

Miss Love had a house, a horse, and a piano—all the things she used to pray for—and now an automobile. Wasn't that enough? Hadn't God let her know once already that she couldn't have a husband?

Like Mama always said, I guess some folks just can't be satisfied. The more they get, the more they want.

41

Being behind the tree, I didn't see it if Miss Love slapped Grandpa or pushed him away. By time I finally peeped around, they were back in the car. Miss Love was pinning her red hat on straight again, so I couldn't see her expression, but I could see Grandpa's, and he didn't look contrite or guilty, either one. He looked like a boy playing tops who has just won everybody's tobacco tags.

Before he could kiss her again and me have to wait it out behind the tree, I yelled, "I got the grits!" and hurried toward them.

After pouring the grits into a napkin out of the picnic basket so I could use the bucket, I filled the radiator from the creek and cranked up. I was just fixing to pour in the grits when I thought to wonder how in heck you could get cooked grits out of a radiator.

"I don't think we better try it, Miss Love," I said. I folded the napkin and held it out to her. "You want the grits, ma'am?"

"I reckon you got a better idea," Grandpa said, sarcastic. He was disappointed. Fixing a leak with grits would be something to tell and laugh about all week, like that time we ran out of inner-tube patching and rode home on a tire stuffed with a piece of old quilt.

"Well, it might plug the leak, Grandpa. I don't know. But I think it'd ruin the radiator. We can risk it, sir, if you willin' to buy a new radiator. But—"

"Let's try something else, Will Tweedy."

"Grandpa, the colored woman said we'd come to a town called Cushie Springs in about two miles. We just foller the creek at the next fork instead of stayin' on the Athens road. That way, we can keep gettin' water to pour in the radiator. And if we make it to the town, maybe we can find a mechanic with solderin' tools."

We made the two miles, but it was an awful drive on a narrow, rutted wagon road. On one side was the creek, on the other a ditch so deep that if you got in it you'd never get out without a mule team. In low spots we hit sand. I had to stay in low gear to get through that. In the meanwhile I was feeding oil to the cylinders and water to the radiator. Kept that bucket going the whole way. When we got there I was wore out, and the heat and burning oil had made a dirty brown mess out of the Pierce's neat new engine.

Cushie Springs was not what I'd call a

town. It was just a handful of houses. Scant hope of finding a mechanic here. But probably we could hire a mule team to pull us into Athens.

Grandpa said let's ring up Mr. Shackleford and get him to send a mechanic. Mr. Shackleford had a garage over in Athens. I said, "You see any telephone poles in Cushie Springs, Grandpa?"

He looked around. "Naw, but what's thet got to do with anythang?"

"How can we telephone, sir, if Cushie Springs ain't got no telephones?"

"Don't be smart-aleck. Will. We'll think of something."

We stopped at the first house we saw. The young man who came to the door could hardly say howdy for trying to look around us at the automobile and at fashionable Miss Love, who was leaning out of the car to shake the dust from her veil.

Grandpa introduced himself and stated the situation. "You know anybody who could git a message over to Athens for us?"

The young man said he'd do it. Be glad to. "I work in Athens and I'm just fixin' to leave. Been down here seein' my folks. This is my mama," he said as an old lady came up behind him and said howdy.

"Howdy, ma'am," said Grandpa.

"And this here's my daddy," he said, smiling at a little old man who came around the house leading a big roan horse that was saddled up.

"Pleased to meet you, sir," said Grandpa, shaking hands. "Are you acquainted with Mr. Shackleford, son? We got a leakin' radiator."

The young man said he boarded right up the street from Mr. Shack's shop. Mounting the horse, he promised to go see him soon as he got back. "But I gar'ntee you, he ain't go'n send nobody over here to work on a Sunday."

"In thet case," said Grandpa, "I got another favor to ast." Writing his name and Papa's on a scrap of paper, he said to please ring up Hoyt Tweedy in Cold Sassy and say we'd be home some time t'morrer. He offered a quarter to pay for the call, but the young feller wouldn't take it. As he galloped off, his mother reached up to tidy her white hair, like we were real company, and said in a slow, drawly voice, "Looks to me like y'all got to spend the night some place, folks. We'd be mighty proud to put you up, wouldn't we, Mr. Nolly?"

It being the custom not to take anybody up on the first invite, Grandpa insisted we'd jest find us a ho-tel.

She laughed. "Ain't no ho-tel in Cushie Springs. Not even a boardin' house." Glancing at Grandpa's spiffy new suit and then at the car and Miss Love's motoring costume, she said, kind of embarrassed, "We ain't got no bathroom or lectric lights like all y'all in Cold Sassy. But if'n yore daughter don't mind, you welcome as can be."

"Hit's my wife, ma'am. And she won't mind." Grandpa motioned Miss Love to come up to the porch, which she did. After introductions all around, the old lady apologized again for the kerosene lamps and the privy. Of course Miss Love said that was all right. But she didn't once in the whole time we were there admit she had a privy, too, or mention her well water and lamplight.

The old lady's name was Miss Gussie. Mr. Nolly's real name, she said, was Knowledge Henry Jamison. I never heard a name like that before. When I got home, I put it down in my journal. What I heard later that night, I wouldn't of dared put down in my journal.

But I didn't need to. I knew I'd never forget any of it.

The Jamisons wanted to look at the Pierce. What with all the mud and dust and oil stains, it wasn't much to show off, but they were real impressed, especially after Grandpa said we'd give them a ride when we got the radiator fixed.

Miss Love seemed upset and awful nervous. I reckon Miss Gussie noticed, because she told her to go set down on the porch. "Make yoreself to home, honey, and rest a spell. We just havin' sausage and cornmeal battercakes and soggum syrup. I don't need no hep."

But Miss Love went on to the kitchen anyway, I guess to get away from Grandpa. Considering her new prospects for the future, you'd think she'd be all smiles instead of upset.

As I learned later, she was upset because she thought she didn't want the kind of future that Grandpa had in mind.

Us men sat down on the back porch steps and watched the sun set behind the barn. After talking hard times a while, Mr. Nolly asked questions about the Pierce, and then politely inquired as to Grandpa's business.

"You got you a store? My brother Big Dawg had a store one time. Big Dawg's name is Early. We jest call him Big Dawg." Pointing way off across the fields to a little log house at the edge of the woods, he laughed and said, "Thet's Big Dawg's drinkin' place. His wife won't let him in the house when he's drunk, so he goes over yonder and she sends a colored boy name Fish to see after him."

Normally Grandpa would of come up with a joke or a story then, but he kept looking toward the kitchen. His mind was on Miss Love. Mr. Nolly was thinking about her, too, because he soon said, "Scuse me for astin', but ain't Miz Blakeslee a Yankee? She kind of talks like one."

After Grandpa explained she was from Baltimore, Mr. Nolly said, "We got a real Yankee here in the county. He's bow-leggid, great goodness! Thet damn son-of-a-gun come in here two-three year ago and bought up a farm at sheriff's sale. Painted the house red, white, and blue and then rode the train back up North and got marrit. All I got to say, thet woman must a-been hard up for a husband, comin' down here where ain't nobody go'n speak to her, to live in a red, white, and blue house with a bow-leggid man. She's bow-leggid herself, though, and horse-faced, so they ain't a bad match. Miss Gussie says she cain't wait to see the fruits a-thet harvest! Say, did you know W. T. Stoddard?" Mr. Nolly asked. "He moved over here from Cold Sassy. W.T. ain't much, if you ast me."

"Naw, nor his daddy, neither," said Grandpa. "His daddy's dead now. Last time I seen him, he'd jest set fire to a dog."

I didn't remember old Mr. Stoddard, but I'd heard about the dog on fire. "He was the one did that?" I asked.

"He was the one," said Grandpa, and then told Mr. Nolly how in summertime there's always a bunch of old men playing checkers on a barrelhead out under this great old big sassafras tree at the depot. "One day a starvin', mangy ole dog come along, scroungin' for a biscuit, and thet fool Stoddard decided to put him out'n his miz'ry with kerosene and a match. Whilst the pore thang howled and rolled and whirled in the flames, them old men set there jest a-laughin'. I happened by bout then. Pulled out my pistol, kilt the dog, and shot thet checker game to Kingdom Come." He shook his head. "I'm jest as glad young W.T. chose to locate over here."

* * *

At supper that night my napkin slid off my knee. Bending down to pick it up, I saw Grandpa squeeze Miss Love's hand that was in her lap.

When Miss Gussie said she'd show us our rooms, Grandpa looked so excited you'd think all he lived for was to go to bed at night. While we took turns at the privy, she got out a soft white nightgown for Miss Love. "It's the one I save for nice. I embroidered them roses on it myself," she said proudly, handing it over. Then she got some towels and washrags out of a cupboard in the hall and, carrying a lighted kerosene lamp, led us up the steep stairs.

"Now this here is yore'n and Mr. Blakeslee's room," she told Miss Love, holding her lamp high as she opened a door into a neat plain room with old-timy furniture and a 1903 Arm and Hammer baking soda calendar on the wall. "I see Mr. Nolly filled up yore water pitcher like I told him to."

Miss Love's face had flushed at the words "yore'n and Mr. Blakeslee's room." To hide her embarrassment, she moved to the bed and ran her hand over the heavy purple and black coverlet. "Who wove it, Miss Gussie?"

"Mama did, when she warn't but sixteen

year old. Spun the wool and dyed it, weaved them panels, and stitched'm t'gether. Ain't it a beauty?" Miss Gussie put her lamp down on the washstand, struck a match, and lit the lamp on the bed table. "They's some quilts in the chest. Y'all might need'm. Mr. Nolly thinks it's go'n turn off cold t'night."

Just as I started to wonder where I was supposed to sleep, Miss Gussie opened a door over by the head of the bed. "This here used to be my sewin' room," she said. "But I fixed it up for my grandboys, Horace and Ulysses. They's eight and ten year old now. They spend ever summer here with us, heppin' Mr. Nolly around the place. Both them cots sleep good, son, so take yore pick." She lit a small lamp in there, then said good night and went back downstairs.

Miss Love looked at Grandpa. "Where do you want to sleep, sir?"

Like there wasn't any question, he nodded toward the big post bed and said, like teasing, "This here's where Miss Gussie said sleep. I reckon we better mind her."

Figuring they'd have to argue a while, I got a book off the bureau and took it to the little room. Though they lowered their voices, I distinctly heard Grandpa say, "One thang for shore, Miss Love. With two cots and a double bed, I ain't a-go'n sleep on the floor like I done in New York City."

(Well, so Mama and Aunt Loma had worried for nothing about New York City.)

Miss Love just laughed at him. "If you'd been willing to spend the money, sir, we could have had separate rooms. Weren't you lucky there were two berths on the boat!"

Peeping around the door, I saw him slap her behind, playful, and she laughed again. It was the first time all evening she'd seemed like her regular self. But then he got serious. "Cain't we jest sleep in here, Miss Love? Please?"

"Shh-h, don't talk so loud, Mr. Blakeslee."

I was about to pass out, I was so tired. "Where y'all want me to sleep?" I called from the little room.

"On one of the cots," Miss Love said quickly. "Mr. Blakeslee will sleep in there, too. I'll sleep in here."

"Thet's go'n look like Will Tweedy spent half the night on one cot and the rest of it on the other," said Grandpa. "Miss Gussie'll think he warn't comfortable."

The upshot was that Miss Love decided to sleep in the cot room and let me and

Grandpa take the big bed. I couldn't help thinking how funny all this would sound to somebody who didn't know she was just his housekeeper.

There being only one washstand, Grandpa and I had to stay in the little room with the door shut while Miss Love bathed. I laid down on one of the cots while we waited. Grandpa paced the floor. The whole time she was washing up, he stopped walking only long enough to hitch up his trousers and scratch his head—like if he scratched hard enough and fast enough he might think how to get his way.

We finally heard Miss Love pour her dirty water out of the washbowl into the waste pot on the floor. But it was some time before she knocked and said she was through. Grandpa rushed to open the door, and it was like he'd opened onto a flower garden, Miss Love had on so much perfume. She stood there in the doorway, holding the red hat in her hand and her clothes draped over one arm. The white gown peeped out above and below her coat, which she was using like a robe.

In the soft lamplight she looked real pretty. Her freckled face was flushed, her eyes bright in the frame of dark lashes, her hair plaited into a thick shiny braid that hung down the left side of her neck.

"I'm sorry it took me so long," she said, her voice steady.

Grandpa surprised me by leaning over and kissing her on the cheek. "G'night," he said. For a long moment they stood there staring at one another, like his eyes were steel and hers a dern magnet. Her lips trembled.

There being no way to get past them, I just sat there on the cot, half-asleep, watching them block the doorway. Finally Grandpa took a deep breath, which shook a little as he let it out. "I know you plumb wore out, Miss Love."

"No, not really. I feel fine. I—uh—feel fine. Are you very tired?"

"Gosh a'mighty, no. If I was a bull I could bust through a fence right now and never feel it." He touched her arm. She didn't move away. He laughed softly. "But I reckon I won't be a-doin' thet tonight. Well, Miss Love, sleep good, hear. Call me if'n you need anythang." They were still staring at one another. "Be sure and call me if they's anythang I can—"

"Thank you, I won't need anything, Mr. Blakeslee. Good night, sir."

She moved past him into the little room. I reckon she'd forgot all about me, because it startled her when I got up from the cot. "Uh, good night, Will."

"G'night, ma'am." She patted my arm as I went out. Then she shut the door.

Grandpa walked over to the washstand and poured some water into the big flowerdy bowl, but I just pulled off down to my union suit and turned back the covers. I was too tired to care about road dust. "Which side you want to sleep on, Grandpa? Left or right?"

"Hit don't matter, son. Like I used to tell yore granny, everwhich side I'm on is the right side. She always said hers was the one next to the cradle or closest to the kitchen."

I was standing on the side by the door to Miss Love's room, so I just got in there.

The wall between my head and hers was only one thin board, and I soon realized it might as well not be there. I heard her pull up the quilt, I heard her turn over, I heard her sigh.

I must of dropped right off to sleep. I didn't know when Grandpa came to bed. But I knew when he got up. The coil springs squeaked and waked me. I thought he just needed to use the pot, which he did, but then he moved around the bed. Every time a board creaked underfoot, he stopped and looked over at me.

It wasn't like Grandpa to notice or care if he was disturbing somebody. Plain as day, he didn't want me to wake up, so I didn't—not for him to know it. But I watched as he tip-toed over to the window where he'd laid his clothes on a chair and, standing in a long slanting rectangle of moonlight, put on his pants over his union suit and pulled up the suspenders.

Instead of knocking on Miss Love's door, he opened it, quiet as a burglar. I heard her gasp. He whispered, "Sh-h, it's me. I'm a-comin' in."

There wasn't any question mark in his voice, but she whispered, "Well, I . . . well, all right," and I heard her get up. Grandpa closed the door, but it didn't any more shut me out than if I was a ghost. I doubt they were standing more than two feet from my head when he grabbed her. "Oh, Lord, Miss Love! You don't know how long I been a-waitin' to hold you like this." His voice was muffled, as if his face was buried in her neck. "Seems like all my life."

She laughed kind of nervous, and whispered in a teasing way, "Now, Mr. Blakeslee, that's no way to talk to a housekeeper."

"I ain't a-talkin' to no dang housekeeper, Miss Love. I'm a-talkin' to my wife."

Still teasing, and I guess holding him off, she whispered, "I won't be the wife of anybody who calls me Miss and I have to call him Mister. So Mister Blakeslee, go back to bed."

He whispered right back. "If'n Miss and Mister is all thet's comin' betwixt us, I shore wisht you'd a-said so in New York City! Yore name's Love? Ain't no problem. My name's Rucker, pleased to meet you." And then before she could say pea-turkey, he grabbed her again. This time, if my ears heard right, she grabbed him, too.

After while she whispered, "Oh, dear God, what are we going to do?" I reckon Grandpa found her mouth before God could answer, because for the longest time the only sounds I heard were little moans and gasps and Grandpa's hard breathing. He sounded like it was all uphill in there.

Miss Love must of pulled away, to judge by her voice as she whispered, "Please, Mr. Blakeslee. If you knew—" And then she went to crying.

"Hesh   now . . . sh-h . . . sh-h-h . . .
ain't nothin' to cry about, Miss Love, less'n
you don't love me, which if you said it I
wouldn't believe you. Love. Love. Oh, Love.
Hit ain't hard a-tall to call you Love. Or to
say you're beautiful or how sweet you smell.
You're like Miss Mattie Lou's rose garden,
Miss—uh, I mean Love." They kissed again.
"You're shiverin'," he said. "I could warm
you up."

"I'm not cold. . . . Don't, Mr. Blakeslee!
You'll tear Miss Gussie's gown!"

His whispered voice was hoarse. "Good
God in Heaven . . ."

I thought he was about to say hit's time to
pray. But for what seemed like an hour or
two, all I heard was them breathing and kissing.

I won't try to say what I was feeling all that
time.

"What are you doing? Don't . . ." she
said all of a sudden, alarmed.

"I'm jest a-loosenin' yore braid. I ain't
never seen yore hair down, Miss—uh, I mean
Love. I want to feel it. I want to feel it on my
face."

"Please go back to bed, sir. The boy might
hear us."

He groaned. "I ain't studyin' him. He's dead asleep, anyhow. Listen to him."

Like I was in cahoots with Grandpa, I snored softly. I couldn't stand the embarrassment if they knew I was awake. They were silent a minute, then she whispered, "There's so much you don't know. . . ."

Smack. "Then say it, Love, but make haste. I been a-waitin' for you a million years. I cain't wait no longer!"

I was shocked, and she must of felt the same. "But . . . but you . . . but I only agreed to be your housekeeper!" Her whisper rose in pitch, an angry sound. "I will not be taken advantage of, Mr. Blakeslee! How dare you try to . . . to use me like I'm a . . . Why, I trusted you!"

"I love you, Miss Love! Cain't you see thet? And today I . . . hit seemed like you loved me, too."

"What are you saying, Mr. Blakeslee?"

"You deaf? I'm sayin' I love you, dang it! I'm sayin' I want you to be my wife! I'm sayin' I been a-waitin' to hold you in my arms ever since the day we got married. . . . No, way longer than thet, Lord hep me. Miss Love— Love, I been a-waitin' for this minute ever since the day I laid eyes on you!"

It made me sick, hearing that.

"Please, Mr. Blakeslee, you don't know what you're saying." Her words were more softly spoken than whispered, and I could tell she had moved away from him, nearer the door. "I don't believe. . . . You never made one gesture, sir. Never said one word!"

"No, but ever time I looked at you, I thought it. God hep me, I been lovin' you and hatin' myself ever time I—"

"You never did anything wrong!" she protested, like she wanted to take up for him. Then she lowered her voice again. "I never once suspected. That's why I was so shocked when you asked me to marry you. I didn't think you'd even noticed me, Mr. Blakeslee."

"I was scairt to notice you. Scairt somebody would notice me noticin'. Scairt Miss Mattie Lou might, and I wouldn't a-hurt her —" I heard him sink heavily onto the cot, and he must of bent his head down, to judge by his voice. "Miss Mattie Lou knowed something was eatin' up my soul, Miss Love. She kept a-sayin', 'Mr. Blakeslee, tell me what's a-worryin' you so.' And when she took sick—"

"Sh-h, you're talking too loud, sir. Please

don't wake up Will. Go on back to bed now and we'll talk when—"

"I got to talk now," he said, but minding her and dropping his voice to a whisper. "By time we git home I might a-lost my nerve. I used to beg God to take away my cravin' for you. When I'd git up off my knees, I'd feel better. But then the very next day I'd watch you workin' at yore table and . . . I couldn't hardly stand it, you was so beautiful. Then Miss Mattie Lou took sick, and I got scairt the Lord might take her to punish me for my sin. I ain't never believed God was thet mean. But what if'n He was? I commenced beggin' for forgiveness. When she was so sick, I got the notion if I didn't go down to the store where I'd see you, I could git you out a-my system. Miss Mattie Lou was . . . She married me when I warn't nothin', Miss Love. She give me all she had when her daddy died. And she ruint her health havin' babies thet didn't live, tryin' to git me a son to carry on the name. She knowed how much—" His voice broke. "She would a-tried agin, but Doc said another baby'd kill her. So I made shore thet didn't happen. I loved Miss Mattie Lou very much. You unner-stand thet?"

I could hear tears in her voice as she whispered, "Yes. Yes, of course I do."

"She was part a-me. I could tell her anything—cept bout you, a-course. It was jest like with Will Tweedy, and now you. I can cut the fool with anybody, but they ain't many folks I can really talk to. . . . Well, after what Doc said, I stayed off from her—"

"Mr. Blakeslee, it's not right to tell me all this."

"I got to tell somebody. You rather I tell Will Tweedy? Or Mary Willis or Loma? I'm sayin' I stayed off from her, and after while the fire went out. Seemed like she was jest my sister, my friend. Not my wife. It was like all the feelin's I ever felt—a man for a woman, I mean—they was jest dead. Then I went to the depot to git you when you come in on thet train from Baltimore, Miss Love. I took one look at you, so young and feisty, and hankered after you like a schoolboy."

"Hush, sir. Hush."

"You don't know what I been th'ew these two years, Miss Love. Lord, I wisht we didn't have to whisper. I'm a-gittin' hoarse."

"Go back to bed, Mr. Blakeslee. We'll talk later." It was like she was speaking to a child.

He paid no attention. "After you left off

livin' at our house and went to the Crabtrees', Miss Love, I couldn't wait to git to the store ever mornin'. If'n I was sick, I went on anyways. I thought I'd die when a whole day went by and I didn't git to see you. Often as I dared to, I'd tell Miss Mattie Lou, 'Set a place for the milliner at Sunday dinner, hear. She's kind a-homesick.' Or, 'She don't git good cookin' at Miz Crabtree's. Not like yore'n.' You and me and her, we'd have sech a good time round thet pi-ana after dinner. Hit kind a-eased my guilty feelin's, seein' how fond a-you she was. But then, by George, you commenced keepin' comp'ny with thet fool Son Black! I couldn't hardly stand it."

"He didn't mean a thing to me. He was just—"

"How was I to know? And then . . . then Miss Mattie Lou was a-dyin'. I set there by her in thet rockin' chair day after day, lovin' her and grievin', but in the back side a-my mind I was wonderin' if'n you might up and marry thet son-of-a-gun jest when it looked like—"

"Sh-h, don't say it, Mr. Blakeslee. Please, let's stop talking. The boy—"

I coughed, and coughed again, like in my sleep, and then snorted and turned over.

"Hit'd take a earthquake to wake him up t'night." There was a pause. "Yore skin . . . hit's so soft, Love. See? Hit ain't hard a-tall to call you Love. Yore cheek, Love, it's like" —he laughed—"like a mule's nose. . . . Like velvet." She laughed, too. He kissed her gently. I know it was gently, because it didn't smack. "Love, when I set there with Miss Mattie Lou, I warn't jest beggin' God's forgiveness. I was prayin' she'd git well. But I was—"

"There's nothing wrong with that, Mr. Blakeslee. God wants us to ask for His healing hand on—"

"Let me finish. God don't want nobody to ast like I done. Gosh a'mighty, Miss Love, all the time I was prayin' Him to spare Miss Mattie Lou, like He was a dang Santy Claus, I was thinkin' thet if'n she died I could marry you!"

I swear I saw the ghost of Granny flit distraught around the room. I wanted to sic her on him, shout, "He ain't in here, Granny! He's in yonder with her! Go haint him!"

Soon as I thought it, I hoped she wouldn't. Back when she was alive and him lusting in his heart after another woman, it's a wonder God hadn't strung Grandpa up by his heels

and split him down the middle. But I couldn't
hate him now. And I hoped Granny up in
Heaven didn't hate him, and I hoped Miss
Love wouldn't. If a man's been horsewhip-
ping himself for two years, it seemed to me
like not even God would want to punish him
anymore.

I couldn't hear everything they said that
night, especially when they moved away from
the door. I missed words and even sentences
when occasionally I breathed deep or snored
a little so they wouldn't guess I was awake.
But I heard most of it.

After Grandpa's confession, Miss Love had
tears in her voice. "You poor, dear man. I'm
so sorry, so very sorry." She whispered it over
and over, and then begged him to go back to
bed.

But Grandpa said he warn't done talking.

"Miss Mattie Lou's last few days. . . .
Well, the good Lord fine'ly set me free a'you,
Miss Love. My mind and heart was all on her.
I knowed she was go'n die, and all I wanted
was for her to live. I kept thinkin' back over
the years and knowed they was good years. I
kept thinkin' how we used to talk in bed at
night, how I was go'n miss thet . . . how I

aw-ready missed it." He took a long breath. "But Miss Love, all sech didn't last past the funeral! After I wrote down her dyin' in the Bible, I turned around and seen you standin' there watchin' me, and from then on—"

"Oh, Mr. Blakeslee! As God is my witness, I never guessed it. Never encouraged—"

"I know thet. I jest wish you had a-encouraged me. Then I could a-risked waitin' a proper time to start courtin' you. As it was, I was twixt the rock and the hard place, afeared somebody else would git you in the meantime. Thet fool Son Black, for instance."

"I would never have married him."

"Well, I didn't know if you would or you wouldn't. On the other hand, if'n I proposed right off, you'd think I was a dirty old man or thet Miss Mattie Lou hadn't meant nothin' to me. You wouldn't have no respect for me." He sighed, like he was lost in thought. Finally he said, "I commenced goin' by the cemetery ever night after I left the store, Miss Love."

"I know. I heard."

He laughed, soft and kind of rueful. "Hit warn't with me like with pore Miss Ernestine Tiplady. You never knowed her. Miss Ernestine would go to the cemetery ever evenin' to see old Mutt. Thet's what she called her husband. She'd tell him how she was feelin' and all, and any news she'd heard, and when she left she'd blow him a kiss and say, 'G'night, Mutt.' Folks seen her do it. Then after while Miss Ernestine got to sayin' g'night to everbody else in the graveyard, callin'm all by name. Pore thang fine'ly commenced passin' the time a-day with'm. Couldn't git home to fix supper for talkin' to dead folks."

He paused. "What I'm sayin', I didn't go to the cemetery to talk to Miss Mattie Lou. But seemed like bein' there calmed me down some." He coughed. "Gosh a'mighty, Miss Love, it's gittin' cold. And my throat's wore out from this here whisperin'. Will Tweedy's asleep. And if'n he ain't . . . Well, I ain't studyin' Will Tweedy right now."

At the cemetery, he said, he did wonder sometimes what Miss Mattie Lou would tell him to do if she could talk. "Late one night I was so tired, Miss Love, I jest laid down on the cool fresh dirt. Right on her grave. Hit felt like when we used to lay in bed together talkin'. Uh, I reckon you think I was off in the head."

"No. No, I understand."

"Well, anyhow, it come to me something

Miss Mattie Lou said long time ago, back when Mary Willis was on the way. She said, 'Mr. Blakeslee, if God takes me in child-bed—' I remember tryin' to hesh her up, but she had it on her mind. She said, 'If'n I pass, I hope I done made livin' with a woman so sweet thet . . . Well, find you another wife and I'll take it as a compli-ment.' "

Miss Love started to speak, but he went on, talking low. "Thet shore made it easier to think on marryin' you, Miss Love. It was like she'd give me her blessin'. And whilst I was still a-layin' over her in the dark night, I remembered something else she said one time: 'If'n the Lord calls me first, Mr. Blakeslee, don't be too stingy to hire you a colored woman. I cain't rest easy Up There if you down here wearin' dirty clothes and nobody to see after you.' Thet's what give me the idea to ast you to be my housekeeper."

He didn't say anything for a minute, or her, either. I reckon they were kissing. Then he went on. "I figgered if'n I could jest git you sewed up, I could do the courtin' later. But I knowed I'd have to make it worth yore while, me bein' old and all the talk and scandal of it. Took me bout two minutes to decide you'd go against age and custom both for something big as a house."

She giggled, a little self-conscious. "I think I'd have done it for the piano."

"The pi-ana cinched it. Then two days later here come Mr. Texas. It like to kilt me, seein' you was still in love with him."

I heard Grandpa get up from the cot and start pacing the floor. When he stopped, he breathed a long sigh that trembled in the night air. "Stealin' Mary Willis's trip to New York City was a selfish thang I done."

Miss Love plain admitted that it was her fault. "I thought Mary Willis had definitely decided not to go. I—"

"Lord hep me, when I seen you wanted to go so bad, all I could think was up there in New York I'd have you to myself, with nobody around to cast looks, and maybe—"

"I'm beginning to hate myself, Mr. Blakeslee."

"For marryin' me?"

"For not guessing how you felt about me. I never even suspected it till we got to New York."

"I didn't know you caught on then, Miss Love."

"I didn't want you to know it."

"You might near as good a actress as Loma. I thought I'd jest lost the hang a-courtin'."

She didn't answer that. "Mr. Blakeslee, if you'd said you loved me when you proposed, I wouldn't have married you. I had decided never to marry . . . for reasons I can't speak of. For reasons no man would want to marry me. But you said—"

"They cain't be no reason any man wouldn't be proud to marry you, Miss Love."

"But you said you just wanted a house-keeper, Mr. Blakeslee. You don't know how I had longed for—prayed for—what you offered. A home, and to belong to a good, decent family. It was as if God had finally figured out a way to give it to me."

"Hit warn't God figgered it out, Love. Hit was me. And now I'm astin' you to be my wife." When she didn't answer, he said, "You cain't say you don't care for me."

"Of course I care for you, sir. But not like—that. I'm sorry."

"Thet ain't what yore arms said or yore lips said when I was a-kissin' you."

"I . . . I got carried away."

"Ain't gittin' carried away part a-what lovin' is?"

"You don't understand." She spoke stiff and formal. "Loving—being a wife—that door is closed to me. After Mr. McAllister, I promised God."

There was an awful silence. Then Grandpa exploded. "Promised God or promised yoreself? Gosh a'mighty, woman, God don't ast for no sech a promise!"

"It was the only way I could find peace. And now I don't want to talk about it anymore. I'm tired. . . . Mr. Blakeslee, please go to bed."

"What you and somebody else done, Love, thet's over with now. Same as my life with Miss Mattie Lou is over with—and thet hand I ain't got no more. Everwhat you done cain't be no worse than me lovin' you whilst I sat by her deathbed. But ain't no point in me givin' you up, now thet she cain't git hurt. And ain't no point in you messin' up what you and me could have jest cause you and thet dang Mr. Texas—"

"It wasn't him." Her whisper was so weak I barely heard. "But don't ask me to talk about it. Clayt couldn't take the knowledge. You couldn't, either."

"You told him what you won't tell me?"

"Yes. I thought"—she sounded about to

cry—"I thought I shouldn't have any secrets from the man I was about to marry. I thought if Clayt really loved me . . . How stupid I was!" I wondered if she meant stupid to tell him or stupid to think he wouldn't mind. "He'd thought I was so pure. Not like the others. You understand *pure*, Mr. Blakeslee? Undefiled?"

Silence.

"Defiled cain't be the right word for you, Love. Or don't them Methodist preachers talk none bout a forgivin' God? Ain't you heard how Jesus said go and sin no more? He didn't say go waller in yore sin!"

"I hadn't sinned."

Silence.

"Miss Love, you don't make no sense a-tall. Not to me. If'n you ain't sinned, how come all this here talk bout you ain't pure no more?"

"Sh-h-h, you're talking loud, Mr. Blakeslee." And she lowered her own voice. "I can only say that Clayt . . . right after I told Mr. McAllister, he talked just like you. Said it didn't matter. But—well, as you know, he finally broke the engagement. And you'd want to get out of being married to me, too, Mr. Blakeslee, if I told you."

"Then, gosh a-mighty, woman, don't tell me! I don't give a good doggone and I don't want to hear bout it. I jest want you to be my wife."

"No, no, please. Please, Mr. Blakeslee, don't touch me. Go back to bed. Please . . ."

I snored softly as I heard Grandpa's hand on the doorknob.

I heard her whisper, "But I . . . I can't bear for you to think—I mean, what happened wasn't—I mean, I couldn't help what happened."

His hand left the doorknob. "Then it must a-been somebody you loved."

"Y-yes." She was crying.

"Well, dang it, why didn't you marry him? Good gosh a'mighty, Miss Love, are you sayin' you got mixed up with a married man?"

"It still wasn't my fault! But I thought you didn't care!"

"I don't! Livin' a lie like I done, I ain't got no call to th'ow no stones. And I ain't astin' are you pure. But I know I cain't stand it if'n you go'n hold a married man up in front a-me like a pitcher for the rest a-my life, sayin' I got to look at you and him. I ain't your Mr. Texas, but I cain't take it if'n you go'n dish out little bitty hints bout it ever time yore conscience starts to hurt. Thet'd keep me wonderin' and maybe jealous. God A'mighty, Miss Love, forgit all thet and jest let me love you and make you happy!" His whispered voice was angry. "Why'd you have to raise this up from the dead, anyhow? You go'n put the past on and wear it like sackcloth and ashes the rest a-yore days?"

Miss Love was crying. "Please, Mr. B-Blakeslee! Be fair. This wouldn't have c-come up if you had let me stay what I agreed to be. Just your h-housekeeper."

Grandpa left the room before Miss Love finished the word *housekeeper*. Came out and shut the door. I knew by the harsh breathing that he was furious. On the other side of the door, Miss Love laid down on the cot and muffled her crying in the pillow. I didn't see how in the world Grandpa could walk out on her like that.

He started to pace the floor, but the boards creaked and I reckon he was scared he'd wake me up. Shivering, he jerked his spiffy new suit coat off the back of the chair, put it around him, and stood at the window in the moonlight, trying to get aholt of himself. Every minute or so he'd scratch his head like he had cooties worse than Hosie Roach.

I must of dozed off, but I waked with a start when he turned the doorknob by my head and went back in there. I reckon Miss Love was too tired to get up. She whispered, "Go on to bed, Mr. Blakeslee. There's nothing more to say. I'll deed back the house and leave Cold Sassy soon as I can arrange it. Then you can get an annulment and marry that other lady."

"What you talkin' bout?" he whispered back. "What dang other lady?"

"You said there was one other woman in Cold Sassy you thought you could stand if I—"

"Oh, thet. I jest made her up—like a good salesman makes up thet somebody else is waitin' with the money if'n you don't take what he's sellin'. Miss Love, after all I done told you tonight, don't you know they ain't nobody in the world I want to live with cept you? Doggit, woman, I love you!"

And then he went down on the cot with her and they were kissing again.

At some point amid the sighs and moans and murmurs, Miss Love pulled away and whispered, "It was my . . ." Her voice was shaking so I couldn't hear the word she said.

Grandpa didn't either. "What'd you say?"

"It was m-my f-f-father. My father. I said it was my f-father, Mr. Blakeslee!"

"You mean—?" He got up off the bed, and she did, too. "God A'mighty! Miss Love, you ain't got no call to tell me a thang like thet!" She couldn't talk for crying. "Sh-h-h-h," Grandpa whispered. "Sh-h-h-h. Hit don't matter now. Sh-h-h . . ."

"Don't shush me. It does m-matter. And I'm . . . I'm g-going to stop cr-crying and tell you everything. Sir, please, don't s-say hush."

And she got aholt of herself and she talked. And she talked and talked. Talked low and fast. "No matter what you say, Mr. Blakeslee, you won't want me for a wife. It's too—awful. But I'm going to tell you. When I finish, maybe you'll pity me or maybe you'll be sick of me, but at least you'll know I couldn't help it. Maybe you won't . . . be angry." Her voice shook so at first that she was hard to understand, but she got out that it happened when she was twelve years old.

"You don't have to tell me, Miss Love," Grandpa protested.

"I do have to. So don't interrupt."

I doubted she remembered that I was just two feet away, and I forgot about trying to sound asleep. But they wouldn't of noticed if I'd started banging on the wall.

"We lived in three rooms upstairs in somebody's house. I had a little cot like this one, in a small room next to what we used as a sitting room. Their bed was in the sitting room. Mama had heart trouble, Mr. Blakeslee. Everybody knew she was dying, and the lady and man downstairs helped her all they could. They had gone somewhere that night—I'm sure it wouldn't have happened if they'd been home. Well, I woke up when Father came in drunk, as usual, and I heard Mama coughing and crying. She asked him for some water, but, Mr. Blakeslee, Father just laughed. Laughed!"

"Don't, Miss Love—"

She didn't hear him. Her voice had got mechanical, like she was reciting a story she'd read in the newspaper—one that didn't have anything to do with her. "After Mama's coughing subsided, she said, 'Timothy, when I'm gone, you will take care of Love, won't you?' I'd heard her say that sort of thing many times, and it always made him mad. I just thought he never wanted her to talk about dying, as if it wouldn't happen if she didn't say the words. But that night he suddenly screamed a man's name at her. 'He's her daddy, tell him to take care of her!'

"There was an awful silence, and then Mama said, 'Hush! Love might hear you. And you know it's not so, Timothy. He married somebody else, remember? Years before I even met you!' Father said that didn't prove a thing. He was so drunk, Mr. Blakeslee. He cursed and said, 'We were married exactly one week, Cleo, when you called me his name! I won't ever forget that.' Mama said it didn't mean she'd been seeing him, but Father wasn't listening. He said, 'You were carrying his baby. Admit it. Why else would you have married a man like me?' She was crying, but she got out something like 'God help me, I didn't know what you were like! But as God is my witness, I was not pregnant!' Father just laughed. 'Why was she born in eight months? Answer me that.' He shouted at her like she was deaf. 'She is his child. Ain't she?' "

"Hesh up, Miss Love," Grandpa pleaded. "You don't have to—"

"I have to. Mama was crying and went into the most awful fit of coughing, but he just cursed her. It was awful, listening to them. Then I heard Father stagger toward my room, yelling, 'By God, I'll show you what I think the truth is!' As he came in where I was, he was still yelling at Mama. I'll never forget his words. 'Would a man kill his own flesh and blood, Cleo?' I heard her scream, and I screamed. I tried to get under the cot, but he caught my arm. Then he said, 'Aw, she's too pretty just to kill! Cleo? Listen to me. Would I take my own daughter? No, by God. But, by God, I can take another man's daughter!' "

Miss Love's voice sunk to an awful whisper. "And then he—he raped me! Raped me, Mr. Blakeslee! I tried to fight him off, but he—"

Grandpa must of started shaking her. "I hear you, Miss Love! Don't say thet word agin!"

"The whole time, he was screaming, 'You know what I'm doing in here, Cleo?' But she didn't answer. Finally he left. Stumbled down the stairs and went away. When I got to Mama, she was on the floor in the hall, unconscious. I held her for what seemed like hours. When the people who lived below came home, they got the doctor."

She sighed a long sigh. "Mama had been

trying to get to me, but she passed out. We talked about it later, she and I. She said I had two choices. I could dwell on this the rest of my life—let it make me scared of everybody and bitter against Father—or I could forgive him and put my hand in God's and live my life. Something she said . . . Well, I realized Mama didn't know he had . . . I realized she hadn't heard anything after he screamed would a man kill his own flesh and blood. So I never told her what really happened. She had suffered enough. But all the years after, I never forgot what she said about forgiving him. And I thought I had. I even got over feeling defiled—till I told Clayt and he did what he did. So, Mr. Blakeslee, now you know. You don't have to wonder. Just accept that I was defiled and hate it and I can never be anybody's wife. I don't even want to . . . be a wife. I'll leave Cold Sassy as soon as I can."

Grandpa's voice was hoarse. "Hit don't make no difference, Miss Love."

"I believed Mr. McAllister when he said that. Never again . . . Leave me alone, Mr. Blakeslee! Go to bed and leave me alone!"

"Damnit, woman! Damnit, I . . . Where's yore daddy now?"

"I don't know. Died drunk, probably. We never saw him again. He didn't come to Mama's funeral."

There was absolute silence in that room then, except they were both breathing hard. I thought sure Grandpa would try to comfort her. Make her see how much he loved her, how nothing mattered now except to forget all that and let him take care of her. Maybe he would have, but she said to him in a voice cold as metal, *"I said leave me alone!"* And he did.

Grandpa stalked out, shut the door, and stood there by the bed, shaking. I never saw him madder. I watched as he tiptoed over to the chest, raised the lid, pulled out a quilt, wrapped it around him. He stood by the window for the longest kind of a time, then knelt down by the windowsill and covered his face with his hand. Grandpa was crying, but he didn't make a sound except a hoarse gasp when he had to breathe. At some point I knew he had gone to praying.

It must of been an hour or more before he came to bed. I don't think he slept at all. I know I didn't.

* * *

Soon as I heard Miss Gussie in the kitchen, I bounced out of bed. "Better get up, Grandpa! Man from Athens might be here early. Boy howdy, I slept like a log! Hope I didn't root you, sir."

"I wouldn't know, son." He looked like he'd been beat up, but he said he slept like the dead.

"Reckon we better get Miss Love up?" I asked. Without waiting for his answer, I called through the door. "Miss Love? Hate to wake you up, but that mechanic could be here any time now. We slept like the dead in here. We rarin' to go!"

It was a nice breakfast with Miss Gussie and Mr. Nolly. Nobody would have guessed how mad Grandpa and Miss Love were at each other.

The mechanic came at seven o'clock. Soon as he fixed the radiator and cleaned the oil and grime off the engine, we took the Jamisons for a quick ride and then left Cushie Springs.

If Grandpa had ridden home in the back seat with his arm around Miss Love, I'd of thought everything I heard was just a bad dream.

But he rode up front with me.

42

Miss Love did a lot of horseback riding the next few weeks, and if she ever stopped to talk to anybody, I didn't hear about it. Whenever I went up there to clean the stable, I walked around the house, not through it. I didn't know what to say to her.

Grandpa? Hearing him joke and tease and tell tales down at the store, you wouldn't of known he had a care in the world, unless you studied his eyes. Since That Night, they were never merry. And he started to look bushy again, and older, and you could see his mean streak better.

For instance, there was the matter of Mr. Clem Crummy having a drawing to get a new name for the Cold Sassy Hotel, recently bought from old Mr. Boop. After sprucing it up a little, Mr. Clem advertised a drawing in the paper "for a name more befitting this fine, refurbished, modern establishment." The Crummys put a big shoebox on the hotel desk, and Cold Sassy filled it up with names like the Waldorf and the Savoy. Mama's entry was the Hotel Prince Edward. Mine was the

Hotel Bedbug. Grandpa entered a name, but wouldn't say what it was.

At four o'clock on Sunday, less than two weeks before Thanksgiving, Mr. Clem held his drawing on the hotel piazza. Nobody but him took it serious, but it was somewhere to go, so Cold Sassy went. Well, Miss Love didn't go. I remember that.

When Mr. Clem pulled his fat hand out of the shoebox and looked at the piece of paper, seemed like he couldn't believe what he saw. I was just sure he'd drawn the Hotel Bedbug! But he hadn't. "For pity sake, Rucker," he exploded, "if I'd a-wanted a name like that, I'd a-used my own!" Then he commenced to laugh. "Folks, Rucker here done named my place after hisself. The Rucker Blakeslee Ho-tel. Ain't he a card, though! I swanny, Rucker, you shore do know how to make a joke. Well, Miss Pauline, bring back the shoebox. I'll try agin."

While everybody laughed, Grandpa walked up so close to Mr. Clem they just about touched stomachs. "You done got you a name, Mr. Crummy. The Rucker Blakeslee Ho-tel."

The crowd got silent and uneasy. Mr. Clem

looked like he didn't know what to say. "But
. . . ain't it just a joke?"

"Hit was when I put it in the box," said
Grandpa. "Hit was jest go'n be something to
tell and laugh about, same as if'n you'd
named it the Crummy Hotel. I never thought
to git drawed." Though a smile was playing
around under his mustache, his eyes were
hard. "But now thet it's the one, I kind a-like
the sound of it. You wanted a fine fancy name
for yore establish-ment? A symbol of success
and ca-racter? Well, sir, seems to me like you
got one." Looking back at me, Grandpa
grinned.

"You cain't make me do that!" Mr. Clem
was sputtering. "It's my ho-tel!"

"But it's my name!" Grandpa put his forefinger on Mr. Crummy's big chest. "Yore ad
said you'd use whatever name got drawed.
If'n you don't carry out the drawin', I'll sue
for breach a-promise. You can put 'Clem
Crummy, Proprietor' on yore sign if you got a
mind to, but what it's go'n be called is the
Rucker Blakeslee Ho-tel."

Everybody thought Grandpa would take
back the name after he'd had his fun. I knew
he wouldn't. Like I said, he was not one to let
go of a grudge, and several years back Mr.

Clem had cheated him in a land deal. Well, now he'd got even—got even and then some. But that didn't mean he wasn't still mad about it.

The next evening, Grandpa came down sick. In a day or two he was coughing and said he thought it was a relapse of lung disease from war deprivation. He said his symptoms were just like what went through the 6th Georgia one winter, and sent word to the family that nobody was to come up there.

"Rucker says it's ketchin' as sin," Doc said. "I told Miss Love she better be careful. Boil his plate and fork and all. I don't want no epidemic gittin' started in this town."

Mama was real worried. Not being sure Miss Love knew how to tend the sick, she took some chicken soup up there for him. Grandpa liked the soup but wouldn't let her in the house. She might ketch what he had. Miss Love said he coughed and groaned a lot, but was eating well. "I just don't understand it," she told Mama.

Something seemed fishy to me, but I couldn't put my finger on it. Maybe he was really sick. On the other hand, if Miss Love had started packing to leave, he might just be

COLD SASSY TREE 569

playing sick to keep her there. If she'd decided to stay but still refused to be his wife, maybe he was pouting. Or maybe he was heartsick, hating her for what her daddy did to her but still not willing to give her up.

What I thought was that he loved her as much as ever and had decided to stay home till she gave in. I recalled him telling me one time, "When you don't know which way to turn, son, try something. Don't jest do nothin'."

The one time I saw Miss Love during his confinement, she said, "He groans all the time, but he eats enough for a regiment. I don't know whether to laugh or cry, ignore him or worry."

She must of decided to ignore him, because after about ten days she got the idea of training Mr. Beautiful to old Jack's buggy. She'd hitch up and go off for hours. Grandpa soon let everybody know that the contagious period was over and insisted on going to ride with her. Said he was still weak, but the cold fresh air would be good for his lungs. After that, they were behind the horse every day, bundled up together under the automobile lap robes, her holding the reins and the whip, him sitting stiff and straight beside her. They would speak a greeting if they passed you, but as Miss Effie Belle said, it was like they didn't know each other or anybody else, either.

Before long, though, they were laughing and talking on their rides, and Grandpa was howdying and joking with everybody he saw.

He had become the grand duke of Cold Sassy again.

Like everybody else, Aunt Loma was relieved that her daddy was better. But, tell the truth, she'd been too busy directing the school's Christmas play to worry much about him.

Mama went over there one morning and found Loma sitting at the kitchen table writing in a tablet. She didn't seem to care that there were dust devils under the beds or that it was time for Uncle Camp to come to dinner. She said she had to work on the play. I expect it was the first time she'd been happy since she got married. Just before school let out every day, she'd bring Campbell Junior down to our house, hand him over to Queenie, and prance off to direct rehearsals like she'd got a call to do it from God Almighty Himself.

Aunt Loma didn't make me be in the play. But anything she needed she called on me and got so bossy I couldn't stand it hardly. Two weeks before play night, she told me to catch her a live mouse for Claude Wiggins to drop out of a shoebox in the third act.

The mouse was supposed to create pandemonium at a Christmas party on stage.

I think now that if Aunt Loma hadn't wanted the live mouse, it never would of dawned on me to mess up the play. The way it happened, my cousin Doodle and Uncle Skinny came in from their farm in Banks County about three o'clock one Sunday evening to spend the night with us and pick up a wagonload of feed corn next morning at the store. Doodle and I had just gone out to the barn to pitch down hay for his mules when in strolled Pink Predmore, Lee Roy Sleep, and Smiley Snodgrass.

After a hard cold spell in late November, there's nothing like a nice warm day to make you restless. You just want to do something, for gosh sake!

Lying in the warm sunshine in the hayloft, we tried to think up something, but didn't have any luck. We were all kind of irritable. Doodle, who had his head resting on a horse collar, raised up to spit a stream of tobacco juice over Smiley's head, and Smiley got mad as heck. "You better be glad none a-that landed on me," he said, growling.

Doodle leaned over in the other direction and spat through the hay hole. Looking down below, he aimed next at the big barrel down there. "Damn," he muttered. "I missed it. Hey, Will, ain't thet the barrel with them drownded rats yore daddy said to bury?"

"Gosh, yeah." I had forgotten about it. Climbing down from the loft, we all went and looked at the three big stinking rats, floating in the barrel amongst the ears of corn that had been the bait.

Everybody knows that when a barn rat looks down into a barrel that seems half full of shucked corn, he never suspicions that it's really half full of water. By time he finds out, he's trapped. He can't climb up the rounded sides.

"Gosh, look how white they are," said Pink, poking one with a corn cob. "How come brown rats bleach out in the water?"

Lee Roy had a thought that made him shudder. "You reckon colored folks turn white like that if they drown?"

"Where you s'pose the color goes?" asked Smiley.

"I reckon it just dissolves," said I, gathering up the rats on a pitchfork. "Doodle, get that shovel over yonder, hear, and hep me dig a hole."

Pink was suddenly inspired. "Whoa!" he yelled, catching my arm. "Let's save the rats for Miss Loma! For the school play!"

"Haw, yeah!" echoed fat Lee Roy, clapping Pink on the back. "Cain't you just see them rats droppin' out of Claude's shoebox?"

"Be mighty rank by then," said I. "School play's not till two weeks, you know." But they knew by my wide grin that in my mind I was seeing stinking dead rats on Aunt Loma's stage.

We hawed and guffawed, and then—I think because I'd taken off my shoes and it felt so warm and good and free with my bare toes twiddling in the dirt—it came to me that we should get Aunt Loma some live rats to keep her live mouse company. "We'll put shucked corn down in the barrel without any water," I explained as we went out to bury the dead. "We ought to be able to catch us a few by the night of the play."

What we got was nineteen, collecting sometimes two or three a night. One looked big as a cat. Smiley found a large metal cage in his attic and brought it over. We padded it with hay and put it in an empty stall in our barn, hidden under some dirty old croker sacks.

On the day of the play, Lee Roy and Smiley backed out. Put their tails down and slunk right out from under the best practical joke ever thought up by man or boy in Cold Sassy, Georgia. It really made me mad.

Pink said maybe backing out was a good idea.

"Well, you can back out, but I ain't." I was furious. If Pink didn't help me, there was no way I could get that heavy cage into the auditorium.

"I'll stick with you, Will," he said, miserable.

That night about first dark, he and I lifted the cage onto a wheelbarrow, covered it good with the croker sacks, and wheeled it around the house through the pecan grove. Mary Toy was playing hopscotch in the yard and like to had a fit to know what we had. "Something Aunt Loma wants for the play," I said. "But we cain't tell anybody. It would spoil the surprise."

As we humped the wheelbarrow over the railroad tracks, I looked back. Mary Toy was in the porch swing, watching us.

At the schoolhouse we had a time toting the cage up the outside steps that led backstage. Dern. Lee Roy and Smiley could of at least stayed with it this far.

There wasn't any real shortage of time, since Aunt Loma and everybody in the cast had gone home for early supper. We pushed the cage into a dark corner and tried to make it look like a natural part of the junk stored back there. Set an old globe on top of the croker sacks, and some cracked slates they kept for mill children to use, and two or three old windowshade maps of Europe that wouldn't let up and down anymore. In front of it all, we put two scuttles of dusty coal and a faded half-furled Confederate flag, saved last year when Cold Sassy's old wooden schoolhouse burned down.

We had a brand-new brick school now, and a brand-new Confederate flag out there on the stage. Aunt Loma's Christmas play was sure to have a packed crowd, because it would be the first entertainment held there at night, and everybody was anxious to see the electric lighting. Carbon bulbs were so dim that nobody thought you could light a stage that way.

Aunt Loma had told Chap Cheney she'd

kill him if he didn't get the stage wired in time for the play. With her telling him exactly how she wanted it, he had wired for dozens of bulbs to be screwed into the floor at what she called stage front, and other bulbs dangled from the ceiling. Aunt Loma had put up a lot of mirrors on the walls of the set, which gave her twice as much light for the same number of bulbs.

That night when the heavy curtains parted to show the lit stage, the crowd yelled and clapped till Chap Cheney stood up, grinning, and took a bow.

The stage lights reflected on faces in the auditorium all the way to the back row, where I could see Papa and Mama and Mary Toy sitting with Uncle Camp, him holding the baby. I had a front row aisle seat, Pink right behind me.

Smiley and Lee Roy sat primly with their folks, acting like they didn't even know us.

Among the latecomers hurrying in were Grandpa and Miss Love. She was dolled up like a Christmas tree in a red velvet skirt, a red and white striped waist, and a red velvet hat trimmed in real holly. She seemed a little subdued, but Grandpa was greeting everybody. This was their first time at a public

function since he took sick. He still hadn't
gone back to work, but I thought he never
looked haler or heartier, or neater or spiffier.
I sure was glad he got his health back in time
for my rat joke.

Just after the curtains opened, Aunt Loma
marched in from backstage, dressed fit to kill
in black silk and importance, and sat down in
the aisle seat that the Tuttles had saved for
her.

I sat calm enough through the first act. But
when Act II started, my mind floated up to
the stage and, like a ghost, went through the
painted set into the dark corner where we'd
hidden the rats. I sure hoped they hadn't got
to fighting or squealing back there.

Just like I planned it, when the auditorium
went dark for Act III, Pink and I slipped
through a door by the stage and tiptoed back
where the rats were. During the Christmas
party scene, with all the actors singing carols
at the top of their lungs, we dragged the cage
to the wings and waited till Claude Wiggins
created pandemonium by dropping the live
mouse out of the shoebox. Soon as the mouse
hit the floor we opened the cage and shoved
it onto the stage. Those big rats poured out of
there like a house afire!

Talk about pandemonium, we had it on stage and behind stage and all over that school auditorium!

You never heard such screaming and hollering. When the rats started leaping off into the audience, men were hitting out with their hats and walking canes, women were jumping this way and that or standing on their seats, some of which were breaking, and good gosh everybody was trying to get out of there!

I saw the rat that looked big as a cat dive off the stage right into Aunt Loma's lap. She knocked him off, but then just sat there, too shocked to move.

I looked at Miss Love. Perched up on the back of her seat, she was shrieking with laughter, her red skirt bunched up nearly to her garters. Grandpa was laughing so hard he hurt—rocking back and forth in his seat, grabbing his stomach, slapping his leg, flopping his arms, and shouting like somebody getting religion at a camp meeting. When his left arm went up, it looked like the knotted empty sleeve was dancing. A rat must of jumped over Grandpa's foot, because he kicked out suddenly, but I expect he was laughing too hard to make contact.

To say we broke up the play was putting it mildly.

The lights came on just as I peeped farther around the curtain and saw Aunt Loma trying to push through the crowd to get to our folks. She stumbled along, crying, her hands over her face like somebody had beat her.

When I glanced toward the back of the auditorium, that brought me down some. I knew Mama and Papa hadn't a doubt who'd done it. They sat there just stunned—till all of a sudden Mama grabbed Mary Toy and they jumped up on their seats. By then, the audience was crowding all the exits, shoving to get out. A lady screamed, and Pink and I bolted for the backstage door. The live mouse and a rat or two scrambled out into the cold night with us as Pink flew off in his direction and me in mine.

I beat the folks home easy. Felt my way upstairs, groped for the light cord hanging near the foot of my bed, jerked the light on, put on my old long pants under my new ones, jerked the light off, and waited.

I couldn't help it; in a few minutes I was rolling on the floor with laughter. Every little bit, I'd stop to listen for the front door to open and Papa to roar out, "Will, you come 'ere!" Then I'd think about Aunt Loma with that lapful of rat or my mother jumping up on the seat, and it was like I was a gun fired off. Laughter exploded out of me and couldn't any more be stopped than a bullet.

But laughing dies off pretty quick when you're by yourself, especially if it's way past your whipping and your folks still aren't home yet.

I was kind of sorry I'd messed up Aunt Loma's Christmas play. Oh, well, heck, if it weren't for my rats, Cold Sassy wouldn't remember that dern play past New Year's. As it was, everybody in town would be talking about it for years to come.

And heck, Aunt Loma could put it on again. It was still ten days before school would let out for the holidays. I could help her—

"Will Tweedy? Boy, you come 'ere! Right now!" Papa was shouting at me before he got in the house and had his belt off before my feet could drag me down the stairs.

I got whipped good. And next day he made me go over to Aunt Loma's to say I was sorry.

Except for telling her I was sorry about the bosom stories I made up, which didn't count since Aunt Loma wasn't mad, I had never apologized to anybody in my life. But for once I was soaked through with honest remorse. Not for what I'd done, but for what it did to Aunt Loma.

I found her in her bedroom upstairs, sitting in a rocking chair nursing Campbell Junior. Her eyelids were red and swollen.

Trying not to rouse the baby, I whispered, "Aunt Loma, uh, you ain't go'n believe it, but, uh, uh, I wish now I hadn't of done that about the rats. It was a real good play and I'm . . . I mean, I'll hep you if you want to put it on again next week. I, uh, I wish—" Something about her face plus having to whisper made me wind down.

I don't know what I expected. Maybe just a shrug of her shoulders, acknowledging she heard what I said. I sure didn't expect her to smile at me. I guess I wanted her to say something noble, like "I deserved it, Will. I've always treated you awful. The one that should be apologizin' is myself."

Maybe I hoped she would handle it like God. I mean the Bible says if you tell God you're sincerely sorry, He puts His arms around you and forgives you.

Well, Aunt Loma was not God that day by

a long shot. What she said, keeping her voice down to a whispered scream because of the baby, was "Don't you talk to me about doin' it again next week, Will Tweedy! Just get out of my sight!" She was shaking all over, tears of fury streaming down her flushed face. Naturally Campbell Junior stopped sucking and went to bawling. "Get out of my house!" she yelled above his frightened wails. "I'll hate you till my dyin' day! Get out! *Get out!*"

With that she leaped up, holding the baby tight, and slapped my face so hard I reeled backwards.

I slammed the door to her room as I went out, and kicked the cats that were asleep in a pile by the back door.

My first thought was I'll never say I'm sorry again as long as I live.

My second thought was if anybody ever says I'm sorry to me, I sure ain't go'n slap him or push him away.

My third thought surprised me: I realized it felt good to be back on familiar ground with Aunt Loma. Ever since that day we'd had such a good time laughing about the bosom stories, I hadn't quite known how to act around her. Last night I could hardly enjoy thinking about those rats flying off the stage for worrying about her crying. Well, if she was determined never to forgive me, I might as well enjoy hating her again.

By time I got home, I was whistling.

After that, Aunt Loma stayed in a bad humor with everybody, especially Uncle Camp. Just for instance, the next Sunday while she was helping Mama and Queenie take up dinner, Campbell Junior fell all the way down our stairs. "I swanny to God, Campbell Williams!" she yelled. "Looks like you could at least see after your own son when I'm in the kitchen!"

"I'm sorry, Loma, I'm sorry," he said as he picked up the screaming baby.

"You sure are! You're just sorry!" screeched Aunt Loma, snatching Campbell Junior out of his arms. "That's the smartest thing you've said since the last time you said it."

When she wasn't fussing about him seeming glad to bring home the bent cans and weevily rice and flour we couldn't sell at the store, she was complaining about his not having any get-up-and-go. "You could at least *ast* Pa for a raise." After Grandpa went back to work just before Christmas, Aunt Loma had the gall to go ask him herself to raise Camp's pay.

Grandpa really blessed her out. "I don't even need Camp," he told her. "I shore cain't afford to pay him no more'n I awready do."

I don't know if Uncle Camp heard that, but I know he heard what was said a few hours later when Hosie Roach, the mill boy, came in to ask for a job. Hosie had washed himself and combed his hair and put on clean overalls, and I could tell Grandpa liked him. He even took Hosie back to the buggy shed to show him the cars. Hosie didn't get a job, but later Grandpa told Papa he shore wisht he could a-hired thet boy. "He'd be equal to three a-Camp."

At first I thought Grandpa didn't know Uncle Camp was standing right behind him. But maybe he did know and said it anyhow, hoping it would make Camp work harder.

The very next Saturday, Camp got some get-up-and-go and went. And the way he did it made my rat thing seem about like putting a frog in somebody's bed.

Aunt Loma never forgave him, either.

43

Uncle Camp got away from Aunt Loma while she was gone to Athens.

She had caught the train that Saturday morning, wearing a black wool dress and the big hat with ostrich plumes that Miss Love had made. She was to spend the day with her LaGrange College roommate, Sue Lee Gresham, who was now Mrs. Humphry Wright of Athens.

Uncle Camp had gone to work early that day, and since Papa thought any lady taking a train should have somebody see her off, he told me to drive Aunt Loma to the depot. To my mind she didn't need a ride any more than if she was going downtown, which she did every day, and besides, she was leaving Campbell Junior with Mama and Queenie. And naturally I wasn't too crazy about being by myself with her. She might take the occasion to raise Cain about the Christmas play. But Papa said to, so I went and got her.

She was far from friendly, but her mind was on Athens, not me or rats.

Aunt Loma really didn't want to go, or so she said as we waited at the depot. "Sue Lee's just usin' me as an excuse to have a luncheon. She hopes I'll be jealous of her. She's always writin' about her big house and her big dinner parties, and her husband bein' president of the bank. I don't call inheritin' a bank from your daddy any proof that you're smarter than the next fellow." Aunt Loma stepped back from the tracks as the train came in sight. "I just wish I hadn't told her I'd come."

I always thought ladies liked to be honor guests at a luncheon, and said so. "Besides, ain't nobody makin' you go."

"Camp made me," she said, real irritable.

"Well, I be-dog." Chalk up one for ole Camp.

"He promised to fix the faucet in the bathtub if I'd just get out of his way. Said he couldn't tackle the job with me standin' there watchin' him fail."

Poor ole Camp.

Papa said afterwards that Camp actually applied himself that morning at the store. Instead of waiting around to be told what to do, he put in a real good morning's work. And whereas he usually had about as much life in his eyes as a turtle, he seemed almost happy.

He and my daddy left together at dinner-time. On the way out the door, Camp asked Papa would he mind stopping by the house before going back to the store after dinner. Kind of apologetic, like he hated to take up Papa's time, he explained. "I'm fixin' to fix a leaky faucet, Mr. Hoyt, and I ain't never done one. I'd shore feel better if you'd come see did I do it right. I . . . well, you know how Loma is."

Papa did stop by, though grudging. I was with him. The door was open, despite it was a cold day, and we went on in. "Camp?" Papa called.

"I'm in the kitchen, Mr. Hoyt. Come on back, hear."

The shot rang out about time Papa set foot in the dining room. Neighbors said they heard somebody scream. It must of been me or Papa, one, though later I couldn't recall anything except the smell of gunpowder and, on the floor, a big long blob of blue and white checked oilcloth from the store. I didn't have to be told that Uncle Camp was under the oilcloth. He had laid down on a length of it, pulled one end up over him like a sheet and the other end down over his head and chest, and after calling Papa to come on back, had put the pistol in his mouth and pulled the trigger.

I reckon he figured if all the blood and bits of bone and brains got trapped in the oilcloth, Loma Baby wouldn't be mad at him.

Papa lifted the part that was over Camp's head, put it down quick, and turned away, his face like ashes. I had seen, too. I stood there, shaking. Finally I said, "Papa, want me to run get Doc Slaughter?"

He could hardly speak. "Run get Mr. Birdsong, son."

Mr. Birdsong offered me a ride up beside him in the driver's seat of the old horse-drawn hearse, the one he called an ambulance if the person wasn't dead. Since neighbors were already gathering, he drove the horses around to the back door, where my daddy was waiting. Papa had closed the kitchen door and hadn't let anybody go in there.

Mr. Birdsong tied Uncle Camp up in that oilcloth like he was a dern side of beef. Me and Papa helped carry him out, and rode with him to the big old white-columned funeral parlor.

Mr. and Mrs. Birdsong and their nine children lived upstairs. Helping take Uncle Camp in there, I wondered how they could stand to live like that with dead bodies, especially when it was one that had committed suicide.

Papa hurried home to tell Mama and sent me to the store to tell Grandpa and them, but they had already heard. As I ran in, Grandpa met me at the door, grim of face. He asked me a few questions, then stalked off to the funeral parlor.

Soon as I could get away from the customers who pressed around, asking more questions, I ran back to Aunt Loma's. I wanted to make sure there wasn't any blood or anything on the floor.

If there was, Mrs. Brown next door had cleaned it up. But I could still see Uncle Camp, same as if he was laying right there with his brains blowed out, and it made me sick. I felt about to faint. Leaving the kitchen, I rushed past the people whispering in the hall and went to the bathroom.

I nearly stumbled over the plumbing tools. Uncle Camp had left them on the floor by the tub.

Just what you'd expect, Camp not putting up his tools.

Then I saw a piece of paper stuck under the big wrench. I knew it was for Aunt Loma, but horses couldn't of kept me from reading it.

You can get the creeps, I tell you, reading what a dead man has just written. This is what it said:

Loma baby i tryed to plan so as not to mess up yr kitchen. i loved you since the day i layed eyes on you you jus as pretty now as then. so it aint you Loma baby its i aint good for nuthin. which you know. its got so jus getin out of bed ever mornin is to much. i pact up my close and all in a box so you woodn have to fool with it. my leavin this werl dont have nuthin to do with you bein mad at me for not fixin the fawsit I bin aimin to do it a long time fore the fawsit went to leekin.

plese save my gold pockit watch for Campbell Junior i leeve it to him i aired it from my grandedy you know. i love you an always will but now you can have some pese. tell mr. Blakesly i preshate him givin me the job like he done now he can fine him somebody who can do him a good dase work i hope god will forgive me so i can meet you in heven.

plese dont be mad i have plan it so you wont be the one to fine me.

yr lovin husban Campbell Williams.
p.s. i fixt the fawsit
p.s. i wont to be berit in cold sassy so you can vist me some time.

yr lovin husban Campbell Williams.

The page blurred. I wished so bad I could of known Uncle Camp for the past three years like I knew him now that he was dead. But even as I stood there holding his sweet and lonely words, I heard water going *drip, drip, drip* into the bathtub.

I picked up the wrench and changed the washer. Nobody was go'n say Campbell Williams was so sorry that he couldn't even fix a faucet. It was a small thing to do for somebody brave enough to put a pistol in his mouth and shoot.

44

Along with half the town, my family met the late train from Athens.

Grandpa said later that folks just came to see how Loma would take the news, but I don't know. It seemed to me that going to the depot was the only way they could think of to show her they were sorry poor Camp had gone to Hell so young. Camp having committed suicide, and not living long enough afterwards to ask God to forgive him, there was no way he could ever be reunited with Loma or Campbell Junior in Paradise.

Naturally we all thought there would just be a quick private burying. Cold Sassy certainly never expected Camp would be brought home to lie in state.

But he was.

By first dark, Aunt Loma's little house was filling up with folks who had brought food and were waiting to speak to the new widow before settling in to eat. Loma was still upstairs in her room when here came Uncle Camp in a fine golden oak coffin with metal handles, riding in style in Mr. Birdsong's fine new glass-sided, gilt-trim black hearse drawn by two black horses with black plumes on their heads.

As soon as the horses stopped, Mr. Birdsong got down from the driver's seat, went in the house, and asked everybody to leave the parlor. Then he and his three sons carried in the coffin, escorted by my grandfather. His grimness forbade any comment as he stalked across the yard behind the coffin. Those watching looked shocked, like it was as awful for Camp to be brought home like a regular corpse as for him to of shot himself in the first place.

Though the undertaker clearly disapproved, they toted Uncle Camp into Aunt Loma's little parlor as if he had a right to be there. I followed close behind Grandpa, who told me to come in and close the sliding double doors.

Mr. Birdsong unfolded his new collapsible casket stand and set it up right in front of the white mantelpiece that Uncle Camp had painted. I don't know why, but I walked over to see if the button, the pencil, and the cockroach were still there. They were, of course, just same as Granny's death was still in the Toy Bible.

Loma had hung the Saint-Cecilia-at-the-

594 OLIVE ANN BURNS

organ mirror above the mantel. I watched in
it as the boys lifted the casket onto the stand
and Mr. Birdsong laid a big wreath of wax
flowers on top, about where Uncle Camp's
hands that held the pistol would now be
pressed together in prayer.

Mr. Birdsong always arranged dead hands
like in prayer.

Hitching his trousers with his arm stub,
Grandpa looked around and said, "Git thet
marble-top table over yonder, Will Tweedy,
and set it by the head a-thet coffin. Then see
can you find a kerosene lamp to put on it."
He must of thought the carbon bulb hanging
from the ceiling was too raw-looking for a
settin'-up.

"Grandpa, you ain't go'n open the coffin,
are you, sir?"

"No, course not. Camp ain't in no condition for viewin'." He spoke calm, but went to
scratching his head like he had the itch.
"Where's Loma at, and yore daddy and
mother?"

"They all upstairs in the bedroom," I said.
"Aunt Loma's still like she was at the depot.
She don't even know what's goin' on.
Grandpa, I thought you didn't like embalmin'
and funerals and all."

"I don't. But I don't like hypocrites, neither. I cain't stop folks from jedgin' Camp, but I ain't a-go'n let'm say how he's got to be buried. Where's Miss Love at?"

"In the kitchen."

"Go git her for me."

"Yessir."

"And bring a lamp."

"Yessir."

Wading through the crowd of silent people in the front hall, I found Miss Love busy getting out dishes. She knew Grandpa had brought Uncle Camp home. When she saw me at the kitchen door, she said, "Loma should be in there when people start paying their respects."

"You think anybody'll go in, Miss Love?"

"Yes. Because your grandfather will get his revolver if they don't." Turning to look at me as she reached for some dishes on a high shelf, Miss Love almost smiled. "But he won't have to, of course. Even grown people mind Mr. Blakeslee, Will—as if they had no choice."

I couldn't help wondering had she minded him. Let him have his way with her, as the saying goes.

I took a stack of plates out of her hands

and set them on the kitchen table by a pile of papers that I recognized as copies of Loma's Christmas play. I reached for the lamp at the back of the table, where Loma had left it last time the lights went out. I felt awful. "Ma'am, do you think Uncle Camp might still be alive if Loma and Grandpa hadn't blessed him out so much? You think Grandpa is tryin' to make it up to him now?" I struck a match and put it to the lamp wick.

"Sh-h-h, Will. We'll never know. Not even your grandfather will know, because he won't let himself think that way."

"And couldn't admit it if he did?"

"And couldn't admit it if he did."

"Aunt Loma was the main one, I reckon, but she won't ever see how she treated him." In a low miserable voice I said, "Miss Love, I, uh, I didn't treat him so good myself."

"We'll talk about it later, Will. Not now." Miss Love took off her apron, I picked up the lamp, and we hurried out.

Mr. Birdsong and his boys were just leaving. I watched them walk across the gold cat-paw prints on the dining room floor and go out through the kitchen. Then we went on in the parlor, and Miss Love asked Grandpa if she should go get Loma and Mr. Hoyt and Mary Willis.

"I want you here by me, where you belong to be," said Grandpa. "Let Will Tweedy go. Tell your daddy to bring Loma on down, son. But first, open them doors. Hit won't do to keep folks a-waitin'. They might leave." As he took aholt of Miss Love's elbow, I pushed open the double doors and he stood glaring at the silent, uneasy crowd. "Y'all can come on in now," he said, as if it never occurred to him they might not want to.

All those Cold Sassy eyes moved past Grandpa and Miss Love and focused on the coffin. But nobody moved.

"Cratic?" Grandpa spoke in a soft voice. "You and Miz Flournoy come first. Camp always thought a lot a-y'all." Mr. Flournoy came forward like a puppet on a string.

Miss Love held out her hand to him. As Mr. Flournoy took it, he turned and looked back at his wife. "Mama?" he whispered. She looked nervous and uncertain, as if being in the same room with a suicide corpse might taint her. But she came on in and Mr. Flournoy ushered her forward.

I watched the Flournoys stare at the coffin. I knew they were wondering if Mr. Birdsong had been able to make Uncle Camp look nat'ral, considering the circumstances. But then Mrs. Flournoy commenced crying. "Daddy," she sobbed, "we c-could of been nicer to that p-poor boy. . . ."

One by one, then in groups, Cold Sassy came in to view the hidden remains. Watching them file by, I felt like their tears weren't just from gruesome imaginings of the blasted head under the golden oak coffin lid. They cried from real sorrow. Like me and Mrs. Flournoy, they knew they could of been nicer.

Hurrying out to go upstairs, I was surprised to see Grandpa following behind. "Hit's all right in the parlor now, son. I best see after Loma myself." As we pushed our way through the hall toward the stairs, I heard somebody ask where was the poor fatherless child. Somebody else said the baby was over at the Tweedys'. "The cook's keepin' him."

Papa was kneeling by the window, praying. Mama sat on the foot of the bed, holding a wet washrag to her forehead. Aunt Loma? Still in the dressy black wool outfit she'd worn to Sue Lee's, she walked the floor in front of the bureau, back and forth, forth and back. She didn't cry or carry on. She looked like a

sleepwalker. Back and forth, and I don't believe she knew where she was or even that
she paced.

"Loma?" Grandpa stood in the door. "I
brung Camp's body home." My parents
looked up, surprised, but Loma just kept pacing. He spoke louder. "Loma, I brung
Camp's body home and folks are down there
payin' their respects. They'll want to say their
condolences to you." She kept walking. Back
and forth, forth and back.

Mama got up from the bed and put her
hand on Loma's arm. "Sugar, here's Pa," she
said softly.

"Y'all go on down to the parlor," Grandpa
told us. As we filed out, he was saying,
"Loma? Come here to yore daddy, pet." I
glanced back just as he caught her arm and
pulled her to him. She looked slowly up, to
see who had her. Then her eyes focused and
tears ran down her cheeks. Clutching her
arms around her daddy's waist, she hid her
face against his chest. "Oh, Pa!" she cried.
"Oh, Pa, I been so mean to him. . . . I
fussed so about the faucet. . . ." She
sounded like somebody lost. "Pa, I want to
come home. Can I? Me and the baby?
Please . . ."

I didn't hear if he said yes or no, because I had to shut the door. But as I followed Mama and Papa down the stairs, I wondered would he let her. And would Miss Love let her? If she and Grandpa were romancing, it sure would put a crimp in things to have Jealousy Incarnate underfoot.

I couldn't help thinking that if all Grandpa needed was a housekeeper, Aunt Loma could keep house for him now. But even if he hadn't wanted Miss Love, it was just as well he didn't wait for Loma. If she had been born colored, not a soul would of hired her to clean up or cook, either one.

Anyhow, Grandpa hadn't hardly passed the time of day with Loma since they quarreled about her being an actress, and things got even worse between them after she disobeyed him and married Uncle Camp. When Campbell Junior was born, he did go see the baby and made a big to-do over it being a boy, which really pleased Aunt Loma. But that was the end of that. It didn't really change anything. Whenever the two of them were in the same room, it was like they didn't know enough English to carry on a conversation. They both could hold a grudge like it was a life work.

Well, it was awful to think what it had taken to make Grandpa treat Loma and Uncle Camp nice.

There hadn't been a suicide in Cold Sassy since the Crabtrees' son, Arthur, got drunk on a cold winter night, laid down across his sweetheart's grave, and took an overdose of laudanum. Next morning when he was found, the bottle was laying by his body.

Arthur never even got back home. The Crabtrees were so mad and hurt and ashamed, they took a pine casket out to the cemetery and put him right under, and to this day there isn't a marker on his grave. The burial service was just one sentence. The preacher said, "God won't forgive this awful thing he did." Dr. Slaughter thought it wasn't the laudanum that killed Arthur; it was laying out there all night in twenty-degree weather. But he was considered a suicide person just the same, since suicide was his clear intent. Two months before, when Arthur's sixteen-year-old sweetheart died of galloping consumption, the *Cold Sassy Weekly* had called her passing "the saddest and yet most beautiful death in memory, lamented in verse by her brother James, well-known invalid poet of Maysville, Georgia." The paper printed Brother James's whole long dern memorial poem about her. But poor Authur got just two lines: "Young Arthur Crabtree of this city became deceased last Thursday."

Camp would of gone the same way as Arthur if it had been left up to his folks. The Williamses, I mean. Grandpa sent word to them right after it happened, but they sent word back saying they wouldn't come. That was the whole message. Despite Camp wrote in his letter that he wanted to be buried in Cold Sassy, Mama had hoped the Williamses would say bring our boy home. That was the usual thing to do when a young person died. "It would of saved a lot of embarrassment for Loma, considerin'," said Mama. "Not to mention the rest of the fam'ly."

But if Mama or Cold Sassy thought Campbell Williams would end up with a quick private burying like Arthur Crabtree's, it had another think coming. Sunday at three o'clock, Camp had him a nice, long regular-type funeral in the Baptist church. Brother Belie Jones didn't give any eulogy, but he asked God to comfort the young widow and raise the baby in the Bosom of the Lamb, and then he read Scriptures for an hour.

As the preacher finished the Twenty-third Psalm, he looked at Grandpa with a question mark on his face. Grandpa, who sat between Aunt Loma and Miss Love, glared hard at Brother Jones, and the preacher said, "Let us bow our heads a-gain in prayer." After reminding God that in the note to his wife, the deceased had asked His forgiveness, Brother Jones prayed, "Lord, Thou knowest this congregation is shocked and saddened by what has happened in our community. We know the Bible says it is a sin to take life, our own as much as anybody else's. But Lord, hep us to see that this boy was a poor lost soul and deservin' of our compassion."

Grandpa nodded grimly, and the funeral was over.

Nobody was sure that Camp's asking God's forgiveness before he pulled the trigger counted as much as if he had lived long enough to repent after doing the deed. But it was a comforting hope.

No suicide person in living memory had ever been treated nice as Uncle Camp. Papa even wondered if maybe Grandpa gave some money to the Baptist church to get it done right, but Mama said that idea was far-fetched—"stingy as Pa is." Anyhow, it was a grand send-off. And as if the church funeral and the fine coffin weren't enough, Grandpa not only insisted Camp be laid to rest in the Toy plot but had Loomis dig the grave right at Miss Mattie Lou's feet.

There were those who thought it was going far too far to put somebody who was already halfway to Hell at the feet of a lady who'd been a saint on earth if ever there was one. But Grandpa didn't ask anybody's permission.

Later that evening, when we were all at Aunt Loma's to eat supper, I asked him if he thought Uncle Camp could of got to Hell already. Grandpa told me to shut up. "They's plenty men thet are mean and hateful, son, or they cheat folks, or beat their wives and their colored, but when they die, them preachers cain't say enough nice thangs. Well, Camp he warn't evil or hateful, either one. He jest couldn't do nothin'. So doggit, Will Tweedy, ain't you or nobody else go'n say he's gone to Hell. He jest couldn't stand it no more. Would a lovin' God kick a boy unhappy enough to do what pore Camp did?"

Mama came up while Grandpa was talking. Right in front of her, he said he didn't want no funeral when he died. "I want a party, like them Irishmen have."

It made me proud, how Grandpa was that day.

But if I'd known from the beginning that Aunt Loma and Campbell Junior would come live with us instead of with him and Miss Love, and me have to give up my room and sleep winter and summer on a sawed-off old bed out on our back porch, I'd of been too mad at Uncle Camp to fix the faucet for him.

45

It would of made a lot more sense for Loma to go live with her daddy and Miss Love. She and Campbell Junior could of had the upstairs room that was hers growing up.

Doing her duty, Miss Love gave her an invite the day after the funeral. But Grandpa spoke up before Loma could open her mouth. "Naw, you better go live with Sister and Hoyt," he said. "I'm too old to hep raise a youngun."

Despite Loma had begged to come home, I

don't doubt she was relieved not to be going.
Besides how she felt about Miss Love, there
was how she felt about kerosene lamps, well
water, and privies.

Still and all, I didn't see why she couldn't
just stay on where she was, and said so.

"For pity sake, Will," said Mama, "I never
thought to raise a boy so hardhearted. What
fam'lies are for is to hep one another in time
of trouble."

"Well'm, but it ain't like Aunt Loma's
homeless."

"She cain't stay where she is. Not unless
some older woman could go live with her,
and I don't know who that would be. A
widow pretty as Loma and not but twenty-
one years old, what would people say? And
how would she live? Lord knows, there's
nothing under her mattress to fall back on."

What she would fall back on was Grandpa,
of course. And since he owned her house as
well as ours, it hadn't taken him two minutes
to see that by putting the two families together and leasing out Loma's place, the rent
money would just about equal her upkeep.

I know Aunt Loma didn't mind coming to
our house a bit. She cried when Papa said she
could bring only one cat, but losing the cats

was nothing compared to gaining Queenie, who would help with the baby and do their washing and cook their food. Aunt Loma was a lot of things, but not dumb.

The first week or two at our house, she stayed in her room (my room), crying about treating poor Camp so mean. But it wasn't long till she was mourning instead for the way he had treated her.

During the Christmas holidays I went up to her room (my room) to see could I find my tobacco tags. I thought I had them in a Prince Albert can under a loose board near the fireplace in there. The door was open, so I went in, and there stood Aunt Loma in front of the mirror, staring at herself in the thin flowerdy dress Miss Love brought her from New York —the one she couldn't wear last summer because of being in mourning for Granny and couldn't wear next summer on account of being a widow.

Seeing me in the glass coming up behind her, she jerked around and started yelling about Uncle Camp killing himself. "The nerve of him, leavin' me like this! Beholden to my daddy and my brother-in-law for the very clothes on my back and the food in my mouth!"

"Aw, Aunt Loma, you don't have to feel beholden," I said, honestly trying to be a comfort. "Mama says that's what families are for."

Whereat she collapsed on the bed and went to crying. "Oh, Will, what's to become of m-me!"

As Aunt Loma got used to Camp being gone, though, she seemed to take on new life. And despite it was crowded at our house, we all settled down. She and I had a run-in every now and again, but even Aunt Loma could see it was to her advantage to be nice. Except for nursing the baby, she was more or less free to hold him or put him down, same as if she was his grandmother or a maiden aunt. She never had to look after him unless she was in a mood to, because if he wasn't toddling around after me, he was with Mary Toy, unless he was with Mama or Queenie. Life was just easier now for Aunt Loma.

Well, it wasn't easier for me. As always when things got behind in the family or at the store, I was the one who took up the slack. I never saw Pink and Lee Roy and Smiley except at school or church. I kept thinking I'd drive the Cadillac out toward Mill Town and see could I find Lightfoot McLendon and take her to ride, but I never got to.

I finally asked Mama why couldn't Aunt Loma make herself more useful. "That way I might could play baseball every year or two with Pink and them, or go fishing sometime."

Mama was at the sink, washing sweet potatoes to bake for supper. She said, not unkindly, "Don't talk bitter, Will. Loma's goin' through a bad time."

"Yes'm, but it sure would hep if she could milk the cow and bring in stovewood."

Mama bristled. "Yankee women do work like that, and colored women, and tenant farmers' wives and daughters. We don't. Loma heps in the house and that's enough."

Loma mostly stayed up in her room (my room) and did what she'd always wanted to, namely, write poems and plays. But pretending to be a writer wasn't much fun without an audience, so pretty soon she brought her pencil and paper down to the breakfast table. Once when the Muse was on her, she sat staring into space so long I got worried. "Reckon Aunt Loma's had a stroke?" I whispered to Queenie.

"Naw, suh, Mr. Will," she whispered back.

"Miss Loma jes' be's sightin' on a poem. She do's lak dat lots a-time."

But it was easy to see the widow was restless, and before long she waylaid Grandpa, when he stopped by for his snort, to ask if she could come work at the store.

He said he'd think on it.

Lord knows he needed somebody, what with Miss Love gone to housekeeping, Uncle Camp gone to Hell, and spring just around the corner. Farmers would soon be coming in to arrange credit terms and buy seed and guano. Ladies were already picking through patterns and piece goods, planning their Easter dresses. And it looked like everybody and his brother was itching for an automobile. On a warm Saturday we could hardly wait on customers for taking folks to ride.

On the other hand, we couldn't afford to put them off, because the cars were beginning to sell. Grandpa read in the paper that in 1906 there were at least a thousand automobiles in Georgia, mostly owned by farmers, doctors, and residents of small towns. That really fired him up to try to sell a lot in 1907.

In the meantime, I was still the stable boy for Miss Love and Grandpa. I never had time to talk much when I went up there, but I couldn't help noticing she seemed happier lately, and that was a relief. Ever since That Night at Miss Gussie's house, I'd been scared we'd hear any day that she was leaving for Baltimore.

Or Texas.

I do remember complaining to her about the committee that had been set up to find a more modern name for Cold Sassy. "Papa's in favor," I grumped. "I don't see why he ain't noticed that the reason it's called Cold Sassy is because that's its name."

"Don't worry so, Will," said Miss Love, smiling her big-mouth smile. "You know your grandfather will never let it happen."

Miss Love was washing a kitchen window that looked clean to me already. It seemed like every time I went down there, she was washing floors or windows, one, despite she'd cleaned the whole house good last summer. "Miss Love, I reckon you ain't heard about fall and spring cleanin'," I said one day. She had come out on the back porch to empty her wash water just as I headed for the barn. I said, "In between spring and fall, and fall and spring, ma'am, you just s'posed to sweep and mop and use the feather duster and like that."

"I like the Yankee way better," she said, bristling. I reckon she thought Mama had criticized how she did. "Up North, ladies do extra cleaning every week in one room. Brush down the walls and wash the floor one week, maybe wash windows and curtains the next, and so on. When they get that room done, they start on another. The house stays nice year round, and it's not exhausting like doing all the heavy cleaning at once."

When I told Mama, she said, "I'd rather get worn out twice a year than stay worn out all the time."

The Rucker Blakeslee Hotel sign was finally up, and they said Mr. Clem Crummy just about got apoplexy every time a stranger asked was the ho-tel owned by the same feller had the brick store up the street. I knew Miss Love thought it was awful of Grandpa to hold Mr. Clem to the drawing, but he just laughed when she said so.

Then one day she came down to the store with a sign she had made. Grandpa read it and laughed. "Go on, put it in the winder," he said.

This is what was on it:

ATTENTION!
Drummers, Cotton Buyers, Railroad Men,
And Other Travelers!
Try the Elegant Refurbished
BLAKESLEE HOTEL
Fine Cuisine!
Clean, Bug-Free Beds!
Fiddle Music and Parlor Games Every
Night!

The Crummys never even said thank you, but the sign got them some business that usually went to the boarding houses.

Miss Love's birthday was on Valentine's. (That's how come she was named Love.) The day before, Grandpa told me she had decided to give herself a present. She was going to use some of her savings to put in a bathroom, and of course a sink and faucet in the kitchen. "Hit's fol-de-rol and foolish-ment," he said, but he grinned proud.

That told me one thing. Whether Miss Love was now Grandpa's wife or still just his housekeeper, she wouldn't put her own money into plumbing if she was still thinking about leaving Cold Sassy. On the other hand, she had another think coming if she expected

Grandpa to say "Don't spend yore money, let me give you the bathroom for your birthday." He had already bought her a present, a Home Graphophone. It cost five dollars from the Talking Machine Department at Sears, Roebuck and Co., and he'd ordered a dozen "best and loudest music records" to play on it.

A machine that could talk and play music was, as Grandpa kept saying, a dang marvel.

You can imagine that when Cold Sassy heard about the Graphophone, everybody remembered he never gave Miss Mattie Lou a birthday present. Granny had always insisted she didn't want one. "Birthdays is for chi'ren," she'd say. "I don't have to mark gittin' older. I can just look in the glass and tell." He did order Granny a coconut and a crate of oranges every Christmas to make him some ambrosia with, but his Christmas gift to Miss Love had been a new buggy top with side and back curtains, and now not two months later he'd bought her that Graphophone.

From Valentine's Day on, Grandpa never went back to the store after dinner on Wednesdays. Like I said, the stores in Cold Sassy closed every Wednesday around noon,

but always before, he went back to work anyway. Said it was a good chance to ketch up on
what needed doin'. But now it looked like he
was ketchin' up on Miss Love.

Sometimes they'd go buggy-riding, closed
up snug with the side and back curtains
snapped shut. One freezing cold Wednesday I
went through the house on my way to the
barn and found them sitting in the warm
kitchen, him in a rocking chair with his
glasses on, reading to Miss Love while she
sewed. One Sunday after dinner I went up
there, just to visit a while, and Grandpa was
laying on the daybed in the hall with Miss
Love sitting right on the bed beside him, rubbing his forehead. When they saw me, she
jumped like somebody caught stealing and
hurried to the kitchen, and he sat up muttering something about a backache.

Plain as day, Grandpa was courting Miss
Love. Why else would he be home with her
so much? Why else would he have spent so
much on the Graphophone and the records
for it?

Despite I couldn't know if they still called
each other Miss and Mister when it was just
the two of them, I sensed a difference lately.
They were always laughing and teasing, and

whenever one came in a room where the other one was, you could read a book by the light on their faces.

To me they were like a book—a book with the last chapter missing. And I couldn't wait to know how it ended.

At school when we commenced studying *Romeo and Juliet,* the drama that might or might not be going on up at Grandpa's house laid itself down on every line Shakespeare wrote about love or marriage.

"Does she call him husband?" I read, and thought of Miss Love, not Juliet.

"Stony limits cannot hold love out!" That was Grandpa shouting at his Love. "O! I have bought the mansion of a love, but not possess'd it" was his lament.

But hark! Mayhap Miss Love doth use Juliet's words to tease: "If thou think'st I am too quickly won, I'll frown and be perverse and say thee nay, so thou wilt woo. . . ."

Well, Grandpa was wooing, no doubt about it. And seemed like Miss Love was enjoying being wooed. But was she yet saying him nay?

Whenever I was up at their house I'd go to wondering if she still slept in the spare room by herself, or did he come in there sometimes at night, or had she taken over Granny's side of his bed. It wasn't decent, the way I kept picturing in my mind what might or might not be going on and none of it any of my business. I just wished I knew one way or the other. Then maybe I could quit wondering and, as Papa would say, be-have myself.

One night I had to go take Grandpa a message from my daddy. As I ran up the front steps, I noticed the parlor draperies were pulled to. And despite the house was shut up tight, I could hear the music machine just a-going. Hurrying in, I saw they'd pushed all the parlor furniture back against the walls, Miss Love had put on a new dance record, and by golly she was teaching Grandpa the turkey trot!

He was bad to stumble, and kept stepping on her feet, but they were laughing and cutting up, just having the best time. I stood there grinning and they waved at me.

"I'm gittin' the hang of it, Will Tweedy!" bragged Grandpa, swinging her around. "Next time we go to New York City, I ain't go'n have to pay no partner for her! Here, Love, learn Will Tweedy how," he said, handing her over to me. "I got to rest a spell."

I was as stumbly as Grandpa, and kept stepping on her feet, too. But boy howdy, I had my arms around her and she was looking up at me, smiling, while Grandpa watched us and beat time to the music. When the machine started winding down, making funny groans and whines, we all three laughed like children.

Later I couldn't help but try and imagine what it would be like dancing with Lightfoot McLendon. In my mind I saw her in a silk ball gown, smiling up at me as I held her, and us circling and whirling.

I still thought about Lightfoot a lot, and still wondered sometimes if she hated me for kissing her. But I was too busy to moon over it much. Things had got real bad at the store.

Aunt Loma kept pestering Grandpa for a job. He didn't pay her any mind, but he did start saying he had to hire somebody. One morning before school I was stacking big sacks of cow feed and guano outside against the brick wall of the store when Grandpa ambled out, spat brown tobacco juice through a crack in the board sidewalk, and said, "Will Tweedy, you know the mill boy thet come in here a while back wantin' a job? What's his name, son?"

I knew right off who and what he had in

Cold Sassy Tree 619

mind, and it made me mad as heck. But all I said was, "Hosie Roach?"

"Thet's the one. Is he in school this term?"

"Yessir."

"How old you reckon Hosie is? He ain't a real big boy, as I recollect. But he's some older'n you, ain't he?"

"Yessir. He's prob'ly twenty. Maybe twenty-one." I couldn't help adding, "And still ain't finished school."

"Well, he seemed right smart to me." Grandpa had sense enough to know the reason Hosie hadn't graduated was that he worked a lot at the cotton mill and couldn't get to school regular. "I liked thet boy. Tell him to come see me this evenin', son. I got to git me some more hep."

I told Hosie what Grandpa said. He didn't jump up and down about it like I thought he would. Didn't even let on he was excited. But he couldn't hide the deep flush that came on his face.

"Tell Mr. Blakeslee I cain't come today," he said, putting his scaly hands in the pockets of his dirty, ragged overalls. "Tell him I'll be by t'morrer."

"He ain't go'n like it, you not comin' when he said to." I spoke hateful. "He's used to folks sayin' yessir when he tells'm something."

Hosie flushed again. I swear he looked like my dog T.R. when he's ashamed and trying to wag his tail and drag his belly at the same time. "Will," said Hosie, "be shore and say I'll see him t'morrer, hear. Tell him I'll be by fore school takes in."

I fell in step with Grandpa next morning as he left our house after his snort. "I'm goin' by the store and get me a pencil," I said.

Crossing North Main, with T.R. trotting ahead, I decided to speak up about Hosie Roach. "There ain't but four things wrong with him, Grandpa."

"What, son? Besides he's a mill boy."

"Some folks in Cold Sassy will think when it comes to workin' at your store, him bein' a linthead is enough and too much." I was being real smart-aleck. "Main thing, sir, he's got cooties and the itch and he stinks."

"He was clean as you thet day he come in astin' for a job."

"Well, he ain't clean when he comes to school. He don't grow much beard, but his hair's so long and tangled and dirty it looks like a dern cootie stable, haw!"

Hosie was waiting in front of the store

when we got there. I didn't hardly recognize
him.

Naturally he was barefooted, and his feet
were cracked and bleeding from the cold. But
he had on new overalls and a clean long-
sleeved denim shirt. His face was shaved
smooth and scrubbed raw, the tow hair clean
and wet-combed.

I knew now why Hosie wouldn't stop by
yesterday. He was too proud to show up dirty.
He must of scrubbed himself from suppertime to midnight.

"I come to see about the job, sir," he said
as Grandpa unlocked the big door. "Sir, I
hope you ain't a'ready hired somebody."

"Come on in, son." I knew Grandpa was
surprised at Hosie being so clean, after what I
said, but I could see it pleased him.

While he went behind the counter to unlock the cash register, I walked over to the
rack where the tablets and pencils were. But
of course all I really had on my mind was
Hosie Roach.

If he got hired, it wouldn't be Uncle Camp
he'd be replacing. It would be me. He'd get
the floors swept and the stock put out every
morning in no time. Within a week he would
find a hundred ways to make himself useful.

Without being asked, he'd get the chickens crated up to ship to Atlanta, and the cars washed, and I don't know what all. Lord, smart as Hosie was, it wouldn't be any time before he'd know how to drive and start taking people out for demonstration rides. And unless folks didn't want his hands on their foodstuff, he'd soon be weighing up sugar and flour and drawing molasses out of the barrel.

Hosie wasn't any better worker than me. But whereas I always had to go home in time to milk and bring in stovewood, he could stay all night if Grandpa wanted him to. And whereas my daddy always asked how much Latin or geometry I had to do that night, and lots of times made me go home early to get at it, Hosie would of course quit school if he got the job.

Bad as he wanted to leave the mill and amount to something, Hosie would be equal to ten of Uncle Camp plus maybe two of me, and Grandpa would respect him. Jealousy rose in me like a pain as I heard them talking terms.

Grandpa had sense enough to know how cheap a linthead would work. However little he paid, it would be more than Hosie made at the mill. He would cost more than me, since I didn't get paid anything, being in the family, but he would be cheaper than Uncle Camp, who had to be paid enough for him and Aunt Loma to live on.

The whole idea of it made me mad.

I was fixing to call the dog and go on to school when I heard Grandpa ask Hosie if he had cooties.

Hosie would of hit any town boy at school who even mentioned such. I stood there hoping he'd hit Grandpa. Because if he did, that would be the end of that.

"I ain't wantin' to shame you, boy," Grandpa said, propping his left elbow on the oak counter top and leaning forward. "I jest got to make shore. If'n we bring cooties in here, or the seven-year itch, I ain't go'n have no customers."

"Yessir. I unner-stand, sir." And Hosie turned to leave.

"Wait a minute now. I ain't said I cain't hire you, son. But most folks gits the itch now and agin, so lemme tell you what to do—if'n you got it or if'n you git it. Will Tweedy?" Hosie jerked around. He must not of known I was still there. "Go in the storeroom, Will, and open up thet case a-Siticide. Bring me a bottle for Hosie."

Why did he have to say that? Oh, well, let him make Hosie mad. Nothing I'd welcome more than to take on Hosie Roach at recess today.

"You heard about Siticide?" asked Grandpa.

"Naw, sir."

"Well, it's itch medicine. Use it at night, not when you comin' to work, cause it's the stinkin'est stuff you ever come acrost in yore life. Got sulfur in it. Makes the skin yaller and you'll smell like a rotten aigg. But by dang it'll cure the itch. Dr. Lem Sharp over in Harmony Grove invented it—Commerce, you know. Dr. Lem ships the stuff all over the United States of America, so it's got to be good."

"Yessir." Hope was rising in Hosie's face.

"Now bout cooties. I ain't a-sayin' you got'm, but we cain't be too careful. What you want to do is git yore ma to cut yore hair short—short as mine. Wash yore head with lye soap ever night for a while, and use you one a-them fine-tooth combs to git the nits out. Y'all got one them combs, boy?"

"Naw, sir."

Grandpa reached up on the shelf back of him, but the comb box was empty. "I'll order some from the wholesale house, son. We do a real good bizness in fine-tooth combs. Lots a-town folks got trouble with them critters." He didn't say that town people with cooties were usually teachers or children who'd caught them at school from lintheads.

Hosie bent over to pet T.R., I guess so his red face wouldn't show. Finally he said, "Mr. Blakeslee, I can start work today. I'm ready and willin', sir."

"Naw, not today," said Grandpa. "Naw, you go git squared away at school, son, and git yore hair cut and all. T'morrer will be jest fine."

Like I said, Grandpa could get away with anything.

And he had finally done what the school superintendent never could. He'd made Hosie Roach willing to quit school.

Mama had a fit when Papa told her about Hosie being hired. She said Grandpa was crazy to think town folks would accept a mill boy in the store. "Well, maybe y'all can keep him in the back," she decided. "You really got to have some hep."

Papa and Cudn Hopewell Stump opened

up next morning, but Hosie was there ahead of them. He had found a broom out back and was sweeping the board sidewalk in front of the store when they walked up. "Lord, Mary Willis, we didn't know who he was!" Papa said at dinner. "That boy was bald as a newborn babe!"

Hosie hadn't just got his hair cut. He'd shaved his head. I really resented him wanting to please all that bad. Especially after Papa asked could I spare an old cap so Hosie wouldn't look so funny.

Papa was real impressed with Hosie.

The next week Miss Love told Grandpa the store ought to have a milliner, and offered to teach Loma. She thought Loma might have a real knack for hats. Grandpa didn't exactly promise the job, but he said it shore would be nice if she could earn her keep, which may of been what Miss Love had in mind. Anyhow, it wasn't long before the two of them came down to the store and set up the millinery table again, and Miss Love put a sign in the window saying Mrs. Loma Williams was under her tutelage and was ready to accommodate customers for new Easter hats at a special low price.

Loma was in hog heaven, being out in public again. I never knew she could act so nice to people. The ladies of Cold Sassy were only too glad to help her get started, knowing Miss Love would lay a hand on every hat, and all the men asked Grandpa how come he waited so long to bring his pretty daughter into the store.

"Jest never thought to," said Grandpa, grinning proud and draping his arm around Loma's shoulders. "If'n she'd a-been a boy, I'd a-had her down here from the day she was born."

Loma looked pleased. I hadn't really hated her for a good while, but I hated her right then. I knew if she worked hard she could worm her way into Grandpa's good graces. And the same with Hosie. Between the two of them, Grandpa might not even notice when I went off to the University.

And would the store ever be quite the same, now that two of the people I couldn't stand were there every day?

46

I shaved for the first time on my fifteenth birthday. Went to school with little pieces of paper stuck on my face to stop the bleeding.

That was the thirtieth day of April. Peonies and flag lilies and poppies were blooming in people's yards, and roses and sweet William, mountain laurel and bleeding heart. And boy howdy, I was fifteen years old!

Smiley and them gave me fifteen licks at recess, one for each year. Then after school they rubbed smut on my face. When I went to the boys' washroom to get it off, I looked in the mirror and, gosh, it was like I'd grown a black beard.

What it was, they were jealous of me being the first to shave.

I like to of never got the smut off. My face was still streaked when I headed for the store. I was already late, and as I hurried by the Presbyterian church, a girl's voice called from behind a big beauty bush in full bloom. "Will?"

It was Lightfoot!

"Will, kin you talk a minute?" She peeped

around the beauty bush. "You got time? Jest for a minute?"

Glancing quickly up and down the street, I ducked around where she was. Gosh, she looked pretty! Her face wasn't pinched from thinness and sorrow like the last time I saw her. The ivory skin glowed against the deep blue of her dress. Like in my dreams, her hair hung loose and shone like platinum.

"Lightfoot?" I'd thought so many times what I'd say when I finally saw her again, but now I was tongue-tied and embarrassed. "Uh, you all right?"

"Yeah, I'm fine. I knowed you ne'ly always come by here goin' to the store from school, but I 'as jest fixin' to give you up. You must a-had to stay in."

"Naw, I just had to wash my face." I rubbed my chin. "Boys put smut on me. It's my birthday today. I'm fifteen."

"Well, thet's nice. I 'as fifteen two months ago."

Gosh, I hadn't thought about her being older than me. "Uh, you gettin' on all right, Lightfoot?" I asked again.

"Pretty good. How you doin', Will?"

"Fine. Uh, my grandpa bought a Pierce car and I drive it for him."

"Yeah, I heerd."

"You did?"

"Hosie told me."

"Oh. Well, uh, with the weather gettin' nice I reckon we go'n be takin' trips again soon. Uh, Lightfoot, I been hopin' to see you again. I wanted, uh, I mean I owe you a apology for —you know, in the cemetery that day. I didn't mean to do it. I—"

"Thet's over and done with, Will." She put her hand on my arm. "And it's one reason I come. You so nice, I knowed you'd feel bad bout thet day. I shore was sorry the lady had sech a fit at you, but I ain't sorry you wanted to comfort me. Maybe I oughtn't to say it, but I ain't never go'n forgit thet time with you."

I dared to put my hand on her hand that was on my arm, and where it had seemed like a million years since I kissed her, all of a sudden it was no more than a day. "Lightfoot, if you ain't mad, why'd you wait so long to say so? Why you sayin' it now?"

"Will, uh—" She flushed and pulled away. "I jest wanted you to know before—" She faltered. "Uh, how's Miss Neppie? She 'as real nice to me."

"She's fine. But she ain't my teacher now.

You go'n get to come back to school next year?"

"No. But I been studyin' Hosie's books, Will. I ain't go'n quit larnin', no matter what."

"School ain't been the same with you not there."

Smiling, she put her hand in her pocket and held out a big buckeye. "Would you take it, Will? For luck, and to remember me by? I brung it with me from White County when we come down here. I, uh, I ain't a-go'n need it no more now."

Something about her tone made me suspicion what this was all about. "Lightfoot, are you sayin' good-bye to me?"

She said. "Will, I . . . I mostly come to make thangs right betwixt us, whilst I'm still free to. I wanted you to know I never thought hard a-you for—you know. And yeah, I reckon thet's it. I come to say good-bye."

"Where you goin'? Back to White County?" I thought I couldn't stand it, not ever to see her again.

"Will, I'm a-go'n git marrit."

The sky wobbled. "Get married?"

"I didn't want you to hear it from nobody else. I'm a-go'n marry Hosie."

Oh, good gosh a'mighty!

"We couldn't even think on it fore yore granddeddy give him thet job. Hosie's got a chance in life now, Will. We'll always feel beholden to Mr. Blakeslee. He shore is a fine man. I better go now, but I ain't never go'n forgit you and please don't forgit me, Will. Thet's why I give you the buckeye. Look at it ever now and agin and remember—"

She kissed me quick, on the cheek. Her eyes were brimming with tears. Next thing I knew, she had disappeared.

As if a chance in life wasn't enough, the next day Grandpa let Hosie off work early to go over to Jefferson for the license, and even lent him his mule for the trip. Also raised his wages fifty cents a week.

It like to killed me.

I felt by myself in a way I never had in my life. Miss Love just had eyes for Grandpa, and Grandpa was taken up with her, and now Lightfoot was about to marry Hosie Roach.

Maybe something would stop it. Maybe something would happen to Hosie. Maybe—

School was out for the summer on Friday that week, and they got married on Sunday, at the little Baptist church in Mill Town. "We jest went up after preachin'," Hosie told Grandpa, "and got the knot tied."

The one that something happened to was Grandpa.

47

Grandpa worked late the following Friday night. Hosie Roach worked late, too, naturally, but went home to Lightfoot about nine o'clock, a good hour before Grandpa locked up to go home to Miss Love.

Just as he turned the door key, a man stuck a Harrington and Richardson revolver to the back of his head, and a rough voice said, "Unlock thet door, Mr. Blakeslee. Hit ain't quite time to close up yet."

There were two of them, one big and burly, the other a younger fellow with a slight build. Despite they had dirty white handkerchiefs over their faces, Grandpa recognized them right off as the strangers who'd come in the store that morning claiming to be cotton buyers.

They made him unlock the cash register, despite he said it was empty, and it *was* empty. Then they sat him down in a straight chair by the potbellied stove, out of sight from the street, and tied him to the chair with a length of medium rope cut from the store's big coil. All that time, Grandpa kept saying how pore he was. "I ain't got no more cash money'n a one-horse farmer," he insisted. "The store don't bring in enough these days for nobody to bother stealin' it."

"Tell thet to somebody ain't got no sense," said the big burly one. "A man ain't pore thet owns two artermobiles and a store and a hotel." He nodded toward Miss Love's fine-cuisine sign in the window. "Luther, tie thet last knot tighter. Now, sir, whar's yore safe?"

"They ain't a dime in thet safe," roared Grandpa, struggling against the rope. He was really mad.

As the burly one slapped him across the face, Luther spied the safe. "Now call out the combination," ordered the big fellow. "And if I was you, sir, I wouldn't give no wrong numbers."

"Have it yore way, but it's a waste a-time," Grandpa insisted. "I used to keep cash money in there. But not since I read bout somebody breakin' in a store in Atlanta and cartin' off the safe to blow up later. I don't—"

"Say the combination for Luther here," the big fellow ordered again. "Say it slow. He ain't too bright."

So Grandpa said the numbers. But Luther being a little bit drunk and his hands shaking like the palsy from nervousness, he couldn't work it. They decided to untie Grandpa and make him do it.

Just like he said, the safe was empty—except for his will and a letter and some stock certificates, land deeds, and other legal papers. The robbers were mad, boy howdy! "Now, sir! You tell us where thet money is or git ready to die, one!" the big fellow yelled, waving his revolver in Grandpa's face.

"I shore didn't waste no time mindin' them boogers," Grandpa said the next morning when he was telling us all about the robbery. "Gosh a'mighty, I couldn't hardly wait to up-turn my dang nail keg!"

He was lying on his left side in Granny's big bed. Miss Love sat in the rocking chair facing him. The rest of us stood behind her— I and Mama and Papa, Aunt Loma, Mary

Toy, and Aunt Carrie, who had come over offering to help.

"Well, sir, I dumped the nail keg and—ow!" Grandpa, trying to turn onto his back, quickly eased back to his left side, which was where the broke ribs were. Doc had bound his chest tight with strips of old sheets to keep the broke ribs from moving every time he breathed. "Hit don't hurt so bad as long as I stay like this," he said, his face twisted with pain. "Ain't I a pretty sight, Will Tweedy?" He tried to grin.

I could hardly bear to look at him. Besides a big ugly knot on his forehead, he had two black eyes, his nose was swelled up huge—broke for the fourth time in his life—and Doc had bandaged a bad gash above his left eye. Besides all that, his right knee was bad twisted, and he was sore and bruised all over.

My daddy got him back to talking about the highwaymen. "Did they get all the money, sir?"

"I reckon, Hoyt. Like I say, I dumped the keg, nails and all, and besides the day's earnin's, out fell all them silver dollars and gold pieces I had in there. Must a-been a hundred and fifty dollars' worth, and them coins rollin' ever whichaway!" Grandpa

spread his right arm wide to indicate the
whole store, but I noticed he was mindful of
his broke ribs. "Gosh a'mighty, they was
greedy! Went down on hands and knees and
crawled around jest a-grabbin'! They'd been
drinkin', you know, and they warn't any too
bright, and was new at the game, too, I
reckon, cause they plumb forgot I wasn't still
tied up. All I had to do was watch my chance
and whack each one acrost the back of the
neck with the side of my hand—*thonk, thonk.*
By time they come to, I was a-settin' on the
counter with their dang Harrington and Richardson pointed right at'm."

Grandpa usually kept his own revolver under the counter, a Smith and Wesson, but had
taken it home for cleaning.

First he made his prisoners take off their
handkerchief masks. "Why, I thought y'all
was men!" he exclaimed, making like he was
surprised. "But dang if you ain't monkeys!"
Grandpa was having the time of his life. He
said, "Well, jest in case y'all got in mind to
start some monkey bizness, I'll do a little tar-
get practice. See thet there cardboard adver-
tise-ment?" He nodded toward a cutout of a
pretty lady holding a box of Pearline Washing
Compound. It hung by a string from the ceil-

ing just above where the robbers were sitting on the floor but, being dazed and dumfounded, they looked all around and didn't see what he was talking about.

"Hit's a-hangin' right over y'all's heads," jeered Grandpa. The men looked up just as he shot the string half in two, dropping the cardboard lady to the floor at their feet. "Now then, I reckon y'all go'n be-have whilst I ring up Pearl Potter, our po-lice. Thet's *Mister* Pearl Potter, for yore information."

But with just the one hand, Grandpa would have had to lay down the revolver to talk on the phone. Not being that big of a fool, he told Luther to do the calling. "Say to Mr. Pearl, 'Me and my buddy been tryin' to rob Blakeslee's store, so come git us and put us in the calaboose!' Make haste, now, Luther. I got to git on home. Gosh a'mighty, I bet Mr. Pearl ain't never got a call like this'n before," he said, laughing.

Luther stood up real slow, eyeing the telephone.

"You ain't never seen a telephone?" Grandpa was trying to goad him. "All you do, you turn thet crank, then you pick up thet dohickey and put it up to yore ear and wait till Central answers. What you talk th'ew is thet thang stickin' out of the box. Tell her Rucker Blakeslee is a-holdin' you and yore partner and you want to speak to Mr. Pearl Potter."

The robber was naturally mad as heck, being made fun of like that, but he did like he was told to—then just stood there and stood there.

"Why ain't you talkin'?" asked Grandpa.

"Cause she don't answer," said Luther.

"Dang!" said Grandpa, "Miss Lucille must a-gone to the bathroom. Crank it agin, sonny boy."

All of a sudden he noticed that the other fellow, the burly one, had stood up and moved a step forward. "You want a bullet th'ew that mole on yore chin, buster?" he yelled, waving the revolver. "Move one more step and I'll put it there. Or maybe you rather watch me shoot another string half in two."

He saw the men exchange quick glances when he said that, but as he himself admitted later, he was havin' sech a good time he never thought nothin' of it.

Instead of stepping back, the big hunky fellow sneered and said, "Thet with the string was jest a lucky shot. You cain't do it agin."

"Less'n yore revolver don't aim true, I can

do it any number a-times." Still sitting on the counter, not taking his eyes off the big fellow, Grandpa said, "Keep on crankin' thet phone, Luther."

"A gun cain't shoot no better than the feller aimin' it," said the big hunky one, and eased forward a little.

Grandpa saw that. "Go to dancin', buster!" he yelled, firing off a bullet that grazed the toe of the man's boot. Even before he pulled the trigger again and got a click instead of a bang, young Luther had dropped the receiver, leaving it dangling by the cord. Crouching low, like a bobcat ready to spring, he grabbed Grandpa's right knee, turned quick, and jerked him off the counter just as his partner raised a chair high and crashed it over Grandpa's head.

48

We all wondered if the robbers meant to kill Grandpa. "He shore looked dead when I come in the store," said Mr. Pearl. "Out cold and bleedin' like a hog."

Dr. Slaughter said it was just a good thing

Miss Lucille got back to her switchboard in time to plug into the fight, and then had the good sense to ring up him and Mr. Pearl.

If Miss Love had had a telephone, she would of been called next instead of us. As it was, she'd just started wondering why Grandpa hadn't come on home when she heard Mr. Birdsong's old horse-drawn hearse rattle into her drive—the one he took Uncle Camp to the morgue in but called an ambulance if the person wasn't dead yet. Miss Love didn't have any way to know for sure which it was when Doc climbed out and said he'd brought Rucker home.

Papa and I got there in the Cadillac a minute or two later. I won't ever forget the look on Miss Love's face as she watched us bring Grandpa in on the stretcher. You'd think he'd been under a rock all his life, he was so pale. The knot on his forehead was big as a double-yolk egg. The gash over his left eye was still bleeding, and his face was a twist of pain. But as we carried him toward the bedroom—Miss Love holding a lamp high to light our way down the hall—Grandpa looked up at her with a weak grin and said, "Don't worry, hear. I'll be up in the mornin' fore the water boils. I got outsmarted, is all."

Then he coughed, and yelped with pain from the broke ribs.

Before I got inside his house good on Saturday night after it happened on Friday night, Grandpa called from the sickroom, "Thet you, Will Tweedy? Anythang new happen down at the store? They ketch them robbers? Come in here, son!"

His room smelled of turpentine, which Doc had prescribed as a liniment for the pulled ligament. Grandpa was sitting on the side of the bed in his nightshirt, holding a pack of steaming hot towels to his knee. By then he was tired of hurting and madder'n heck at the robbers. "If'n I ever meet up with them two agin," he yelled, shaking his fist, "I'll kill'm!"

"Better wait till you feel better, Grandpa," I said, joking.

That just made him madder. But he had to get aholt of himself, because the ranting and raving made his ribs hurt. Groaning, he eased back down on the bed, turning onto his left side. "Hit ain't so bad . . . long as I lay still and breathe shaller."

"Dr. Slaughter says you must breathe deep," Miss Love reminded him, coming in with a supper tray.

"Gosh a'mighty, woman, I'd like to see him

breathe deep in my condition! All this wouldn't a-happened, Will Tweedy, if'n I'd jest knowed what them dang robbers knowed —thet warn't but two bullets in their dang revolver."

Miss Love set the tray on a towel on the bed so Grandpa could eat laying on his side. "You couldn't have known about the bullets," she said, patting his shoulder.

"Don't pat me when I'm mad, woman! I would a-knowed bout them bullets if I'd a-looked." He groaned, reaching down to rub his knee. "And I would a-looked," he added, "if'n I hadn't a-been talkin' so big and showin' off."

"Dear, try to stay calm. Dr. Slaughter said—"

"Let Doc stay calm. I'm mad and hurtin' and I need to git on to the store." Grandpa took a bite of cornbread and kept right on fussing. "If'n they'd a-fought fair, with fists, I could a-licked them boogers! Either one or both of'm!"

He wasn't just mad. He was embarrassed. What hurt most—worse than the broke ribs, broke nose, banged head, and twisted knee all put together—was his pride. The only fight he'd ever lost before was the War Between the States.

Miss Love bent over him and touched his cheek. "You're alive," she whispered. "That's all I care about."

"Well, it ain't all I care about. Doggit—no, damnit, by gosh—I never thought to git done in by a dang settin' chair. If I'd a-seen it comin', I could a-ducked." He groaned.

My mother was coming down the hall as I left Grandpa's room to hurry back to the Saturday night customers at the store. "I thought maybe I could hep some way," she told Miss Love. "Maybe wash your supper dishes. And I'll take the soiled sheets home for Queenie to wash and iron." Almost timidly, she peered in at Grandpa lying in the bed. "Pa?" she said sweetly. "Would you like me to come sit with you a few minutes?"

He was still mad at the robbers. "I reckon, Mary Willis," he grumped, "if'n you'll set over in the corner and not say nothin' and not cry. I cain't stand it when you mother-hen me."

I just knew she'd burst into tears. Instead, she snapped back at him like she'd been taking lessons from Aunt Loma. "Just cause you didn't get your way with the robbers is no reason to talk to me like that, Pa. And I don't have to stay and listen to it." She turned to stalk out.

"Aw, Mary Willis honey, come on in here and set down." Motioning toward the rocking chair, he grinned up at her. "Did you bring me a snort, by any chance? Miss Love ain't no diff'rent from yore ma when it comes to whiskey in the closet."

Mama actually burst out laughing. I did, too, and so did Miss Love. Grandpa almost laughed but had to keep it to a smirk. Laughing hurt his ribs.

I knew Mama had come mostly to be with her daddy. Miss Love was not one she had in mind when she said what fam'lies are for is to hep in time of trouble. But Miss Love seemed real glad to have her there.

I didn't get back again till after dinner Sunday. By then the whole house smelled like turpentine.

Thinking Grandpa might be asleep, I tiptoed down the hall instead of calling out. Just as I was about to peep into his room, I heard him and Miss Love talking soft and easy in there, the way people do when they're resting and in no hurry.

I knew I ought to announce my presence.

But instead, drawing back behind the open door, I looked at them through the slit between it and the door frame. I could see them easy. Miss Love, in a pretty yellow dress, was lying a-top the sheet on Granny's side of the bed, her head cradled in the crook of Grandpa's left elbow. He lay on his left side, a thin nightshirt over the tight binding around his chest, the sheet pulled up to his waist. And gosh, he had his right arm laid across Miss Love's stomach! His eyes were closed.

To save me, I couldn't move or speak.

"Are you about to go to sleep, Rucker?" she asked softly.

He said, "Naw, I'm jest lookin' at the inside a-my eyelids."

"What?"

"I got my eyes shet and I'm a-lookin'. Which ain't the same as jest havin' yore eyes closed. Did you know you can shet yore eyes and see in the dark? At night it's like lookin' at a moldy old prune—jest all kinds a-gray dots and lines and curlicues amidst the blackness." Turning his face toward the window, which was a block of bright sunshine, he exclaimed, "But gosh a'mighty, Love honey, it's so much more to look at now! Hit's like

watchin' a dang sunset. Mostly red and orange, but they's streaks a-brown, too, and a
big purple blob thet moves, and here come
some little green dots!"

"What on earth are you talking about?"
Miss Love thought Grandpa was joking. I did,
too. I near bout laughed out loud.

His eyes still closed, he grinned. "Shet yore
eyes and look. You'll see."

Miss Love did what she was told, turning
her head toward the window as her black
lashes brushed her freckled cheeks.

I shut my eyes, too. In order to see the
sunshine, I held my face up close to the crack
in the door.

"I see what you mean!" she exclaimed.
"Why, it's beautiful, Rucker! I never noticed
before! Goodness, it would make a lovely de-
sign for dress goods. But . . . what's the
point?"

"Ain't no point. Jest something to do when
you cain't sleep. Leastways thet's how I got
onto it last night. When I went to lookin', and
marvelin' how much I could see in the dark, I
quit thinkin' words and then I started to git
sleepy. The surprise was when God come into
the pitcher. I don't mean I saw God. I . . .
well, I felt him, like He was inside a-me, or at

least closer than my nose, stead a-bein' way off up in the clouds somewhere thet I cain't reach to." His voice softened. "Hit feels like thet now, Love. Hit must be what the Bible means by 'Peace, be still,' or 'Be still and know thet I am God.' "

For a while neither one said anything. Then Miss Love asked, "Are you praying now, Rucker?"

"No'm. Like I say, I'm jest a-starin' at my eyelids. If'n I went to prayin', I'd be sayin' words, thinkin' bout myself and what I want and what I'm scairt of. This way I ain't thinkin' nothin'. I'm jest feelin' God's presence. Hit makes me feel safe—like I can do anythang I got to, includin' stand all this dang pain. I reckon it sounds like foolish-ment. You prob'ly think I'm off in the head, Love, like them folks that has visions."

"No," she said softly, "because I feel it, too."

"Don't it seem like yore brain ain't cluttered up? Like if'n the Lord wanted to tell you something, you'd know what it was?"

"Yes, it feels like that," she murmured.

A covey of goosebumps thrilled up the backs of my arms, because it felt like that to me, too.

"Well, let's say a-men now. I'm th'ew lookin' at my eyelids. I rather look at you a while."

Opening my own eyes, I saw Miss Love smile, and him smile back, so tender. They lay there a few minutes, neither one speaking. Then, rubbing his whiskers, he said, "Is this Sunday?"

She nodded.

"Then I ain't shaved in ne'ly three days. Hit's got so I cain't stand whiskers, Love." He grinned at her. "See what you done? I used to didn't care." Another silence, and he said, "You miss goin' to the Methodist church, don't you?"

She hesitated. "Sometimes. Well, every Sunday. It's the way I was brought up."

"You miss thet collection plate goin' around, and Miss Effie Belle plowin' up and down the pi-ana? And all them dull an-nounce-ments, not to mention them dull ser-mons?"

"I wouldn't swap one of your sermons to have all that." She laughed, then got serious. "But I like being part of a congregation. I miss the people, Rucker."

"All them dang hypocrites?"

"My mother always said never expect

church members to be perfect. Christians are still people."

"Well, she spoke the truth there."

"Most of us Christians need to go to church, Rucker. By ourselves, we feel uneasy about God, and we're too bashful to pray except when we're sick or scared. We read our Bibles, but we never think things out the way you do. But you—it's a wonder God didn't call you to preach, Rucker."

"Ain't I been preachin' to you?"

"I mean in a church. I mean really preach." She smiled at him so sweet.

I was getting restless. I wanted to leave. But a board creaked the first step I took, so I decided to wait a little. It being Sunday, they'd probably go on to sleep. Long as I could remember, Mama and Papa had gone to their room every Sunday after dinner and shut the door, and we knew better than to wake them up.

"I got called to preach one time," said Grandpa. "Up in the mountains when I was a-peddlin'." He laughed. "But it warn't the Lord thet called me. I done the callin'. Called myself Brother Blakeslee, itinerant Baptist preacher and peddler of fine merchandise."

"Oh, you didn't!" Grinning, she raised up on her elbow to look at him. "Why in the—"

"I'd jest come out of the War. I'd had my fill a-sleepin' in the woods and cookin' over a dang campfire. I reasoned thet them mountain folks would feed a preacher and put him up, and then buy his blankets and needles to hep with the Lord's work. Well'm, it shore did backfire! I got me a invite to preach, but I warn't into my sermon hardly when a mean-eyed man on the front row stood up and cussed me out. Said I must be the Devil In-carnate, or at least his agent, cause I shore warn't no True Believer. A-mens rose up all over thet little room."

"Goodness! What did you do?"

"Thought fast, I tell you. 'Wait a minute, folks!' I shouted. 'All what I jest said, thet was s'posed to be the Devil a-talkin'. Now if y'all will shet up, I'll tell you what God said back to thet old forktail varmint.' I warn't go'n let a bunch a-dang hill people run me off. I went at it, makin' up stories bout sin-ners thet God had punished, and spoutin' hellfire and damnation and all the other preacher stuff I could think of." He grinned. "Didn't make a dang bit a-sense, but they liked it. Wanted me back next Sunday. But I'd learnt my lesson, Love. I vowed it was the last time I'd try to tell bout my Jesus and my God to folks with rock minds."

He blew at a curl near her ear. She shivered, giggled. "Quit. That tickles."

"You rather me preach? I wisht I felt up to havin' our Sunday time in the parlor. I got a good sermon worked out for you."

"Well, I could go play some hymns."

Oh my gosh, where could I hide right quick?

"Not now, Love," said Grandpa. "I rather have you layin' here by me. You hep me forgit the pain, and I don't feel so sick."

Another silence. "What's it about?" She sounded lazy, sleepy. "The sermon, I mean."

"Something Will Tweedy's been questionin'. He don't unnerstand why Jesus said, 'Ast, and it shall be given.' He says why would Jesus say sech a thang when it ain't always so?"

"That's easy to explain, Rucker. Tell Will that sometimes God has to say no for our own good, or to teach us something, or show His power. Sometimes it's just not His will to give us a certain thing. Or He wants to test our faith and see if we trust Him no matter what."

Grandpa laughed. "Love, you sound like ever preacher I ever heard. But Jesus didn't say God might say no when we say gimme. He said God's go'n say yes. Anythang we ast for, we go'n git it. Well, hungry folks pray for food, but they shore don't all git fed. And sick folks beg Him for healin', but lots of'm die, or maybe live on in bed. Jesus had to mean something diff'rent from what folks think He meant, else to my mind He was a dang fool to go round promisin' what God wouldn't do. But Jesus warn't no fool, Love. So what did He mean?"

Distressed, she sat up and said to Grandpa, "Please, Rucker. Don't talk sacrilege."

"Hit ain't sacrilege. Miss Effie Belle says when she cain't think what to have for dinner, she asts God and right off He gives her a idea. To my thinkin', thet's sacrilege."

Miss Love really laughed. "There's not a woman in the world who hasn't prayed what to cook for dinner, Rucker!"

"Well, God give y'all cookbooks for thet. Anyhow, when I got to ponderin' on it last night, the word *ast* commenced to jump at me like sheep comin' over a fence. *Ast. Ast. Ast.* But ast for what? For meat and bread? For healin' miracles? Are we s'posed to ast 'Lord,

give me the answers on the arithmetic test,'
'Lord git me hired over the next feller,' 'Lord,
give me a son'? Gosh a'mighty, how I used to
ast thet'n, Love!" He looked long and tender
at her, and kissed her cheek.

"And didn't God send you Will Tweedy?"

Gosh, I hadn't thought of that!

"Maybe He did," said Grandpa. "Then
agin maybe He sent me you so I could have
another crack at it." I could see Miss Love
blush, and, out in the hall, I blushed.
Grandpa didn't. "But I don't think He
planned Will Tweedy for me. I don't even
think He sent me you. You and Will jest happened in the way of thangs. God ain't said
you won't git nothin' good less'n you pray for
it. But I'm shore thankful for you, Love." He
touched a finger to her chin and her mouth,
then rested his hand on her cheek.

His voice softened as he went on. "Another thang to think on: some folks ain't said
pea-turkey to God in years. They don't ast
Him for nothin', don't specially try to be
good, and don't love nobody the way Jesus
said to—cept their own self. But they go'n git
jest bout as much or as little in the way
a-earthly goods as the rest of us. They go'n
have sorrows and joys, failures and good

times. And when they come down sick they go'n git well or die, one, jest same as the prayin' folks. So don't thet tell you something bout prayin'? Ain't the best prayin' jest bein' with God and talkin' a while, like He's a good friend, stead a-like he runs a store and you've come in a-hopin' to git a bargain?"

Miss Love frowned. "Rucker, you can't write Holy Scripture. It's already been written."

"Well, I shore can question what it means." With a heavy groan, trying to shift a little to get comfortable, he put his arm across her stomach again. "And hit fine'ly come to me in the night, what Jesus must a-meant by *ast*. You want to be like them folks with rock brains, or you want to hear it?"

She smiled. "I want to hear it."

I put in my journal all the above. Also the answer that had come to Grandpa.

"When Jesus said ast and ye shall receive, I don't think He meant us to pray 'Lord, spare my child,' or 'Make it rain for the crops,' or 'Don't let my bizness fail.' I don't even think Jesus meant us to ast for—"

"—for a house or a piano?" She put her

hand on his open palm. He laughed, and lifted her hand and kissed it.

"Naw, and not even for a husband or any other sech favor. The Lord's Prayer does say, 'Give us this day our daily bread,' but thet's the only dang thang Jesus ast for in the whole prayer thet you can *tetch*. They ain't nothin' in the Lord's Prayer says 'Make me well.' I'm tempted to pray thet right now, hurtin' like I am. But I don't think Jesus meant us to think we can git healed jest by beggin' for it." Grandpa laughed kind of rueful. "God made us so we want to stay alive. He put healin' power in our bodies. We don't have to beg Him to save us. All we got to do is accept bein' sick, do what Doc says, and trust thet God wants us to git well if'n we can."

Miss Love broke in. "In the Bible, Jesus only healed the people who asked Him to—and believed He could. If Jesus could heal, can't God? If we pray and have faith?"

"Well'm, faith ain't no magic wand or money-back gar'ntee, either one. Hit's jest a way a-livin'. Hit means you don't worry th'ew the days. Hit means you go'n be holdin' on to God in good or bad times, and you accept whatever happens. Hit means you respect life like it is—like God made it—even when it ain't what you'd order from the wholesale house. Faith don't mean the Lord is go'n make lions lay down with lambs jest cause you ast him to, or make fire not burn. Some folks, when they pray to git well and don't even git better, they say God let'm down. But I say thet warn't even what Jesus was a-talkin' bout. When Jesus said ast and you'll git it, He was givin' a gar'ntee a-spiritual healin', not body healin'. He was sayin' thet if'n you git beat down—scairt to death you cain't do what you got to, or scairt you go'n die, or scairt folks won't like you—why, all you got to do is put yore hand in God's and He'll lift you up. I know it for a fact, Love. I can pray, 'Lord, hep me not be scairt,' and I don't know how, but it's like a eraser wipes the fears away. And I found out long time ago, when I look on what I got to stand as a dang hardship or a burden, it seems too heavy to carry. But when I look on the same dang thang as a challenge, why, standin' it or acceptin' it is like you done entered a contest. Hit even gits excitin', waitin' to see how everthang's go'n turn out."

Grandpa stopped to move a little and his face twisted with pain. But he went on. "Jesus meant us to ast God to hep us stand the pain, not beg Him to take the pain away. We can ast for comfort and hope and patience and courage, and to be gracious when thangs ain't goin' our way, and we'll git what we ast for. They ain't no gar'ntee thet we ain't go'n have no troubles and ain't go'n die. But shore as frogs croak and cows bellow, God'll forgive us if'n we ast Him to."

"He will also help us be forgiving," said Miss Love, smiling. "Rucker, why don't you try to forgive Clem Crummy? You really ought to take your name off his hotel. You got even with him. Isn't that enough?"

Grandpa laughed. "Not quite. I want to rub his face in the dirt a while fore I let him up, Love. Somebody's got to learn him better than to cheat folks, else he's liable to land in jail. Besides, me and God ain't got time for Clem right now. We too busy tryin' to make a challenge out a-them broke ribs and this here twisted knee. And I'm busy tryin' to accept the loss a-my dignity."

Out there in the cool hall, afraid even to wiggle my foot lest they hear me, I wondered if I could ever accept Lightfoot McLendon marrying Hosie Roach.

"Well, Miz Blakeslee," Grandpa said, running his hand down the side of her waist and hip and thigh, "do you think thet's what Jesus might a-meant? Don't it make sense?"

She thought a minute. "If you talked like this at a Wednesday night prayer meeting, Rucker, most people would walk out. They'd say you're not a Christian and shouldn't be allowed to speak in God's house. But to me it makes beautiful sense. Thank you for it."

"Remind me to tell Will Tweedy, hear."

I slid down to the floor. Just by peeping around the door frame, I could still see them if I wanted to. But what I wanted to do was ponder what all Grandpa had just said.

Then Miss Love changed the subject and I had to listen instead of think. "Rucker, do you know they've made up a committee to find a new name for Cold Sassy?"

"I heard. But they'll change Cold Sassy over my dead body."

"What if they named it Blakeslee? Wouldn't you like that? Our name being on the map might help us sell cars."

He laughed. "Blakeslee is too much like Blakely. Thet's a town in south Georgia. Anyhow, the Blakeslees warn't nothin' special to the town."

"You're special to the town."

"Yeah, but not like Miss Mattie Lou. Now

she was descended from two pioneer fam'lies, the Toys and the Willises both. But Toy would be a silly name for a town, and Willis ain't much better." Grandpa paused. "Will Tweedy's name ain't William, you know. Hit's Willis."

Trying again to get comfortable, Grandpa moved his arm up from Miss Love's stomach and by gosh let his hand rest right between her bosoms! And like she didn't even notice where his hand was, she moved her head over on his shoulder. Her breath quickened as his fingers traced the curve of her neck and wandered careless toward the soft flesh below.

"God hep me, Love," he said softly, "I ain't so bad hurt I don't feel nothin'!"

She didn't say a word. The smile left her face and her lips parted.

If you thought about it, me spying on them through the slit of space between the open door and the door frame was right humorous. But what was funny as heck was Grandpa with that bruised, swelled-up nose, the big knot like a horn on his forehead, the black eyes like a dern raccoon's mask, the scab over one eye like a sword slash on a pirate, the itchy three-day sprouting of gray whiskers—and Miss Love gazing at him like he was

Prince Charming come to the costume ball dressed up as a toady frog.

"What do you think about Enterprise?" she asked sleepily. "Or Progressive City? What about Sheffield? Those were suggested in last week's paper."

"Any one a-them names on a postmark would bore me to death, jest like Commerce does. They say a Englishman come th'ew Harmony Grove in nineteen aught-one, sellin' silverware. The next year he come th'ew agin and like to had a fit when he seen 'Welcome to Commerce' where it used to say 'Welcome to Harmony Grove.' He'd sent in Harmony Grove to name a new park over in England and it won him a five-hundret-dollar prize, but over on this side a-the ocean, folks thought it sounded tacky and countrified."

"Cold Sassy wouldn't win a prize any-where," Miss Love said. "Admit that."

"Naw, it wouldn't. But it suits the town."

"You suit me, Rucker." Her eyes all shiny, she looked at him and murmured, "The last few months with you . . ." Her lips trembled. "Dear Rucker, I think you know, but I want to say it. This has been the only really happy time of my whole life."

Grandpa smiled and touched her hair. "I

cain't say it's the onliest happy time for me, ma'am. But they shore ain't never been any to equal it!"

She giggled. "Now quit sayin' *ma'am* to me. That's what people call old ladies, or their betters."

"You're my better."

"No, I ain't, I'm just your—" A look of surprise crossed her face and she burst out laughing. "Good Lord, Rucker, I just said *ain't*! Before you know it I'll be saying *hit ain't*!"

He tried not to laugh, to save his ribs. "Well, come 'ere, honey. Learn me how to talk right." Wincing, Grandpa pulled her close and kissed her, hard. Then, keeping his mouth on hers, he loosed the pins from her hair. Just as it fell around her neck in a wavy brown mass, he jerked away. "Yore dang nose!" he yelped. "Hit hit my nose!" Quick tears filled his eyes. Then he whispered, "Didn't hurt a-tall," and kissed her again— but a lot more careful.

Long minutes later, I heard her whisper, "If I held you tight as I want to, Rucker, your nose and your ribs and your knee couldn't stand the pain."

"Then don't do it," he whispered back,

kissing each freckled cheek. "I can tell you, pain don't do nothin' for ro-mance!"

"Remember that when you rub stiff whiskers on my face and I say *ouch* instead of *oh darling*."

He rubbed his chin against her cheek. "Well'm, they ain't stiff now."

"Don't say *well'm*."

"All right'm." He laughed, and kissed her again.

"Oh, dear, dear man. I love you. I love you."

They quit talking then, and drifted off to sleep, and I tiptoed out.

I was ashamed of myself, and embarrassed. But by golly, I had my missing last chapter. If Grandpa and Miss Love weren't already living happy ever after, they would be soon as he got well.

But the last chapter wasn't finished.

By middle of the week, Grandpa was coughing and running a little fever. By Friday it hurt him to breathe and it like to killed him when he coughed. Mama went down and stayed all day. Doc came by every chance he could.

Saturday morning, just as we sat down to

breakfast, here came little Timmy Hopkins, saying Miz Blakeslee wanted Mr. Hoyt to ring up Dr. Slaughter. Said tell him Mr. Blakeslee was having a bad chill and he'd coughed up some dark, rusty sputum.

49

I went in the Cadillac to fetch Doc, who began fussing at Grandpa before he got in the room hardly. "I don't care if it does hurt to breathe, Rucker, you got to git some air down there." He put his hand on Grandpa's forehead. "Hot as a firecracker!"

Despite all the blankets on him, Grandpa was shaking like a dog pulled out of a frozen pond. As Dr. Slaughter bent over him with the stethoscope, he asked, "Wh-wh-what you th-think I g-got, D-Doc?"

"Shet up, Rucker. I cain't hear with you a-talkin'."

Doc listened all over his chest and his back, too. "Where does it hurt when you cough?"

"B-b-between my sh-shoulder blades. You r-reckon it's a t-tetch a-pleurisy?"

Doc straightened up. "Naw, it's a tetch of

pneumonia, Rucker. More'n a tetch, tell you the truth. I can hear the rales. But you're strong as a ox, you know. You go'n pull th'ew all right."

Out in the hall, though, Dr. Slaughter told us he was worried. "Rucker's tough, but losin' all thet blood ain't go'n hep, and he shore could do without them broke ribs. He could do without the pneumonia, for thet matter." He sighed.

"I don't understand," said Miss Love, dazed. "I thought I was doing all I should for him. But he got worse so fast."

"Hit ain't your fault, honey. Thet's the way pneumonia is. Hit comes on with a bang, then it has to run its course, and we won't know which way it'll go till the crisis comes." Doc put on his hat. "Now listen to me, Miss Love," he said. "Rucker's fever is aw-ready a hundret and five. Hit could go lots higher. For shore, he's go'n git lots worse fore he gits better. So you let Mary Willis and Loma come up here and hep with the nursin'. You hear me?"

"I couldn't ask them to do that."

"You ain't got to ast'm. You jest got to let'm. Soon as he gits over the chill, y'all go'n be spongin' him off night and day. We got to keep his fever down, else it might cook his brains. You understand, Miss Love? And keep the windows open. He needs fresh air. Don't let the whole dang fam'ly set in there around the bed, usin' up the oxygen."

My mother and Aunt Loma arrived right after he left, just as Doc knew they would. After school I went to the store as usual, but Papa told me to go on to Grandpa's and stay there. "Get the chores done," he said, "and be there in case they need to send for hep. Too bad Miss Love ain't got a telephone."

It was awful, listening to Grandpa cough and hack and moan. I was glad to go get busy outside. In my mind I can still picture Granny's rose garden that day, the bushes decorated with buds and blossoms. But at the time I just glanced at the garden and went on to the barn to see after the animals.

While I was pitching hay, Miss Love came out and stood by the pasture gate. I climbed down from the loft to see if she needed anything, but she just shook her head, watching as Mr. Beautiful galloped up and put his head over the railing to be petted. She rubbed his ears and stroked his neck, but her mind wasn't on him.

"If your grandfather dies," she said bitterly, "I won't stay in Cold Sassy any longer than it takes to sell the house. I hate this town. It's like life. It gives, and then it takes away."

I couldn't bear the thought of Cold Sassy without Grandpa or her, either one. As we started back to the house, I begged her, "Ma'am, don't give up on him. Like Doc said, he's strong. He's go'n get well. Hear?"

That night we were all there for supper, even Mary Toy and Campbell Junior. Miss Love sponged Grandpa off while the rest of us ate.

Mama was just leaving the table to take her turn with him when we heard Grandpa say, real loud, "Miss Love, you better git on back to the store now. . . ." He paused for breath. "We're much obliged, but Miss Mattie Lou don't need no more hep."

Forks clattered onto plates as Papa and Aunt Loma and I jumped up and dashed to the sickroom, leaving Mary Toy and poor little Campbell Junior sitting there, confused and scared. We got to the bedroom door in time to hear Grandpa say, "Best go on now, Miss Love. They short-handed at the store."

"But I live here, Rucker! Remember? I'm your—"

"Miss Mattie Lou?" Looking toward the door, not seeing us at all, he said brightly, "You want to serve Miss Love some cake? She's got to get back to the store terreckly."

Grandpa had a bad spell of coughing then. Soon as he could speak, he said, "Did you ever git Miss Pauline's hat finished, Miss Love? She come in yesterd'y, astin' bout it."

"Call me Love, Rucker," she begged, kneeling down by the bed so she could look right in his face. "Please, call me Love!"

Trying hard not to cough again—it hurt so bad—and looking right at her, he asked Miss Mattie Lou for some water.

At that, Miss Love rose to her feet, tears streaming down her cheeks. My mother reached out like to a hurt child, and Miss Love stumbled into her arms.

I couldn't stand it. I fled to the back porch, knelt down by the tall slab table, and begged God to let Grandpa get well.

Mama and I stayed all night, her taking turns with Miss Love at the sickbed. The fever raged despite all the sponging, and Grandpa couldn't sleep for coughing and talking.

Sometimes he just mumbled gibberish. Other times it was real sentences, but they didn't make sense. Then again he'd speak clear as anything, telling jokes or carrying on a conversation with some person we couldn't see.

For a while Grandpa was back in the War with his daddy. There would be a handful of words; then he'd get quiet and Miss Love would say he's gone to sleep, thank God. But soon he'd take up where he left off. I remember him mumbling something about a battlefield. "Hit was awful, Pa. . . . All them dead Yankees layin' there. I tried to find you . . . some boots, but they jest warn't none left. . . . Our boys had done hepped theirselves."

He talked about seeing a Yankee balloon. "Pa, you reckon they spotted our battlements? If'n they did, Lord hep us!" And Grandpa sat bolt upright in the bed. I helped Miss Love ease him back down on his side. "Who're you, ma'am?" he asked as his eyes focused.

Remembering that Grandpa had been a boy like me in the War, she said, "I'm your nurse, son. They—uh, they brought you to the hospital."

"Where's my daddy at?"

"Uh, on the next cot. But let's don't wake him up. He's worn out."

"We ain't go'n march t'morrer?" He pulled nervous at his whiskers.

"No. Don't talk anymore now. Try to rest."

I brought in another pan of water. Miss Love wrung out the towel again and slowly, so weary, she wiped his back and his neck, his face and arms and then his legs. After while he seemed to sleep, but in no time was coughing again and talking.

He wasn't in the War now. He was with Miss Mattie Lou—coughing and mumbling disconnected sentences picked out of the air from this or that time in their life. He was a Graphophone record kept on a shelf for thirty years and getting played again now. His eyes were unnatural bright, his breathing short and fast and difficult, and what he coughed up was tinged with bright red blood.

About ten o'clock, Mama talked Miss Love into lying down a while, "even if you cain't sleep."

As Mama bent over the wash basin on the floor to wring out a towel, Grandpa fixed his eyes on her. But it was Granny that he saw. "Miss Mattie Lou . . . they's something I got to confess, hon. . . . You deserve . . .

to know what kind a-man . . . you done pledged yoreself to marry."

Oh, law, was Mama fixing to hear how he'd loved Miss Love from the minute he laid eyes on her?

"I been shamed to tell you . . . but I ne'ly . . . got run out a-them hills . . . last month." Then he told her bout callin' hisself to preach. With her and him fixin' to git married, it was go'n be his last peddlin' walk th'ew the mountains and he was jest sick and tarred a-sleepin' on the ground. Figgered the church folks would put a preacher up and feed him, too. "I acted a lie, Miss Mattie Lou . . . and it shore did . . . backfire. Fore I was hardly . . . into my sermon. . . ."

His voice trailed off.

"Hush now, Pa," said my mother, wiping his chest as best she could around the binding, which wasn't easy, with him lying on his left side to favor the broke ribs.

I sure wished Granny was here. She could always think of something to do for a sick person. But that night Mama was like Granny. "Pa, try to take some water," she'd say, lifting his head and holding a glass to his cracked, parched lips. Then she'd rub his mouth with Mentholatum, or maybe lay a wet washrag over his eyes.

"Sit down and rest, Mama," I finally told her. "I'll wash him."

Staring right at me, pulling at his whiskers kind of frantic, Grandpa said, "Miss Mattie Lou?"

"I'm Will, sir. I'm your boy. . . ."

Granny's clock had just chimed midnight when Miss Love came back in, her eyes dark-circled, her green print dress wrinkled. "I'm afraid I dozed off, Mary Willis," she whispered. "Is he better? Has he slept any?"

My mother shook her head. "No, he cain't rest for talkin'. I cain't understand why Dr. Slaughter don't come. He said he'd come."

"He said he'd come if he could. Miss Herma is having her baby. I guess he couldn't leave her. I'll take over now, Mary Willis. You try to get some sleep. Use the bed in the front room." Miss Love had become businesslike and mechanical. "Will, you go lie down on the daybed in the hall."

"I ain't tired, Miss Love. I'll stay."

Grandpa drifted into a fitful sleep, then waked with a start about two-thirty and between gasps for breath went to raging at something or somebody, all the time pulling at his whiskers.

"We've got to get him quiet," said Miss Love. "Will, can you manage by yourself?" I nodded and reached for the wet towel. She tiptoed out, and in a minute there came to my ears—and to Grandpa's, I could tell—the sound of piano music. Miss Love played hymn after hymn. "Faith of Our Fathers," "A Mighty Fortress Is Our God," "Rock of Ages," "Abide With Me." All his favorites, chording slower and slower, quieter and quieter. And Grandpa calmed down.

At daybreak the fever was still high. He was back with Granny when Dr. Slaughter arrived.

Mama had gone on home. Aunt Loma arrived to fix our breakfast and then took over the sponging so we could eat, but we all carried our plates to the sickroom. Miss Love let her eggs turn cold while she hovered over Grandpa.

Finally he spoke to her. Spoke her name. "Miss Love?" he whispered. Oh, she was so excited. "Miss Love, make . . . Miss Mattie Lou . . . rest some, hear. . . . She's been up . . . all night, seein' . . . after me."

Miss Love looked like she'd been slapped.

"I feel sick, Loma," she said, and left the room crying.

When she didn't come back and didn't come back, I said, "Aunt Loma, you think I ought to go see about her?"

"Maybe you better."

I figured she was out at the barn, and she was. The black gelding had trotted up to her, but she paid him no mind. She heard me coming and turned quick toward me. "Will! He's not—"

"No'm."

"Dr. Slaughter thinks he won't make it. He said so this morning. Will, he just can't die! Oh . . . I've got to tell him something. Something I can't say with Miss Mattie Lou always in there!"

She burst out crying, then all of a sudden threw her head back and went to laughing! Laughed like a crazy woman. Like she couldn't stop. Finally I got mad and shook her. "Stop, Miss Love! Ain't nothin' funny!"

"Oh, you just don't know!" Out there in the May morning she could hardly talk for laughing. "I'll tell you, Will, so you can laugh, too. You see this second wife?" She pointed to herself. "She thought she was going to have a baby, but she wasn't sure. After she was sure, she decided to wait till her husband's birthday to tell him. But"—Miss Love stopped laughing, her voice went flat—"but now he's dying, and I can't tell him because . . . dear God in heaven, Will, how can I tell your grandpa right in front of your granny that he has fathered my child! He'd hate me! He wouldn't believe it was possible. Will, he has forgotten all about me and him!"

Gosh, a baby! It was going to end up just like Mama and Aunt Loma said it would.

"I can't bear it if . . . if he dies without knowing. And knowing might even make him fight to live!"

"He's already fightin' to live, Miss Love. He'll fight to his last breath."

"But if he knew this, it might make all the difference!" And she burst into tears.

I didn't know what to do. Finally I said, "Miss Love, hush up. Hear?" I sounded just like Grandpa. "Ma'am, he always says when you don't know which way to turn, do something. Don't do nothin'. Listen, ain't it the fever causin' him to be funny-turned? I mean the delirium; ain't that from the high fever?"

She nodded, holding both hands to her cheeks. "We m-manage to cool him down some, but it's n-never enough."

"What if we could cool him down quicker? If he came to himself even for a minute, you could talk to him! Why don't we put him in the bathtub? It'd soak him cool a lot quicker than all that spongin'. Wouldn't it?"

"I never heard of doing that!" She was excited, then worried. "But it might chill him too much. We'd have to ask Dr. Slaughter first."

"But don't it make sense?"

"Let me think, Will." Out there by the pasture gate, she quickly took the pins out of her tousled hair, pulled it back, twisted it into a knot at the back of her head, and pinned it tight. Even with her hair so plain and her eyelids swollen from crying, Miss Love looked beautiful to me, for she had come alive!

"I could run get Loomis," I went on, excited. "Loomis could pick Grandpa up like a rag doll, Miss Love. Not jostle his ribs or anything. Just bend over easy and lay him in the water."

Hope upon us, we ran back to the house. It scared me to death when Aunt Loma rushed to meet us at the back door. "He's had a big sweat!" she shouted. "Drenched the bed! The fever's down, Love! At least for now, and he's gone to sleep! He knew me, Love!"

"Oh, thank God!" Miss Love's eyes filled with tears. "But—oh, Will, what if I've missed my chance!"

Loma said she'd go on home and tell Sister and Brother Hoyt the good news. "You stay here, Will, just in case. Love, try to get some rest."

I thought Miss Love would want to sit there alone with him, but she asked me to stay. Grandpa was laying on his left side, as usual. She sat beside the bed, facing him, in the same rocking chair he had sat in to watch Granny.

Sometimes she would lay her head on the mattress and stretch out her hand just to touch him. I know she prayed; I could see her lips move. Every few minutes she'd feel of his forehead or his arm. At some point she murmured, "I'm dying to wake him up, but I don't dare. This sleep could make all the difference. . . . Will, honey, won't he be thrilled if it's a boy? I just know it will be a boy."

I didn't tell her, but Mama used to say Granny was always sure it would be a boy.

She got up to pace the room. "Will, what if

the fever goes way up again before he wakes?"

At that moment Grandpa went to coughing. His eyes opened wide as he gasped for breath. Miss Love looked at the sputum he spat into a rag. "It's so bloody, Will," she whispered.

When the coughing subsided, Grandpa started to drift away again, but she called him back. "Rucker, look at me!"

He opened his eyes. "You . . . so beautiful," he mumbled.

"How do you feel, dear?" She spoke softly.

"Well, I'm . . . takin' it leisurely. . . ." He pulled at his whiskers.

She leaned over the bed to get her face close to his. "I've got something wonderful to tell you, Rucker. Can you hear me, dear?"

Gazing at her, his face softened. He put his hand on her hair, and something like a weak grin passed over his face. "I'm Rucker. . . . Pleased to . . . meet you, Love. . . . Oh, Love, I'm so sick. I jest cain't . . . git . . . enough . . . air. . . ."

"You're going to get well, Rucker. I'll make you get well! Don't go back to sleep yet. Please. I've got to tell you what I have for your birthday. The most wonderful thing has happened, Rucker. . . ."

It's to my credit that I left the room. I didn't stand out there in the hall and listen, either. I went to the kitchen and drank some milk, then mixed some meal and water for Granny's chickens and went out to dump it in their pan. They ran up to me, clucking and shoving, and then here came old T.R. Sensing my joy, he jumped up on me and licked my face, and I hugged him good, pulling his ears and scratching his belly.

Church bells were beginning to ring all over town. I wondered would Papa attend preachin', now that Loma would of told them that Grandpa was better.

I thought I ought to go back in and see if he was still awake. I couldn't wait to hear what he'd say about the baby. I went in the house, tiptoed up the hall.

It looked like he was sleeping again, and Miss Love, too. She had stretched out on the bed beside him, her hand on his. The house was quiet and peaceful at last, and I was wore out.

I thought I'd just go lay down on the day-bed a few minutes. . . .

I don't know how long I slept. Miss Love's scream woke me up.

Grandpa was dead.

50

I ran in there. Miss Love, still on the bed, was raised up on one arm, staring at him. I waited for her to say something, but she just kept staring.

I heard somebody come in the front hall. "Miss Love? Mary Willis?" It was Miss Effie Belle.

"Oh, God help me!" whispered Miss Love. "Keep her talking out there, Will. I've got to . . . oh, God, just a minute more."

Miss Effie Belle had heard the scream as she was coming in from church. Her pink lip wart quivering, she said, "Rucker's passed on, ain't he, Will?"

"Yes'm."

"Well, God knows best." Her eyes misting, she touched my face with her wizened hand. "You go'n take it hardest, Will. You was his favorite in all the world."

I thought I ought to say that Miss Love was his favorite now, but what was the use?

"One time when your granddaddy was a baby, I helt him in my lap. Who'd a-thought I'd outlive him!" she said, trying hard to keep aholt of herself. "And we been next-door neighbors for I don't know how long. Lord, why couldn't it of been Bubba? I'm so tired, and Bubba just cain't seem to die." She sighed and patted my shoulder. "I'd like to go in and see him, Will."

At that moment we heard the bedroom door close, and Miss Love came up the hall. She looked like stone. Her eyes were dark-circled and her skin pale. There was no expression at all on her face as she said, "Will, you'd better hurry home and tell your family. They'll have to call Dr. Slaughter."

"Yes'm. I was just fixin' to go. Here's Miss Effie Belle to see you."

The wizened hand reached out to pat Miss Love's arm. "I'll be more'n glad to stay with you till Mary Willis and them git here."

"You're very kind. But I . . . I'd like to be alone right now. I hope you understand?"

Granny's clock chimed half-past noon as I followed Miss Effie Belle out of Grandpa's house and ran home.

Papa had attended morning preachin', but he was already back home when I rushed in.

Dead must of been written all over my face, because I didn't have to say a word except how and when.

"Run clean up and put on your suit, Will," said Papa. "Folks go'n be comin' in all day. Out of respect for your granddaddy you ought to look presentable. But make haste."

As the family hurried out to the car, Papa said we had to go by the store.

"Are you crazy, Hoyt?" asked Mama. She had cried all the time she was getting dressed, and looked it.

"There's a sealed letter in the safe," he said, taking the driver's seat. "Your daddy told me about it a month or more ago. Said if anything happened to him, I was to get the letter out and read it to the fam'ly." He motioned me to turn the crank. The engine sputtered but didn't catch.

"Cain't it wait, Brother Hoyt?" Loma screeched. "I want to see Pa!"

"No, it cain't wait. If you want to know exactly how your daddy put it, he said, 'Git thet letter fore my body's cold, and don't let nobody move me till it's read.'"

* * *

Miss Love came out of the room where Grandpa was and walked slowly up the hall to greet us. She hadn't fixed herself up or anything while I was gone. Smelling a little of turpentine, she was still in the soiled green print dress she'd worn all yesterday and all last night and all this morning. She hugged everybody, the way folks do when they don't know what to say, but she did it as if there was nothing to be said.

Mama whispered, "Can we see him?"

"Certainly. Of course," said Miss Love. Leading the way, she said Dr. Slaughter had already come and gone. "He said to convey his condolences, and tell you he was sorry not to stay. Miss Herma is having a bad labor."

I couldn't believe the change in Grandpa! He was turned on his back, his head on a single pillow, his right arm outside the fresh clean sheet that had been spread over him and the bed. His face was shaved, the mustache trimmed to a neat pencil line again, the hair combed and slicked down. Miss Love must of used some of her freckle-cover cream to fade the bruises and lighten the blackness around his eyes.

"Don't he look nat'ral," Mama whispered.

My throat swelled till I could hardly get my

breath. To me he looked spiffy, and I just wanted so bad to tell him.

I saw that Papa, holding Campbell Junior, was having just as hard a time as I was. Whereas I was grieving for my grandpa who had died, Papa was mourning for the man who had given him his chance in life. I don't know why, but right then it finally dawned on me that Papa had wanted to please Grandpa out of respect and gratitude, not from kowtowing. I watched as he tried not to cry. All of a sudden, still carrying the baby, he left the room.

Aunt Loma, Mary Toy, and Mama stood around the bed, crying. Miss Love stood there dry-eyed, looking down on the father of her unborn child.

I found Papa in the parlor. He had lifted Campbell Junior up to the window so he could watch a hen leading her baby chicks toward the front yard. "See the biddies?" asked Papa, and little Camp jumped with delight.

"What do we do now, sir?" I asked. "Call Mr. Birdsong?"

"Not yet, son." He sighed deep. "I have to read that letter first. I reckon we better go back in there and start."

For the reading, Miss Love sat down in the rocking chair, pulled as close to Grandpa as she could get it. Papa had handed over the baby to Aunt Loma. She stood jiggling him in her arms to keep him quiet. Mama was holding Mary Toy's hand, but my little sister begged, "Will, stay by me," and I put my arm around her, held her close. Papa walked around to Granny's side of the bed and tore open the envelope.

"Mr. Blakeslee didn't tell me what's in this," he began. "He just said if anything happened to him I was to get the letter out of the safe and read it to y'all right away." He looked over at the widow. "Are you all right, Miss Love? You rather go in the parlor?"

"No, Mr. Hoyt. Please read it." She placed her hand on Grandpa's shoulder.

The letter was in his big sprawling hand on a long ruled sheet torn out of the store's ledger book. I copied it later, word for word like Grandpa had it.

"To my dearly beloved wife Love Simpson Blakeslee, to my beloved daughters Mary Willis Blakeslee Tweedy and Loma Blakeslee Williams, to my beloved son-in-law Hoyt Tweedy, who is like a son to me"—Papa had to wait a minute before he could go on—"to my grandsons Hoyt Willis Tweedy and Campbell Williams Junior, and to my granddaughter Mary Toy Tweedy:

"This is about the disposal of my earthly remains.

"Please recollect the funeral I gave Miss Mattie Lou. I tried to make it a nice thank-you to her for living. Likewise I gave Camp a nice funeral. I believe God means us to stand up to suffering, not end it with a bullet. A man killing himself aint nothing I can understand. But I can forgive it. Anyhow, I wanted Camp's funeral to say 'Judge not that ye be not judged.' "

I could hear Aunt Loma snuffling.

"Now I want my burying to remind folks that death aint always awful. God invented death. Its in God's plan for it to happen. So when my time comes I dont want no trip to Birdsong's Emporium or any other. Dressing somebody up to look alive don't make it so."

My daddy paused. I could tell he was reading ahead to himself, because his face flushed all of a sudden and he had to take a deep breath before he could go on.

"I dont want no casket. Its a waste of money. What I would really like is to be wrapped in two or three feed sacks and laid right in the ground. But that would bother you all, so use the pine box upstairs at the store that Miss Mattie Lou's coffin come in. I been saving it. And tho I just as soon be planted in the vegetable patch as anywhere, I dont think anybody would ever eat what growed there, after. Anyhow, take me right from home to the cemetery.

"Aint no use paying Birdsong for that hearse. Get Loomis to use his wagon. Specially if it is hot weather, my advisement is dont waste no time."

Mama, scandalized, had both hands up to her mouth. Mary Toy had turned white as a sheet. I held her tight. Aunt Loma seemed excited, like when watching a spooky stage play. I felt excited myself. I wondered was this Grandpa's idea of a practical joke or was it a sermon. Maybe after he made his point, he'd put a postscript saying that when he was dead it really wouldn't matter to him what kind of funeral he had. But I doubted it.

Miss Love? She kept her eyes on Grandpa, lying there so unnatural quiet, so unnatural still.

Papa read on. "I want Loomis and them to dig my grave right next to Miss Mattie Lou. I dont want no other preacher there but him, but don't let him give a sermon. It would go on for hours. Just let him pray for God to comfort my family.

"I would like Will Tweedy to read some Bible verses, and I want you all to sing 'Blessed Be the Tie That Binds.' Also I want Hoyt to read some verses I am going to copy on another sheet and put in with this letter. The title is 'Be Still, My Soul.' I want Miss Love to know that the line in the poem about 'Love's purest joys restored' means I want her to try to find a way to be happy after I am gone. I expect her to outlive me by some years, and I dont want her to live drab. I want folks to say there goes Rucker Blakeslees happy, good-looking, piana-playing widder. I dont want them to say she sure has gone downhill since he passed."

All eyes turned on Miss Love, but she sat like stone.

Papa read on. "I dont want nobody at the burial except you all and them at the store that want to come. Dont put *Not Dead But Sleeping* on my stone. Write it *Dead, Not Sleeping.* Being dead under six foot of dirt wont bother me a-tall, but I hate for it to sound like I been buried alive.

"Now then, the funeral party. In case you

all aint noticed, the first three letters of the word funeral spells FUN. So a week or two after I die, you all have dinner on the grounds at one of the churches, or if they aint in favor, have it at the ball park. I dont care which. I think a Wednesday at one o'clock would be fine since the stores close anyhow. I hope everybody in Cold Sassy will come, white and colored. Have a happy get-together with kinfolks and old friends. Tell funny stories about me and such.

"I would like for you all to ask the town band and the Negro band to come play parade music and also tunes like 'Ta-Ra-Ra-Boom-de-Ay' and lively hymns like 'When They Ring Them Golden Bells.' Get everybody to sing out on *Don't you hear the bells now ringing, Don't you hear the angels singing? Tis the glory hallelujah Jubilee-ee-ee.* And so on.

"Let it be known ahead that we going to have favors. That will bring out the crowd. But dont buy nothing that cost much. Unless its in the cold wintertime, lets set up apple bobbing and dunking booths for the children. Maybe have a shooting gallery for the men. And lets have a hog-calling contest and a crowing contest, funny things that will make folks laugh. See can you get some little colored boys to do buck-and-wing dancing. Maybe we can have a backwards automobile race, and race bicycles backwards too. Oh, it's going to be a fine fancy day!

"Now you all can cry and wear black at my burying if you want to, but I dont want nobody at the funeral party to wear black or cry either one. Dont go if you cant be pleasant. If you do go, dress up and act happy. You can cry later.

"Anybody who dont foller my wishes as written here is out of my will. I do not wish my will to be read till after the funeral party.

"Well, thats all I can think of. I hope it will be a long time between this writing and when Hoyt has to read it. I want all of you to always remember what my family meant to me and how blessed I was to have two such fine wives. I think they was both dang marvels. Enoch Rucker Blakeslee."

The paper was signed, dated, sealed, and witnessed.

There was no choice but to hurry with the burying, despite folks were already bringing in food and sad faces. Loomis got his two oldest sons to go dig the grave. Then, while

Cold Sassy gathered on the front veranda and in the parlor, we gathered in there around the deathbed with the door closed, watching as Loomis, weeping, lifted Grandpa and gently laid him in the coffin box. Miss Love had fixed a sort of padding out of clean feed sacks printed in bright red and white checks. It liked to killed Mama, those feed sacks, but Miss Love acted like they were the usual thing for a coffin liner.

After my daddy said a prayer, she draped two more of the checked feed sacks over his body and then, hesitating only a moment, covered his face. Loomis nailed the box shut, and he and Papa and I toted Grandpa out the back door to the wagon.

It sure would of tickled him to see all the neighbors on his front porch staring with their mouths open as Loomis drove the mule team toward the street.

Miss Love rode in the wagon with Grandpa. Besides lots of perfume, she had on the black dress she wore to church that time Cold Sassy criticized her for acting like she was in mourning for Granny. As expressionless as the time she was a store mannequin, she sat in the wagon on a sawed-off chair, bracing herself with one hand on the driver's plank and the other on the coffin box.

Behind the wagon came the two cars, me driving the Pierce, Papa the Cadillac, and all of us looking straight ahead. It's no credit to me or Aunt Loma that we were enjoying our roles in this melodrama. Mama and Papa sure didn't feel that way. They were ashamed. But if Miss Love was feeling anything like shame, she didn't show it.

What Grandpa would of really enjoyed, haw, was the sight of Mr. Birdsong reining in the black horses pulling his ambulance-hearse just as our procession turned into the street!

Cudn Hope, Uncle Lige, and Hosie were waiting for us at the cemetery gates. I could tell that Hosie had been crying.

It was awful, the burying. Such a pitiful little band of mourners, so bumbling without Mr. Birdsong or anybody else to tell us what to do.

There hadn't been time to think or feel much of anything except disbelief while we were making all the arrangements. Now that we were actually here in the cemetery, we felt shocked and helpless.

Grandpa had only considered what he

wanted when he wrote all those instructions; he didn't give a thought to what it would be like for us to gather around a gaping hole before we'd hardly realized he was dead, before we'd hardly even got started on the grieving.

And what were we supposed to do? How was the service supposed to start?

I could tell the spirit was on Loomis to help us out, but he knew white folks' funerals aren't like colored funerals. He was scared we might not like him taking over.

As Papa put one arm around Mama and the other around Mary Toy, Miss Love's composure crumbled and she went to crying. I got the wagon chair for her to sit in, and stood by her while she sobbed and wailed. What to do? Black Loomis knew what to do. He lifted his face to the sky and sang, "Swing low, sweet chariot, comin' for to carry me home. . . ."

By time the last hum of the word *home* drifted in and out among the tombstones, all of us felt calmer, and Miss Love hushed as Loomis prayed "for Missus an' all us in de fam'ly. We asts You to hol' us in Yo Bosom, Lawd. Hol' us 'n' comfort us, till we's able to

git up 'n' carry on in de lan' ob de livin', bless
Jesus a-men."

Then Papa pulled the letter out of his
pocket. "I will now read this poem of Mr.
Blakeslee's choosing. He wrote that he found
it in a old book." He cleared his throat.

"Be still my soul: the Lord is on thy side;
     Bear patiently the cross of grief or pain;
Leave to thy God to order and provide;
     In every change He faithful will remain.
Be still, my soul; thy best, thy heav'nly
Friend
     Thro' thorny ways leads to a joyful end.

Be still, my soul: thy God doth undertake
     To guide the future as He has the past.
Thy hope, thy confidence let nothing shake;
     All now mysterious shall be bright at last.
Be still my soul: the waves and winds still
know
     His voice who ruled them while He dwelt
below."

Papa said, "Here Mr. Blakeslee wrote that
he was tired of copying, but he thought the
third verse was the best one of all for a funeral.

"Be still, my soul: the hour is hast'ning on
    When we shall be forever with the Lord,
When disappointment, grief, and fear are
gone,
    Sorrow forgot, love's purest joys
restored.
Be still my soul: when change and tears are
past,
    All safe and blessed we shall meet at
last."

I hadn't really decided which Bible verses to recite. One thing boys and girls growing up in Cold Sassy know a lot of is Bible verses. Maybe I'd do the Twenty-third Psalm. They always say that at funerals. . . . But then like a light turned on, it came to me what Grandpa might like.

" 'Ask, and it shall be given you,' " I began. " 'Seek and ye shall find; knock, and it shall be opened unto you; For every one that asketh receiveth; and he that seeketh findeth; and to him that knocketh it shall be opened.' We have the same message in the Book of Saint John," I said, sounding for all the world like a preacher. " 'If ye abide in me, and my words abide in you, ye shall ask what ye will, and it shall be done unto you. . . . Verily,

verily, I say unto you, Whatsoever ye shall ask the Father in my name, He will give it you. Hitherto have ye asked nothing in my name: ask, and ye shall receive, that your joy may be full.' "

Well, but how could I just stop there? Those words were worse than nothing if I didn't tell what they meant to Grandpa. Looking at the long rough box, I spoke timid, in a mumbled voice. Not preachified at all. "Grandpa didn't think Jesus meant, by that, that we should ast God for things, or for special favors. He said we could trust that in the nature of things, without astin', we'll get lots of blessin's and happy surprises and maybe a miracle or two. When Jesus said ast and you'll get it, He meant things of the spirit, not the flesh. Right now, for instance, I could ast, 'Lord, please raise Grandpa from the dead,' but it wouldn't happen. But I can say, 'Please, God, comfort me,' and I'll get heart's ease. Grandpa said Jesus meant us to ast for hope, forgiveness, and all like that. Ast, 'Hep us not be scared, hep us not be greedy, give us courage to try.' " I was really carried away. "Ast any such and God will give it to you. But don't ast Him not to let fire burn, or say spare me from death. At least, uh, that's what Grandpa said."

Right then it dawned on me. By some of what I was saying, I had just revealed to Miss Love that I had spied on them last Sunday. She would know I heard not only Grandpa's sermon, but probably everything else that he said and she said. I couldn't look at her.

Later, when I did, she smiled a little smile at me, like saying it didn't matter now.

I couldn't go to sleep that night for wondering would it put Mama in the bed when she heard about Miss Love's baby. I knew she'd be upset, but I doubted she would talk about it to anybody except Papa, because whereas Miss Love had just been her daddy's wife, now she would be the mother of Mama's half sister or brother. That would put her in the family. And in our family, we don't talk against each other to outsiders.

Tossing and turning, I kept remembering the look on Mr. Birdsong's face as he watched our procession move off. But I also remembered our embarrassment and shame at the cemetery, and wondered how much Grandpa had really cared about all he made us do. I bet he just wanted to stir up Cold

Sassy one last time. Give folks something to gossip about.

I didn't wonder why nobody in my family even questioned burying him the way he said to. If Grandpa wanted to keep his whiskey in your closet, marry three weeks after Granny died, and be buried in feed sacks in a coffin box, if you couldn't say yessir you didn't say no sir. Him saying what he did about cutting anybody out of his will who tried to interfere was entirely unnecessary.

Oh, law, we forgot to sing "Blessed Be the Tie That Binds."

The store stayed closed on Monday. Miss Love made a big black satin wreath for the door and I went down there and hung it. I meant to go on to school, but for once in my life I didn't want to see Smiley or Pink or Lee Roy or Dunse or anybody. I didn't want to have to answer dumb questions about the burial.

I wished so much for Bluford Jackson. If he were here, he would just sit with me, and not talk or ask anything. Well, that's what he was doing in his grave: not talking or asking anything. Likewise Granny and Uncle Camp and now Grandpa.

I sure didn't want to go sit around at Grandpa's house and listen to Cold Sassy pay its respects. I'd done enough and too much of that the past year.

What I ended up doing that morning, I went over to old Mr. Billy Whisnant's, next to the schoolyard, and knocked on the door. The winter hadn't been kind to his rheumatism. He was more bent than ever. "What you want, boy?" he asked, looking real suspicious when he saw who it was.

I said, "Sir, if you'll trust me to do it right, I want to cut you some stovewood. I don't mean for pay. I . . . well, I just want to."

The next Sunday morning, Miss Love went back to the Methodist church. She wore a navy blue dress and lots of perfume. There were those who said she ought to have on black no matter what Mr. Blakeslee wanted, and they didn't think it was fittin' for her to be out in public so soon after buryin' her husband. But as everybody knew by then, Rucker Blakeslee had seen to it that nothin' about his passin' was fittin'. So what did it really matter what his widder did?

The following Wednesday she wore a red dress and lots of perfume and her brightest big-mouth smile to the ball park for Grandpa's funeral party. She and Aunt Loma were the prettiest ladies there by far. Loma was all dolled up in the flowerdy dress from New York.

Mama didn't wear black, but she didn't wear red or anything flowerdy. She wore gray.

I never saw so much food or so many smiling people. Nobody approved of the party, but knowing what the family was up against, they weren't about to make it worse for us by not coming.

Tell the truth, they wouldn't of missed it.

With the band music and all, it was like a festival. Miss Love got Mary Toy and me and Pink Predmore and the other boys to give out balloons and stick candy. She first thought of chewing gum, but Mama said nobody but common people would chew it.

I overheard Miss Alice Ann Boozer say it served Rucker right, after the way he done Miss Mattie Lou. "Married that Yankee and didn't live a year."

You ought to've heard Miss Effie Belle take up for him: "I never thought to say it, Alice Ann, but I'm glad now he married her. Miss Love kept his house nice and seems like she made him happy."

In between the crowing contest, the backwards bicycle race, and all that, you'd see folks gathered together, talking and laughing. One group I went up to, for instance, somebody was telling that Grandpa was the best knuckle-knocker in school when he was a boy. Somebody else told about him gettin' up in church and prayin', "Lord, forgive me for fittin' thet man, even though if'n I had it to do over agin I'd hit him harder." Somebody else said, "Ever hear bout the time he beat Wildcat Lindsay in a fist fight? Funniest fight you ever seen."

Mr. Pearl was telling another group about the time Rucker turned over the privy at the depot with a Yankee railroad president in there, "and the Yankee offered a fifty-dollar re-ward to anybody who'd tell him who did it. But nobody would," said Mr. Pearl. "Rucker said he needed the money and was go'n go claim the re-ward hisself. But Miss Mattie Lou wouldn't let him." Everybody died laughing about that, and then they joked about Grandpa naming Mr. Clem's hotel after hisself.

But nobody joked about him saying, when he married Miss Love three weeks after Granny died, that Miss Mattie Lou was as dead as she'd ever be. At least not in my hearing.

Mama had been scared folks would criticize and say the family didn't show proper respect, not having Grandpa embalmed and not having a church funeral, and then getting up a party. To make sure that everybody understood the circumstances, she had showed certain people his letter ordering the cheap burial, and then she let the *Cold Sassy Weekly* print Grandpa's plans for the funeral party, including, of course, that the whole town was invited.

So not only was it written up ahead of time, but it got a big write-up afterwards.

"Just as the deceased had requested," said the paper, "a good time was had by all. It's just too bad that the one who would have enjoyed it most couldn't be there."

The family gathered at Grandpa's house that night after supper for the reading of the will. The lawyer was Mr. Predmore, Pink's daddy.

My daddy was named executor.

First the document reminded us that the old Toy house and furnishings had been deeded over "to my beloved wife, Love Simp-

son Blakeslee" at the time of their marriage.
"I also leave her one thousand dollars, as
promised at the time of said marriage." He
left Mama the house we were living in and a
thousand dollars. Loma would get a thousand, too, "and the house on Julius Street,
now rented, which I believe to be of equal
value to the others." After payment of all
debts and certain bequests, and after the rest
of the estate was sold, including houses, farmland, and stock—but not the store—the
money was to be divided, share and share
alike, between Miss Love, Mama, and Aunt
Loma.

Well, that would be less for Miss Love than
Mama and them had feared, but a lot more
than Miss Love had bargained for back when
she said I do. Still and all, to me it seemed
fitting, her having moved up from housekeeper to *bona fide* widow.

But wait. "In the event that I should have
another child or children born or unborn at
the time of my death, the estate will be divided, share and share alike, between my
wife, my two grown daughters, and this other
child or children, if living. Should any of
these heirs precede me in death, the deceased's share will go to her (or his) off-

spring. If there be no offspring, born or unborn, said share will revert to the estate."

Mama and Papa and Aunt Loma didn't bat an eyelash at that. But then they didn't know what I knew. Gosh, what if Miss Love had twins!

I waited for her to speak up about the baby, but she didn't.

Now Mr. Predmore was reading about the store. Grandpa wanted it to be owned jointly by his widow and children, share and share alike. Papa was to serve as manager for as long as he wanted the job.

The first of the individual bequests was for four hundred dollars "to my grandson Hoyt Willis Tweedy for his education, provided he agrees to come into the store as an associate for a period of at least ten years after leaving college." Grandpa didn't leave Campbell Junior or Mary Toy a dime. I guess he just forgot about them.

To the First Baptist Church of Cold Sassy he left "the sum of one dollar in appreciation of its kindness in the matter of my son-in-law Campbell Williams's funeral." Mr. Predmore read that with a straight face. Boy howdy, what I'd give to be at the deacons' meeting after they heard about the dollar!

But there was a sop for the deacons: two hundred dollars "in memory of my late beloved wife, Mattie Lou Toy Blakeslee." Grandpa left the same amount to the Methodist Episcopal Church, South, of Cold Sassy "in honor of my beloved wife, Love Simpson Blakeslee."

The last bequest was for Loomis Toy, "the sum of fifty dollars in appreciation of his loyal service to the store and my family."

Not much was said after the reading. It's to my family's credit that when we got home, nobody spoke out loud what I'm sure we were thinking about, namely, Miss Love's share of the estate. Naturally I didn't say that most likely she was going to get half of it instead of a third. I wondered when she would tell them about the baby. It would have to be soon.

Gosh, what if sure enough the baby *was* a boy? I couldn't help thinking how in that case, if Granny Blakeslee was alive she would call it worth mentioning that Grandpa finally got what he wanted most in life after he died.

I wondered when Miss Love would leave Cold Sassy. Probably not till the baby was born and the estate settled. I wondered if she'd try to sell hers and the baby's interest in the store to my daddy. I wondered if he could afford to buy it.

I wanted to talk to Papa and them about my four hundred dollars, but it hardly seemed like the time. It really made me mad, Grandpa thinking he could buy me like I was Uncle Camp's funeral. It was all right with me if he wanted to pave the way with money for Miss Love to get welcomed back to the Methodist fold, but if I wouldn't spend my life in the store despite caring so much about him, I sure wasn't go'n do it for a bribe. Dead or alive, he meant to have his way. Well, in the matter of my future, I meant to have mine.

Miss Love came down to our house to tell the family about Grandpa's baby, and I drove her home. We sat there in the car talking, and that's when she told me she had decided not to leave Cold Sassy.

"For one thing," she said, matter of fact, "where would I go? And why should I leave the only family my son will ever have? No matter how your folks feel about me, Will, they'll do right by their baby brother. That's the kind of people they are. They'll make room for him in the family and bring him into the life of the town. He'll know people who enjoyed and respected his father. And he'll know you, Will. You can show him how to fish, play ball, work hard, drive a car—all the things a boy needs to know that I can't teach him. Oh, Will"—her voice trembled—"you're so like Rucker! Knowing you, my son will know his father."

The child and I were keeping Grandpa alive for Miss Love.

Who would keep him alive for me?

Grandpa had said Cold Sassy's name would be changed "over my dead body," and that is exactly what happened. A month after we buried him in the coffin box, the U.S. Post Office approved a new name, and Cold Sassy became Progressive City.

The next spring the town council voted to widen the road on each side of the railroad tracks, which meant the Cold Sassy tree had to go. It was taken down and the roots chopped up, and I think everybody in town took some home to boil for sassafras tea.

I still have a piece of that root, put away in a box with my journal, my can of tobacco tags, the newspaper write-up when I got run over by the train, a photograph of me and Miss Love and Grandpa in the Pierce, my Ag College diploma from the University—and the buckeye that Lightfoot gave me.

DATE			
MAR 2 7 1993			
AUG. 2 3 1993 MY 2 3 '02			
NOV. 2 8 1994 AG 1 4 '04			
FE 2 4 '97			
-OC 2 3 '00 AG 1 3 '05			
DE 1 2 01 FE 1 9 '07			
JA 2 5 02 JY 0 6 '07			
AG 0 9 '07 AP 0 2 12			